The Distance Between

The Distance Between

Ceapeaya's Awakening Book 1

Blair Cousins

Contact me: Blairsoffice@gmail.com

Cover Design by Vivid Covers
Interior Design by KH Formatting

ISBN: 978-0-9984621-4-1

First Edition - 2019

10 9 8 7 6 5 4 3 2 1

This book is dedicated to all the family, friends, and amazing beta readers who lent me their ears. Thank you for letting me talk a hole through your head.

Chapter One

The clock ticked by in the silent classroom. Nothing could be heard except the sound of pencils on paper. The air was tense, riddled with intense anxiousness. Ester glanced up at the clock as she twisted the curls of hair tightly coiled on the back of her neck. She had plenty of time; there was still two and a half hours left to complete the test. She wished, however, that her heart would get the message. Staring down at her paper, she treated every question as if it were a fragile egg because this test could change the outcome of the rest of her life.

The final bell rang, and the instructor called time. Sighs of relief filled the air as the students shuffled out. Ester gathered her things and followed behind the mass. She hated school and wasn't one to stick around stuffy places like this. She would rather see the city. In the hall, she watched the others walk by. Everyone looked neat and clean—no doubt they were metropolis kids. She doubted any kids from the outskirts would be here. In fact, she didn't know a single kid from her home town that planned to go to the Academy of the Rean Coalition of Rangers. It just wasn't encouraged. You lived and died in the outskirts because that's what was expected of you.

She checked her watch as she walked out of the testing center and into the humid air of the busy streets. She took a deep breath, letting the smells of the city fill her nose. Everything about the nation state of Tel-sa was so much different than her home town, from the buildings carved from trees, to the shops, and people roaming the streets. Hover jetters zoomed overhead—newer models like the ones she saw on the tele. She wished she could explore more, but she had a train to catch. The bus stop wasn't too far down the street; she spotted it from a block away. She looked around one last time calculating how much time she could spare just to explore a few blocks, but the risk of missing her train was too much. She barely had enough money to fund this trip, but she swore one day she would come back. As she made her way to the bus stop, she noticed a few girls looking at her. She made eye contact with them, but they only laughed and giggled to themselves. No doubt they were laughing at her rags. Ester glared but kept walking. She didn't have time to get into any unnecessary fights. It wasn't worth it, but she hated when people looked down on her. Even amongst her own country folks, people looked down on orphaned and abandoned children like her.

The bus came shortly after she arrived at the stop. Ester boarded and took a seat near the window in the back. Now that the test was over, she could sit down and enjoy the city, even if it was from the inside of a crowded bus. The bus beeped and hovered a few feet off the ground. It slowly picked up speed joining the traffic around it. Faces zoomed by, blending into a massive mush, and drew Ester's attention to the architecture. The buildings, carved from the trunks of the thick jungle, had a modern city aesthetic and stretched high into the sky under a spotted canopy of trees. Gliding between them, huge telescreens displayed floating advertisements of products she couldn't even buy back home. She passed a Fried Tuzan and Co, one of Rean's most popular chain restaurants, making her mouth water. She had always wanted to go to one. There were so many cafes and shops. She wished she could have stayed longer, but her train left in an hour and it would take her about that just to walk there from the bus station. Ester let a sigh escape her lips. As she readjusted herself, a familiar voice caught her ear. From the speakers she heard the muffled sound of one of her favorite songs. It was Galaxia, her favorite pop idol. Ester strained to hear over the crowd, the song faded to the sound of a radio DJ. Galaxia was having a concert in Tel-sa's capital city in the spring. Ester slumped. What she wouldn't give just to see her idol live. The bus ascended into the station. *One day,* Ester thought to herself, but it was hard enough believing that she'd ever make it out of the outskirts.

***

The train and bus ride home was long and exhausting, but finally Ester arrived at the orphanage a little after sunset. She walked down the dusty road to her home, passing hover carts carrying goods towards the city. Out here was nothing—to the west sand and deserts and farmland everywhere else. She was hundreds of miles from the nearest metropolis, separated by the great Adum-vo desert as they called it in school. To the local kids, however, it was referred to as the Dust Wave because of the unbearable wind and dust storms that leaked out into the outskirts—the edge of the farmlands where Ester lived. Ester walked a few miles and arrived at her worn three story house she and fourteen other children called home. The lights were on, and the rich smells of Sister Genevieve's famous stew wafted through her nose. Her shoulders relaxed as a smile made its way to her worn face. Home at last. Her legs rejoiced as she willed her tired feet to the front door.

"Ester!" A unison of voices shouted when Ester opened the front door. Three young girls ran towards her, nearly toppling her over. From around the corner, Sister Genevieve smiled, her hands clasped together in front of her.

"Girls, let Ester wash up for dinner," the sister called.

"Yes ma'am." The young girls stepped aside and watched Ester disappear up the old wooden stairs to her room.

Ester walked down the hall and opened the door to her communal room and tossed her backpack on her bed, collapsing onto the mattress. She took a deep breath as she let the memories of the day roll from her mind. She worked all year to afford a ticket to Tel-sa for her entry exam and was extremely grateful for Sister Genevieve's help. She never in a million years dreamed she would be so close to her dream. In just three short weeks, she would find out if she got accepted into The Academy of the Rean Coalition of Rangers. She could only imagine what it would be like to travel all the way to Ans-on. No one she knew had ever been there, but it was said that it was three times the size of Tel-sa, with technology beyond her wildest imagination. She giggled as she rolled around in bed. She peaked over her dresser and eyed her inspiration. Next to a wrinkled picture of her family was an article about Rean's strongest ranger. Clocking in on the natural power scale, a scale that measured every Reanian's natural electrical conductivity, was Captain Wildgrass Inspread who was a ten. The highest natural recorded number in history, which was pretty impressive considering the average Reanian rarely clocked in over a four—meaning the strongest anyone's power every got was no more harmful than a static shock. It was an utter mystery how he became that strong, but it was what he did with that power that inspired Ester to become a ranger. He saved hundreds during his short time as a ranger. He was a global hero, but six years into his career he quit. It made Ester a little sad, but she wanted to be just like him. She wanted to save people from all the cruelty in the world, so that no one had to know the pain she has suffered throughout her life. Ester turned and looked at her faded picture of her family. Her father's soft eyes soothed her heart, while her mother's strong arms reminded her that she was capable of doing anything she put her mind to. She reached out and touched the photo, pulling it closer to her face. She looked at her older brother Corta, the brains of the family. She could only imagine the teasing she would get for all the studying she was doing, because even as a child Ester didn't like school. He loved to learn, and she would never forget his motto: there is always more than one way to get to the bottom a problem.

"Ester?" Little Suue poked her head through the door. "Are you coming down for supper?"

"Of course, Suue. Give me a second." Ester said, as she placed the photo neatly back into place.

"Okay!"

Ester could hear her housemate's feet running down the hall. She liked to think that all the girls and boys living here were her family. Well, some of them. After all, it would be the closest thing she'd ever have to a family, thanks to The Order of Peace, which was the organization that ran most of the orphanages in west Adum. What they lacked in quality and aesthetics, they made up for in stability and safety, which was all Ester could have asked for.

She changed out of her nice clothes and threw on a pair of patched up tan pants and a t-shirt. She thought about the people she'd seen in the city today. Everyone was wearing a version of the ever popular ride suits, which to Ester looked like a tighter version of a one piece long pajama. She laughed a little. They were all the craze, but they weren't her style. She preferred comfort over flair. She checked herself in the mirror, catching the necklace her mother had made for her in the mirror. She clasped it, warming the little amber stone in hand. She really hoped her family will be proud of her. It had been five years since they were killed, and she missed them so much it made her heart ache.

"I promise I'll never let you down." Ester opened her palm, gazing at the stone.

Laughter from downstairs broke her train of thought. In her exhausted state, she had almost forgotten how hungry she was. She ran downstairs and joined everyone in the dining room. Packed tight, Ester squeezed in next to her friends, taking a seat at the long wooden table. Supper time in the sister's house was always filled with excitement, and tonight it was double with the arrival of Ester back from the big city. Ester didn't expect everyone to be so interested, but then again she would be the first kid to visit a bustling metropolis.

"What was it like?" Jermane, another teenager that lived in the room with Ester, asked.

"Did you see any famous people?" Algaza, another teen girl, asked trying to raise her voice aboce all the chatter.

"Oh please." Tommy, one of the younger, boisterous teen boys, smacked as food fell from his mouth. "You act like she went to a tele-show. She just wasted her money on some dumb test."

The other boys laughed as Ester glared. From her hand, sparks began to form. She concentrated it to her fingers, and zapped Tommy on the leg, with a small shock.

"Ow!" Tommy shouted. "Sister Genevieve! Ester shocked me!"

Sister Genevieve looked up. "That's enough, children." She cast stern looks in both their directions. "This is not a house of barbarians. There will be no fighting or rough housing." She eyed them all, sending their backs straight in obedience. "Finish your dinner; you have school early in the morning."

There were nods and yes ma'ams all around, except for Ester who stared furiously at Tommy and his friends. She really hated that kid. He was pretty much the house brat, and it showed. Ester dove into her dinner. She wasn't going to let him get to her after such a wonderful day.

That night, Ester tried to will herself to sleep. She couldn't take her mind off the events of the day. She couldn't believe that she had gone all the way to Tel-sa and actually saw the city, which was far more amazing than she could have ever imagined. Ester took a deep breath and sighed. Going to Tel-sa was a dream, but getting into The Academy of the Rean Coalition of Rangers was her ultimate fantasy.

"Ester," Algaza whispered in the darkness, "tell us about the big city."

Ester turned her head. She could hear Jermane shift as well. It looked like she wasn't the only one who couldn't sleep.

"It was amazing." Ester tried to bottle up her excitement. "Just like on the tele, everything was so big. The buildings were ten times the size of grain silos. It was like traveling into another world."

Algaza and Jermane giggled, making Ester even more hyped.

"Really?" Algaza said. "Was it all junglely and wild like from that show?"

Ester nodded in the dark. "Yes, I swear if the metropolis were to stop trimming, I'm sure the jungle would take it back. I've never seen tree trunks so big like that. They literally carved them into buildings almost like a city made of tree houses."

"Can you guys keep down over there?" Adis cut in, another one of Ester's roommates. "Can't you see some of us are trying to sleep?"

There was silence, but Ester's eyes were on Adis. She was the queen around here, or at least she acted like one. It didn't help dampen her ego knowing she was also hands down the prettiest girl in the orphanage, and in their school and she never let anyone forget it.

"I'm sorry, Adis. Am I talking too loud for you?" Ester's voice rose. Adis said nothing at first, but in the cover of darkness Ester could tell she was rolling her eyes.

"Nobody cares about your stupid story, Ester. You're probably not even going to get in, so pipe down," Adis huffed. Ester was steaming under the blanket, but a calm cool hand touched her arm. It was Algaza.

"Don't worry about her, Ester. I believe in you," she whispered. Her warm smile could be felt in the darkness.

They were all trapped and frustrated here. Abandoned, it was important to keep calm and stay focus, but it was hard. Ester couldn't wait for the day she could leave and start her life. She turned over and pulled the covers close to her chest. It didn't matter what the others said, she had as good of a shot as everyone else.

***

The sun rose, and with it came the hustle and bustle of the morning. Everyone had to be up extra early for the trek to school. They weren't rich enough to take hover carts to school or even bikes like some of the other Adum-la kids. They had to walk. Down the hall, shouts and arguments broke out amongst the younger kids. The bathroom lines were long as the children pushed and shoved around the sinks.

"Move, Seir!" Bellarue shouted as the two began to fight.

"Make me!" Seir shouted back as more and more children pushed to get in.

"Hey!" A voice cut through the crowd. "You want a fist sandwich?" Ester stepped between the two. The younger children straightened up and shook their heads. "Good, then tighten up."

They nodded and formed a line. Ester let out a small smile and walked towards the back of the line. As an elder of the house it was the older kids job to help keep the younger ones in check. Ester didn't believe in sweet talk and swiftly squashed squabbles with her fist, but it wasn't for kicks. Fights broke out all the time, and it was better to put an end to it before it spiraled out of control. Amongst the crowd of children, Ester spotted Sister Genevieve staring at her. The sister nodded her head, as she led the young ones down the stairs. Ester smiled to herself as she got in line. Sister Genevieve was much more than a caregiver to Ester. She was the closest thing to a real mother she had, and even though now she was eighteen now and would have to move out when she finished school, she knew she would miss her terribly. Orphans weren't allowed to stay with their caretakers pass the age of eighteen because room was always needed for the constant influx of orphaned children. Strain on the system was even greater due to Adum-la's open door child policy that stated that any homeless child was welcomed here. Parents in the other nation states wishing to give their children up were fed the idea that their children would be given a better life in Adum-la. The reality, though, was the big governments in the metropolises couldn't stand dealing with all the orphan children. So, they took advantage of Adum's policy and dumped them out here out of sight. That really made Ester mad; children shouldn't be shelved away hundreds of miles away from home, even if they are orphaned.

Sister Genevieve prepared breakfast and helped everyone gather up their things. On their way out, they picked up their lunches and waved the sister goodbye. Ester walked out amongst the crowd after Jermane and Algaza hoping to speed past the sister.

"Ester." Sister Genevieve stopped her.

Ester froze and kind of smiled, but from the look on the Sister's face she knew she was heading into trouble.

"Ester, I found your plant this morning."

Ester slumped; she was in trouble now.

"It's dead." The sister's eyes saw right through her.

"I know." Ester avoided her gaze as she stood on the porch.

"Ester, this is your final project for school, and it is very important."

"I know. I don't—"

"Ester, I won't argue with you. You have three weeks to grow a sprout for graduation, and maybe if fate allows, they will let you pass."

Ester rolled her eyes. "But Sister—"

"That's enough." The Sister let out a sigh, her expression softened. "Ester, listen to me. This is very important, your future."

"It's not here," Ester retorted, and the sister sighed again. Sister Genevieve cupped Ester's chin and placed a kiss on her forehead.

"I expect nothing less than your best, but know that the world does not bless those who do not in turn put in the work."

Ester sighed in defeat. "Yes ma'am."

The sister waved Ester off, uncertain of her future and clasped her hands together. "Please Grand Mother in the sky, take hold of that child and give her wings."

The wind picked up, blowing through Ester's thick curly hair. Her future wasn't here in the fields of Adum-la. She wasn't meant to tend the soils, settle down, and marry. Those weren't the dreams that occupied her mind anymore. She dreamed of fighting alongside her fellow rangers. In galactic battle, against all sort of enemies, protecting her fellow citizens and visiting planets far, far away. As she thought about her dreams, her heart beat faster. She was so close she could almost see herself walking into ranger school. There she would be equal, side by side with her fellow rangers and not some poor kid from the outskirts. She shut her eyes and took a deep breath. It was meant to be, she told herself as she clutched her necklace, the only thing she had left to remember her parents by. *I'm going to make it mama, papa,* she said to herself. She picked up the pace, her gait slowly turning into a jog. There were no breaks; she needed to stay in shape if she was going to get into ranger academy. She needed both a sharp mind and a trained body she thought to herself as she passed a few of her classmates on her two mile trip to school.

***

Ester could barely stay awake during her morning classes. They were so boring, she wished she could go out for a run. Brother Isa was going over galactic history, a subject Ester thought would be more interesting but instead it just put her to sleep. Brother Isa droned on about the history of their neighboring planet, Labadora, a large green planet much bigger than Rean that sat visible in the sky like the moon. Little was known about the planet, but it was rumored that the Labadorans were far from friendly. Some even going as far to call them uncivilized. Ester's head dipped a little, but a tiny shock popped her in the butt. She yelped as all eyes turned to her.

"Is everything okay. Ester?" Brother Isa said, lowering his book.

"Yeah," Ester forced a smile, as she tried to block out the snickers of her classmates. She looked behind her and saw Adis grinning at her. Ester cursed under her breath.

The bell rang, ending another uneventful day. Ester was sure she could get into ranger academy with physique alone, but she didn't understand why she needed to waste her time in school. She was sure none of the kids in the metropolises took agriculture classes, but this was educational gold in Adum-la. She lifted her head and yawned as Brother Isa walked towards the front of the room.

"And remember class, you have a little over two weeks to prepare your advanced agriculture project. This will be your final grade. Enjoy the rest of your day. Safe travels." The teacher dismissed them.

Ester slumped in her chair, like she needed another reminder. She got up and filed out of the room with the rest of the students. Just a day had passed since her big adventure, and it was far too soon to be pulled back into the real world.

"Ester." A hand reached out and touched her shoulder.

Ester jumped and was greeted by the warm smile of another one of her housemates, but this one was much more of a pain.

"Luck, you scared me," Ester snapped back, but Luck only chuckled.

"Feeling a little on edge, are we?" Luck said, as he flashed one of his more cockier smiles.

Ester rolled her eyes. He was by far the most handsome boy in school. His eyes soft and blue like the sea, with sun kissed sandy colored skin. His hair was curly and short, untamed, just like his spirit. Staring at Luck was like watching the sun set on a perfect day with the promise of a wonderful night to come, but Ester cared very little. She was one girl his charm did not work on. Ester reshuffled the books in her hands in annoyance and walked away.

"Ester, wait, I'm sorry." Luck chased after her, but Ester only glared as Luck tried to keep pace beside her. "You know you're really cute when you're mad." Luck laughed lightly.

"And you really know how to clear a room after a bottle of goat's milk."

"Aww, that's low," Luck pouted, only half hurt. The two walked to the courtyard together, passing other students and faculty. "I noticed you looked a little nervous in class today."

"And?" Ester kept walking, not slowing down even a bit.

"And I was wondering if there was anything I could do to help." The two stopped. Ester was really bad at hiding her emotions, especially around Luck. The boy was gifted at reading people.

"Ugh, okay," Ester sighed. "I really messed up my final project. The plant, it's totally dead." She sighed again.

"I know." Luck said with another one of his award winning grins.

Ester could feel her eye twitch as her glare intensified. "You hungry or something, cause you're asking for a fist sandwich."

Luck took a step back and raised his hands up in defense. "Easy there, I am friend, not foe." He smiled with his eyes. "Look Ester, I'd be happy to help you with your project."

"Yeah, right, not even you can grow a plant in three weeks."

"Oh, is that a challenge?" He folded his fingers into the shape of a gun and conjured up a tiny spark on the tip of his index finger. "Are you forgetting who you're talking to? I am Luck Verden Hayes, grower of all things." He winked.

Ester stared at him for many long seconds, then laughed. "Okay, you know arrogance doesn't suit you, change it." Ester walked around him, but not before Luck grabbed her hand. They were now standing with their backs facing each other.

"I'm always happy to help, I mean it."

"I know," Ester said.

He let go of her hand and watched her walk away, smiling to himself.

On the walk home from school, Ester stared up at the sky. The sun inched across a sea of blue, as slow as a sand snail. She couldn't afford a bad marking after she worked so hard in all her units to maintain good marks. She was sure all the metropolis kids had perfect marks, but out here marks didn't matter. They valued hard work in the fields. Long ago, it was something she took pride in. There was a time many years ago where she would have been happy with tilling the ground from sun up to sun down, but that all changed when her family was slaughtered. If her brother Corta was here, he would know how to get her out of this mess. He was good at figuring things out. She stopped alongside a farmer's stand to pick up a few seeds for her project.

Maybe it might be a little easier to grow a tum tree, she told to herself as she browsed the shelf, twirling the curls of hair on the back of her neck. The shopkeeper smiled at her as she passed, shuffling her feet across the hay littered floor. This final project had been nothing but a headache, and she'd tried. She watered the plant, and put it out in the sun, just not every day, but who was she kidding. She only had herself to blame; she didn't care about learning to farm. She wanted no part of that life, and now she was in a bind and without this plant she won't graduate. *Stupid*, she cursed under her breath and settled on a package of opalia seeds.

When she arrived home, everyone was already busy with their daily chores. The younger children were in charge of sweeping and dusting, while the older children helped with fixing up the house and cooking. The boys were all outside tending to the garden, pulling weeds and watering the plants. In the kitchen the girls were mending clothes and sorting through donations. Ester walked into the kitchen. Algaza, Jermane, and Adis were sitting at the table.

"Well, look who decided to join us." Adis said. "Surely you don't think your little trip to the metropolis resolves you of your homely duties?"

Algaza and Jermane looked at her, but Ester swallowed her pride and tried to ignore her. "Of course not, I had to stop at Horvor's."

"What for?" Algaza asked, getting glares from Adis.

Ester shuffled her pack around. "Nothing big, just some seeds." Ester pulled out the package of opalia seeds and showed her friends.

"Opalias." Jermane's eyes sparkled. "Those are my favorite."

"Yeah, I just hope they're easy to grow." Ester clutched the seeds, eyeing them as if they had a plot against her. "Welp, I'm going to throw these in a pot."

"You can't be serious." Adis laughed. "You do realize those are one of the hardest plants to grow?"

Ester clenched her fist. "I-I knew that, duh, just mind your business, Adis." Ester stormed out.

"Ester, make sure the soil is balanced or they won't grow," Algaza frantically warned.

"Oh brother, I can't wait to see how this turns out," Adis smirked.

Ester rushed towards the shed in the back of the house. Who cared what Adis thought, she was going to make this plant grow. It was too late to earn the perfect mark, but anything was better than nothing. She was grateful for the fact that she hadn't slacked off the whole year. Her marks were pretty padded, but so was her competition. So, she would need to put her everything into this project. Just as Ester was about to open the door to the shed, she was the bombarded by clumps of dirt. She spun around with such ferocity, the guilty party stopped their assault at once.

"Um, it wasn't me." Riker held up his dirt covered hands, as Ester fumed towards him.

Then *slam*, another clump of dirt struck her on the side of her face, getting in her hair and ear. She growled and wiped away the filth, catching Tommy laughing some feet away.

"Tommy! You're dead meat!" Ester shouted as sparks crackled from her fist. Tommy's eyes got big, and he and his friends turned and ran away. "I'm not going to forget this, you worms!" she growled as she dusted the rest of the dirt out of her hair, displacing her short tied ends even more.

She sighed. She would have to shower tonight, which meant she had another thing to do. She opened the shed door, trigging the flickering motion sensor light. Some of the other kids plants were resting in the window and Ester stared at them with envy. Along with Ester, Jermane, Adis, and Luck were also graduating this year. She wouldn't miss Adis or Tommy and his friends, but it would be hard to say goodbye to Jermane and Algaza and the younger kids. Ester pulled out a soil crusted pot and dusted it off. It was small and had some cracks in it, but it would have to do. She rinsed it under the sink, inspecting it for larger cracks.

"I hope that's not the pot you're using for your plant?" Luck smiled, leaning against the door frame.

Ester jumped and shut off the water without looking at him. "If you're going to help, help. If not, piss off."

"Ooo, sassy." Luck walked over and placed his hand over Ester's. "Here, let me find a better pot for you." Ester froze momentarily and allowed Luck to take the pot. "This one will be much better." He presented her with a rounder pot, handmade, with an aged gold glaze. "This will hold more soil."

Ester inspected the pot. "Thanks."

"What kind of plant did you decide on?" Luck asked as he pulled a large sack of soil from underneath the wooden work table.

"Opalias." Ester said as she rinsed the pot. Luck stopped and looked at her. Their eyes met, and she could tell he was on the edge of laughing. "What?" Luck's smile weaned as the corners of his mouth trembled, then he burst into laughter.

"Opalias are one of the hardest plants to grow." He clutched his gut. "Surely you know this?" She rolled her eyes. "But," he reached over head to pull out a jar of nutromix, "they don't take long to sprout." Ester's face perked up. "If you do it right, of course," he added.

"Well, blast me in the foot, I'm screwed." Ester plopped onto a stool. Luck looked at her warmly and smiled, cooling the fire in Ester's heart if only for a minute.

"Don't worry." He stood in front of her, looming dangerously close. "You have me remember?" His face hovered only inches from hers.

"And you do realize just because you're helping me with this, it doesn't mean I'm settling down with you." Her words halted his advance, but he recovered quickly.

"Of course." Luck took a step back. "But, if you change your mind—"

"Yeah, yeah, you'll be here." Ester shook her head. Sometimes she wished he would just get the message.

"Waiting." Luck teased with a smile

Ester rolled her eyes. "They'd bury you before you ever got the chance to marry me." Ester chuckled under her breath.

"What was that?" Luck raised an eye.

"Nothing." Ester cracked a smiled.

The two continued to talk as Luck guided Ester on how to pot her plant. In the window, a shadow lurked, watching the two as they worked. With fists clenched, Adis swore she would make Ester pay for stealing the attention of Luck from her.

***

Night rolled in and all the children gathered around the tele to watch the Var Alex Show, a nightly program featuring the latest artist and performers from all over the planet. This show was one thing the children could agree on and was sort of a tradition around the house. Tonight's show featured Dr. Blaze and Friends from the hit children's show. The children were enamored, and though Ester didn't want to admit it, she was into it, too. Dr. Blaze and his sidekick danced around the stage, preforming their trademark hero dance. The children laughed, but did not notice Sister Genevieve hovering in the doorway.

"Ester," she whispered softly, but loud enough to be heard above the tele.

Ester turned and eyed the sister warily. She hoped she wasn't in any more trouble. She stood, moving carefully not to trip over anyone. The sister smiled and led Ester into the kitchen, where all the sewing materials were laid out. Ester relaxed and noticed Jermane was there too, all pinned up in a layer of fabric. The two girls exchanged smiles as Ester was led to a chair and seated as Sister Genevieve moved gracefully around the room gathering things.

"Ester, your ceremony is coming up soon, so we must get you ready." The sister clasped her hands together.

When donations fell short, Sister Genevieve made the children's clothes. They didn't have the tones to purchase nicer fabric, but Sister Genevieve made due hemming and altering second hands. But it was a household tradition that all ceremonial clothes were handmade. To the Sister, their graduation ceremony was more than just a graduation, it marked the end of their time in her care. And each child received these ceremonial garments as gifts for the special place they held in her heart.

Sister Genevieve picked through her boxes of needles, when she remembered that she left her favorite one on her nightstand. She told the girls she'd be right back and hurried off. Ester nodded and looked over at Jermane. Draped delicately over Jermane's body was the start of a beautiful Kiko robe, customarily worn by the Dagee people. This was Sister Genevieve's ancestral tribe, before joining The Order of Peace. With striking similarities to a large quilted blanket, a Kiko robe was designed by piecing together square pieces of fabric with different colors and patterns. This created a robe with a college of different symbols, each with their own meaning. Jermane was Ling-del, which was a small tribe from the nation state of Cha-la, but her mother and father died from sickness. So, with no one to care for her, she wound up here. To Sister Genevieve, heritage and family were everything. In honor of Jermane's lineage, the Sister created a Kiko robe decorated with Ling-del symbols and colors. Ester fell in love with Jermane's beautiful jade colored robe. Jade was the stone of Jermane's tribe and symbol of their nomadic culture. Once finished, Ester was sure it was going to be beautiful. Adis and Tavanee walked into the kitchen and marveled at Jermane's robe. Tavanee, who was only fifteen, couldn't wait for Sister to make her Kiko robe.

Tavanee awed at the detail. "Wow, Jermane! Your Kiko robe is really pretty."

"Thank you," Jermane replied as Adis walked by without a lingering glance.

"Sister Genevieve has already made my Kiko robe, and I believe it is her best work yet." Adis stopped at the edge of the table, flipping her long black hair out of her face.

"I bet," Ester muttered sarcastically.

Adis faked a smile, ignoring Ester's sour expression. "But I'm sure yours will be just as nice, Jermane."

"Oh-oh no, I'm sure yours is going to be the very best Adis," Jermane stuttered over her words.

Adis grinned and looked over at Ester. "Yes, indeed. By far I'll be the best dressed girl at the ceremony."

"Oh, give it a break," Ester spat back.

Adis shot her a glare. "Hmp, you're just jealous." Adis snapped. "Besides it looks like you won't even be graduating." Adis' grin returned when she saw the level of rage building up in Ester's eyes. Shocked, Jermane and Tavanee both looked at Ester.

"Ester, is that true?" Jermane looked at her friend with worry.

"Of course it's true," Adis laughed. "Go head, tell them."

Ester clenched her jaw tightly. She was so close to jumping out of her chair she could barely contain herself. "It's not even that big of a deal. So what, I botched my final project. I've got good enough marks."

Adis' grin widened as she went in for the kill. "Ha, good enough, but not the best. I mean you're still trying to get into ranger academy right?"

That statement struck a nerve, and Ester was out of her seat before she could control herself. Jermane quickly shuffled between them, forcing Ester to a holt. Adis laughed, but stepped back for measure.

"It's your dream, not mine," Adis shrugged. "Come on, Tavanee. We best let Sister do her work, even if some of us won't be graduating."

Adis left with Tavanee shuffling behind her, leaving Ester standing there in a ball of rage. Ester hated that girl, but what hurt the most was that she might be right. All her hopes were riding on this plant, and she needed to straighten up if she was going to get out of here.

Chapter Two

Over the next few days Luck worked closely with Ester to get her plant to grow. She was extremely grateful for his help and was starting to believe that she would have a successful plant by the end of the month. In the meantime, she stuck to training for academy. Not only did she need to be at the top of her class, but she needed to be in peak physical condition as well. So she worked extra hard on her physique, knowing her competition would be doing the same. That's why she worked a part-time job to stay in shape. A few days a week she helped make private deliveries to residents around the area. This was ideal for keeping her body in shape, with all the lifting and walking it required, but the best part about the job was riding in the hover car. Weighing over nine-hundred pounds, the hover cars were so much fun to ride in. To Ester, it was like riding on a hover jetter, even though the hover cars out here were much slower.

Ester left for work after she checked and watered her plant. Her part-time job was at the Duken's farm, which grew grain. She laced up her shoes for the three mile walk and packed her bag with cantinas of water and fruit. It was getting close to summer season, the hottest time of the year in Adum-la. On her planet, Rean, they only experienced two seasons, winter and summer. Even though they had short intermittent seasons, that was nothing but a blip compared to Rean's winters and summers. In school, she read other planets had wildly different climates. For example, Fandour, the closet planet to the Verlin asteroid belt, was like one big dust wave, a hundred times worse than the Adum Desert. No one lived there except for outlaws and drifters. On the second planet, Kees, the climate was tropical. This little blue planet was filled with clear blue oceans with mountainous islands that dotted the surface. This one was her favorite because it was the most beautiful. It was said that the people there could fly. The scholars believed that the same force that gave Ester and her people their electric power also blessed the people of Kees with the abilities of telepathy and levitation. It was pretty cool in Ester's opinion, though she wouldn't trade her electric shock power for anything, even if it was nothing more than a simple shock. Her planet, Rean, was the third planet in the Compus system, and after that was the fearsome and looming planet of Labadora. She'd read stories about the monstrous people of Labadora and the great beast that fought alongside them. They were formidable, even for the rangers.

Thankfully, all of the planets were at peace because of a treaty signed long ago. The last planet in her solar system was a little ice planet called Ceapeaya, or better known by her people as the Motherland. Mystery shrouded its surface and its people. Passed down from generation to generation, her people told stories of how all magic drew its power from the Motherland. Of course, people didn't believe in magic now. Everyone knew that the radiation from the sun gave the people in her galaxy their unique abilities, but still the legends were passed down in roaming tribes.

Ester stared up at the clear blue sky. Sitting there next to the sun was the neighboring green planet of Labadora, and if she looked hard enough she could see the blue dot of her other neighboring planet, Kees. She dreamed of traveling through space one day. Rangers got to do cool things like that, and just thinking about it made her excited. She gradually picked up the pace to a steady jog, which created a light sheen of sweat on her round brown face. She adjusted the pack on her back and moved her arms effortlessly back and forth as she sped up. She jogged down the dirt road parallel to the fields of grass where animals grazed. Folks waved to her as they passed by in their carts, carrying goods. She waved back as her jog turned into a run. She wondered what deliveries she would be making today. Last week, she got to go to Honey's Flower farm. She liked that farm because she got to feed the miniature goats that lived there. Up ahead on the side of the road she spotted a man sitting next to his cart. As she got closer, she noticed it was one of the Dukens.

"Miss Ester!" An elderly man waved.

"Mr. Duken!" Ester stopped. Mr. Duken sat on a large rock next to his horse drawn cart. "Is everything okay?"

"Oh yes, absolutely perfect." The elderly man looked up at the clear blue sky. Ester looked up as well, trying to figure out what he was staring at. "Did you know there are people up there right now?"

Ester raised her hand to her forehead to block out the sun. "Who? The rangers?"

The elder chuckled. "Spirits."

"Spirits?" Ester raised an eyebrow, but Mr. Duken only laughed.

"Watching over us all the time."

Ester laughed. "Mr. Duken, are you sure the sun isn't getting to you?"

Mr. Duken chuckled and shook his head. He stood from his rock with the help of his cane and walked towards Ester, taking her hand. "Oh, I can tell the universe has great things in store for you, child."

Ester looked at her palm, but she couldn't tell what he was looking at. So, she smiled and just went along with it.

"Say, would you mind helping me get old Barren back to the farm? He's terribly stubborn today and would much rather enjoy the klase weed instead of pulling."

"Sure thing, Mr. Duken!" Ester loved animals. She walked over to Barren and greeted him by extending her hand palm down towards his nose. Barren gave it a quick blow and nayed, shaking his long black mane. Ester lowered her hand. "It's good to see you too, Barren." The horse stepped at little closer and gently head-butted her. "Oof, well thank you." Ester smiled and rubbed his nose. Mr. Duken walked up next to them.

"See, he likes you more." He chuckled and walked over the driver's seat.

Ester walked out in front with Barren's reins in her hands. Together, they made the trek back to the Duken family farm, which was one of the biggest farms in her area. Lots of families were employed by the Dukens. They were a very nice family, admired by the community.

Mr. Duken thanked Ester for her help and offered her a few tones for her time. She thanked him and quickly made her way to Scott Duken's office. He was the grandson of Mr. Duken and current manager of the Duken estate. She hoped he wouldn't be too upset about her being late.

"I'm so sorry I'm late." She barged into the office, nearly tripping over the ledge. The woman at the counter eyed her as Ester walked up to her desk. "Good morning, Miss Aima."

"You're late, DuTain." Aima watched her from the desk.

"I'm so sorry, ma'am. I was helping Duken senior with Barren. You know how stubborn that horse can be." Ester laughed as she rubbed the back of her head.

"Very well." Miss Aima reached down and opened her desk drawer, pulling out a digital name tag heading it to Ester. "Don't make this a habit."

"Yes ma'am,"

"Miss DuTain, is that you?" A familiar voice called from the back office. Ester looked up and saw Scott Duken poke his head out from his office. "Miss DuTain." The middle aged man extended his hand. "I sure am glad to see you." Ester shook his hand as she tried to affix her name tag to her shirt. "We had a call out in the field department; I'd pay you double if you'd be willing to help."

At the mention of extra tones Ester perked up. "Of course, sir. I'd be happy to help." Ester didn't mind working shifts in the field. It was mostly soil prep and weed pulling, but it was a good work out which was just what she needed.

"Excellent!" A smiled exploded across Scott's face. "You know, we sure could use an extra hand, full time around here."

"Thanks but no thanks, Mr. Duken. I'm going to the metropolis after I graduate."

"All the way out there, huh?" Scott chuckled. "Well, I wish you luck, but if you change your mind, you're always welcome here, Miss DuTain."

"Thank you, sir!" Ester smiled a great big smile. She felt a little sad though. If she did get into ranger school, she would miss the kind people at her part time job.

***

In just two weeks' time, Ester's little opalia plant had grown a total of three inches. She was so happy to see everything coming together, thanks to Luck's magic fingers. If this kept up, she would have a presentable plant in no time. Out in the shed, she watered and added extra nutromix to balance the soil. The delicate sapling would not grow without the perfect mix of nutrients and minerals. She was sad she wouldn't be around to see it bloom, but planned to gift it to Sister Genevieve. It would be a beautiful addition to the Sister's already stunning garden.

"You know what, little opalia plant? You're not so bad. I mean, once I got the hang of everything it became easier. If only life in general were that easy." Ester smiled as she caressed the leaves between her fingers. She picked up the sapling and placed it in the sun.

"What are your dreams, little opalia plant? Do you wanna go in the ground or travel through the stars?" Ester started at the tiny green plant waiting for an answer that would never come. "Welp, I guess that's for you to know and you only. My job is to get you grown enough to make that decision."

She smiled and headed out of the shed. Today was going to be a busy day because she signed up to volunteer at her school's mini market in the Bizlo locale for extra credit. Thank goodness she went overboard with signing up for volunteering this year. Somehow she must have known she would slack off somewhere. Ester grabbed her bag and walked around to the front of the house. If she ran the whole way it would be good exercise. She checked her shoes and was about to head off when she heard someone call her name.

"Ester!" Luck waved. "Hey, wait up."

"Not now, Luck, I have somewhere to be."

"I know, that's why I'm walking with you." He smirked.

"I'm not going on a joy walk. I have volunteering at the school today."

"I know. That's where I'm heading, too."

Ester rolled her eyes. Why were boys so dense? She couldn't be mad at him; after all, he was helping her with her final project. And there could be worse company. She shuttered at the idea of working with Adis.

"You do realize we're going all the way to Bizlo?"

Luck nodded.

"And we're more than likely taking the school's busted hover cart."

"I know, I'm driving." Luck started walking.

"What!" Ester caught up with him. "How?"

Luck shrugged. "I signed up first."

"Bullshit. I was like the first one to sign up for everything."

"Not everything." Luck smiled, but Ester only looked more pissed.

She really wanted to drive, even if the hover cart was super slow.

"Fine then." Ester walked by him.

"Ester." Luck reached out to her, but she continued to walk. Luck jogged to keep up with her, but it was clear that this wasn't going to be a carefree walk. Ester looked over her shoulders and smirked.

"I'll see you at school." Ester took off in a sprint.

Luck shouted out to her and started to run, but he did not have the same stamina as her. Ester laughed as she left him in the dust. As Luck faded in the distance, Ester started to slow down to a fast jog. She loved running. There was something about the way the body felt when it was forced to work at its best. Training for the academy kept her spirit alive during the tough days of living in the orphanage. She had lost so much and sometimes that really got to her, but the memories of her family fueled her motivation to continue. Her necklace bounced from side to side on her chest, egging her on. She inhaled as she felt the energy course through her body and took off in another sprint.

The clouds were rolling in from the Adum desert, but the day was still shaping up to be a good one. Besides Luck and Ester, three other students had signed up to volunteer under the supervision of Brother Isa. The school participated in the market sale to give students a chance to see what it's like to vend at the markets. Goods were made by students and sold to help pay for things like building repairs and school supplies. The school went to the markets twice in the fall and three times in the spring. Ester had gone to all of them. She liked going to the markets. It reminded her of the smaller ones she went to as a child.

Brother Isa directed the students to load up the cart. The students worked very hard to bring goods to market this year. This trip they brought with them melons from the garden and homemade bags from their home goods class. Ester helped make this batch of bags this trip and was quiet proud of her bag making skills. She even made one for Bellarue, one of her housemates, for her birthday and she loved it. Ester carried crates to the cart and helped organize them. It would be an hour trip by cart, but the ride was beautiful. Brother Isa turned on the hover cart and the wagon choked and popped. A few students screamed and backed away, but it was finally running.

"You sure you want to drive that thing?" Ester asked, looking at Luck.

"Wouldn't pass up the chance for the world." He winked at her.

"Would you pass up on it for me?" Ester batted her big brown eyes.

"Nope." Luck grinned then walked away.

Ester grunted and hopped on the back with the rest of the students. The hover cart jutted forward, sending the students rolling back. Ester cut Luck a look, but he threw his hands up and pointed to the cart. Ester glared, but there was no bite to it. She guessed she would have to play sightseer and that wasn't so bad.

She looked at the school drifting slowly away. Out in the outskirts there was nothing for miles, only dense sandy grasslands on one side and sand dunes on the other. Ester wasn't native to this part of Adum. Her tribe claimed the fruitful lands northwest. Out here, the soils weren't as good because of their proximity to the dessert, but the people made do. Even though the trip was long and secluded, Ester enjoyed staring off into the distance. She felt the void calling out to her. Beyond the dunes and miles of dessert was where she belonged. She knew it. She yawned and settled in for the long trip. She had a feeling today was going to be a good day.

The markets were bustling today. Many people stopped by their booth, buying up most of their stock of melons and bags. Ester and Luck unloaded so many melons, they could barely keep them on the table. Luck was especially proud because he'd spent a lot of time in the school's garden. Fruits were his favorite thing to grow, and he was happy to see that they were selling well. The day ended and the students walked away with quite a lot of sales. The money they made today would be of great help to the school.

On the way back, Luck rode in the back to give another student a chance to drive. Ester didn't pout about it this time, even though she was still jealous that Luck got to drive on the way here. She had driven three times before, and she was tired and didn't mind taking it easy. Luck watched the other students rest. It had been a long day, and he had to admit he was a little tired too.

"How are you not dosing off?" Luck asked.

"I've been on this trip like four times already," Ester said.

"But still, this was one a heck of a day." Luck rested his head on his knee.

"Maybe for a pretty boy like you." Ester teased.

"Hey now, I still pulled my weight. After all, those were my melons we were selling."

"Yours? More than just you helped grow them."

"This is true, I will not deny them their credit. However, I have logged in the most hours in the garden and can be credited with saving three crops," Luck said.

"Fine, plant king."

Luck pushed her over. Ester flailed to regain her balance and pushed him back. Luck laughed as he put his hands up in defense, but then noticed something behind Ester. The clouds were rolling in fast. A stampede of dark grayish brown eclipsed the sky. Ester stopped laughing when she noticed Luck's shaken expression. She tilted her head and made a face, trying to see what his blue eyes were looking at.

"What?" Ester asked when a strong gust of wind whipped her fly away hair across her face.

She turned around and gasped. The winds started to pick up, jarring some of the students awake. Brother Isa looked out towards the desert. A dust storm was heading their way. Brother Isa pulled the hover cart over immediately and hurried the kids off the back. The wind ripped through the land, almost knocking over one of the students.

"Get the tarp!" Brother Isa shouted.

Brother Isa helped the student up as he walked towards the cart to help Luck with the tarp. Ester fumbled for the carabiners, but they were nowhere to be found. The dust bit and stung at their skin as the wind picked up. Some of the students begin to wail and cry. Dust storms out here were much worst because of how close they were to the dunes. Brother Isa instructed them to get behind the hover cart and stay down. Luck unfolded the tarp but the wind was blowing so hard it was threating to rip the cover right from his hands. The flaps thrashed and popped Brother Isa in the face. He bit back the pain and caught the flap, wrestling it to the ground instructing the other students to sit on it while they secured the top.

"Ester! Carabiners?" Luck shouted.

"Can't," Ester shouted as she tried to look for the box.

Brother Isa looked beyond them the worst of it was upon them.

"There's no time!" Brother Isa waved for Ester and Luck to jump down. "Can you help hold it?"

Luck and Ester nodded. Together, all three of them held the tarp close to the hover cart while the other students secured the bottom by sitting on it. The winds tore through the land causing everything to bend to its will. Sand and dirt swept into any opening getting into their eyes, noses, and mouths. Ester couldn't use her hands to cover her face, so she looked down to avoid the worse of it, while holding up her end with both hands.

The storm broke against the grassy fields behind them, raging like waves in the ocean. Then, as quick as it washed over them, it subsided.

The tarp fell against them as they all panted in silence. Brother Isa looked around. Everyone was a little dirty, but fine. He lifted the tarp away and the sunlight flooded in. Ester and Luck stood up. Sand blanketed the grass behind them, but the little shoots still poked out from the ground.

"Yikes!" Luck pointed to Ester's face. "You look like crap."

"Have you seen yourself in the mirror?" Ester shook her head at Luck's clothes, which were covered in filth.

Luck laughed as the hover cart jolted back to life, startling them both. Brother Isa was already sitting back in the front, waving for the students to get back on. Ester and Luck exchanged looks and laughed as they packed up the tarp and hopped back on. They still had a good forty minutes until they reached the school, and now Ester was really tired. On the back of the wagon, she nodded off, and Luck pulled her close this time. She didn't fight it and fell asleep against his shoulder.

A small smile appeared on his face. Even though he wanted so much more, he was happy for the time that he had left to spend—these moments he would cherish forever.

It was very late when they got back. Brother Isa was nice enough to drop them off at their house. From the shadows, Adis watched Luck and Ester joke and laugh as they walked through the front yard. It made her blood boil to think the attention of such a handsome boy could be wasted on the likes of her. Adis clenched the basket of vegetables she was holding. Where did Ester get off believing she could ever amount to anything? She was no better than any of the other orphans, and she certainly wasn't better than her. Adis was at the top of her class. Ahe was the queen, and Ester was a daydreaming brute. Aomeone needed to remind her where her place was.

Chapter Three

The morning after they got back from the market came, Ester was bubbling with excitement. Her graduation ceremony was in five days, but more importantly, the acceptance letters for ranger academy would be arriving soon. She could hardly wait as the extra boost of excitement carried her through her morning routine. She pulled out a t-shirt and put on a pair of long shorts as she brushed her hair into a bun. Algaza was getting dressed a few beds down, and the two exchanged smiles as they hurried to get dressed. Pulling a hair tie with her teeth, Ester glanced at the picture of Captain Wildgrass Inspread, her idol and one of the most famous rangers to ever live. What if she got a chance to meet him? What if she turned out to be a renowned ranger like Inspread? Ester giggled at the idea. She was getting ahead of herself; she would just be happy to get in. Ester slipped on her shoes, and she was out the door.

She was just about halfway down the driveway when she realized she had forgot to water her plant. Missing just one day could derail the entire process. She turned around as some of the other kids gave her passing glances. She'd catch up. After all, it would only take a moment to water. She ran to the shed and pushed open the door only to find her tiny sapling shattered on the floor. In a panic she rushed to scoop up the soil, but the entire plant looked like it had been smooshed and the leaves had already started to dry.

"No," she whimpered, tears welling in her eyes.

How could this have happened? She held the tiny plant in her hands as she trembled. It felt like her dreams were slipping through her fingers like the tiny grains of soil. There was no saving it, and no time to grow another. Even all of Luck's divine power couldn't help this time.

Ester panicked. "No, I can't."

She ran from the shed into the yard. The once welcoming light blinded her. It felt like her world was spinning. Without this final project, she couldn't graduate, and if she didn't graduate what did it matter if she got her letter into ranger academy? Her heart started to race and her breathing spiraled out of control. What was she going to do now? There was no plan B, no time to start over. Ester ran back into the shed and leaned over the sink. Too many things flooded her mind, making her cheeks burn as she tried to hold back the tears. It was over for her and she knew it. Ester collapsed onto the floor and cried as the tears poured from her face.

***

Noon arrived and Ester found herself awoken by the sounds of birds chirping overhead. For a second, she had forgotten why she was in the shed until she saw the soil splattered across of the floor. Then the memories, along with the pain, flooded back. Ester sniffled, but her tears were all dried up and her head was pounding. She stood and looked at the mess scattered across the floor. It was grotesque. Ahe couldn't bear to look at it, but since she already missed school she didn't want to get into any more trouble by leaving a mess. Besides, her little opalia plant deserved better than to be left discarded on the floor. So she swept and cleaned up, best she could, feeling so much guilt. She tossed the pieces of pottery in the recycling and the remaining soil in the compost. As for her plant, she looked at it one last time as the tears built up in her eyes.

"I'm so sorry, little plant." She brought it to her chest and wept for both of their dreams.

Ester took the plant to the compost and dug a little hole and buried it. She felt like this would be the final resting place of her dreams as well. Ester stood and looked back at the house. The offenses were building up as she thought about how angry Sister Genevieve would be when she realized Ester missed school, but that was nothing compared to how she felt about her project. She needed to walk. Ester snuck to the back door and peaked inside. The key to the back door was under a pot, hidden just in case someone got locked out. Ester lifted the pot and took the key, using it to slowly open the door. She turned the handle and opened it, hoping and praying the sister was gone or upstairs, but then she remembered that it was the first of the week and Sister Genevieve went to market. Feeling a little relieved, Ester scanned the kitchen, foraging for scraps left to eat. She found an apple and drank three whole glasses of water before heading out again.

Ester walked the dirt road, in the opposite direction of the markets. There was no doubt Brother Isa would be paging Sister Genevieve about her absence, but Ester didn't care. Who knew how her plant fell, but it didn't matter. It was her responsibility to secure it. Ester's chest started to feel heavy again, as the sun beat down on her back. A breeze touched the land, blowing her hair out of her face.

Was this a sign? Was this the universes way of trying to let her down easy?

After all, she hadn't received her letter yet. For all she could have known, it could have been a no. Then none of this crazy plant stuff would even matter. She looked up at the sky, lonely clouds moved by in a sea of blue. The skies were the same no matter where you looked in Adum, just like the scenery. Just miles and miles of nothing. As a child when she was frustrated, she used to spend hours in the fields just staring up at the sky, but even on her worse days she at least had a place to call home.

But now, even the idea of home was starting to drift away.

She had no back-up plan. There was only ranger academy. She reached up and clenched her necklace around her neck. Why were things always so hard for her? Could she at least have one break? A lone tear rolled down her left cheek. She wiped away the tear as if it was some intrusive bug. Her parents always taught her not to give up so easily, but it was hard, really hard. She started to jog. Her feet beat the ground as if it were trying to exorcise the feeling of dread from her body. She picked up the pace into a run, determined to free herself from this pain.

Ester arrived home just as the other children were getting back from school. She walked silently, hoping to avoid the awkward question of why she wasn't in school today. The little ones spotted her and ran to her side. Bellarue was ready to launch an attack of questions, but buttoned up tight when she saw Ester's tired expression. The young girl slumped back, leaving Ester to walk alone, a courtesy she wished the boys would give her.

"Hey!" Tommy ran out in front of Ester. "Brother Isa was wondering where you were today?"

His comment resonated over a yard of nosey ears. Ester looked away fully intent on ignoring the younger boy.

"Rumor has it you spilt to go make out with a boy," Tommy said.

Ester ignored the darting glances and whispers and walked past Tommy. Out of the corner of her eye, she spotted Luck, but she made no indication she'd seen him.

"I mean even ugly girls deserve a chance!" Tommy yelled after her, torturing her again.

Ester stopped as Tommy and his friends fell out in laughter.

"Oh please," Adis stepped forward, Tavanee warily in tote, "as if the little mud rat could ever be so lucky to be with a boy."

"Adis," Luck finally spoke up, "that's enough."

Ester turned to look at him.

"Oh? You didn't hear?" Adis snickered. She spun around on the balls of her toes, batting those playful blue eyes. "Why don't you ask Ester why she's so mad?"

Luck shook his head, completely ignoring Adis' taunts. He didn't want any part of this charade. He passed Adis and approached Ester. Enraged, Adis turned to face them and balled her fists.

"I mean, after all, how's she supposed to make it if she can't even take care of a stupid plant!"

Silence washed over the children as if someone popped a balloon in a library. Adis inhaled, fruitlessly trying to take back her words as curious eyes rolled over the girls.

"What did you say?" A low feral growl came from Ester.

"Ester I—," Adis peered around frantically for support but

Tavanee had long since disappeared into the crowd.

"Ester?" Luck tried to step between them.

"You bitch! What did you do!" Ester tried to push Luck to the side, charging right for Adis.

Luck grabbed her mid-stride and tried to hold her back, but Ester fought him as Adis stumbled back.

"Ester!" Luck shouted. "Calm down!"

"Let go!" Ester ripped away from him.

Energy pulsated through Ester as she raised her fist. Adis held her hands up in defense, but Ester clobbered her to the ground.

It rattled Adis' skull and sent her rolling in the dirt, but she wasn't going down like this. Years of pent up jealously raged through Adis' body as her natural electric ability began to build up as well. This was not her defeating moment; she would not let Ester win.

Soon the girls were in a total brawl. Sparks flew as punches landed everywhere. A crowd of cheers and pointing fingers formed around the girls. Adis was no match physically, but her spirit would not quit.

This was as much of a personal battle for Ester as it was for Adis. Ester pushed back; she was sick and tired of Adis always messing with her. Ester slugged Adis in the stomach with a fist full of rage. Adis coughed but wasn't through yet and swung clumsily over Ester's head.

"You're an ugly brat!" Adis screamed.

"Better a brat than a bitch!" Ester grabbed her by the hair. She was ready to end this, as the electricity built in her fist.

"Ladies! That's enough!" An ear shattering holler silenced the group. Sister Genevieve flew off the porch and tore the girls apart by their ears. "I have had enough of your pettiness!" The girls whimpered under her might. "For this foolishness, you will be confined to your living quarters for the rest of the night!"

The evening was ushered in with silence. As punishment, all the children were forced to do extra chores after dinner for egging on the fight. As for Ester and Adis, they would not be getting off that easy. The two girls sat before the sister, their eyes glued to the floor. It was hot under the Sister's gaze. Neither one of them had the courage to talk or move, but Sister Genevieve wasn't going to wait all night for an answer. She leaned back in her sturdy wooden chair and crossed her arms.

"I don't know what has gotten into you both, and I very much don't care. You two are some of the oldest in the house and are expected to set the example for the younger children. Your behavior out in the front yard today was unacceptable. I should march right up to that school and let Brother Isa know of your actions, so that both of you can spend some time in summer discipline."

"But Sister Genevieve…" Ester cried.

"Silence!" The sister barked harshly, cutting her off.

Ester scrunched up her face, fighting back the urge to burst into a fit of angry tears. She knew Sister Genevieve would not tolerate any excuses or back talk. Ester felt like her future was in shambles.

The sister sighed and relaxed her shoulders. Judging by the broken expressions on the girls' faces, she felt her point had been heard loud and clear. She cleared her throat and adjusted herself in her chair.

"Now, if you two can manage to keep your hands off each other until graduation, I will forgo telling Brother Isa about your behavior this evening." Both girls breathed a sigh of relief. "But do not test me." She looked at Ester. "I have also received a message from Brother Isa stating that you did not show up for school today. Is that true?"

"Yes ma'am." Ester admitted, lowering her head.

A small smile creeped across Adis' face, but only a flash.

"You are not ill, obviously, so why did you feel the need to skip class?" Sister Genevieve asked.

Ester slumped in her chair. Why did she have to be this vulnerable in front of Adis, of all people? She was sure she had something to do with her plant, but she had no way of proving it.

"My plant, ma'am. It broke overnight. I was too upset to go to school and face Brother Isa." It burned her up inside to see her world crumbling around her. "So, I decided I needed some time away."

The sister eyed Ester. "Accidents happen. However, that is no reason to miss one of your final days in school."

"But it wasn't an accident!" Ester blurted.

"Ester, I don't want to hear your excuses." Sister Genevieve was starting to lose her patience again. "You will tell Brother Isa what happened tomorrow, and that is the end of that." Ester pouted and slumped back into her chair. "You two are dismissed."

Ester stormed off with Adis not far behind.

"Adis," Sister Genevieve said. "Is there anything you would like to tell me?"

The young girl froze, then shook her head. "No ma'am." The sister eyed her, but nodded and dismissed her.

***

The following morning, Ester struggled to get out of bed. She pulled the covers over her head, but it was fruitless. There was no avoiding it now. She would have to face Brother Isa alone and tell him the news, but that wasn't the part that ate her up inside. She would never get into ranger academy now. Any delay would make it twice as hard to re-apply, and her odds would be cut in half if she graduated with poor marks. On top of that, she would need to come up with the money for re-testing and train tickets. Where was she going to get that kind of money?

Ester lagged behind her housemates on their trek to school. She was in a sour mood and could tell the day wasn't going to get any better. Algaza walked beside her in silence, giving her reassuring glances, but Ester's heart had all but drained of any traces of happiness. The early morning sun beat down on her taunting her.

Morning classes rolled by without incident, but Ester barely paid attention as she gazed out the window in a haze. The bell rang for lunch and Ester tried to sneak out, but Brother Isa caught her before she could. Ester frowned as she walked past the rest of the students to his office. Humid and small, Brother Isa's office was decorated with pictures of smiling pupils he was surely proud of and his certificates to teach. The clock ticked against her nerves as she tapped her leg up and down. She wished she were outside eating, though she wasn't hungry. Brother Isa walked in. He was a tall man with a soft face like Luck's. He had been Ester's secondary school educator since the cross over from pre-adolescent school. He knew her almost as well as Sister

Genevieve, so nothing got past him. Brother Isa took a seat behind his neatly organized desk, and Ester once again found herself under the scrutinizing gaze of an authoritative figure. He ran his fingers through his dark brown hair, as he waited for Ester to speak.

"Ester." The sudden mention of her name shook her out of her stupor.

"I'm so sorry, Brother Isa, for missing class yesterday," she blurted out like a busted dam. "My plant died, I don't know how. I just..., I just found it on the floor in my shed." Ester wanted to melt, just like the tears threating to run down her face.

Brother Isa blinked twice then sighed. "Ester, you know I cannot pass you without a final project, and it is unlike you to be so careless." Brother Isa frowned.

Ester felt so bad. She knew there was nothing that could be done; she just wanted this day to be over.

"Brother Isa!" Luck barged in and bowed. "Please forgive my sudden intrusion." Confused Brother Isa turned to Luck. "Please allow me to offer my account on behalf of Ester."

"Account?" Brother Isa looked between the two, even Ester looked shocked.

"When Ester's plant died three weeks ago, I offered to help her produce a new one."

"Luck, you know the rules," Brother Isa cautioned. "This was a solo project; you were to work alone."

"Yes, sir, I understand this. However, all I did was point her in the right direction, to help her get started. The rest was up to her." Luck looked at Brother Isa with a more calm expression.

Brother Isa exchanged glances between the two. "And is this the plant that died? Your second one?" He looked at Ester.

Ester nodded in shame. "Yes, sir, I found it smashed on the shed floor yesterday morning."

"Smashed?" Brother Isa said.

"Well, broken," Ester slumped. Just remembering Adis' words was enough to get her angry but pointing fingers without proof would do nothing for her. "It was an opalia plant. I believe some creature got in and knocked it over or something."

Brother Isa looked at Luck in dismay. "Is this true, Luck?"

"Yes sir," Luck presented pieces of the broken pot to his teacher. "The window must have been left open. There was quite the mess. In our yard, we have creatures found of opalia."

"I'm so sorry." Brother Isa turned and looked at Ester. "I can see that you tried to take responsibility for your actions, but I still cannot pass you without a final project."

"What if I do something else?" Ester blurted. Brother Isa and Luck both looked at her. "If a project on plants is what you need, what if I write a detailed paper about the care of opalias? I learned a lot these past couple of weeks. I can tell you the whole process by heart."

Brother Isa looked at her and pressed his fingers into his temples. She had done very well these past couple of years, and it would be a shame to see all that progress derailed because of an accident. Brother Isa looked up with a stern look.

"I can't give you full credit."

"Half?" Ester perked up.

"A quarter, and the paper has to be five pages plus a presentation."

"Oh, thank you, Brother Isa!" Ester jumped up and down.

"But this is the best I can do. If your turn in an exceptional project you'll pass my course with decent marks, but it's due in three days."

"Thank you sir, thank you!" Ester bowed, as Brother Isa returned the gesture with hands clasped together.

Ester and Luck left together. She was so relieved, even if she only had a few days to start and write a paper. She walked briskly beside Luck, eager to get through the day, almost completely ignoring him.

"Ester, wait up." Luck called. They were practically jogging. She twirled around and looked him in the eyes, catching him off guard. She looked happy, happier than he had ever seen her. "It's not a race." He smiled at her.

"I know, it's just, well, I just can't believe I'm going to graduate and that means," she gasped suddenly, "that means I still have a chance to get into ranger academy! Yes! There's still hope I'll be able to blow this dust wave." In her excitement, she completely forgot Luck was standing there. He had stuck his neck out for her without knowing the full story. He had truly been a good friend. She froze in her excitement.

"Luck, I—"

"You're welcome, and I hope you get your ticket out." He smiled warmly.

"I don't mean it like that." Ester averted her eyes.

"I know," Luck chuckled. "I've known you since you were thirteen, and all you've talked about was getting into ranger academy. I'll be fine, besides you owe me. Go out and kick some ass and show those metropolis kids that we folks from Adum-la aren't to be messed with."

Ester fought back the urge to tear up and threw herself into Luck's arms. He was surprised but embraced it. He would miss her dearly, but he knew her spirit wasn't meant for the rich farmlands of Adum-la.

***

Ester whipped together her final project almost overnight. Luck was right about one thing: she had learned a lot about opalia plants. Her presentation went off without any hiccups and impressed Brother Isa enough that he boosted her credit to half. She was still mad at Adis, but she was finally graduating and, in a few days, she hoped she would be receiving her acceptance letter as well.

On the last day of school the entire school gathered for the graduation ceremony. It was a lovely sight to see. Family and friends of the graduating students stood in the fields to honor the students' final passage from youth to adulthood. For many of them, they would be taking jobs at their families' farms or entering trade school. For the children under Sister Genevieve's care, their fates were decided by the placement program, a program that offered post-orphanage support. Under this program, the government would give young orphaned adults tones for housing and job placement options. It was a heartbreaking and stressful time, but a fate they had all prepared for since the day they entered the orphanage.

Just three days after the ceremony, the younger children prepared to say their final goodbyes. Everyone had placement plans, everyone except Ester, who had yet to receive her acceptance letter. Jermane had been placed as an apprentice cook on a farm in the northern lands. Adis would be traveling to the mid-town region and become an office worker apprentice, and Luck was being sent southeast to work on the Fular's fruit farm. Sister Genevieve worried Ester would not receive the news she hoped for, but there was no convincing her otherwise. Even still, the deadline was fast approaching, and she was running out of time.

"Algaza, have you seen my summer skirt?" Jermane threw things around their large rectangular room in a panic.

"I haven't, I'm sorry." Algaza watched her search.

"Oh no, I can't go off without my favorite skirt. Sister Genevieve made it for me," Jermane said as she ran her fingers through her hair.

"Don't worry, you'll find it," Algaza reassured her.

"Ugh, why do these things have to be so complicated?" Jermane plopped on the bed. "I don't want to move, Algaza. I don't want to."

Algaza hurried to her side and hugged her. "I know, I don't want you to go either."

There was a light knock on the door, and the girls looked up to see Ester grinning. In her hand was the very skirt Jermane was looking for.

"Oh my goodness, where'd you find it?" Jermane rushed to the door and held the skirt in her hands. It was fresh and clean, just like new.

"Well, we can't send you off with dirty clothes." Ester wrapped her arm around her friend and hugged her tight.

"Oh Ester," Jermane began to cry.

"It's okay, Jermane. I know you'll be happy whereever you go."

Jermane sniffled. "But-but what about you?" She looked up with watery eyes.

"Don't worry about me." Ester forced a smile.

Jermane was the first to go. It was hard to say goodbye, but another child had already been sent to fill her place. That's how things worked; it made it hard to get attached, but Jermane had been a true friend. Ester would not forget about her. Just two days later, everyone said their final goodbyes to Adis. Ester wanted to skip out on it, but Sister Genevieve would not allow family to part on bad terms. Ester and Adis played nice, but Ester wouldn't be lying if she said she'd be happy to never see her again.

Now all that remained were Luck and Ester. It was hard in these final days waiting for a response. She wondered if her letter had been lost in the post and wished they would just call. She assumed for normal kids this wouldn't be as stressful. They all had homes and families. Normal kids didn't have to worry about being evicted.

The next day, Ester sat outside on a stump alone. The clouds were rolling in; it would probably rain later today. What would she do if the letter never came in? What would she do if the later did come in and it was a no? Ester didn't even want to think about it. She looked up at the sky and followed the sun's shadow behind the clouds. Sometimes she wished that she could have had a normal life or at least given the chance to live with someone from her tribe. She felt so lonely sometimes. She looked down at her necklace. It was all she had left, along with an old wrinkled picture of her family. She smiled a little thinking about the day she took that picture. She could remember it so well. It was just after she had turned eleven, after her naming ceremony. Her family was at the markets, and a vender was selling portraits. She and her older brother, Corta, begged their parents for a picture and finally her dad gave in. She remembered her mother being skeptical at first, but when the picture was printed and framed everyone was shocked. Back then Ester thought it was magic because the picture captured their essence perfectly. Ester hugged the memory. There must have been a reason for her to survive. Ester looked up at the sky. Why else would she be here and not the rest of her family?

It rained in the afternoon, just like Ester thought it would. She watched Luck send off another taxi. He wasn't fooling her; he was only staying because of her and on somedays she briefly wondered what a life with Luck would be like.

Luck covered his head in vain as he ran back inside. Ester smiled a little, feeling grateful that Luck even wanted to stay. She started to daydream when a light knock at the door stirred her awake.

"Hey." Luck appeared, trying his best to play it cool in his damp clothes. "Just our luck it would rain today. I kind of wanted to go for a walk."

Ester turned and sort of smiled. He walked over to the windowsill and joined her. Normally boys weren't allowed in the older girls' room, but he was sure Sister Genevieve would make an exception.

"Hey, don't worry. I think everything will work out," Luck said.

"You're just saying that." Ester laid her head back on the windowsill, wishing the rain would wash her away.

"I'm not." Luck put his hands up. "If you're the same girl who put together a five page paper and presentation in three days, then I'm sure you aced the entrance exams."

Ester smirked. "I padded that paper so hard."

Luck laughed. "I kind of figured. You were using one too many descriptive words, but you had Brother Isa hooked."

"He does have a thing for flowers." Ester smiled. "But that was just dumb luck. Those exams I took back in Tel-Sa were the real deal, no padding those."

Luck placed his hands on her shoulder, catching her gaze. "Some things aren't the result of dumb luck. Somethings happen because you work for them, that is the Adum way." Luck inched in closer, and Ester started to close her eyes when she heard the hum of a hover engine outside.

"Mail," Ester peered through the foggy window. "Is that the mail deliverer?"

Luck squinted through the foggy glass. "I guess so…"

The excitement in Ester's eyes was uncontainable. She took off down the stairs with Luck trailing behind her. She swerved past kids, leapt over toys, and squeezed past groups of talking children. She ran down the third set of stairs and through the foyer and swung open the door. It was pouring now and the mail deliverer had just closed their mailbox. Without thinking, she ran out into the rain.

"Ester!" Luck called breathlessly after her.

Luck cringed at the pouring rain and the prospect of going out again, but at the last minute he grabbed a jacket and umbrella, covering his head, and ran after her.

"Ester!"

She was facing the mailbox. The door was open and there was a single, unopened letter inside steadily getting wet from the rain. She was frozen with her eyes locked on it. Luck immediately popped open his umbrella to cover them both.

"Well, aren't you going to open it?" Luck looked at her.

She stared at him, then swallowed as she pulled out the letter. Her eyes glued to the florescent ranger academy lettering. Her heart raced as the envelope shook in her hands. Sister Genevieve and some of the younger children gathered at the front door, waiting in anticipation. She took a deep breath and tore open the letter, pinching it open a little then sliding her thumb across the crease. She pulled out the cream colored stationary and unfolded it.

> *Thank you for applying to the Academy of the Rean Coalition of Rangers. On behalf of the recruiter and commanding officers, we would like to extend an invitation and welcome you into our program. We look forward to seeing you soon. May Rean be with you.*

Ester looked at Luck and back at the letter again, then back at Luck again.

"Ester!" Luck struggled to balance the umbrella. "You made it! You got in!"

Ester clasped her month with her hand then looked down at the letter again. "I made it!"

She shouted this time. Sister Genevieve and the other children shouted and cheered as they watched Ester dance in the rain. She was right about one thing; this rain had washed away something. It washed away all her doubts that she was on the right path. This was her fate.

Chapter Four

Ester sat at the bus stop alone. The sky was clear and perfect. It was a beautiful day but bittersweet day. She stared down at her shaking hands. She made it, finally, after all those years of hard work; she was going to ranger academy. It almost didn't seem real. It was an hour till noon and the wind picked up, blowing spirals of sand across the dunes. She wouldn't miss the dust storms or the blaring heat, but a peg of sadness grew in her heart at the thought of this being the last time she might be in this place. She shielded her eyes with her arm as the dirt blew through the makeshift bus stop. She would miss her friends dearly; she would have to at least make a plan to visit them one day. She was sure they would find happiness in their placements.

As she sat, her mind drifted to what her new life would be like. No more walking for miles to get to the nearest town. In the metropolis, they had super trains and everyone owned a hover car or jetter. She wondered what it would be like to soar high in the sky on the back of a new model hover jetter. She loved air bikes. She remembered her trip to Tel-Sa, seeing those amazing bikes soaring high through the trees. It would be her first purchase, she thought, even though she hadn't a clue how much they cost.

Up ahead and from the west, she saw a hover cart breach the horizon. She squinted as she jumped to her feet. Her heart raced as the hover cart toted forward, slowly. She kept her eyes on it like a bird, but it wasn't the bus. It was too small. She sat back down and sighed as she watched it slowly pass. She waved at the family on board. They must have made the long journey from the markets outside of Tel-Sa, a very popular trading spot. Ester remembered passing them on her trip into the metropolis. It was so much bigger than the markets around here.

Sister Genevieve use to tell her stories from her youth about how her tribe would make garments to sell there. Ester yawned and stretched back on the empty bench. She doubted any other travelers were heading to Ans-On; nobody went that far. She laid back and closed her eyes and tried to piece together what Ans-On looked like. Skies crowded with hover cars, people wearing clothes wildly unfamiliar to her, and buildings that seemed so tall that they looked as if they held up the sky. She imagined zooming trains and giant floating telescreens. Galaxia. A smile appeared on her face. Ans-On was where her idol lived. What if she got to see her? Ester tossed the idea. That was asking too much, but Ans-on was where all the big idols lived. It was the hub of the planet.

Another hour passed, and Ester began to drift to sleep. She was stirred awake by a low rumble in the distance. The sound was coming from the east, so it wasn't her bus, but the noise would not let her sleep. She sighed and leaned up as the sound got louder. It must be more merchants leaving for Tel-Sa. She repositioned herself and closed her eyes again, allowing the sound of the engine to lull her back to sleep. The hover cart approached and slowed to a stop a few yards away. She listened to the door slam and feet shuffle in the sand. It must be someone being dropped off at the stop. She forced herself awake, rubbing her eyes.

"Tired already?" A familiar voice said to her.

Her head sprung up as she pulled her hand from her face. "Luck?"

"In the flesh." He chuckled, in his dirt covered farm uniform.

"What are you doing here?" She rose and stretched. He was the last person she would expect to see.

"Aww, not happy to see me, and I came all this way." He walked closer, leaving only a foot between them. "I came to wish you luck."

"Again?" She laughed.

"Again." Luck stared at her like he would never see her again.

"Well, it's not like I'm never coming back…" she trailed off, but they both knew that was a lie.

Luck laughed. "Right, well if you do come back, I'll be—"

"At Fular's Fruit Farm, I know. You've told me a thousand times." She stared at his face. Why did he have to look so sad? "Luck?"

"Yes?"

"Thanks for seeing me off, even if it was for the four-hundredth time."

"You are welcome, and I'd gladly see you off four-hundred times more."

"I know." Ester stared into his eyes as a low rumble hummed in the background. Luck looked pass her and saw a large hover bus approach.

"I think your ride's here."

Ester spun around, her eyes wide. She nearly leapt into the road to get a better look. There it was, just like the one she road to Tel-Sa. It hovered above the dirt, displacing the sand around it. Ester danced in place and threw her fist in the air. Luck chuckled, and in that moment, Ester remembered him.

"Luck." She turned to him.

"Good luck." He turned and waved as the bus pulled up. It was the only way he could say goodbye without it hurting.

Ester stood there and watched him head back to his hover cart as the bus came to a complete stop. Her brow furrowed, but this didn't have to be goodbye. She was always welcome at home. The doors skidded open, and a few people got off. The driver eyed Ester.

"You got a ticket?" The middle-aged man shouted over the hum of the engine.

"Yes sir!" She pulled out her ticket card and scanned it and turned around. Luck waved as he slowly started to make a U-turn in his hover cart. She quickly found a spot in the back and watched Luck drift away off into the distance. It felt so odd, but watching him leave made her feel like she had finally closed the book on this chapter of her life.

"Good luck, Luck," she said under her breath as she settled in for the long ride.

***

The sun had crawled all the way to the other side of the sky when

Ester arrived at the east bus station in Tel-Sa. She hopped off and stretched before heading to her next stop. The ride had been unnaturally long, but at least they didn't have to stop because of a dust storm. However, her journey was far from over. Even from this station she would have to take another bus to get to the grand station on the west side, but she had time before her next bus arrived. This time she wasn't leaving until she went to Fried Tuzan, the chain restaurant of her dreams. She exited the station and walked out onto a platform and was surprised to see so many people. Even at dusk people still littered the streets. It was pandemonium. She wondered if businesses ever closed.

Across the street from the station there was a food platform. Only the metropolises had eating platforms. They were like the shops in the marketplaces back home but with big name eateries. She checked her watch; the time was seventeen hundred hours. Her next bus left in an hour and a half, plenty of time for her to grab a bite to eat. She walked across the platform and went to the railing and stared at all the people below. Hover cars zipped by, and people chatted and rushed in and out of the station. There were a lot more people from Adum-La here than she expected. They were easy to point out because of their simple clothes. She glanced at the people wearing ride suits, a very popular style of body suits that people wore in the metropolises. All the rangers wore suits similar to ride suits, but ranger suits were specially designed for combat. She looked at her rags. She had on her favorite tan short sleeved shirt with her patchy faded green button up over shirt and matching patchy mud brown pants. It wasn't a ride suit, but she could still kick some ass in it, and she was not ashamed. She walked across the short sky bridge to the food platform. Sister Genevieve had been nice enough to give her some extra tones for a few meals and packed her fresh bread and salted meat for her trip. She'd eat that later. Today, she wanted Tuzan. She walked up to the door and opened it. The scent of freshly fried foods invited her in. The clerk at the desk greeted her with a warm smile.

"Hello, welcome to Fried Tuzan and Co, the birthplace of Rean's famous triple dipped bane squid." The woman's bubbly demeanor took Ester by surprise. "Can I offer you a combo with a large flavored water or wheat juice?"

"Um…" Ester was a little intimidated by the options. She only recognized a few items from the advertisements.

"Would you like to try our sampler?" The bubbly woman pointed to item number four on the display screen.

Ester looked up, still completely clueless what anything was. "Sure."

"Excellent!" The woman clasped her hands together.

The woman smiled and rang Ester up, and by the time Ester paid for her food, it was already done. She couldn't believe the speed. She took her meal and thanked the woman, heading towards a small table facing a large tented window. On the horizon, she could see the city of Tel-Sa, a jungle of buildings and trees. It was beautiful. She unboxed her food and the aroma hit her like a pail of fresh water. How in all of Rean could something smell so good? She eagerly took her first bite and was instantly attacked by a mouthful of flavors and spices.

Wow, just wow, she said to herself. It was every bit as good as the advertisements suggested. She really wished Jermane was here to enjoy this. Ester took her time enjoying her dinner and felt nothing but joy as she wondered what other tasty foods she could try.

When she was done, she boarded the bus to grand station; the trip from the east to the west part of the state took over three hours. She was tired but still excited. From the grand station, she would take a train across the Who-da plains and then she'd be in Ans-on. With sleep tugging at her eyes, Ester sat and looked out the window. It was dark, but she could still make out the small villages in the distance by their flickering lights. The nation state of Who-da was nothing but miles of grassy fields. It was the only state to still consist of free roaming tribes. As a child, Ester's mother told her that the beasts of Who-da were the fallen gods from the motherland and served as the protectors of the people and their resources. Who-da is said to be the birthplace of all Reanian people, the heart of her planet. She fell asleep thinking of her family as she reached up and touched her amber colored necklace. She would make her tribe proud, and one day, become a protector of the people just like her idol, Captain Inspread.

Daylight broke and woke Ester from her sleep. She was only miles from Ans-on, but the metropolis was starting coming into view. She didn't think it was possible, but the nation state of Ans-on was more technologically advanced than Tel-sa. Free from any signs of agriculture, the metropolis looked shiny and sleek. The train crossed the city lines and was thrust into a futuristic world with high flying hover cars and tall blue and silver tinted buildings that touched the sky. As the train slowed, giant hover screens bombarded Ester with advertisements and news broadcasts just before they entered the station. In the train station, there were holograms that displayed the weather all over Rean and fully digital walls with tele-shows and news broadcasting. This was something kids in Adum-la only joked about, but the people who lived in Ans-on really did live in a different world.

The train came to a stop and the conductor announced that they had arrived in east station. Everyone got up and walked to the doors. Ester followed, but she wasn't sure where to go next. She'd never been this far west before. The doors opened and Ester, along with the crowd, flooded out. It was loud and people pushed by her to catch their next train. No one remotely looked like her, with her torn clothes and messy hair. Everyone wore brightly colored ride suits with gadgets snapped and pinned to their bodies. They looked like tele-show models in their vibrate green, blue, and pink ride suits, even their hair was colorful and bright. Ester got carried away with the crowd and was dumped off in the atrium, the main transportation center. She looked up and around, even the clear blue windows where 100 percent digital. She recognized one of the tele-shows: Dr. Blaze. She stared at it for too long and was nearly knocked over by an uncaring businessman.

She jerked around to snap at him, but he carried on as if Ester wasn't even there. She figured rudeness was a trait found all over Rean. The time was zero seven hundred hours. Her next train left at zero eight hundred hours, but she needed to make it to Core Station. She pulled her out hologram map from the welcome package she received from the academy, which gave step by step directions to get from her home to ranger academy. The only problem was that the directions were meant for someone who frequently traveled around the city. If it wasn't for Brother Isa, who had been a missionary in Tel-sa and Cha-la, she would have never made it this far. Now she was in Ans-on, and this place was a whole other confusing mess.

She looked around as she walked, trying not to seem lost. She found the exit to the outside in hopes of finding some landmarks and the outside was even worse. Hover cars zipped by, at speeds that insects would envy. People cruised on hover boards and jetters through the crowds, much too close for her comfort. Nothing looked familiar to her. She couldn't even tell what was a restaurant or a shop. Sweat formed on her brow as she walked back into the station; there was no way she was going to find her way to Core Station out there.

"Are you lost?" A neon-blue haired man with matching blue lipstick stopped and asked her.

She blinked a few times, trying to process what she was staring at. Folks back in Adum-la were not this eccentric, mainly because make-up and dirt didn't work well together. She nodded and watched the blue haired man pluck a candy pop from his lips.

"Oh, you poor thing, where are you headed?" The man asked.

"Um," Ester peered at her map. "Core Station?"

A smile formed on his lips, making Ester cringe at his blue tinted teeth. "Oh hun, you're in the right place." He pointed to a hallway on the left. "Take the underway. It goes right to Core Station."

"Uh, thanks."

"Anytime!" The man waved goodbye.

She was grateful for his help; now she knew at least what direction to head in. Back in the atrium, she took the left tunnel. On the walls flashed arrival and departure times for the underway trains. She did a double take at the speeds; it would only take thirty minutes to get to Core Station from the east station. That seemed impossible, but she continued forward anyways. She reached the turnstiles and watched people scan their cards. She nearly forgot that she received something similar in her welcome package. She slid her backpack off her shoulders and dug around for her card. It was paper thin but hard as a rock—thank goodness for financial assistance. The school had covered most of the cost in transportation, as long as she didn't miss any of her rides. It was getting close to zero seven thirty hundred hours, and she didn't want to find out what happened if she had to pay for a train ticket. She walked up to the turnstile and watched a gentlemen scan his card and enter. It seemed easy enough. Ester lifted her card and scanned it, but the light blared red and did not let her through. She tried again, but it was still red. She turned and looked around, everyone was doing the same thing. She watched a child wave their card on the scanner and the light turned green. Was her card deactivated? She tried again and again.

"It's backwards and down, you twill!" A man shouted from behind, and it was then that Ester noticed the line forming behind her.

Ester jumped and turned her card around and the light turned green. Surprised, she didn't waste any time and hurried through. From there, she headed to a large display with the names of places she'd never heard of. There were no listings for Core Station. Her heart sunk; she hoped the blue haired man hadn't lied to her. She looked all over, when she noticed that this was a listing for trains arriving and departing from the west station—the station she had just came from. She rolled her eyes in frustration. These stations were so confusing. She walked down the corridor until she found the listing for east station, the one she was currently at. There it was, Core Station, the train was leaving in fifteen minutes. She glanced at her watch.

"Crap!" She raced down the corridor.

There were dozens of gates and stops; this place was a lot bigger than she thought. She looked up at the gate numbers. The train from east station to Core Station was 102 and she was only at gate thirty-five, so she ran like the floor was on fire.

Out of breath and sweaty, Ester had made it to gate 102. People eyed her behind their phones and tablets. She smiled and played it cool as she recomposed herself. The train arrived promptly at zero eight hundred hours. She boarded and was on her way.

"Please buckle your seat restraints and remain seated until we stop at the next station," the woman on the speakers chimed as Ester settled in her seat.

Ester did as instructed when she noticed a child flailing about and shrieking in the row next to her. His mother was trying everything to calm him, but he continued to fuss. Ester sighed and smiled, the cries of children were all too familiar to her. Normally a sweet treat or a tickle was enough to subdue even the crankiness child. Ester was sure the child would settle when she noticed a small stuffed toy on the floor in the aisle next to the mother. She looked up at the boy, he wasn't flailing randomly, he was trying to reach his toy. Ester got up and handed the toy to the mother, who thanked her repeatedly. Just as Ester was about to say no problem, the train took off, knocking her off balance. Ester stumbled into her seat and watched the happy pair. It was something about the smiles of children that made Ester happy. She turned and glanced out the window. The scenery passed by in a colorful blur. She couldn't take her eyes off all the things zipping by. It didn't feel like they were going that fast, and yet she thought if they didn't slow down she would be hurled into the future.

From Core Station, she boarded her final train to ranger academy on Juw-ja island. Most of the islands on Rean were uninhabitable, but it was agreed that moving the global military to an isolated island was the best place to set up headquarters and Juw-ja did not disappoint. The rocky temperate island offered great protection from invaders and was isolated and small enough to run and manage. Northwest of Adum-la it was colder, but not too cold that the island was ravished by snow. It was just perfect for what the United Nations of Rean needed.

Aboard the train to Juw-ja, Ester noticed more faces close to the same age she was. This was her first look at the prospective students who would be attending ranger academy. These young adults would be her peers. No one on the train looked like they were from Adum-la. Though she would happily take the title of the first person from Adum to get into the academy, she hoped that wasn't the case. Everyone sat down and got settled as the train began to take off. Ester was excited and a little nervous about crossing the ocean for the first time. The train sped through the tunnel, then out into the city where it cruised between the skyscrapers high above the streets. Ester's eyes were plastered to the window. There were so many new model hover cars in the sky. Some entered buildings while others exited, as if one could just fly up to a building and enter it. Hugged close to the sleek shinny buildings were platforms that people were dining at. The platform floated around the building as visitors ate like it was normal. Ester couldn't believe her eyes. Then they hit the coast. She looked down at the ports and the ships then gasped when she saw the ocean. It was huge, wider than any plantation or field she had ever seen. It looked like one big blanket of moving dark bluish green. It sparkled from the sunlight as large sea serpents breached the surface. Ester leaned so close to the window that her breath fogged up the glass. She had never seen a sea serpent in the wild before.

Juw-ja island appeared on the horizon, and Ester's mouth dropped as she watched it get closer. It was rocky and flat and from the skies hover crafts lifted and took off. She watched the sky as a Rean forty-seven pointed its thrusters downward for landing. She had only seen forty-sevens on the tele-shows in school. The forty class was the only class of star ship that could travel to other planets within their galaxy. It could make the trip from Ceapeaya to Fandour and back to Rean without burning out its solar engines. As the train veered around to the east part of the island, Ester could see other cadets. Some were in marching formation, while others were practicing with CuCores, specialty designed weapons that harnessed her people's natural electric abilities and amplified them. The train pulled into the ranger academy station, and all the cadets on the train drew quiet as they looked out the windows. There were hundreds of cadets and rangers walking on the platform. The trained slowed to a stop.

"Attention all new cadets, please exit and report to the check-in station for processing. Attention all new cadets, please exit and report to the check-in station for processing."

The message repeated. Ester filed out with the rest of her peers but couldn't ignore the stares she was getting from the other kids around her. She did look a little out of place compared to the other kids, but she'd earned her right to be here just like the rest of them. Once off the train, she was one in a crowd of hundreds. The new cadets weren't the only ones arriving back to school; senior cadets, instructors, and active duty rangers all walked about.

"Attention all new cadets, please exit and report to the check-in station for processing."

She looked around for the check-in station and caught eyes with a pale skinny blond boy. His icy blue eyes stared at her, as if it wanted to ask a question, but nothing was exchanged but a smile. Ester blinked twice before the intercom cut off her thoughts.

"Attention all new cadets, please exit and report to the check-in station for processing."

Ester looked back at the place the boy was standing at before, but he was gone. She looked around for him then shrugged. Looking for the check-in station was hard. It was impossible to see over the immense crowd and even harder to focus over the chatter and intercom blaring in her ears. She wished there were some kind of sign or arrow that pointed her in the right direction. She saw some of the students from the train and decided to follow them. They weren't wearing ranger suits so they must be new students. As she followed them her decision proved to be the right one. She saw a large hover screen that read "Check-In." She smiled and headed right over.

The check-in post was a long hall with many rooms. It was where cadets went for their physical exams and paperwork check. Cadets stood in line and waited to be sent to a different room. Ester looked around at people entering and exiting the rooms. It was so clean and orderly. The walls were a dull chrome gray, and the doors a soft cream. Each slide open on their own as students shuffled in and out. Ester presented her academy card, one she received in her welcome package, to the coordinator for verification. The coordinator took one glance at Ester then scanned her card. There was a nod, which helped calm her nerves. She was meant to be here, and it wasn't a mistake. The coordinator sent her to room 45-6. Ester took her card and hurried over to the line that corresponded to her room number. Ester lined up behind another girl with dark brown skin and a head full of thick curly hair who wore a loose tan dress buckled around the waist with a black belt.

"Oh my goodness I'm so nervous." The girl said once she saw

Ester.

"Yeah, me too," Ester said, as she looked around.

"I've come a long way, and I'm just racked with emotions right now," the girl said as she ran her fingers through her thick dark brown hair.

"Same," Ester laughed a little.

"I'm Samay by the way, Samay As-Sulard." Samay extended her hand.

"I'm Ester, Ester DuTain." Ester reached out and shook it.

"It's nice to meet you." Samay smiled.

The door opened, and a cadet walked out. Samay looked in front of her then back at Ester.

"Oh, gotta go! Hope we meet again." She waved and entered the room.

Ester waved. Samay seemed nice. Ahe hoped they would be in the same class together. As Ester waited, she got a good look around. Cadets were flying in and out of the rooms and there seemed to be a good mix of cadets here. While most wore ride suits, some wore beautiful dresses and wraps similar to what Samay was wearing. There were even cadets wearing tattered pants and shirts like Ester, but the one thing that got Ester's attention were the different hair styles. She admired those who dyed their hair vibrant colors like red and purple, but personally she wouldn't mind getting hers cut. She looked around for the blond boy she saw earlier, but the examiner interrupted her thoughts by calling the next cadet. Ester hurried into the room and took a seat. It looked like a fancier version of a doctor's office. Everything was completely digital, even the scales. Ester was amazed.

"Good morning," a man with long dark brown hair said with a smile. "Can I get your name?

"Yes, it's Ester DuTain," Ester said as she straightened up.

"Thank you," The examiner said as he brought up her information, pushing his hair from his face. "You're from Adum-la? I haven't seen anyone from there all day. I was beginning to think we weren't getting any this year."

"This year? So people from Adum-la do join the academy?"

"Absolutely." The examiner laughed. "Now, let's get you processed so you can start your day."

The examiner ran her blood work, took her measurements, and had her complete a series of simple physical tests. Ester was out of breath after she finished running on the treadmill. The examiner nodded and pulled out another piece of equipment. To Ester, it looked like a tablet connected to a pole with four legs on wheels. She wondered what it was for.

"Okay, now we're going to measure your natural conductivity level." The examiner tapped a button on the screen. It turned green, and a light green outline of a hand appeared. "All you have to do is focus your electricity into your hand and discharge with your hand pressed against the screen. And don't worry about breaking it, it can take a beating." The man chuckled.

Ester nodded and raised her hand to the screen. Her heart started to beat as she tried to draw all her energy to her hand. She was a little nervous as sparks began to form throughout her arm.

"Good, now focus it to your hand."

Ester tried, but she couldn't push it past her elbow. She grunted as she pushed harder. *Come on*, she mumbled under her breath and then the sparks began to pop. She smiled as she placed her hand on the screen.

"Now discharge."

Ester did as she was told and let go.

"Wow, I'm impressed. Your natural power level is five out of ten, that's good." The man checked off the boxes on his tablet.

Ester's cheeks felt warm. She was grinning from ear to ear, even though having a power level of five still put her at average. She was happy to find out she was in the upper average range, with the average range being three to five. She sat back down as the examiner processed her blood work. She scratched her neck and noticed something odd. Her necklace felt warm. Her heart was racing, meaning her temperature must have been up too, which may explain why it was so suddenly warm. Still, she thought it was a little weird. The examiner turned and gave her medical approval. Ester beamed with happiness as she signed the release forms on the tablet and was issued a uniform and dorm assignment. It looked like she would be rooming with more people again—nothing she wasn't used to. The examiner gave her some quick instructions and sent her on her way.

She exited the room and headed towards the hall. Everything about the academy was high-tech, well-polished, and new. There wasn't a single speck of dust on the carpeted floors. She stopped and watched a news broadcast on a screen embedded in the wall, from a station in the nation state of Huma-ko. It was fascinating to watch news live from another part of her world and not just hearing the leftovers like back home. After a minute, she headed toward her dorm.

There were arrows on the wall for new cadets to follow to get to their dorms. The examiner back at check-in said the arrows would be up for the first week of school, much to Ester's relief.

Orientation started promptly at sixteen hundred hours, and it was thirteen thirty hundred hours, so she had plenty of time to get to her new dorm, change, and report to orientation. Following the arrows, Ester slowed a bit to take in the new sights. She took the escalator down to the exit and walked through the sliding doors out into a large courtyard enclosed by trees. The air was crisp, heavy with the scent of sea water. It was colder here than in Adum-la, which was currently about to super heat as summer tightened its grip. She stopped and took a deep breath of fresh sea air. It was amazing being so close to the sea. She wanted to stand there all day taking in the sounds and fresh air, but there was another smell threatening to break the moment she was having. She turned her head and sniffed around. Not sure where the strange odor was coming from. She then lifted up her arm, and her nostrils were attacked by the pungent odor of forty hours of hot sweaty pits. She grimaced. The last thing she wanted was to stink up the place on her first day. Ester headed to her dorm, quicker this time. She could explore later.

The dorms were on the other side of the courtyard through a large garden. She walked quickly, but slowed to look at all the trees and flowers found all over Rean that were planted here. She stopped to smell a rose lily, a plant found in north Adum. Its buds smelled of sweet berries, and its pedals a deep pink. This species was prized for its beauty but was treasured for its ability to grow anywhere. Just beyond the path, Ester caught sight of another famous plant, black wood grave, commonly found in the nation state of Huma-ko. These hardy trees were known for their rich black wood, very good for making furniture and small boats. Ester admired the plants and felt a little proud that she could name them. She was sure Luck would be in love if he were here, but there was something else she noticed in the distance that caught her eye. She walked closer and found a stone fountain with five iron statues posed around it. It was of the five leaders of peace, the ones who were responsible for bringing peace to Rean after a long and bloody hundred-year civil war. Ester walked around it a few times marveling at the detail. Water rolled down the iron figures from a tilted pot to signify peace and unity for all. Then she remembered why she was in such a hurry in the first place; she needed to shower. She looked around and behind the fountain were five paths. Each marked by one of the five animal symbols representing one of the five nation states on her planet. Ester was in house Snake and found her symbol right away. She followed the sign and hurried along the long sidewalk down to her dorm.

Just down the hill, amongst the trees, was her dorm—a sleet dark gray building that looked completely out of place compared to its surroundings. The bright green of the trees clashed against the cold gray metal of the building. Engraved in steel above the entrance was the symbol of a giant winged ear serpent with a forked tale, the symbol of Dane Ans, one of the great leaders of the past and founder of Ans-on, master of peace. Ester was more than excited to be placed in the house representing Ans-on. She walked up to the door amongst the sea of chattering cadets and scanned her wristband. Some looked like they had already formed groups and talked as if they were good friends. She headed through the sliding doors of the lobby and gasped at how nice it looked inside. Everything was decorated in the house's colors: navy blue and silver. There were couches to lounge on and tables to study at. In the back, cadets strolled in and out of a room that looked like her sleeping quarters. Ester headed there but caught a glimpse of the telescreen. They were running a story about Labadora. Ester wanted to watch more, but she needed to get changed as fast as possible. She turned towards the dorm area and ran into someone. Items spilled onto the floor as all eyes were on them.

"Oh my gosh, I'm so sorry." Ester reached down to help them pick up their things.

"It's okay."

Ester looked up and caught eyes with the blond haired boy she had seen back at the station. Ester was enamored by his crystal blue eyes. His cheeks were hot red in contrast to his extremely pale skin, and his lips were a vivid pink, the same as his finger nails. His smile just lit up his entire face, and he wore an all-white ride suit with the stomach cut out in the shape of a star. She blinked a few times and continued to help him pick up his items. She'd never seen a boy like him before. That's when she realized she was mostly picking up cosmetics.

"I know what you're thinking," the boy said. "Why on Rean did I bring so many perfumes? But you never know what you're going to need."

Ester squatted with her mouth open. That was the last thing on her mind, but the boy continued to go on and on about perfume.

"Thank you," he said, then gasped. "Where are my manners? I'm Angel, Angel Johnson." He held out his hand, also ghostly pale, but well-manicured.

Ester shook it. "I'm Ester, Ester DuTain."

"It's nice to me you." Angel stood up with an armful of perfumes and foundations, threatening to explode from his arms again.

"Um, do you need some help with that?" Ester held out her hand under his arm to try and catch any stray products.

"Umm, I guess so, thank you so much."

"No problem," Ester said as the two walked towards the back room together.

"I just got here. I mean we all did, duh, but I think I'm going to like it here. I mean we are some of the first few to be in this dorm after the remodel."

Ester nodded, not even questioning how he would know this.

"Though I'm not a fan of the navy blue," Angel said as he readjusted some of the product in his hands.

Angel was surprisingly chatty. To an outsider, one would think they were best friends and if it were left to Angel, they probably were going to be. The sliding doors opened, and Ester was shocked to see that she was sharing a space with both girls and guys. The room was large and similar to the one she had back at the orphanage, but this was an upgrade. The walls were chrome gray, with windows expanding high toward the ceiling. Beds with shelved canopies lined both walls, a total of fifteen beds on each side. She looked around the room. Each bed space had a glass end table with a tiny lamp on it, a single person bed that sat on drawers, and another set of drawers at the foot of the bed. Most of the beds had been taken, but out of the corner of her eye, she saw a skinny brown arm waving at her.

"Um, do you know her?" Angel pointed to the girl.

Ester squinted and a smile appeared on her face. It was Samay.

Ester walked right over with Angel in tow.

"Hi again," Samay said as she stood next to her bed.

"Hi!" Ester threw her bag unto the bed next to her, careful not to drop any of Angel's stuff.

"I'm so glad we're in the same house." Samay smiled.

"Same." Ester smiled back.

"Oh my gosh," Angel gasped. "I love your dress."

"Thank-thank you," Samay said, then gasped when she saw what was in Angel's hand "Is that Something Symple?"

"Yes it is! It's the bi-year edition," Angel raved.

"Wow! They only have The Season Peaks collection back home." Samay admired.

"Oh no, well here in Ans-on they have everything, and I don't mind sharing."

"Really? Thank you so much," Samay laughed. "Do you already have a bed? There's a free one next to Ester's. If that's okay with you, Ester?"

"Um, sure," Ester said. She felt a little uneasy about sleeping so close to a boy, but judging by everyone else's reaction it must not be a big deal.

"Yay!" The two said in unison.

Angel rushed away to change bed assignments and moved his things next to Ester. Ester watched them rave about perfumes as she unpacked. The three of them looked like a bowl of odd ball soup, but Ester didn't mind. She was happy to have met some friendly people.

Ester unzipped her bag on the bed. She didn't have many outfits, but she shuffled around for her picture. As a gift, Sister Genevieve had made her a wooden frame for her wrinkly old family photo. Ester loved it; she was nearly brought to tears when the sister presented it to her. The picture and her kiko robe were some of her few valued treasures.

"So where are you from, Ester?" Samay asked, breaking Ester from her train of thought.

"I'm from Adum-la. What about you?"

"Wait, you're from Adum-la?" Angel cut in, "Whoa, that's like a million miles away, but I guess I kind of understand because of your clothes."

"What's that supposed to mean?" Ester said as she raised an eyebrow.

"It's not a bad thing, it's just, a little different," Angel said.

Ester wanted to laugh; he shouldn't be talking based on what he was wearing.

Angel stared at Ester for a minute and tilted his head as the super blond curls on his head bounced as he tried to find out why she was looking at him like that. "What?"

"I mean I'm not trying to start a fight, but you look like a shop mannequin."

Angel smiled and blushed, which Ester swore looked like a trained response.

"Aww, thank you." Angel turned up the charm and clasped his hands together at his cheeks.

Ester laughed. "I'm kidding."

"I know." And in an instant, Angel's face was back to normal again. "But I'll take what I can get. A pretty boy never turns down a kind word."

He struck a pose, making sure to show off his small but firm butt, earning him a giggle from Samay. Ester rolled her eyes in amusement. Who was this child? And was he sure he was in the right profession? Ester pulled out a fresh pair of under garments and grabbed her uniform. She looked around for the showers and saw a bathroom sign in the back of the room.

"Boy, do I stink." Angel pressed his fingers to his nose. "Don't know about you guys, but I'm going to hit the showers."

"Um, I might take one a little later." Samay shied away.

"No judging. I think you smell really nice anyway," Angel said, as the heat rose on Samay's cheeks. "As for me, these bad boys need a good scrub."

Angel pulled out his bag and laid it on his bed. It was packed to the brim. He struggled to unzip it and when he did, it nearly burst open. He sifted through the items that spilled out, picking through them in search of another bag. From that bag, he took out a smaller bag and dumped out its contents of dozens of tiny bottles and jars and laid them all over his bed.

"The packing limitations were a real doozy," Angel said as he scratched the back of his head.

"What's all that?" Ester asked as she registered herself to her bed using her wristband.

"On nothing, just my travel kit. Make-up, nail polish, hair formulas, you know the usual," Angel said, as if it were common to walk around with a shop full of cosmetics in your travel bag. "A boy has to look good at all times." Angel turned on his charm machine again.

"You know this isn't a clean job; we'll be sweating and getting dirty." Ester watched him organize.

"I know. That's why I brought my best strain resistant products." He smiled, reaching sickening levels of cuteness.

Ester thought at any moment he was gearing up to sell her something.

"Well, I gotta hit the shower," Ester said as she flung her uniform over her shoulders.

"Oh, me too! And I know just the perfume to wear to orientation." Angel picked through his things and gathered up his uniform.

Ester stared at him with a blank stare; he couldn't be serious. This boy was in for a rude awakening or maybe it was just a culture thing. Either way, Ester was amused by it. The two headed to the bathroom which was all the way in the back of the room. There was only one door and nothing was marked male or female. So Ester shrugged, and the door slid open, assuming the distinction would be made clear once inside. Inside she was greeted by a haze of smoke and a thick aroma of fragrances and body odor. She looked around. Both boys and girls were standing awkwardly next to their assigned lockers. The girls huddled together with towels around their chests while the boys tried to hide their peering eyes. The academy couldn't be serious, even the bathing room was shared. Angel walked past her like it was nothing.

"Wait, Angel, where are you going?" Ester tried to cover her eyes as she hurried to catch up with him.

"I'm going to my locker." His curls bounced all around his head. "Let's see, mine's 1-46. Which ones yours?"

Ester couldn't believe he wasn't nervous at all. Ester looked up at the ceiling, trying to pull the number from her mind. "Um, 2-34, I think."

"That's on the right side." Angel pointed with his bath caddie close at his chest. "Meet you in the shower."

"Wait, what?" Ester stopped him right there.

"What?" Angel titled his head in genuine confusion.

"I'm a girl, and you're a boy. We don't take showers together."

Angel nodded. "Yes, huh, in ranger academy we do."

"What?" Ester almost looked grossed out. Just the thought of peeking eyes roaming her body made her want to puke.

"You didn't know?" Angel blinked twice.

"Of course not! Whose backwards idea was it for girls and boys to shower together?" Electricity buzzed through her thick coiled hair as she clenched her fists. Others were looking at her, but she didn't care.

Angel shrugged, then went off to his locker. Ester was in a mood now. She wasn't expecting things to be like this. Even back at home she had the privacy of showering alone. This wasn't a deal breaker, but she definitely didn't like it. She found her locker more easily than she would have thought, and inside she was pleased to find it was stocked with squares of soap, a towel, and a robe, all in their house colors.

With her towel around her body, Ester walked over to the showers. Some of the boys stole glances at her, but she made sure to turn on the ice. She was setting the ground rules early, just like she used to do back at the orphanage. She placed her hand on the door at the same time as some girls were walking out. A girl in the front with bright purple hair gave Ester one look and laughed.

"I'm sorry, but I wasn't expecting this." The girl covered her mouth. "What are you half Labadoran or something?"

Her friend next to her with a black Mohawk with both sides shaven laughed.

"What do you think, Zime?" The purple haired girl asked.

"She looks local, but maybe from the slums."

Both girls busted out in laughter. Ester was not in the mood, but swallowed her anger with a glare.

"Oh, I'm sorry," Ester faked a sympatric look. "Are you lost little girl? Judging by your breasts, I'd say you need to go back to your mama's side."

Both girls stood there with their mouths open as Ester walked by them. You didn't grow up in a house full of unruly children and not have an arsenal of witty comebacks at your disposal. Why were such mean people even allowed in? Ester shook her head. When it finally registered that she was in the shower, she froze when she saw all the dangling male parts. As if she was an insect in the path of a small child, she wanted to jump back through the door in embarrassment.

"Hey! Ester! Over here." A completely nude Angel waved to her.

Ester definitely didn't want to look Angel's way, but there were no other showerheads available. Angel continued to wave, so it was useless trying to wait for a free space. She averted her eyes cautiously, which was doing her no favors as she nearly tripped several times as she made her way over to him.

"You okay?" Angel eyed her clumsy footwork.

Ester nodded.

"Good because I changed my mind and went with Something Symple. My shower soap was from the same brand and even my drying powder is from that line, and I don't mix brands. Like, it's not against the rules, but you just wind up smelling like a shopping cart with spilt fragrances all over it. Like when you're shopping in the upper cities and the clerks are spraying and…" He trailed off, watching Ester just standing there looking at her feet. "Ester? You okay?"

She nodded again as Angel continued. Why was she so nervous? She had seen so many dangly parts in her lifetime. She changed and bathed boys back home and even went to watering pools and swam with the boys nude—granted she was very young when that happened. Why was she so nervous now? There was nothing she had that nobody had ever seen or didn't already have. She clenched her fist around her towel as her jaw tightened. It was just breasts and females parts, nothing to make a fuss over.

She flung her towel off, not caring about the eyes clearly on her and hung her towel on the towel rack. She peaked around, and no one seemed to care, so she guessed it wasn't a big deal. Ester touched the shower controls, turning on the hot water, allowing herself to enjoy it.

***

All the cadets packed tightly in the huge, dome-shaped auditorium. Ester had seen places like this on the tele, but she had never been in a place with so many people. The time was sixteen hundred hours and orientation was just about to begin. Ester could barely contain herself. She sat in the middle of Angel and Samay. The lights were still up, giving Ester a chance to get a good look around. Every year, the academy accepted around 150 cadets. Among them were other rangers and instructors eager to hear the president's welcome. The lights started to dim, and everyone got quiet. Lights flooded the stage as a woman walked up to the podium.

"Welcome cadets. I am Grand President, Tomea Le," the woman addressed the crowd. "It is a great honor to start off another academic year with the future protectors of The United Nations of Rean. I would like to be the first to say how proud I am to address you here today. You have all proven yourself worthy to sit here. You are the best in your communities, in your studies, and in physical condition. If you complete this program successfully, you will be the world's first line of defense against attack.

People cheered as the president smiled and raised her hand to calm the crowd

"Peace forged through alliance, perseverance, and honor! That is the Reanian way, may Rean be with you." The Grand President bowed and stepped aside as she prepared to welcome their next speaker.

Ester leaned over the edge of her seat to get a better look at the next speaker. She may have lived hundreds of miles from ranger academy, but she'd done her research. Sitting on stage behind the Grand President was the rest of the ranger academy high officials. She spotted Jefreeson Willows, the Vice Grand President, Grand Commander Darwin J'Chives, and First Sargent's, Li-san Moore and Chi Vellumee. These people were the celebrities Ester looked up to. The Grand President shook the hand of the next speaker. Ester recognized him right away: Assistant Director Colin Vibes.

"Thank you, Grand President, for that moving statement." Assistant Director Vibes smiled. "On behalf of all the staff and captains here at the Academy of the Rean Coalition of Rangers, we whole heartedly welcome you. It is an honor to stand before so many young faces from all over our beautiful planet. As many of you know it took a feat of great bravery to be here amongst so many statehoods, as peace was not always the way of our people. We have the great leaders of old to thank for this peace and the values instilled into every ranger to guarantee our way of life remains so. Over the next few weeks, you and your peers will be put through the final portion of your entry exam.

The director took a step away from the podium as a hologram formed behind him.

"The path to ranger-hood does not end at the acceptance into the academy. Every day, you must prove your worth, and prove to us and your captains that you deserve to be here. That is why the entrance exam is split into two parts.

"One-hundred and fifty cadets were hand selected and divided into houses based on the five leaders that brought peace to our world. These houses are as followed: House Scorpion who honors Logon Adum from Adum-la; House Crane who honors Al-lazarah Cha from Cha-la; House Bull who honors Tuma Huma from Huma-ko; House Monkey who honors Sharza Tel, from Tel-sa; and House Snake who honors Dane Ans, the orchestrator of peace from Ans-on."

Cheers filled the auditorium as Ester fidgeted her hands in excitement. House Snake was her house, and she felt extremely honored be in it. Dane Ans was one of her favorite historical figures. It was said because of his kind and compassionate heart peace was finally reached after a hundred years of war. Even though it was ancient history, Ester believed in the idea that people really could make a difference. The assistant director held up his hand and silence fell over the room.

"I am glad to hear your enthusiasm, however, this is still a test and like all tests a certain performance is required to pass. Your first real term begins at the start of winter, and the program only has seats for ninety students."

"What?" Ester gasped, she looked at Samay, who looked just as worried, then turned to Angel.

Angel stared at Ester with his big blue eyes. "You didn't know?"

She shook her head as Angel's facial expression turned from surprise to shock. The assistant director walked the stage as the next screen changed for the cadets to view.

"That means only the houses that can work together will have their members move onto ranger academy," the assistant director said. "Teamwork is highly valued here, regardless of your rank or position. We cannot succeed if we do not all move as one."

Ester twirled the tiny curls on the back of her neck. All this time, she'd relied on herself to get her where she needed. Now she had to work together with a bunch of strangers, and their work ethic directly impacted her chances of saying in ranger academy.

"So, without further ado, allow me to introduce your house captains." Assistant Director Vibes opened his arms to welcome the five individuals standing on the stage.

Ester spaced out. How was she going to get in when she didn't know anyone? She looked around at some of her peers sitting with her. What if she got a crappy house filled with lazy people? Ester remembered the girls from the shower. There were already two mean people in her house, what if there were more? They all took the written exam, but that didn't mean they were fit enough to get into the academy. She twirled her hair so tight that her finger got stuck. She needed a game plan.

"And finally, the house Captain for House Snake: Oval Pole." The crowd applauded as a thin man with faded orange hair limped forward and bowed.

"Oh wow! We got Captain Pole! He's the best." Angel bounced enthusiastically.

"Huh? How do you know all of this?" Ester whispered as she clapped.

"It's old news. My parents are civil councilors." Angel stood and clapped and cheered when the names were finished being called as Ester sat with her mouth open. Now she really needed answers. Children of civil councilors did not go to ranger academy.

After orientation, talk about the limited space had everyone a buzzing with chatter, but Ester had other things on her mind. As they exited, Ester lost Angel in the crowd. She stood on her tippy toes next to Samay as she tried to find him. Then she saw a flicker of blond and headed straight towards him.

"Angel, Angel! Hey, wait up." She grabbed him by the arm.

"Oh sorry, guys. I thought you were right behind me," Angel said.

"Your parents are civil councilors?" Ester said, as others passed them on their way to the diner hall. "That's so cool. Why are you even applying to be a ranger then when you could be a civil councilor?"

Angel stood in the hall in silence, his face expressionless and cold—something new Ester had not seen before. Two girls walked by but that did not break Ester's stare. Then Angel perked back up again as if he just finished charging up.

"Probably for the same reason you did, to protect people." He smiled a great big smile, and turned and walked down the hall.

Ester watched the spot where Angel once stood. She wasn't expecting that, but she guessed he was right. She'd joined to protect people too, but couldn't he be a bigger help as a civil councilor? They had so much influence, perhaps there was more to his story than she thought. Samay tapped her on her shoulder snapping Ester back to reality, and the two walked down the hall.

That night Ester found it hard to sleep. There was so much to process, so much to reflect on she didn't know where to start. So far, this had been more than Ester could have ever imagined. Even if this was still considered school, she looked forward to the next four years she had in academy.

Chapter Five

Training started bright and early the next day. All the cadets dragged themselves out of bed at zero five thirty and into the shower. Ester had no trouble getting up early. She was used to it. Angel, however, was having trouble. He fought the clock as if time was going to stop for him. Finally, he turned over and opened one eye.

"Like seriously, what are you?" Angel grumbled as he pulled himself into a little ball.

"What?" Ester looked down at him.

"Like how can you get up so early? It's exhausting." Angel gave into the time and lifted himself up. He looked like an angry little lint ball with his curly hair all over the place.

Ester laughed and turned her attention back to unfolding her uniform. "I used to get up early every day and walk to school."

Looking even more perplexed, Angel sat on his bed with his mouth open. "Walk? How far was your school?"

"Not too far, only a few miles," She trailed off as she searched for her boots. She could already tell where this conversation was going. Any minute he would ask about her past, and she would tell him and he'd feel sorry for her. It was a common theme whenever Ester met anyone outside of the orphanage.

"Miles!" Angel said a lot louder than Ester would have liked.

"That's actually pretty common for me too," Samay cut in. "Although sometimes I caught a ride to school with my dad."

"Lucky you," Ester said. "So you guys heading to the shower?"

"Sure," Samay said and bundled up her things in her arms. "Angel, you coming?"

That shook Angel from his stupor, and in a second, he was out of bed and gathering up his things. "Coming!"

The trio walked to the locker room together. Ester decided to opt out of taking a shower. She didn't feel dirty and there was no use wasting water if she didn't work—that was the saying back at the orphanage. Samay's locker was only a few spots from Ester, so they decided to hang out at her locker.

"You're from Adum, right?" Angel said.

"Yeah," Ester said as she put on her ride suit.

"I've been there once, but I was super little," Angel said.

Ester looked up. "Oh?"

Angel nodded. "Yup, but I don't remember much. I do remember that it was very windy."

"Yeah, the winds get up there." Ester chuckled. She couldn't imagine what it must have looked like to see Angel all dressed up caught in the middle of a dust storm.

Samay and Angel walked towards the showers together, and Ester sat down on the bench to wait for them. She figured she might as well go to breakfast with them, seeing how they were the only people she knew. On the other end of the locker room, she heard some arguing. She stood up, but couldn't see anything. Other cadets wondered over to the other side, and Ester followed.

"Look, man, I'm sorry." A boy with short black hair in the front of his head and shaved hair in the back said.

Standing over him was another boy with dark tan skin and sandy blond hair. He scoffed at the boy with the black hair.

"You better watch where you're going, you bald headed twill!"

The boy on the floor glared but inched away. "Whatever, man."

He stormed past Ester and the other cadets. She wasn't sure what caused the fight, but standing next to the sandy haired boy were the two girls Ester had encountered yesterday.

"What a loser," the girl with the purple hair said. "I can't believe we got put in house snake with a bunch of weaklings."

Ester had heard enough. She walked back over to Samay's locker and caught a glimpse of the black haired boy as he walked out. Did ranger academy really have this big of a bully problem?

***

Their first class started promptly at zero seven hundred hours. The classroom was spacious and tidy. Maps and diagrams hung on the walls next to thin tall windows that flooded the room with light. The cadets waited in silence for their captain to speak. He was a thin man with faded dyed orange hair and a prickly salt and pepper colored beard. The bags under his eyes said that he was an intense thinker. The burns that blotched his face and hands said that he had seen many battles. He stared at the class but not at them. His eyes were glued to the clock. It turned from zero seven hundred hours to zero seven zero one hundred hours.

"Okay cadets, I'm happy to see that everyone made it to class on time," he said in a leveled, monotone voice. "My name is Captain Oval Pole. I was born and raised in Tel-sa, Plizard locale. I graduated ranger academy years before most of you were thought of and retired to become a captain."

He hit a button on his wristband and the podium lifted and hovered out of his way. When it moved, the class whispered under their breath about the robotic brace drilled into his left leg. The cadets all stared at each other, but Captain Pole's expression stayed the same.

Captain Pole spoke over the thoughts in the cadets head and captured their full attention. "If this offends you, then this is not the career for you. If pain, death, or anguish frightens you, then this is not the career for you. If you care about your precious good looks, then this is not the career for you. This is not a job about collecting the glory and gloating to your friends." He paused to pointedly look around. "This is a job about protecting people and upholding global and intergalactic law. But as rangers we must always look out for each other. We must live by the mantra that no matter what nation state you are from, we are one."

Captain Pole summoned a chair and sat heavily. "With that being said, it is mandatory that we administer the second portion of your entry exam here. So this exam, what's it about? Well, here's the breakdown from the beginning: each house starts off with a hundred points, that's all. You can't gain points back if you lose them. You lose points by performing poorly on the exams, and if you are caught behaving poorly, you can have house points taken away from you. So, if you're prone to being hot-headed, then you might want to cool it. Why are points important? Just think about a mission. If you screw up, you can't take it back. So, if you screw up your house's points, they are gone for good."

The cadets gulped as they looked at each other.

"That's one factor," Captain Pole said as he leaned back in his chair. He rolled over to his desk to take a sip of his hot tea. "Hmm, yeah. So here's the meat of it. Throughout this semester I'll be preparing you for your two exams. And if you guessed the theme of the exams involved was teamwork, then you would be right. Both exams are designed to test how well you work together. I cannot stress this enough: teamwork is the key to ensuring your spot here at ranger academy." An icy glare cut across the room as Captain Pole drank from his tea.

"Part one is a four-part relay race and part two is a scenario simulator, and no, you won't be fighting each other with CuCores. It's just a set with interactive parts designed to test how well you work together in a mission setting."

The cadets groaned as Captain Pole took another sip from his tea.

"Relax. You'll have plenty of time to prepare yourself for the exams. With that being said, academics still play a very important part. Each of you must maintain good grades or your house will quickly lose points. Now, any questions?"

No one said a word, no one moved.

"Good. Beyond the exams, here's a breakdown of what your academy life will look like if you make it that far. The academy is broken down into terms, there are eight terms total, covering two years, this examination period included. Terms A1 through A3 are academic and classroom focused. Those are the next terms you will enter if you are successful in your entrance exams. Terms JC1, standing for Junior Cadets phase 1, through JC4 are your combat and specialization terms."

Captain Pole paused for questions, then nodded, and pressed a button on his wristband. Behind him, their class schedule popped up. It looked like they had a full day of class and training.

Ester was not excited about diving into the books again, but at least she only had a year and a half of classroom work before she would spend her final two years as a junior cadet–that was, if she made it that far.

"Okay, good," the captain continued. "So, let's start with a simple activity to get to know each other better. I'm going to call out the nation states and you raise your head if you're from that state. Simple?" When he received all nods, he put his tea down. "By the way, if you ever crush your leg during a mission, and you're looking for some killer herbal tea, Bex Se tea is the best damn tea in all of Rean." Captain Pole pulled out a thermal and poured himself another cup as he scratched his braced-up leg.

A few cadets averted their eyes, not wanting to be reminded of what could happen to them.

"Okay, show of hands, who's here from Cha-la?"

Samay's hand went up, along with a few others, but Ester didn't see many.

"Alright, welcome. What about Huma-ko?"

Some loud hoots echoed through the room, proudly showing their Huma-ko pride.

"Okay, okay." He lifted up his hand. "How about Tel-sa?" A few cadets cheered and whistled. "Yay, Tel-sa," Captain Pole said with the enthusiasm of a person on their death bed. "And Ans-on?"

And that was by far the loudest cheer.

"Calm down, calm down." Captain Pole lowered his hand. "I'm sure all of Rean can hear you." The Ans-on cadets took that as a compliment and snickered under their breath.

"And how about Adum-la or Who-da?" One hand went up slowly, and the entire class turned and looked at Ester.

"Who-da or Adum-la?" The Captain asked.

"Adum-la sir," Ester said.

The Captain blinked a few times. "Adum-la. You're a long way out." He looked directly at Ester.

"I am, sir, but I am proud to be here," Ester said confidently.

"Okay, good." Captain Pole nodded, then turned his stern gaze across the room. "Well, as of today, your nation state of origin does not matter. You are rangers; you are one. Remember your home and let that serve as reminder of what you'll be risking your lives for every day."

The first class let out, and the cadets were assigned chapters of reading and activities for the week. The next period was physical training. The group walked together, following behind Captain Pole. With a tumbler of tea in his hands, he led the class at a quick pace to their next location. Ester walked in the back with her friends. She paid little attention to their conversation, and instead focused on the sandy haired boy and his friends from the locker room.

"Just our luck we'd get a busted captain to teach our class," the sandy haired boy said within earshot of Ester.

"Oh my gosh, Murk, stop." The girl with the purple hair whined as she grabbed his arm and giggled.

"What? Am I wrong?" Murk grinned. "Look, even Zime and Bue agree!"

"Heck no," Zime, the girl with the braided Mohawk, said. "You're just mean." She grinned at him anyway.

"Whatever. Kiakit agrees with me, right?" Murk turned to his friend with the purple hair.

"You are so bad, Murk," Kiakit said.

Murk grinned. "Well, maybe we need a handicap teacher to slow the pace for the rest of the losers." The group snickered, but Ester held her tongue as they wandered away.

"Ester, you okay?" Angel asked.

"Fine," Ester said coldly, her eyes focused beyond him.

Angel looked at Samay with a worried look. Samay gently touched Ester's shoulder, melting away Ester's glare. A gentle smile returned to Ester's face, much to her friend's relief.

The class filed in as Ester marveled at the size of the gymnasium. Compared to the modest outdoor dwellings she used to do sports in, this was like a mega upgrade. The ceiling was domed-shaped and high, dotted with skylight windows. The walls were lined with weights, colored balls, and strange machines, some of which Ester had never seen before, but all that paled compared to the huge obstacle course that sat in the middle of the green track. Captain Pole stopped as the class moved around him. Everyone was amazed at the sheer size of the space.

"Great, everyone made it," he said with the same enthusiasm he had in the classroom. "This is where you'll be doing your daily workouts. The first workout block will be focused on cardio and running the course. FYI, the course behind me will help you train for your first exam, so train hard. The second workout block is in the evening after your last class. That block is for body maintenance, so weight training, meditation, stretching—nothing too intense."

"During training block one, you'll be focusing on the obstacle course. To get you prepared for the exam, you'll run the course three times a day, but if the same three people fall in last place by the end of your training for that day you will lose points for your house." The captain ignored the communal gasp and continued. "This means you have to hold each other accountable. Remember, you're only as good as your weakest link. Don't let them fall behind, try to push them, help them get better." Captain Pole placed his tea on the rail surrounding the quarter and a half mile track. "The course will get easier, and over time, you'll be skipping through it." Captain Pole bent down and started to stretch. "The layout is simple. You sprint the first part, then use the bars to cross the sand pit, then run to your weight packs and lift and carry them to the finish line. Easy enough? By the end of this semester, you should be able to run this in six minutes."

He peered at the skeptical students. It would seem he would have to show them. He bounced on the balls of his feet and loosened up his arms. He stared at his cadets before turning around and heading for the course. Everyone stared at each other is disbelief. He couldn't be serious if he thought they could finish the course in six minutes, let alone him attempting to finish the course in that time in his condition. Murk and his group pushed through to the front, all with smug looks on their faces. Other cadets watched anxiously from the back as Ester, Angel, and Samay found a spot on the rail.

"I don't know about this," Angel said biting his lip.

Ester watched intensely. She did not discount people for their appearances, however, his leg injury looked pretty serious. She had known of a man who had a similar injury back home. He used to be in top condition but after the accident, he was completely immobile. *What was Captain Pole trying to prove?* She thought. *He's a veteran ranger. He doesn't need to show us his skills; he earned that respect by serving.*

Captain Pole took his place at the starting line. The big digital clock on the wall turned on, flashing all zeros in red. Everyone drew quiet. The clock began to countdown starting at five, four, three, two, one. He was off, a little slow at first. Ester could hear the snickers coming from Murk's group, but soon their laughter started to fade as Captain Pole sprinted down the track. He jumped unto the bars and swung over the pit as if he were ten years younger. Once on the ground, his momentum did not stop. He took off towards the weighted sack, flung them over his back, and ran as if he were carrying feathers. The clock raced with him showing a time of five minutes. He was almost there when, the clock hit the twenty second mark and it was a real race now to the finish. Captain Pole made it across the finish line and threw his pack to the ground. Everyone looked up; the clock read five minutes and forty-two seconds. All were silent when he approached them, out of breath.

"I'll admit," he gasped for air, as he wiped away a light sheen of sweat, "I'm a little out of shape, but you get the picture. Complete this course three times a day, don't forget to stretch, and help your fellow teammates. It's not hard. You have until twelve hundred hours, then lunch, then back in class. Is that understood?"

"Yes sir," The class said firmly.

Captain Pole nodded and watched them from the finish line. He gulped down his tea, with pain riddled across his face, but that mattered little with his time showing brightly over the course. If he could still be in that good of shape, then the cadets knew that with hard work and training they could overcome it as well.

After a good warm up, it was time for them to try the course themselves. All the cadets lined up at the line intent on beating their captain's time, but once the buzzer went off, they found that it was not as easy as it looked. By the time the cadets got to the bars. they were out of breath. While others sped through the course, Murk and his crew pushed through, leaving everyone behind. Ester was impressed, and she guessed he wasn't all talk, but she wasn't going to give him the satisfaction of being the first to cross the finish line.

Meanwhile in the back, Angel and a few others struggled. Angel looked back and saw Samay fall into the sand pit.

"Ouch," Samay said as she rubbed her back.

"Are you okay?" Angel asked.

"I will be." Samay stood and tried to reach for the bars once more.

Out in front, Murk, Kiakit, Zime, and Bue were holding down the lead. Ester couldn't let them win, so she sprinted when her feet hit the ground from the bars. She raced to her sack and threw it over her shoulders. It was heavy, but nothing she couldn't handle. She took off, passing Bue, then Kiakit and Zime. Murk looked back in shock at the fact that Ester could keep up. Now the two were in the lead going toe to toe. Locked into their own race, they had completely forgotten about the class. Both zoomed down the course with their sacks on their backs. Murk had the strength, but Ester had the endurance. She forged a gap between them as Murk struggled to keep up and balance the weight on his back. He wasn't use to competition and tried catch up, but Ester broke away and crossed the finish line first.

Murk crossed shortly after and collapsed on the ground. He'd never lost a race. Kiakit rushed over to help him up, but he shoved her hand away. He wasn't sure who this girl was but he wasn't going to get showed up by her.

"Nice job!" Captain Pole shouted from the other side of the course. "But why are you stopping? You still got two more runs."

Ester and Murk looked at each other and grunted. Neither were prepared to run at full speed two more times, but their pride wouldn't let them give up. They jogged to the start of the course and set off again.

***

Lunch came, and everyone was exhausted. This was the only time all the houses came together, making the dining hall packed with people. Ester lagged behind as the other students passed her. She was so tired, she just wanted to go back to her dorm and sleep. She groaned under her breath when she realized she still had weight lifting left after her next class.

She entered the dining hall and the smells of freshly prepared food rejuvenated her. All the smells reminded her of the markets. She couldn't believe a school dining hall could smell this good. She looked across the hall and saw Angel in line. He saw her too and waved.

"Wow, you really overdid it." Angel winced at her ragged appearance.

"Yeah," Ester sighed. She wasn't trying to be a show off, but now she was paying for it.

The two entered and walked up to the counter to grab their food. Ester paused as Angel grabbed a plate of baked fish and veggies.

"Ester?" Angel looked back.

Her eyes looked like they were watering. She had never seen so many food options, and had been expecting water and sandwiches after their amazing dinner the night before. A cadet behind her grunted, snapping Ester out of her trance. She looked through all the options and went for the baked goat and veggies.

"Wow, people eat like celebrities here," Ester whispered to Angel, who laughed. "What?"

"Your life in Adum must have been really different," Angel said.

Ester wanted to roll her eyes, but she had to remember that Angel grew up in Ans-on, the most advanced city on the planet. The two looked around for a table to sit at when Angel spotted Samay.

"Hey, look there's Samay." Angel pointed.

Ester looked out into the crowd and saw her sitting at a table next to the black haired boy who Murk was fighting with this morning. Ester followed Angel to the table and looked around the cafeteria.

Ester noticed patches of cadets in different colored ride suits. No one tried to sit and talk to other students in different houses. Even on the first day of class it seemed like every house had already staked their claims. Angel greeted Samay, who waved. They sat down at their round table surrounded by their classmates who sat at other tables nearby.

"That first training was no joke." Angel fanned himself. "I'm sure I'm going to need a hot bath after that one."

Samay agreed. "I hope every day won't be that intense."

Ester listened as she ate, but she was more curious about the boy sitting a seat away from them.

"I don't know what was harder," Angel said. "That entrance exam or this training."

Samay nodded.

"What do you think, Ester?" Angel asked.

Ester jumped and scratched her head. "What was the question again?"

Angel laughed. "You are like the queen of zoning out. I was saying that I don't know what's harder the entrance exam or this training."

"Oh, the entrance exam for sure. I studied so hard and I still felt like I didn't cover enough." Ester said.

"Yes!" Angel said. "My parents even hired me a tutor, and I felt like I barely earned a good score. I mean I got my score card and managed to get a seven out of ten. Like that test was seriously hard."

"I got the same score," Ester groaned. "What about you, Samay?"

Samay jumped, then sunk her head lower as her cheeks got warm. "Um, I..."

Angel gasped. "If it's bad you don't have to say."

"I uh, actually got a ten out of ten." Samay shied away. "But I still thought the test was super hard. My parents made me study every day."

Ester and Angel looked at her with their jaws wide open.

"Really, guys, it wasn't a walk in the park," Samay said as Angel fussed over how cool that was.

Ester laughed, but noticed the boy sitting next to them staring at them. She noticed a grin appear on his face as he watched Angel rave over Samay.

"Hey, I'm Ester." She extended her hand to him.

The boy froze. "I-I'm Fermit."

"Sorry that jerk Murk was picking on you this morning. He seems like a real prick."

Fermit laughed a little. "Yeah, for sure."

"Oh my gosh," Angel said. "You're that boy who totally killed it on the bars today."

Fermit forced a smile as he tried to make himself look small, but it was no use with Angel around. Once Angel focused on something, it was thrust into the spotlight. Samay and Ester smiled as Angel fussed over him too. Ester sat and listened as the conversation turned from training to tele-dramas. This was fun, even if half the time she didn't know what everyone was talking about. She was just happy to have made some new friends. If she played her cards right, these would be the people she would help protect the world with.

Chapter Six

After a good night's rest the class was ready to begin their next day. Ester wasn't going to overdo it today like she did yesterday. The last thing she wanted to do was lose her house any points. The cadets shuffled in under the baggy gaze of their captain who sat in the front of class at his desk in the corner near the window. The topic of the day was projected on the holoscreen, and the cadets pulled out their books to follow along. At zero seven hundred hours, the captain stood and put his half-finished breakfast on his desk.

"Okay cadets, welcome back. I hope you had fun yesterday running the course because it's going to be your new best friend for the next few weeks." The Captain masked a burp behind his arm. "Excuse me."

He looked behind him at the topic projected on the holoscreen. "Right, so I talked briefly about the first exam yesterday, but I'm going to go into a little more detail because it'll be here sooner than you think. I personally think the first test on teamwork and accountability personally is the easiest, but surprisingly, every year houses fail. The test consists of a series of group relays with a combination of academics and training elements. Meaning, you have to know your Rean and intergalactic history, and you have to be able to navigate the obstacle course. And yes, even for non-combat roles, you need to be combat ready for any situation."

Captain Pole grunted as he stretched a little. "Also, let me re-remind you about house points. Just because there's only one of me, that doesn't mean I don't see all of you or let me re-phrase, it doesn't mean the higher ups can't see you. Furt." The Captain called a name, and a young skinny boy jumped up.

"Y-yes sir."

"You cut the last part of the course back in training yesterday. The house loses one point." There were groans and boos coming from all his classmates as Furt cowered in shame. "I'll make it two if I hear any more complaining. You are all responsible for each other's progress. Instead of focusing on who finishes first, focus on keeping your team together." The Captain eyed Ester and Murk, who both lowered their heads in embarrassment. "Okay, for our lesson today, let's start with pre-treaty intergalactic history."

***

The class ended and everyone made their way to the training course. Ester felt so embarrassed back in class. She really showed off yesterday when she should have been focusing on the objective. She walked beside her friends to the gym and listened as they talked about the chapters assigned in class.

"I can't believe how much more there is to intergalactic history," Samay said.

"Oh yes!" Angel said. "Trust me, wait to we get to the section on Labadora."

Fermit groaned as Ester loosened up a bit. She wasn't a fan of studying, but in academy they were learning new things which interested her way more than the dulled down topics she learned in school back home. Angel walked through the door first, along with Samay and Fermit. Ester followed behind, but felt a strong hand on her arm.

"Hey," Murk called, "you're not like the rest of these second rank cadets."

He grinned with his arms folded on his chest. Behind him stood his friends: Kiakit, Zime, and Bue, a boy with short dark brown dreadlocks. A flash of anger flickered in Ester's eyes.

"What do you say you ditch those losers you call friends and join up with us? We're going to carry this house to the top, and it'd be wise to join someone who will get you there," Murk said.

"Like hell I would!" Ester said loud enough for everyone to hear.

Samay stopped and turned around, as other classmates stopped and listened. Angel and Fermit heard the commotion outside and exited to see what was going on. Murk scoffed.

"Fine, suit yourself. Go ahead and align yourself with worthless twills, see if I care. Just stay out of my way." Murk and his friends pushed past Ester.

Angel and the others stepped out of Murk's way as he stormed into the gymnasium. Angel rushed over to Ester as the cadets in the hallway dissipated.

"Are you okay? What was that all about?" Angel asked as he checked Ester over.

"It was nothing," Ester said, calming herself. She did not care for that kid; he was way too arrogant for his own good.

Samay hurried over and gave Ester a reassuring smile, but Ester was pretty much back to normal. She didn't want to waste another second thinking about that brat.

"Come on guys." Ester walked to the door. Her friends all looked at each other, but Ester had already walked to the door and was holding it open for them.

***

Class today was no joke. Captain Pole really worked them hard. It was only day two, and Ester was already overwhelmed. Ester and Angel walked through the lobby of their dorm as Angel rambled on about something, but in her haze her mind started to drift. Being here at ranger academy had been her lifelong dream and she was happy to be here, but she wondered how her parents felt. She wanted so badly to talk to them because so much has changed since she was young. She rubbed her necklace and thought of the promise she made when she entered the orphanage. She promised to protect anyone who was in need, to become a ranger, and see to it that no one else ever suffers the same pain she went through. She just needed to keep focusing on that.

"Hey? Hey you there?" Angel waved.

"Oh yeah." Ester scratched her head.

Angel eyed her, but then popped back into his normal upbeat

mood. "The chapter on intergalactic history should be easy. I mean who doesn't know the history of our galaxy?"

"Yeah." Ester laughed, secretly thanking Brother Isa for practically hammering history into her head.

Back at their beds, they grabbed their stuff and hit the showers. Even though Ester hated the communal shower, shower time was starting to become her favorite part of the day. The water was always hot, and the pressure was perfect. There was even a hot bath for soaking. This school was amazing. Angel left ahead of her, but she didn't stay too long because her legs were killing her. Ester walked back to the bed, and her face twisted in confusion.

"What is that?" Ester cringed at the smelly green paste Angel was rubbing on his face.

"Facial deep cleanser. Want some?" Angel held out the jar of lumpy goo.

Ester waved her hands. It looked like week old moldy potatoes.

"I'll pass." Ester sat down on her bed beside him.

"Suit yourself." Angel applied more paste to his face as Ester settled on her bed. The two sat in silence for a few minutes, as Angel sat on his bed watching over her.

"What?" Ester finally turned her head around and noticed Angel staring at her.

Angel didn't say anything at first, only stared, but Ester had a feeling there was something he was trying to get off his chest.

"What?" she repeated, this time with more demand than curiosity.

"So how come you don't wear make-up or anything?" Angel suddenly blurted out.

She blinked a few times. "What do you mean?"

"I mean lots of people love make-up." Angel put his face cream down, then felt around his bed for a can of spray. "Unless they don't have that in Adum," he whispered, not that anyone was paying attention.

Ester stared for a few seconds, then burst out into laughter. A few people looked over, and it made Angel a little nervous.

"Of course we have make-up," Ester said as she tried to stop laughing, but tiny bursts threatened the sides of her lips as she tried to contain it. She calmed when she noticed Angel was looking very nervous. "We have it. I'm just not interested, that's all."

"Oh okay," Angel said as he started to smile again. "Your name is very pretty by the way."

"Thank you, it's my tribe name. It was given to me by my mother and father," Ester trailed off.

"That's cool," Angel said as he rocked back and forth on the bed.

"Yeah, it was." Ester quieted down. "My tribe was slaughtered when I was thirteen, including my family." Ester let the words fall out. She figured he'd get around to asking her anyways and she might as well get it over with.

"I'm so sorry," Angel gasped, his hands over his mouth.

"Don't be," Ester said, waving it away. "It happened a long time ago."

Ester could see Angel was starting to feel bad about asking, but the look in Ester's eyes did not reflect the image of a broken child. Instead it showed the face of a fiercely determined person.

"What-what was your tribe like?" Angel asked shyly.

Ester looked up, half expecting him to be looking at her with pity, but instead he looked genuinely interested.

"They were amazing. We were Rean worshippers, like the nomadic tribes in Who-da. We valued and respected all that Rean had to offer. Everything, from the soil we grew our crops in to the animals we raised. Everyone and everything had a purpose and a place." Ester stretched as she allowed herself to fall back into her memories.

"Wow, so how did you get a tribe name?" Angel probed with interest.

"Oh. It's this whole big thing. When you turn eleven you have what's called an Appa. It's like a coming of age party. That's when you're considered an adult and given your tribe name. My mother also made me this necklace." Ester presented it to Angel.

"Oh my gosh, that's so pretty." Angel marveled at the amber colored stone.

"Thanks. It matches the one my mom made for my older brother.

Our tribe was famous for the trade of nice stones like this." Ester tucked her necklace back into her shirt. "My before name was Glass Flower because I was born on the eve of spring when the new flowers were still covered in light frost. It's because of my family and tribe that I want to become a ranger. What about you?"

Angel was still staring in shock. She got that look every time she told her story. Ester cleared her throat and continued.

"So why would a child of a civil councilor want to become a ranger? I mean you could be a civil councilor. You could make the laws and have sweeping influence."

"It's not like that," Angel said with a hint of coldness in his tone. "I mean, it's not that easy."

Ester nodded. She didn't doubt the job of civil councilor was easy. They were in charge of representing an entire nation state.

"My parents' job is boring." Angel laughed it off as he started to wipe his face.

"Yeah, but you're rich, and you get to live in Ans-on. It's like my favorite state. Nothing against Adum-la, of course."

"Really?" Angel tilted his head. "It's just one big metropolis. Don't you have metropolises in Adum?" Ester gave Angel a vacant stare. "Oh, right." Angel started to rock back and forth again. "Ans-on isn't really all that special, though I think the appeal is that a lot of the government is stationed here. Maybe that's why."

"The government? Who cares about that? You guys have a Fried Tuzan and Co." Ester rubbed her stomach.

Angel gasped, his face showed a flash of pure shock. "You guys don't have a Fried Tuzan?"

"Well, yeah, but not where I live. I think there are some in south Adum in the fishing towns maybe."

"Wow." Angel sat with his mouth open as Ester nodded.

"See, lucky." But then that same shadow of coldness washed over Angel's face again. There was something he wasn't telling her. "I don't mean to pry, but why did you decide to apply to ranger academy?" she asked softly.

An announcement rang over the intercom— lights out in an hour, the voice said. Some cadets were already fast asleep. Today had been a long day. Angel smiled, but it was weak.

"If you don't want to share, I understand." Ester reached up for her light, but Angel stopped her.

"Sorry, I get asked this all the time." Angel's face lacked all of his usual joy.

He looked somewhat tired and annoyed, like a frustrated toddler— a look Ester understood all too well.

"Yes, my parents are civil councilors and yes, we have more money than some others, but what they do, it's not for the greater good. It's for them," Angel said bitterly.

"It's just a facade they put on. They all do it. They all pretend. That's why I want to become a ranger, just like Grand Commander J'Chives. I want to do some real good. I want to change the world with my own hands, not by dressing fancy at some party, eating hors d'oeuvres and smiling for raises."

Ester nodded. She didn't understand the world Angel came from, but she understood fakeness. "That makes sense. I want to make a real difference too, just like my idol Captain Wildgrass Inspread."

"Oh my gosh, yes!" Angel gushed.

"Well, to the both of us then," Ester held out her hand.

"To the both of us." Angel shook it.

The two broke the handshake just as Samay walked over from the shower. Angel greeted her, and the two started talking about homework. Ester listened and laughed as they made jokes about how serious Captain Pole looked sometimes. She was really grateful that she had made such good friends. She was a little worried about traveling a world away, but it was nice to find out that good people could be found anywhere, even if a few rotten eggs got in. The intercom rang and in a sweeping motion the lights started to go out. It was still early in her journey, but she felt confident that her house had what it would take to make it.

Chapter Seven

Captain Pole stood on the side lines watching his class stumble over the course. It had only been two weeks since they started training, but every day counted. His cadets were determined, but that did nothing for their poor run times.

"I'm not sure how that's going to be very helpful!" Captain Pole shouted across the track. He held a stop watch in his hands as he watched his students scramble to carry their weights to the finish line. "Nope! Come on, hustle!" he yelled, still half-asleep as he muffled a yawn with his arm.

Some cadets lagged behind, while others made headway, but the test would require the entire class to be in tip top shape. Captain Pole called time and gave the class a break. Ester panted with her hands on her chest. Fermit rested on his back, as Angel and Samay walked over with cups of water.

"Thanks," Ester said.

Angel handed one to Fermit and plopped on the floor next to Ester.

"I swear Captain Pole is trying to kill us," Angel whined.

Ester chugged her water. "I don't know, I still rather do this over classwork."

"Really?" Angel leaned back.

"Speak for yourself," Fermit said. "It gets a helluva lot harder from here."

Angel nodded. "Oh, I know, I read up on it. I heard the second exam is ten times harder."

"It is, trust me." Fermit sat up.

Fermit stretched and froze when he saw his friends staring at him.

He shrunk away, wishing he hadn't said anything at all.

"Fermit, have you taken these exams before?" Samay asked.

Fermit could feel his face getting red. "Um, no." He tried to laugh it off, but Angel saw right through him.

"Bullshit." Angel made a sour face.

Fermit rubbed the back of his shaved head, but sighed. He guessed it was time to come clean. "Okay, but promise me you won't laugh." All of his friends nodded. "This is my second time applying for ranger academy."

Everyone gasped and looked at each other.

"Oh my gosh! What happened?" Angel asked.

"My house lost," Fermit said, but he knew that was not the whole truth. He had been running from it all this time, but it had been eating him up inside. "But truth be told, I slacked off. I didn't take it serious the first time, and it really hurt when my house lost. You get priority to re-apply, but you have to take the re-entrance exam and it's grueling. A lot of cadets drop out. I promised myself that if I made it, I wouldn't slack off like I did the first time. I have to become a ranger. I have to honor my dad and everything he did for me to get me here."

Fermit balled up his fist. It was shaking, but a hand reached out and touched him. He looked up and saw Samay looking at him and not down on him. He faced Ester and Angel, both nodded. A small smile appeared on Fermit's face.

"We're all going to make it." Ester stood up.

Everyone nodded as Captain Pole ended the break and called everyone over. Everyone circled around him, and he motioned them to sit. He got up from his seat and limped around to make sure everyone was here.

"Great, so your progress on the practice course isn't that great, but it's coming along." Captain Pole found a stool and pulled it over. "But now that you're getting used to working together, I thought I'd take the time to explain to you the layout of your first exam."

Everyone listened as Captain Pole used a hologram to show them what they were getting into. The test was an obstacle course similar to the one they ran through as part of their daily routine, but much harder. The course was broken up into four parts: a barrel walk, a puzzle solving portion, a trivia portion, and an event called links. This portion of their two-part exam was a real house breaker, and the danger of falling behind was real. Most houses never recovered after landing in last place.

Ester was feeling nervous looking over the course. Captain Pole played digital reenactments of how each of the parts were run, and it looked a lot harder than the practice course. Captain Pole closed the hologram and looked at the distraught faces of his cadets.

"Relax, we're not going to throw you in like wood to a fire." Captain Pole stood. "Come with me."

His cadets got up and followed him to the other side of the gymnasium. When he reached the other side, he ran his wristband over a panel next to a door. The light turned from red to green, and the entire wall started to move. Everyone stepped back as the wall folded out of the way, revealing four stations.

"Alright, so here are the practice stations." Captain Pole lifted up his hands.

Behind him sat the four main components of the exam. The first station was the barrel walk, which required four cadets to lift and walk a pallet with barrels on top of it to the finish line. The next station was the puzzle solving station, where groups of three worked together to solve puzzles that required both a sharp mind and teamwork. Beside that station was the trivia station. This was the simplest station because it was strictly an academic focused event. Another three person event, cadets worked together to answer questions about Reanian history. The focus of this activity was to test the knowledge they learned during class and encourage their peers to strive for academic excellence. The last station was by far the most confusing. This station was the last event of the exam and required a great deal of teamwork and coordination. The event named links, was a five-person event, where five cadets were connected by magnetic rings at the waist in the shape of a star. In this formation, the cadets were to use each other's eyes to navigate a complicated obstacle course. Links was, by far, the most intense part of the exam. To ensure that no one cadet dominated in each event, each portion of the exam was ran twice, ensuring all thirty cadets participated.

"Okay, now that you've seen the course, I would like to add one more thing. The point of you training together and living together is so that you can understand each other's strengths and weaknesses. I cannot assign who will do each event; you'll need to work that out yourself. With that being said, keep in mind that you're only as strong as your weakest link. Don't let your pride decide what event you do." Captain Pole walked over to a desk and pulled out a chair. "There are demonstrations in front of each station. I don't think I need to show you how they work, but if you have any questions feel free to ask. But for today just give it a try; tomorrow the real training begins."

Ester stared at the course. She didn't like the idea of the class picking who did which event, but that was the rules. She shuddered at the thought of being forced to do the puzzle or trivia part, but the links portion looked hard too. Ester noticed Murk and his friends with their arms folded together. She definitely didn't want to work on the same team as them. Ester found Angel and her friends, and they walked to the different stations.

"Boy, is that trivia station calling my name." Angel clasped his hands together.

Ester was just about to agree when she saw Murk and his friends walk through the crowd.

"That's fitting for someone like you." Murk grinned, overhearing what Angel said. "But leave the picking to us."

Ester was about to snap back, when Fermit stepped in front of her.

"Captain Pole said that we have to work together and decide who is assigned to each event." Fermit bit back.

"Ha, don't make me laugh," Murk said. "Bue, what did you tell me about this kid?"

"He was a fourth year back when I was in school," Bue said. "He talked a lot of shit, too, about becoming a ranger, but look he's repeating the semester over again."

Murk laughed. "I heard the captain all right, but I'm sure as hell not going to take suggestions from someone who couldn't even make it into ranger academy the first time."

Angel grabbed Fermit's arm. Fermit's cheeks were hot with embarrassment as the rest of the class whispered around him. Fermit shook out of Angel's grip and stormed away.

"Fermit…" Samay reached out.

"Let'em go," Murk said. "We don't need advice from losers like him. Listen up House Snake. I don't know about you, but I'm not trying to repeat this entrance exam over again. Stick with me and you'll make it in the first time around, I guarantee it."

Kiakit and Zime cheered him on, rallying up other cadets to join him. Ester was shaking mad as she stood in the back watching Murk bark orders. Everyone was buying into Murk's promises, even though she thought he was full of shit, but there was little she could do now. She had no other choice but to follow along.

Class ended for the day leaving Ester frustrated and mad. Where did this Murk kid get off bossing everyone around? She would give him a piece of her mind, but it wasn't worth losing house points over. The group studied and rested up for a bit before heading down to the dining hall. Ester stood in line disinterested. Today had gone so poorly. All she wanted to do was go back to her dorm and sleep.

"Pudding?" Angel asked.

"Huh?" Ester said as she was ripped back into reality.

"Pudding. I asked if you wanted pudding." Angel looked at her. "You know, Ester, you sure space out a lot. Here, I'll make your mind up for you."

Angel placed the brown dessert on her tray and continued down the line. Ester looked at it in fascination. She'd never had pudding before, but it was topped with a strawberry and that was a huge plus. Ester followed Angel to their table, where Fermit and Samay were already sitting.

"Oh my gosh, guys, today was so crazy," Angel said as he sat down.

"Yes." Samay nodded. "I'm not sure how I feel about Murk leading us…"

"Fuck him." Fermit blurted, earning him a fair number of shocked stares. "S-sorry."

"Don't apologize," Ester said. "That guy and his friends are a real pile of animal crap."

Angel and Samay nodded.

"I mean where does he get off? He's no more of an expert than any of us," Ester said. "If anything I would listen to you, Fermit, more than him. At least you've done it before."

Fermit sort of smiled, remembering that he was only here because he blew it the first time around. Ester reached out and patted Fermit's back.

"Don't listen to what Murk says. You've earned your place here," Ester said.

Fermit smile widened as the others agreed.

"Oh my gosh Ester," Angel said. "You have to try your pudding. It is totally amazing today."

"It is." Samay took the last bite of her pudding. "I love sweet treats so much. There's a place back home that sells the best treats."

"Really?" Angel said.

"Yes," Samay nodded. "I used to go there a lot after school and grab a snack and watch live performances."

"Ooo, so it was like a mini concert hall?" Angel said.

Samay shook her head. "Nothing big like that, more like a café with a small stage."

"Ooo, Samay, do you ever get up there?" Angel asked. "Oo! Do they have karaoke? I love karaoke!" Angel bounced up and down.

"I-um," Samay stuttered over her words but then nodded.

Ester finished up her vegetables and placed her fork down. "That's so cool, Samay. So, do you like to sing?"

"A-a little. I'm not a pro or anything like that." Samay tried to damper the spotlight on her.

"Yeah right, girl," Angel said. "I beat you can sing."

Samay shook her head, but Angel continued to shower her with compliments. Ester laughed as the stress of the day melted away.

"Wait a minute, guys," Ester said as she pulled the spoon from her mouth. "This pudding is freaking amazing!"

"I told you!" Angel said.

"Why isn't this a national dessert," Ester wailed.

"Yes!" Samay clapped.

Everyone laughed and somehow their day didn't seem so bad.

***

Over the next couple of days, the class practiced hard, but under Murk's orders things were going about as smoothly as a cart on a bumpy road. No one dared challenge him because he and his band of bullies were quick to set them straight. Even Ester's friends didn't speak up. There was no point when it was just four against twenty-six.

"Well, I guess you guys want to fail and that's fine with me." Captain Pole said as he walked over to a stool and sat down. "I'll still have a job, so it's up to you if you really want it."

The cadets groaned as they pushed through practice. At the barrel walk station things were not going well for the team. Fermit was tripping over his feet under the heat of Kiakit and Zime. The group walked back over to the starting point and lined up. Kiakit counted down to one, and the group of four sprinted towards the pallet, picking it up in unison. They worked as a team to move the pallet, but Kiakit and Zime were pushing the team too fast causing Fermit to trip backwards sending the whole thing crashing down again.

"Idiot!" Kiakit shouted. She fumed as she got up. "What is wrong with you!" She berated Fermit.

"I'm-I'm sorry." Fermit whimpered.

"Sorry? Don't be sorry! Work harder, you stumbling twill!" Kiakit shouted as she stormed away.

Kiakit Joy was a hot-headed girl, a part of Murk's group. She along with Zime Luveir had been bossing everyone around at practice all day. There was no doubt they were strong, but they were relentless in their criticism and short on their patience.

"Jeeze, Fermit, could you be anymore useless?" Zime added. "And you, whatever your name is, you were off balance too. How did you even make the cut?" Zime rolled her eyes as she began gathered up the barrels. "Wait, what am I doing? You weaklings need to reset the pallet since you can't seem to keep it up." Zime walked away.

Ester watched in annoyance from the sidelines as her two classmates hustled to reset the pallet. She understood the point of the exercise. It wasn't about who got to the finish line first, but about working together to safely transport the load. It was designed to make students trip and stumble, but Kiakit and Zime were too focused on winning to realize that. Fermit helped reset the pallet, but Ester could tell he was at his breaking point.

Meanwhile, Ester was having trouble with her own event. She was assigned to the puzzle, no doubt out of spite, and she hated it. For the puzzle, they needed to place themed or patterned pieces in the right order, but the pieces were spread apart. It relied on the team working together to direct each other to the right place based on the clues they received. This was all easier said than done, as she struggled to piece together the clues. Ester glanced down at her red and blue pieces in a daze. She struggled to find the connection.

"Purple, you twill!" One boy shouted behind Ester.

"No! It's based on alphabetical order!" Another shouted.

Ester looked around. She thought she'd be better suited for carrying the pallet, but Murk's yappy mouth convinced everyone to separate in this order. She could feel her fingers tingling as she over worked her brain trying to figure out the puzzle.

"No guys, the clue is 'color', meaning it's about the colors, not the names!" Another cadet shouted over everyone.

It was pure chaos. The electricity started to build under Ester's skin. This was getting them nowhere. She was tired of coming to class and arguing all morning during training. This wasn't working, and she didn't care what happened, she wasn't going to put up with this any longer. Ester threw down her puzzle pieces and marched towards the sidelines.

"Samay!" Ester shouted. Samay jumped around and looked at Ester. "You're smart right? Trade with me." Samay froze as all eyes were on them. "I mean, you're always answering all the questions in class. Trade with me."

"Don't you move." Murk stormed over. "What do you think you're doing?"

"I don't know anything about this stupid puzzle and neither does anyone else. Why can't someone who actually aced the written exam be on this side?" Ester pointed out in frustration.

Some of the cadets stepped back as they watched Murk and Ester stare each other down. Murk could feel his eye twitch as the current pulsed through his veins.

"Why? Because I already sorted it out. It's not my fault all that Adum dust is clogging up your brain!" Murk stood in the middle of the group as Ester fumed.

"I agree with Ester." All eyes turned and faced the naysayer.

Murk hunted out the voice bordering on pure rage. It was Angel. He stood his ground, but his courage was weaning.

"I just think it's smarter to let the people who are good at puzzles do the puzzles and let the stronger people do the barrel walk." By now Angel's tone shifted from strong to meek. Murk stormed towards him as Angel took a step back.

"You better watch it, shrimp." He stood in Angel's face.

"Time!" Captain Pole shouted from his stool. "I hope you guys like failure because that's what you are going to get arguing like that." The class groaned as they headed back to the classroom. "Also, that's two points off for fighting, but don't worry, you can always re-apply if you fail." Captain Pole shouted from the other side of the track as he watched his students walk back to the locker room in disdain.

Back in the locker room, no one said a word in the mist of all the tension in the air. Murk was boiling under his skin and could barely contain his anger. He fumed at his locker as his friends changed beside him.

"That bitch," Murk slammed his fist into the locker, not caring who could hear him. "Here I am trying to raise this house to greatness, and that girl, that worm, she tries to under mine me."

"Well, maybe the blond one does have a point. I mean she is pretty dumb, maybe," Bue froze when he saw the sparks raise from Murk.

Kiakit got in between them and scuffed at Bue's comments and turned to Murk. "Cool it, don't let that girl get under your skin. She's already cost us enough points."

Murk stared Kiakit down, He hated to admit it, but she was right. He couldn't allow himself to get distracted by his classmates. After all, he had come from a strong line of rangers. He had been raised in the ranger lifestyle, groomed to be the perfect solider. His pedigree alone proved that he was a natural born leader, and he wasn't going to let anyone stand in his way.

Class ended for the day, and Ester, Angel, Fermit, and Samay walked slowly back to their dorm. Today had been a total disaster, and they were quite exhausted. Angel clenched his fists in frustration which made his platinum blond curly hair fill with electricity. Ester and the others noticed and wanted to laugh but were far too tired.

"I don't see how we're going to get anywhere," Angel complained as he walked alongside his friends. "Murk and his gaggle of twills act like they run the place." Angel placed a hand on his hip and stopped. "I mean, you get me, right?"

Ester nodded, and so did Samay. After all, Angel was right. The class was spiraling out of control under Murk's rule. His group tried so hard to be right all the time that they pushed down anyone who stood in their way. Someone needed to take them down a notch, but no one had the courage.

"You know what guys?" Angel said. "I know what we can do to turn this day around."

"What?" Samay asked.

"A trip to the sauna!" Angel said.

"A what?" Ester asked.

"A sauna, you know a steam room. It's hot, but very relaxing. There's a small one in the mini gym in the back," Angel said.

"I forgot about that," Fermit said as he rubbed his chin.

"Um, I don't know." Samay looked at the time.

"Aww, we have time. Let's go, please," Angel whined as he started jogging in place.

Everyone looked at each other. If they knew one thing about

Angel it was that there was no saying no. They reluctantly agreed just to stop his begging and followed him back to the dorm.

***

Warm steam filled the air as sweat poured from their bodies. Angel was right, this was exactly what they needed. Ester leaned back as her friends chatted. Her shoulders relaxed as the tension washed away. The room was just big enough for them, and they were lucky to get there at this time as a pair of cadets left shortly after they arrived. Ester stretched out her toes and sighed. She could get use to this.

"This reminds me so much of my homeland," Samay said.

"Oh? Where are you from?" Ester asked.

"I'm from Cha-la. We have something similar to this back home, but it's more like a steamy bath. They are found in places called host shrines. It's a place where you go to rejuvenate the body."

"Nice," Ester said. "I'm pretty sure Adum-la doesn't have anything fancy like this."

"That's right, you are from Adum-la," Fermit said. "That's quiet far away."

"Eh." Ester shrugged.

"You're from Ans-on, too, Fermit?" Angel probed as Fermit reluctantly nodded. "Yay, go Ans-on!"

Samay laughed. "There are a lot of Ans-on people in our house."

"That's because we're the best," Angel said.

"Yeah, right," Ester threw a hand towel at Angel.

"Hey," Angel whined.

"Still," Samay said meekly. "It would be cool to meet other people not from Rean."

Ester nodded. "Yeah! Honestly I'm really excited about that. Another perk of being a ranger, you actually get to meet other species. Now, if only they would come here." Ester laughed.

"They do actually," Angel laughed. "There are thousands of immigrants from other planets living here."

"You're kidding?" Ester said with her eyes wide open. She turned and looked at Fermit and Samay and they all agreed. "Wow, I guess I really do live inside a bubble."

"It's okay," Angel laughed again. "They mainly come here for diplomatic reasons and anyone outside of that stick very close to the big metropolises."

"Whoa," Ester said.

"Have you ever met anyone from Labadora?" Samay asked.

Angel shook his head. "It's not well known, but like people from Labadora don't really travel here." Angel lowered his voice.

"Why not?" Ester asked.

"We're on bad terms, so to speak," Angel said. "I mean, I don't know the exact details, but something's not right up there." Angel nodded upward.

"Oh," Ester said leaned back as the others continued to relax.

That night Ester laid in bed wide awake. She was tired, but her mind wasn't quite ready to let her sleep. She never really thought that much about the giant green planet in the sky. She was aware that there was some kind of conflict, but she couldn't imagine it being that serious that no one was allowed to travel. Ester pulled her covers closer to her, but she couldn't escape the light of the moon. She looked up and caught a glimpse of Labadora in the sky, a planet in conflict. She felt a small shiver, but curled up into a little ball and fell asleep.

Chapter Eight

Captain Pole sat at his desk reading the news on his tablet as his students filed into the classroom. In just a few short weeks, the cadets had learned so much and were now focusing more on test preparation. The captain sat behind his desk, sipping his favorite Bex Se tea and came to life only when the clock struck zero seven hundred hours.

"Good morning," he said in his usual lackluster tone. "I hope you slept well. Today's lecture will be cut short. I'm sure you'd like to hear me talk about the history of CuCore development, but I think you'll benefit from more training. Over the past couple of weeks, you've made some progress with training, but, of course, there is more."

The class groaned.

"There's always more." The Captain finished off his tea and slowly raised himself up from his desk. He winced at every step but made no effort to sit back down. He pressed a button on his wristband and the holoscreen popped up. "As you know, your first test is a group activity spilt up in four parts. The first two parts are the barrel walk and the puzzle solver." The holoscreen displayed information about the test as the cadets feverously took notes.

"Pssst, Ester," Angel whispered. "Pssst, Ester."

"Hmm?" Ester struggled to keep an ear open while she jotted down notes.

"Today during training, we gotta put Murk in his place."

"Hmm hmm," Ester murmured.

"I mean it," Angel whispered with his head ducked down. "I'm tired of him, and I think it's time we put a stop to that classless twill."

"Johnson." Captain Pole stared Angel right in the face. "Is there something you want to share with the class?"

"Um, no sir." Angel straighten up as his face turned bright red.

Some of the other cadets snickered, as Captain Pole returned to his lesson. Ester caught Murk pointing and whispering amongst his friends. Ester glared. Angel was right, something needed to be done. Captain Pole coughed, and the screen changed to a different slide.

"As I was saying, the final two parts will consist of an academic trivia round and a group race called links. I cannot stress enough that it is not important that you make it in first place. Although it does look good, you're being tested on how well you work together, not on who finishes first. Your only competitor is the clock. All groups must finish within the time frame given." The Captain turned walked back to his desk. "Finish the notes and the assigned chapter by ten forty-five hundred hours after and meet me at the track for training."

The class got to work reading through their tablets, but Ester noticed that Angel was really riled up about Murk. She glanced over her shoulder and saw Murk whispering to his friends again. They snickered as they looked their way. Ester clenched her fist. One day, Murk would get what's coming to him.

***

The clock showed ten twenty hundred hours and most of the class was finished with their morning work and heading to the gym. The weeks of their first semester were going by fast, and with that came the anxiety of their first exam. The group stepped outside. A cool breeze swept over the island. It was the end of summer and the weather was already starting to change.

"I'm kind of excited about the academic trivia round, though," Fermit said as he walked next to his friends.

Angel nodded. "Me too! I love me some trivia."

"Um, well you guys can have that, but I'll stick to the other events," Ester said.

"I think we should make a game plan and have everyone pick the events they want to do," Angel said.

Samay rubbed her arm nervously. "But with Murk around."

Angel jumped out in front of his group, making his angry face, which still made him look like a frazzled child. "Don't you worry about Murk!" Angel hissed, pointing his finger at Samay. "We're going to take care of him."

"What did you say?" A voice cut through the chatter in the courtyard as Murk and his friends walked through the parting crowd.

Angel tensed as some of the other students from their class gathered round. Ester stepped forward, but Samay stopped her, pointing to Angel's body language. He wasn't going to back down this time. Angel clenched his fist as Murk smirked, waiting to see what the thinner boy would do. Anger flashed through Angel's clear blue eyes, but he bit his tongue and took a deep breath.

"I said," Angel stared Murk straight in the eyes, "we're not listening to you anymore."

"Is that so?" Murk laughed. All of his friends chortled along with him. "So, the little brat has a plan."

"He can't be serious!" Kiakit said.

"Shut it!" Angel shouted. "We're all tired of you bossing us around. Your reign ends today and if you have any complaints, take it up with me after we pass this test, since following you has gotten us nowhere." Angel turned to the class. "I don't know about you guys, but training has been super sucky. I'm tired of working in events I'm not good at, and no surprise, it's getting us nowhere. So, if you want to follow Murk so be it, but if you actually want to work in the events you're good at, then let's get together and talk this out. Who's with me?"

Murk's friends stood there with their mouths open. Some of the other students looked at each other and then at Murk. Some started to come around, with their eyes averted they slowly started walking towards the gym. Murk was boiling under his skin. Fermit looked at Samay and they both looked at Murk. He looked like his head was going to explode at any minute. Murk turned and glared at them, turning Fermit and Samay stiff as a board. The two friends laughed nervously and inched away from Murk.

"Looks like you've been voted out," Ester said as she walked away.

Murk took a step forward, but Kiakit stopped him with her hand on Murk's shoulder. "Forget about them."

"Back off," he snapped. "I'm not throwing away my chance to get into ranger academy because of some blond headed twill." Murk stormed off to training, as his friends scrambled to keep up with him.

At training the track was a mess of tablets and holographic images of Rean and the galaxy. Cadets huddled in groups pouring over pages of previous trivia questions, while others tried their hand at the links. Things were running a little bit smoother after Angel had spoken up, but they still had a long way to go. Captain Pole watched the clock from his stool, his emotionless face was not encouraging, but he made fewer statements today, which some cadets took as a good sign.

Ester watched Angel and Fermit chatter from the sidelines. She definitely didn't want to get stuck doing trivia or the puzzle and was grateful for Angel's bravery. Instead, Ester decided to try the links. It looked doable from the preview screen. She and a few other cadets huddled together and watched the replay. She ignored the fact that she had to work with Zime, who didn't look any happier with the arrangement. After watching the demo for the tenth time, the group moved into position. Ester picked up a link and placed it around her waist. It was lighter than she was expecting. When she turned it on, she was not expecting it to pull her and her other teammates tightly together. Everyone stumbled forward as the magnetic force recoiled, positioning them exactly four feet apart. The group stumbled around trying to find their balance, which was difficult because if one person stepped forward the rest of the group was shuffled along with them. Ester was tugged forward as Hue, another boy in their class, tripped over his feet. Zime rolled her eyes. She wanted to be in the middle, but she was out voted, and Hue was chosen to lead. Ester liked the idea because she knew Zime could be too bossy. The clock started, and the group tried their best to move as one. The course was a jungle gym of blocks, walls, and crawl spaces, designed to be carefully navigated like a ship formation traveling through an asteroid belt. The fastest way through would require everyone to watch their teammates' backs. Especially for the cadet in the middle, who had a 360-degree view of their teammates and the course.

"I am so over this!" Zime complained after they found themselves stuck at their first obstacle. Zime was on the outside, opposite of Ester.

Ester rolled her eyes and ignored her comment, looking to Hue. "Hue! You're the middle man! We need you to tell us where to go."

Zime cast a dirty look at Ester. "It's no use; he's too fat and stupid to do anything."

Ester was grateful for the forced distance because she about ready to clobber Zime. "I swear, why are you such a bitch?" Ester snapped.

"We wouldn't be here if it wasn't for your little friend!" Zime hissed.

"And you liked falling over next to Kiakit on the barrel walk? Because you guys were such the power team?"

Zime said noting, but Hue coughed, gaining the attention of his teammates. Hue wasn't as outspoken in class, but whenever someone heard a sigh, they knew it was Hue. He didn't perform well in the other challenges, but he was observant. Angel actually recommended he try the links, despite Murk and his friend's complaints, because Angel noticed how Hue seemed to point out different ways of doing things. Hue peered around the course. He realized quickly there were many correct ways to navigate the field, but there were some routes that were easier than others. He saw a path that didn't require much crawling and pointed to it.

"Guys, uh, take two steps left. I think I may have found an easy way through this," Hue muttered.

Zime looked ahead. "You can't be serious."

She whined, but the other four had already started walking. Hue noticed up ahead that there was a small incline. If they kept going the way they were some of them would be hobbling overtop of it.

"I see an incline," Hue, said as he peered over one of his teammates. "I think we should back up towards the wall to avoid it."

Ester heard Zime make a smacking sound with her teeth, but she did what Hue said and they cleared he obstacle. They stumbled and repeated their steps many times, but they were making progress. Hue pointed and gave instructions, taking in feedback from his teammates. Ester watched the clock; they were making good time. Even Zime noticed that they were doing well and decided to be more helpful. There was a wall coming up. Zime spotted it. They would have to back up and try a different way. Hue nodded, and they all moved as one. Crawling and squeezing their way through the course, the group finally saw the finish line

"We're almost there." Hue pointed. "Now, let's slow down, I see something up ahead."

There were more awkward inclines coming up and there was no way to avoid them. The group slowed and made sure to provide as much space to ease the comfort of their teammates that were stuck on the incline.

"Let's do a one-person rotation left!" Hue shouted and group turned with ease.

They cleared the course and walked across the finish line. The group cheered as they undid their links. Ester collapsed on the floor next to Hue. This had to be their best run yet, but still the clock blared down on them. They needed to improve their time. Ester looked up and made eye contact with Zime. She ignored Ester's gaze, but there was something different in her body language. Zime stood and barked at the group like she always did. She ordered them to run it again, but this time she didn't make a fuss about Hue leading.

Meanwhile around the track, others were making head way on their tasks. From the looks of it, this did not sit well with Murk. He watched from the sidelines as Kiakit and Bue made headway on the barrels, barking orders back and forth. Ester could tell the others were taking it in stride, but why couldn't he just see how much better things were? Ester shook her head. He was just one hiccup in their plan, but she was sure he would come around once he saw how good everyone was doing.

***

It was now a week before the first part of their exam. Ester's house had been working hard every day in training. The cadets hit the books as well as the gym in preparation for their first house test. In their first class of the week, Captain Pole covered how the test would be set up. Houses would compete together in a massive relay race. Each house would have a panel of judges scoring them at every station. This was the headlining event of the fall semester and the only part that was open for others to view. This made Ester extremely nervous. Hundreds of rangers would be watching their exam, and as prospective a ranger, it was important to her that she make a good impression.

Angel and Ester left class for the day and headed towards the courtyard. With Murk and his band of bullies at bay, the class was able to decide who was best suited for each task. It wasn't easy separating everyone out, but after a week of back and forth, they settled on something. If all went according to plan, the test should run smoothly. Angel found an open space on the lawn and plopped down in the grass. Fall had taken root, and there was a distinct chill in the air.

Angel shivered. "It's starting to get chilly."

Ester watched her friend rub his hands up and down his arms. To Ester, he was nothing but skin and bones, but he ate like a grown man. She smiled as she watched his curly locks of hair bounce around his face as he took out his tablet.

"You need a haircut," Ester joked.

Angel looked up at Ester's unkempt hair. "Um, have you seen yourself in the mirror?"

"What?" Ester pulled at one of her fly away curls. Her hair was as thick and wild as a forest of trees, only tamed by a single hair tie that was stretched too thin into a ponytail. "Okay, so it's a little frizzy."

"A little." Angel looked at Ester's hair. "I have product to tame that mane, but I might have to go back to the mainland to get some more, because it's looking more like a jungle than a garden."

"I'm okay." Ester pulled her knees up to her chest, thinking about the mainland as well. "So, what are the shops like in Ans-on?" She asked, unknowingly unlocking a hidden side of Angel she was sure to regret.

"A-maz-ing." Angel mouthed every symbol. "I could live in a mall and never go home. Back in school, I wore every fashion trend, and yes, even the tacky ones. I had to try them out for myself, you know to make sure it was what it was. I personally love the Numa Numa brand for boys. They make the best high cheek shorts and I lo-ve fitted crop tops and everything vibrant, honestly. Oh! I totally forgot about the newest brand of color changing ride suits. I think it's going to drop in the winter. After all, winter is ride suit season and I cannot wait."

Ester laughed. She was completely lost in Angel's fashion talk. "There's nothing like that where I'm from."

"Really? How do you survive?" Angel placed his hands on his soft pink cheeks.

"Fine, thank you." Ester said. "Well, I shouldn't say Adum is void of shops. We have shops, but in the southern region, where the big trading post are, there are a lot of markets there. But I've never been. I heard the fish markets were really cool though."

"I think I've heard about that. We do import a lot of fresh vegetables and fish from Adum."

"I'm not surprised. A lot of hard work goes into growing the crops for the country." Ester said with pride.

"Hey, we should go shopping on break." Angel bounced up and down. "With my express card, I can take you to the malls, and oooh! You can meet my friends! They are so cool."

"Oh yeah, I forgot about break," Ester said, she had been too busy worrying about the exam to even think about it. "Are we allowed to leave Juw-ja during break?"

"Of course we are! Granted it's a short break, like three days or so, but I have an express card and can pretty much go anywhere in Ans-on because of my parents. So yeah, we can totally go to the sky mall or something."

"That's awesome!" Ester grinned. It wasn't like she wanted to buy anything, not that she had any tones away, but she would love to see the shops.

"Gotta love rich mommy and daddy; they're useful sometimes." Angel picked up his tablet and pulled up a list of trivia questions. "Now, quiz me." He handed Ester the tablet.

"Okay," Ester said. "What is the region of our galaxy with a ring of asteroids called?"

"Verlin's Belt! Too easy." Angel bounced up and down.

Ester waved her hand up and down. "That was just practice. Next question!"

Chapter Nine

The locker room was bustling with chatter on the day of their first exam. The cadets had worked tirelessly for weeks, and there was nothing more important than the test they would be taking today. For the test they were given special house themed ride suits. Ester's house, House Snake, sported a blue and silver suit, with the house's emblem embroidered on the chest on the right. Ester stood in front of the mirror with her ride suit half on admiring the soft light weight feel of the fabric. It was so comfortable; it really felt like she didn't have anything on. She pulled the rest over her shoulders and stuck her arms through. She zipped up the front of her blue and silver suit looking very official as she flexed in the mirror.

"You look totally hot." Angel stood behind her with Samay and Fermit smiling in agreement.

Ester's cheeks warmed as she laughed a little. "I wouldn't say hot. I mean, everyone looks good."

Murk and his friends were the last to enter the locker room. Some of the cadets stepped out of his way as he and his friends headed to the back. Samay turned and made room for him. Murk caught eyes with Ester.

"You may look the part, but don't think for a second that you're anything more than Adum dust. We'll be the ones carrying the class, so try not to get in our way." Murk and his friends walked off.

Ester clenched her fists, but a gentle hand patted her on her shoulder.

"Don't worry about him. We can't do this without everyone." Angel said.

Ester calmed down. "You're right. Okay guys, let's do what we practiced. I know we'll come out on top if we do our best." Ester threw out her fist as the others joined. "House Snake, the backbone of peace and the distributor of justice. For House Snake!" Everyone shouted and cheered.

***

The cadets stood in anticipation behind the doors leading to the course. Captain Pole stood in the front counting heads and making sure everyone was in line as he limped back and forth. Despite the fact that they had practiced this course a hundred times, the cadets still felt nervous. Angel rocked from side to side. He was sure his heart would give out before he even started. Fermit felt the same way even though he had been through this before. Samay and Ester stood side by side ignoring the bullets of glares coming from Murk. Today was their big day, and nothing was going to stop them from coming out on top. Captain Pole clapped his hands, drawing the attention of his cadets.

"Alright, this is the moment you've been training for. Remember, this is not a race against the other houses. Watch the clock and use each other to navigate the course. There's no need to be nervous, but there is a large crowd of captains and rangers beyond this door. They'll be looking to see how well this batch of cadets preforms, but all you should be focusing on is working together to complete your task.

Captain Pole walked up and down the line "It's not my job on the line whether you pass or fail, but it is your career. So, if you want the honor of being called a ranger, then you'll have to earn it. I don't say this often, but I am proud of you. Together you have shown great improvement. Remember what you've learned. May Rean be with you."

A muffled roar from behind the door set the cadets straight, followed by a man on the intercom. Captain Pole lined up at the door in the front of his class. A ranger directing the class walked up from behind with a big smile on their face, giving them the all clear. Captain Pole nodded as he listened to the announcer.

"Good morning, rangers, captains, and esteemed guests to the first portion of the second entrance exam into the Academy of the Rean Coalition of Rangers. Today's exam will test our prospective cadets' ability to work together and think critically in a relay style race. The top three highest scoring houses will be awarded a passing grade, and the lowest two will be awarded failing grades. Let us commence with the test by introducing our houses. Without further ado, please welcome House Scorpion!"

The crowds cheered as the name of each house was called. Ester's heart raced as she stood in line with her classmates.

"Please welcome House Crane!" The cheering got louder.

Ester jumped as her arms started to shake. She took a deep breath and closed her eyes. *Please mother, father, and Sister Genevieve, move over me and give me your strength so I can do my best today.* Ester touched the spot where her mother's necklace lay.

"Please welcome House Snake!"

The doors opened, and the cadets followed their captain into the arena. Bright lights blinded the cadets as the class walked out onto the track. There were hundreds of people there, and they were being televised on a hover screen above the course. Ester looked around; there were so many people here. Bearing down on her were the numbers on the big clock that hung above the course. Ester gulped. Somehow the course looked more intimidating than the practice course they had been working on over the past few weeks. Her house lined up next to the other houses in front of the stage as the other houses were called. Her heart was beating out of her chest, as she stole glances here and there. She lined up next to her friends and stood like a statue as Grand Commander J'Chives smiled and took the stage. He raised his hand to settle the crowd, bringing the arena to silence.

"Welcome, cadets. I know that you have trained hard for this moment for the past few weeks, and I have faith that each and every one of you will do well here today. So, without further delay, please take your positions at the start of the course. You'll have forty minutes to complete the course and remember teamwork is the backbone of the coalition. We are nothing without our fellow rangers. Good luck cadets and may Rean be with you."

The captains took their place on the side lines as the houses lined up. Each house had a brief amount of time to size everyone up. It was a pretty diverse mix, with cadets that were really tall to cadets that were on the heavier side. Each looked like they brought their A-game. The clock flashed five minutes, which was all the prep time they got. The eight cadets who were doing the barrel run lined up first, while the others waited on the side lines. In this race, cadets had to wait at their assigned post to start their part of the race. Ester and her friends headed to their post, but there was a bit of arguing coming from the back of the group.

"I'm switching!" Murk shouted and pushed another cadet out of the way.

"What are you doing?" Angel turned around.

"I'm doing the links." Murk grinned.

"But we already have our assignments for the links," Ester responded, with the others gathering around. The clock flashed three minutes.

"Gotta save the best for last." Murk smiled.

Ester and Murk exchanged glares as the rest of the class looked around.

"You're messing up the order!" Ester snapped. The clock flashed one minute.

"It doesn't matter!" Angel shouted. "We have to get to our stations. Come on!"

Ester glared at Murk as she walked away, but there was nothing she could do now. Murk, Bue, and Kiakit were supposed to take the lead for the barrel run, but now he switched sending Zime to do the barrels. Ester bit her tongue and started to run to her station. Now she would have to work with Murk. The time flashed thirty seconds, and everyone hurried to their station. At the puzzle station, Samay and another cadet named Conner took the lead. At the academic trivia station, Angel and Fermit took the lead, and in the final event, the links, Murk, Hue, and Ester were stationed. The clocked flashed five seconds until the buzzer went off. Bue, Zime, and Kiakit lined up at the line and eyed the other cadets with fierce looks. It was time.

Everything they had been working hard on would show today.

The buzzer went off, and the first group of cadets raced to their pallets. Kiakit shouted to the other three to move quicker. Her group got to the pallet second and lifted the platform with the load as quickly as they could. Under Kiakit's command, the group took off. The course had many obstacles on it that made walking around them difficult. Already a group from House Bull fell over.

A cadet in Kiakit's group shouted for everyone to watch their steps as there was a patch of uneven ground up ahead. They slowed to navigate it better and maintained their lead in second place. On the hover screen, all the cadets could see their house's progress. Everyone from House Snake cheered and shouted as Kiakit's group passed the finish line in near first place. The light flashed green and the second team, led by Zime, ran to their pallet. They lifted the pallet and took off down the track. They were close to first and moving quickly. Zime shouted from the back.

"I see a row of um, things." She tried to nod to her left.

"What?" Bue shouted.

Zime struggled to describe it. "Things, you know, the big…"

"Wall!" Another cadet in their group shouted, but they were moving too fast and slammed into the padded wall, making their pallet and its contents fall to the ground.

"Fuck," Zime said as she and the rest of the group raced to re-load their pallet.

They were now in third place with Houses Monkey and Crane passing them. They re-loaded their pallet and took off again, but this time more carefully. The clock above the course flashed nine minutes.

"Come on!" Murk shouted.

Ester rolled her eyes from her station, as the rest of the class cheered on their teammates. Zime and her group made it across the finish line and the light turned green for the first group to head to the puzzle. They were led by Conner, a boy Samay recruited to help. The theme was numbers, and the objective was to find the right pattern to complete the puzzle and open the door. The clues were 80, 20, 10, and 40.

"Ten and twenty are connected how?" Conner thought as the group bounced ideas around. He slapped his hands on his head. "Ten, twenty, ten plus ten is twenty. Twenty was ten, no, twenty plus twenty is forty. Got it!" Conner shouted to his peers.

"Ten is the start, they add up, ten plus ten." Conner shouted as the other cadets started to see the pattern. "Put what adds up next to each other and you should get the next number." His classmates followed his directions and the door opened. "Yes!" Conner and his group ran to the side lines as Samay and her group ran to their puzzle.

"Way to go!" Samay waved on her way to her station.

The next theme was colors, Samay and her group got excited, but their puzzle was much harder than the practice ones. Another house started on their second puzzle, making them tie for third place. Samay stared at the clues, white, red, purple, and black. The group stared at the colors as the clock above them flashed fifteen minutes.

Samay waved to her group. "Hey guys, let's huddle." They huddled together quickly. "What do you guys think? What do these four colors have in common?"

The group stayed silent for a minute. One of her group members looked up and saw the other house making progress.

"Focus." She pulled them back down. "What do they have in common?"

Josh, another boy from their class, coughed to clear is throat. "Well, technically white and black aren't colors." The other group members groaned in annoyance.

"Well yes," Samay said with an eye roll, then looked at the clock above her. "Black and white aren't," she rubbed her hands together. "But purple and red are."

Sweat formed on her brow as she struggled to think above all the noise. She peeked and looked at the other group. They looked just about done, and if she didn't hurry her class would drop to fourth place.

"Come on, think, I mean, what do they all have in common? What does this puzzle want?" Her friends looked at the clues. The order didn't matter, and there was no way to add another color to get all of the colors.

"Purple and red, no, you need blue, but what makes black?" she stressed.

Josh slumped in frustration. "It's impossible. For one, there's nothing you can mix to get purple and red. Heck you can't even mix anything to get red because red is a primary color."

Then it struck Samay like a bolt of lightning. "You can't! You can't get red because it's a primary color and what's purple?"

Josh looked around, stuttering over his words.

"What's purple?" Samay asked again.

"Um, a secondary color? I don't know!" Josh panicked.

"Yes! White is a tint, black is a shade, purple is a secondary color, and red is a primary color. These are all examples of the types of colors!" Samay jumped up and down. "Try it!"

Her teammates rallied around her and wrote in the clues. The door clicked open, and the group exploded in excitement. Just in time too as they were able to maintain their place in third. The light flashed green for Angel, and his group to start the speed trivia. There were five questions per group, and the clock above flashed twenty-five minutes. Each member needed to get one question right to move on. Angel lined up next to his classmates. Cheers egged them on as the first question flashed on the screen.

Who was the second emperor to sign the Rean Peace Treaty?

"Al-lazarah Cha of Cha-la." Angel shouted out.

Huma-ko is best known for exporting what kind of resource?

"Ore!" Another classmate shouted.

The rest of the class shouted from the side lines. Angel's group raced through the questions. The first group finished in less than five minutes. Next up was Fermit's group. The five of them congratulated the previous group as they raced to the platform. There was no pause in the questions. The next one popped up on the screen as soon as all five of them were in position.

Which nation state has no formal governing leadership?

"Who-da!" Fermit shouted with ease.

What is one of the unique traits evolved for the people of Kees?

"They have the power to levitate and fly," Another answered, as his teammates cheered.

The core of a CuCore is made up of which element?

"Copper!" another teammate shouted.

What was the name of the first Ranger to pilot in space?

His teammate paused and turned to the group. They huddled together and came up seconds later with an answer. "Sergeant JJ Fox?"

The last question appeared as the group clapped and cheered.

The island south of Adum-la is often referred to as what?

The group looked around, but Fermit knew right away from studying with Ester. He pulled his group in, and in seconds, their last team member answered. "The Isle of Fish."

The light flashed green, bumping them into second place. House Snake roared in excitement. The last group lined up for the links race. The house in the lead was only on their first run, but they were moving slowly. Murk saw this as an opportunity to push forward. The clock flashed thirty minutes; they had ten minutes to run the course.

"I'm getting in the middle!" Murk shouted as he pushed past everyone.

"Hey, it's supposed to be Hue first!" Ester shouted.

"You guys want to win or come in last?" Murk spun around, sparks flying off his arms.

His teammates looked around then looked at the clock, their time was running out.

"Thought so." Murk pointed to the four people he wanted on his team.

"This is wrong," Ester tensed. "Hey, you come back and join Hue!" She shouted to one of her classmates on Murk's team. "I'm going in too." The other cadet stepped back. The clock flashed thirty-one minutes.

Murk rolled his eyes, but led the group. He carried them fast. Their little argument had given the house in the led a little more than an advantage, but they could still aim for second.

"I see something up ahead! It's a wall!" One of the cadets on the team shouted.

"Doesn't matter, push through!" Murk shouted.

"We need to slow down to complete it." Ester shouted as she and the others felt like they were being dragged along.

"We're already in second, just listen to me." Murk pushed forward which caused the magnetic links to push the other cadets along with him.

"Slow down!" Ester tried to put on the breaks, but the other three teammates were grinding on ahead.

"Come on!" Murk shouted from the middle of their group. Then out of nowhere, he felt a tug on his back left side. One of his teammates had fallen, which pulled the whole group down.

"Get up! Get up!" Murk growled as his teammate struggled to her feet. "Get up!" he shouted again as another house passed them. The time flashed thirty-five minutes. "Get up! Come on!"

Their classmates on the sidelines were hanging onto their seats; even Captain Pole was watching his students closely. Their fallen teammate was finally to her feet and the group pushed on.

"Left! Left, you idiots!" Murk barked orders like a war commander, but it worked, and the first team finished the course in a little over four minutes. The group collapsed at the finish line and looked back at Hue and his group. It was up to him now.

"Come on, Hue." Ester looked up at the clock. The time was thirty-six minutes.

Hue and his group were ready and suited up. "Ready!" His teammates nodded as the light flashed green for them to start. "Let's go! Head left, there's a wall a few steps up."

"Hue! I see an incline." A girl shouted from the front.

"I see it. Let's slow down and take two steps to the right. I see a wall around that corner." Hue pointed.

The group moved fast. They were tying for fourth place now, with the house in third and second not too far ahead.

"I see a low rise; we have to crawl and get down!" Hue shouted. His group responded and dropped to a crawl. The time flashed thirty-eight minutes. "Head three steps to the right, it's narrow up ahead."

"Hue, the course to the left is low. I'm crawling under," his teammate shouted.

"Good call. Everyone, let's try to keep up." Hue's team moved swiftly through the course.

The time was thirty-nine minutes, and with a minute to spare, Hue and his team crossed the finish line. They collapsed to the ground, surrounded by a roar of cheers from the crowd and their classmates. Time dropped to the final thirty-seconds, and Hue and his group ran to the side lines and clapped and shook hands. The buzzer went off, and the crowd clapped and cheered for all the cadets. Grand Commander J'Chives stood from his chair and took to the podium.

"Congratulations, cadets! All five houses have made it across the finish line. Rejoice and rest up. Your test result will be revealed in your next class at the beginning of the week. Let us give another cheer for all the cadets here today."

The crowd went off as the cadets walked back to the locker rooms, but it was clear there was still a lot of tension in the air.

Chapter Ten

The next day, everyone was in class bright and early. They were all anxious about their test scores. This morning Captain Pole was late, which made the class even more anxious. Ester watched the clock. It was now zero seven ten hundred hours. She looked over at Angel, who shared her same concern. Ester bounced her leg up and down under her desk as she twirled her thick curly hair with her finger. She was still mad over the fight at the end of the test. How could Murk embarrass them like that? She stole a glance at him, and he didn't even look phased. She wanted to say something to him after the test, but Angel said it wasn't worth her time. Nevertheless, Murk was officially on her shit list. At zero seven fifteen hundred hours, Captain Pole came limping into the classroom. His face was red and covered in a light sweat.

"Please forgive me, class. My leg locked up when I was trying to go down the stairs, and if you can imagine, it was quite unpleasant."

He winced as he limped to his desk, collapsing into his chair as if he had just run a marathon. From his desk, he took out a small clear box and opened it. Inside of it was a row of syringes with a blue liquid in it. He took out one.

"Pain meds." He showed the class, more so to prove that it was official ranger medicine and not something illegal. He pulled the cap off with his teeth and injected the meds into his leg. He grunted but sighed a breath of relief.

"Okay, I apologize again." He sat back in his chair. "This is going to be a short class and not because of my leg. Your mid-term break is coming up, and we captains use this brief time to prepare for your next exam, which will actually start three weeks after the break."

The classes looked at each other in disbelief—that was half the time they had to prepare for their last exam.

"And before you start sending angry e-messages to each other, this is done intentionally. Part two of the exam is a lot different than your first exam. This is the scenario portion, meaning you'll be tested on how well you can work together as well as how you react under stressful conditions. This is not a pass or fail exam, meaning there are multiple ways you can approach each scenario; however, you'll need to show how well you work together. I cannot stress that enough. With that being said, there is a great deal of new things you'll need to learn before you take the exam. Meaning we'll have plenty to go over before your break. Use your break to relax your mind and body because the next few weeks are going to go by fast."

Captain Pole poured himself a cup of Bex Se tea from his thermal and hit a control, so an ottoman would appear at his feet. He gently lifted his leg and rested it on the ottoman and groaned as he relaxed. He sat for a second with his eyes closed in complete comfort as he sipped his tea. The antsy cadets shifted in their seats and looked at each other wondering if he would ever tell them their results.

"Ah yes, I forgot." Captain Pole put his cup down. "Your test results." The cadets stared at him in dead silence. Captain Pole's eyes closed as he enjoyed one more sip of his tea. He hummed in contentment then set his cup down again. "It wasn't all bad, but it was far from good. You managed third place."

The room exploded with a mix of cheers and groans. It wasn't the highest score, but it was better than last place. Fermit, in the back, slowly raised his hand, grabbing Captain Pole's attention.

"Yes Doil?" Captain Pole called him by his last name, as he picked up his cup again.

"But, what about our score?" He asked.

Numbered scores were everything. Each class started out with one hundred points and that score would decide if their class would make the cut. Captain Pole placed his cup down and looked at the class. There wasn't a hint of emotion in his gaze as he stared at the class.

"Your final score was 64."

As if someone had dropped a glass sculpture on the floor, the cadets sat in their seats in complete shock. With a score that low and no way to bring it up, that meant that their class was in real trouble.

"But we're in third place," Angel blurted out.

"Yes, Johnson, we are, and two of the other houses scored lower than you," Captain Pole replied.

No one said anything. They didn't want to know how low those scores were or even think about the possibility. The classroom was dead silent in disappointment.

"Your scores reflect your performance, meaning there is obvious work to be done in the way you work with each other. The house with the highest score, House Crane, was able to score high because they learned to put their differences aside and work together. They were losing points in the beginning, yes, but realized they would accomplish nothing if they bickered. They are also the house that came in fourth during the race."

The cadets looked around in shock.

"How?" Murk asked.

Captain Pole leaned up and stretched. "I told you, this was not a race against the other houses. This whole entire portion of the exam is about how well you work together. Not to mention, other houses have been losing points before the test even started. And yes, you are being watched as I have mentioned before. With that being said, Neben, DuTain, your constant bickering has not gone unnoticed by the judges."

"But Captain Pole, it's not me!" Ester cried out in her defense.

"What! That's nonsense," Murk hissed.

"We are watching you." Captain Pole held up his hand to Murk, signaling him to be quite. "It doesn't matter who starts what, a true ranger knows when to walk away. This is not play school. If you graduate ranger academy you will be working with hostile and provoking forces. It is vital that you keep a cool head, reckless behavior could jeopardize the mission."

Ester wanted to protest more, but Captain Pole had already moved onto another subject. She couldn't believe she was being punished for something Murk started. If they were truly watching them then they must be doing a poor job. It was ridiculous and frustrating in her eyes. She sat at her desk simmering in anger. This was all Murk's fault.

The classed ended, and everyone was assigned chapters of work on intergalactic relations. Ester exited the classroom and stormed down the hall near breaking point. Angel followed behind her.

"Ester, wait up." Angel chased after her.

"It's not fair." She slammed her fist into the wall, generating enough electricity to cause a nasty shock.

"Forget about him," Angel said. "At least they know he's an asshole."

"Yeah, but I got in trouble too." Ester slumped. From day one, that kid had it out for her. It wasn't fair that she was getting in trouble too.

"How about this? For break we can do something extra special to take your mind off this. I'm sure there's something fun going on in central Ans-on; there always is."

Ester straightened up. She was looking forward to seeing the shops.

"Hey, what about going to Snow Mountain? It's a really nice jelly bar, oh, and Button's Core Spa is a place that can resurrect any crappy mood. I love that place, and don't worry about paying." Angel pulled out his tablet. "Oh and Galaxia will be preforming at Centra, but if you'd rather go shopping, that's fine too."

"Wait, Galaxia is preforming in Ans-on? This weekend?" Ester grabbed Angel by the shoulders.

"Yeah," Angel nodded. "She usually tours around this time of year, why?"

"Can we see her?" Ester said with one hundred percent seriousness.

"Sure." Angel clicked on a few links on his tablets. "First row seats okay with you?"

"Wait, how?" Ester looked over Angel's shoulders.

"My family gets invites to these things all the time, so it's no biggie."

Ester could not believe what she was hearing. "Oh my gosh, I would die if we went."

"Well, I need you alive, so I can have a study partner."

"Fine, just can we go?" Ester begged.

"Clicked and booked." Angel smiled from ear to ear.

"Oh my gosh! Thank you! Thank you!" Ester shouted and hugged him.

This news melted away all of Ester's anger. She was so excited about break she could barely focus in class for the rest of the day. It was one thing to be in ranger academy; it was another thing to see one of her idols preform live. She walked behind Angel to the gym feeling much better about the week.

***

To Ester it felt like the week just flew by. Ester and Angel were ready for a break after an intense week of studying. Ester was especially excited about the break because she was seeing Galaxia live for the first time. Galaxia had been her favorite singer songwriter ever since she was fifteen and she couldn't believe Angel got front row seats. This was more than a dream, it was something she never thought possible. Back at the dorm, Ester packed her bag for the two-day trip. She didn't have many clothes, but they were comfortable, and she didn't care either way how she looked. Angel joined her, pulling out his bag of make-up and luggage. He turned and looked at what Ester was packing and cringed.

"You're not taking that are you?" He eyed her half full zipped bag.

"What?" Ester said.

Angel stepped over to her bed and peeked into the bag. He poked at her tattered clothes and made a face.

"How long have you had these?" Angel backed away from the bag as if it were cursed.

"They're secondhand, but they're new to me, so what does it matter?" Ester picked up her favorite t-shirt with the faded logo of a beverage company that had long gone out of business. She smiled fondly, as Angel looked like he wanted to vomit.

"Yeah, no." Angel placed his hands on her shirt and brought it back to the bed.

"What's wrong with this shirt? It doesn't have any holes," Ester complained.

"Maybe not, but it is not proper Ans-on attire."

"And what do I wear then? All my clothes are like this." Ester crossed her arms.

Angel looked like he was going to gag. "All? Okay, intervention time. First thing we're doing when we get to the mainland is going shopping." Angel looked at Ester's natural appearance and hair. "And makeovers."

Ester touched her face. "What's wrong with my face?"

Angel winced. "Do you want an honest answer?" Ester was starting to get mad as the electricity made her hair frizzy. "It's okay, it's not terminal. I can help you out." Angel put his hands up in defense.

Fermit and Samay walked over to join them. Samay had her bags packed too.

"Heading out?" Angel asked Samay.

Samay nodded. "I'm visiting my uncle who lives in Ans-on. He was nice enough to send me tickets." She smiled warmly.

"Nice," Angel said.

"What about you, Fermit?" Ester asked.

"I'm staying here," Fermit grinned as he scratched the back of his shaven head. "Gotta cram for the test. Don't want to fall behind," He laughed.

"That's fair," Angel said. "Well try to get some kind of break in there."

Fermit nodded.

Ester and Angel said goodbye to their friends as they headed to the train station. Angel was a little sad that his new friends couldn't come with them, but it was a short break and it was good to see that everyone was making the most of it.

Angel and Ester stood at the terminal in the train station and waited for their train to arrive. This terminal was a lot different than the busy one Ester arrived at a few months ago. There were less people and a lot more security. Even the people waiting for the train looked different. Ester looked closer and recognized some of the people by their honors. There were a lot of junior sergeants and civil servants. Angel seemed unfazed. After all, Angel was the son of civil councilors, so he was probably used to this. There was a low rumble coming from the blue lit tunnel as the train arrived. Angel pulled out his express card and digi-id and waved for Ester to follow. The train was nothing like the one she road in on. This one was huge. She followed Angel to the door and waited behind him as the people got off. It was so big she wasn't tall enough to see inside the windows. Once the last person got off, everyone filed in and scanned their cards. Ester pulled out hers, but Angel stopped her.

"I got this," Angel reached over and scanned his card, then scanned his wristband over the panel. "My guests ride free." He winked.

Ester nodded in amazement as the light turned green and the two walked up the short flight of stairs. There were little cameras in the walls, and at the top was a man in a red and gold ride suit directing people to their seats.

"Anywhere is fine." Ester heard Angel say. She was barely listening as she was so amazed at how fancy it looked. The seats were all booths with tables in the middle. The cabin was super clean and spacious. There were staff taking food and drink orders and the walls were completely digital with news, weather, and investment updates flashing by.

"Ester, over here." Angel waved.

Apparently, she was so lost in her surroundings she forgot to move. The door man eyed her as she shrunk away to Angel's booth.

"This is a train?" Ester felt the seats, which were unbelievably soft.

Angel looked around and shrugged. "Yeah, this is about standard. I like the trains in the Ans-on underground better. Some of them have dance clubs in them."

Ester looked at Angel. She wasn't even going to ask how a dance club could fit onto a train or why it would be on a train in the first place. The doors closed, and the train made its way out of the station. The lights in the tunnels sped past, but the service workers working the tables walked around unaffected.

Ester leaned over to Angel and whispered. "How come nobody is falling over?"

Angel gave her a weird look at first, but then he looked at who she was pointing to.

"Oh, you mean the wait staff?" Ester nodded. Angel laughed out loud, which made his platinum blond curls bounce up and down. "It's because of their ride suits. I think it's the J-model. It's magnetic and has balancing features. Some of the space rangers wear J-suits to make it easier to walk around. Civilian models are available in the shops, but they're pricey. In my opinion, they're not that cute either."

Ester nodded as she tried to process the information. When it came to Angel talking about expensive things, it seemed as common as talking about the weather. This was the distance that Ester felt sometimes in his presence. She couldn't imagine a life where tones flowed like water, and everywhere you went you were connected digitally. A waiter came to their table and Angel ordered a drink, but Ester declined. She was too distracted by the beautiful view outside. They were crossing the ocean, and it was a marvelous sight to see. She would never get used to seeing it. High in the sky birds glided in the air as they circled schools of breaching fish. Ester kept her eyes on it the whole time, which amused Angel.

When they arrived in Ans-on, there was a security officer there to meet them. Angel waved to him, and they followed him to an all-black hover car.

"This is fancy." Ester watched the man with the dark brown hair close the door behind them.

"It's standard; we always travel like this." Angel turned on his wristband. "We can stay at my place for the break. The concert is tonight, so that doesn't give us much time to get dolled up. Plus, I need a deep cleanse skin treatment because all that sweat has made my skin wrinkly."

Ester looked at Angel's face and arms. Her face was a mix of amusement and confusion. The hover car ascended and joined the traffic pattern in the sky. Ester's face was glued to the window. They were hundreds of feet in the air. She could see all the roads below her as they cruised among the tall buildings. They rose higher and jetted by sky malls, and past hover screens with large ads on them. One of which advertised the very concert they were going to tonight.

"Look, Angel!" Ester pointed to her idol.

Angel looked over. "Wow," Angel said with little enthusiasm in his voice.

Ester rolled her eyes.

"I have to remember that you have never seen this before, which is like crazy." Angel swiped through a few screens projected from the table. "Okay first, we have to get you something to wear."

"Angel," Ester groaned.

"I am not taking no for an answer." Angel made a face. "You're meeting my friends, and I want you to make a good impression."

Ester slouched in her chair and threw her hands up. Angel clapped with delight and began going over all the shops they would visit. Ester tuned it out to watch Galaxia sing. She melted at the thought that in just a few hours she would be seeing her live, which was well worth the hassle of a shopping spree.

Angel's home was located in the civil building. Civil servants and councilors were required to live in the civil buildings, which were amongst the most luxurious buildings in Ans-on. They pulled into the garage as a door on the side of the building closed. They hopped out, and Angel said goodbye to his driver and ran to elevator door. Ester nodded to the driver as well and rushed to catch up with him. She looked around and had never seen so many jet black and silver hover cars in her life. They were all newer models, top of the line. To her, it reminded her of a parking area, except it wasn't on the ground and located inside of a multi-level sky scrapper.

"I cannot wait to show you my closet. I have so many outfits and shoes." Angel jumped up and down.

The door opened to a room that was metallic gold and silver.

Angel hit a button for A-22 and the elevator glided up smoothly. Ester marveled at how quiet it was; it was even quieter than the ones back at the academy. Angel pressed a button on his wristband and spoke into it.

"Master, is mother and father home?"

"Hello, Angel. Welcome home. Mr. and Mrs. Johnson are not in the building. Is there anything else I can assist you with today?"

The AI startled Ester.

"What the heck was that?" Ester looked at Angel.

"No, thank you, Master." Angel sighed. "It's just Master, our home private assistant AI. I thought they would be here. I sent them a message." Angel lowered his eyes.

"It's okay, Angel I'm sure they have important work to do."

"Yeah, right." Angel tapped a few buttons on the elevator display. "Master, what is my parents' current location?"

"Mr. Johnson's current location is at the Mayfield Skybar, and Mrs. Johnson's current location is at Salle's Hair Salon and Spa. Estimated time of home arrival: Unknown."

"Thank you, Master." Angel rolled his eyes. "See."

"Is there anything else I can assist you with?"

"No, thank you, Master." The door opened to a small hallway with three doors. "That's my parents' office." Angel pointed to the right. "And that's the briefing room." He pointed to the left. "It's for when they actually do work," Angel joked as he placed his palm on the fingerprint reader. "And this is our home."

When Ester walked in she could not believe her eyes. The condo was so modern and sleek, with a metallic silver finish, much like how ranger academy was. All the tables and furniture were made from a tough clear resin and art decorated the walls accenting the apartment with color. Ester looked to her left at the living room that had flowering plants on the tables and a white and gold couch set. On the walls leading to the kitchen were family portraits. She stopped and smiled. Angel looked just like his mother, with her matching pale skin, almost white blond hair, and clear blue eyes. His father had golden blond hair and soft facial features that almost looked feminine. He was very handsome. Now she knew where Angel got it from.

"Is it just you?" Ester stopped and looked at all the pictures.

"Yup." Angel shouted from the kitchen. "Mother lost all the rest of my siblings before they were welcomed into the world."

"I'm so sorry."

"It's okay, that's why she named me Angel, from the lore of my great-great-grandmother. It was said an angel was a creature of luck, and if you saw one, you must drop to your knees and praise it and in return for the warm welcome it gives you good luck."

"Sounds kind of weird." Ester stepped back from the wall and walked to the kitchen.

Angel shrugged. "I think I'm good luck. Mother also said I was. She said I was the best thing to happen to her, that and the invention of deliverable wine." Angel laughed as Ester looked around the kitchen.

"Wow, I can't believe you live here." Ester admired the glass table and smooth white steel refrigerator and cooking oven. If someone told her that this place was brand new, she would believe them, because that's how clean it looked.

"Hungry? Want some water… or wine?" Angel offered.

"No, thank you." Ester continued to walk around the kitchen and Angel watched her in amusement.

"Now I know where you're from they have kitchens."

"Shut up. It's nothing this fancy." Ester pressed a button and a cabinet door opened revealing neatly placed glasses and plates.

"Okay, okay," Angel disappeared in the back. "Hey, come here I gotta show you my stuff, and you have to help me pick out something cute to wear."

"Okay." Ester pressed the button again and the cabinet door closed. If she ever got this rich she would love to buy this kitchen for Sister Genevieve. "Where are you?" Ester walked down the hall.

There were a lot of closed and open doors. She looked in one room and the lights turned on automatically. It was a bathroom and it was just as nice. Ester gaped at the tile floors and glass sink when she was shaken from her thoughts by Angel's voice.

"I'm in my room, last door on the left." The sounds of drawers could be heard opening and closing from down the hall.

Ester stepped out of the bathroom and walked down the hall. She stopped and looked at the artwork on the wall briefly before looking ahead.

"You parents sure like…" Ester stopped in her tracks.

Angel's room was huge. It was so big Ester was sure it could fit about five people comfortability.

"Do you share this with your parents?" Ester looked around at the soft pink and blue decorated walls, with posters of every big name model on Rean.

"Eww, no. This is my room." Angel ran around the room with a handful of clothes in his hands.

"This whole thing?" Ester wanted to take a seat, her legs felt weak.

"Yeah." Angel gave her a weird look. "Help me find something cute." Angel threw his clothes on his bed.

Ester looked around. There were even rooms in his room, even a bathroom. "Are those closets?"

"Yeah, I have three." Angel held up a royal blue ride suit with cut outs on the front and back. "What do you think of this?"

Ester shook her head to bring herself back down to Rean and stared at the suit. "Is it torn?"

Angel laughed. "No silly, it's a fashion suit, a FIN-ver, to be exact. What about this one?" The second suit was white and pink and looked like a crop top strapped to tight pants.

"Um, I don't know Angel. It all looks a little exposing to me."

"Good, so which would you say makes my butt look better?" Angel picked up two more suits and turned and showed off his backside.

Ester stared in confusion. "I-I don't know."

"Aww, you're no fun." Angel pouted.

"What?" Ester walked closer to his bed, there were so many suits on the bed. They all looked like a jumbled mess. She picked up one that was yellow and white.

"Eww," Angel slapped it away. Ester jumped back. "That one is old, what about this?"

Angel held up a blue and white suit. The top part was long sleeved and cropped, made from a soft white fabric. The bottom was navy blue, with a funnel shaped piece that connected to the top part. The sides were completely cut out and most of his back was exposed. Ester looked at the contraption with mild repulsion, but she knew if she didn't say something Angel would just show her more.

"It's not bad." She sat on the bed.

"Good, because I like this one too, and I have the perfect boots to match." Angel disappeared into one of his closets, appearing shortly after, holding a pair of boots, in a different outfit, a tight all white and silver accented ride suit. There were matching diamond shaped cut outs on his stomach and back. He wore matching boots and carried an all-white purse with an M embroidered in it. "Ta-da!"

Ester wasn't sure if she should look at the boots Angel had in his hands or ask him if he had an automatic outfit changer in his closet, too. She blinked several times before giving the thumbs up. Angel clapped and giggled as Ester sighed. She could tell that this was going to be a long day.

***

For the rest of the day, Angel dragged her to all the shops and salons. It wasn't as bad as Ester thought. She enjoyed most of it, even though Angel got mad when she said her favorite part was getting food. But she did have a good time. She'd never forget the looks on the beauty technician's face when she said she'd never had a facial. It was priceless and maybe over time she would grow to like Ans-on's weird taste in fashion. Back at Angel's condo, Ester watched as Angel finished getting her ready.

She twirled around in the mirror wearing a lilac colored ride suit, with a short frilly yellow skirt and flowy yellow sleeveless crop top. Her hair was pinned up into a braided bun, with sparkly yellow and purple tinsel braided into it. She fought Angel tooth and nail not to have her nails done, but Angel was not having it. In the end though, she kind of liked it. She looked down at her matching nails as Angel plucked and shaped her eyebrows and did her make-up. This could be Angel's thing if he wanted to, because it was practically a pro. Her matte purple lipstick matched her eye shadow along with a pair of purple clip on earrings. This was prettiest she'd ever felt.

"Picture time!" Angel ran over to her.

His make-up was just as good. His lips were navy blue and his eyeshadow was on so thick it looked like dog spots. White glitter highlighted his face, sparkling just as bright as Ester's. Angel pulled Ester close and the two posed for a quick picture taken by his hovering camera. In seconds, the picture they took was projecting as a hologram.

"Perfect!" Angel waved the camera away and finished getting ready. He sprayed on some perfume and went to put his boots on. "My friends are coming over, so you'll get to meet them." Angel switched out his wristband for one that matched his outfit. "Okay, how do I look?"

"Great." Ester gave a thumb up as she kicked her legs up and down.

"Angel, your friends are requesting entrance into your home. Shall I let them in?" The master AI system chimed.

"Yes please, Master." Angel turned to Ester who looked so cute. "My friends are going to love you! Stay here."

Angel ran from his room leaving Ester all alone. She wondered what kind of people Angel hung out with. Angel didn't seem like the type to hang around rude people, but not everyone was nice like him. Ester heard some voices in the hallway. It sounded like three people. She straightened up and smiled when Angel entered the room.

"Oh my gosh, Angel!" A chubby boy in a dark brown ride suit gasped. "She's so cute! I'm so jelly."

"Oh stop." Angel waved.

Two other girls followed, one that was really tall and thin, wearing a shimmery all black ride suit. The other was short with a muscular build, wearing a sleeveless opal colored top, with light brown pants. Ester relaxed a little when they all returned her smile. Angel rushed over to Ester and pulled her off the bed.

"Guys," Angel pushed Ester forward, "this is Ester, my new bestie from ranger academy."

"Aww," The boy groaned as he adjusted his black framed glasses.

"Oh hush," Angel teased. "Ester, these are my best friends from prep school."

Angel opened up his arms wide. The taller one let out a sharp controlled laugh and looked directly at Ester.

"I think he meant to introduce us by name, but I'll save us the time. My name is Saela," She reached out and shook Ester's hand. Her grip was strong and firm, which surprised Ester. "To my right is Hi-Wing." The more muscular girl grinned. "And the whiny one is Josh."

"I am not whiny!" Josh's face turned red. "Angel's the one who went off to ranger school and got himself a cute girlfriend."

Angel huffed. "I do not have a girlfriend, Josh. You know I'm reserving these buns for Allura."

Josh collapsed to the floor dramatically as Angel laughed. Ester watched the friends interact; she could tell by their chemistry they had been friends for a long time.

"Angel," Saela cut them off. "Shouldn't we be going?"

"Oh right!" Angel gasped. "Master! Call up our car!"

"Yes Angel, and a message from your parents: be safe and have fun."

"Thank you, Master, tell them I said, 'will do!'" Angel and the others rushed from his room and ran towards the elevator.

***

The concert hall was the stadium of Ester's dreams. It was pitch black with hundreds of soft multi-colored lights that made it look like they were viewing outer space. Ester's hands reached towards the stage as her idol, Galaxia, made her grand entrance. She walked out with arms wide open, head up, ready to embrace the crowd. Her thick curvy frame and big light brown afro created its own atmosphere of confidence and beauty. Shining bright like a comet in her sparkling light blue ride suit, she opened with one of Ester's favorite songs. Ester screamed. She wanted to cry, but her heart was beating too fast, demanding only to release all this excitement she had built up. She sang along, next to Angel and his friends as they danced, moving as one with the crowd. Everyone threw their hands in the air as their wristbands lit up, turning the entire concert hall into a beautiful galaxy. Ester hollered when Galaxia hit the high notes, turning to Angel who smiled back at her. She would never forget this night for as long as she lived.

Chapter Eleven

Their break ended all too soon, but the cadets were back, refreshed, and ready to continue their training for their next exam. The scenario exam, part-two in their entrance exams, was not a test they could run their way through. They needed to study hard and learn basic ranger protocol and rely on each other to make the best possible decisions. During these short few weeks before their last exam, physical training was cut down to one session a day giving them more time to study. It was eleven hundred hours, and Ester and her friends were sitting together outside in the courtyard going over galactic history. There was a lot of stuff they hadn't learned in school, and they were grateful that their final exam wasn't a written test on the material.

"What's the point of all this?" Ester put her tablet down.

"It's important to the scenario." Angel read each word and highlighted the portions he thought were important.

"Yeah, but how?" Ester didn't see the connection. Rangers were fighters not bookworms.

"We're going to need to know about galactic relations to complete the mission." Angel put down the tablet. "I've read about the scenario test; it's not like the relay test. I've heard of cadets freaking out and breaking down. It's super stressful, and you're responsible for knowing all about the universe because the test is simulated in space."

Samay put down her sandwich. "We don't need to know how to fly a spacecraft do we?" she fretted.

"No, not at all," Angel said, "but we do need to know about the different space stations and no fly zones and such."

"Like the dangers of Verlin's belt?" Samay pulled up the hologram.

"Exactly." Angel expanded the projection. "See, we are here, the third planet from the belt. Each planet, minus Ceapeaya—"

"The Motherland?" Ester asked.

Angel nodded. "Besides Ceapeaya or the Motherland as some refer to it, each planet has at least two or three major space stations and tons of little satellites and mining stations in between. Fandour is the most dangerous, not because it's a planet of outlaws, but because it's the closest planet to the belt. It doesn't have any major stations super close; they're kind of far out in the safe zone. Kees has three major space stations. We have three as well, and Labadora has two, but one went offline about three years ago."

"Because of the wars, right?" Samay asked.

"Yeah, their planet has been in a vicious civil war for years now—since, the dictator Harvik Pishcel rose to power."

"I've never heard of him?" Ester clicked on the planet.

"That's because it isn't talked about much. The government has been keeping it hush-hush because relations are so bad."

Samay gaped at Angel. "Oh goodness."

"But it's okay. They mostly fight amongst themselves anyways." Angel shrugged.

"If there's so much war, why doesn't anyone step in to break them up?" Samay asked.

"Intergalactic law," Fermit quietly chimed in. "We cannot interfere with another world's law."

"Oh, hey, Fermit," Ester peeked over at his tablet. "I see you're not taking any chances on this exam."

"Nope," Fermit said as he continued to scroll and jot down notes.

"Hey," Ester rolled over in the grass. "Didn't you take the second exam? How was it?"

Fermit froze at being put on the spot. He looked at his friends and forced a smile.

"It-it wasn't all bad." Fermit laughed.

"Bullshit," Angel said. "Your eyes are telling on you."

Fermit sighed. "It wasn't a walk in the park, I can say that for sure, but it's… I don't know, weird."

Everyone inched closer. Fermit swallowed hard. "Forget what I said. I don't want any bad luck to fall upon us. We just have to cram this stuff."

Groans erupted from the friends as Fermit went back to studying. Ester watched his face. He was a nervous guy as it was, but his body language said it all. This was not a test to be taken lightly, and Ester didn't want to risk letting everyone down, so she opened her tablet and got to work studying.

***

Night rolled in and many cadets hid away, either studying or resting up for the next day. Kiakit searched the bedroom area for Murk. Lately, he had become more hot-headed than usually, but Kiakit didn't let it bother her. That's just how Murk was; he wasn't whiny and weak like the other cadets in their class. She found Bue and Zime in the lobby pouring over the books. Neither had seen Murk either, but then Kiakit snapped her fingers. She knew exactly where he was. Kiakit ran across the lobby towards the small gym they had in their dorm.

"I thought I might find you here." Kiakit walked over to Murk, who was doing a series of intense pull ups.

Murk jumped down and flexed in the mirror. He was in peak physical condition. Kiakit walked over to the bench beside him and sat down.

"You hit the books yet?" Kiakit asked.

"Don't need to." Murk rotated his wrist.

"Bullshit, even you can't predict what's on the exam." Kiakit smirked.

Murk scoffed. "I swear all these lazy cadets will do nothing but poison the lines of all the great rangers that came before them. I was born and raised to be a ranger. I have members of my family who are active duty rangers. I know all about the test. Why do you think I keep saying that I am the best? Because I am the fucking best." Murk balled up his fist and hit a punching bag, whacking it out of his way.

He struck it again and again, beating on it as if it were nothing. Kiakit admired his strength. If there was going to be anyone that would lead their house to victory, it was going to be Murk. Kiakit joined him and started lifting weights. This time around they were going to come out on top.

***

Test day was only a day away and the air was heavy with nervousness. This was their last chance to prove themselves worthy of a seat at ranger academy. There was no guarantee that they would make it, even if the other houses had lost more points than them. They had sixty-four points total and the house in fourth place was only ten points below them. Any little slip up could mean that their class would fail. Captain Pole could feel the tension and felt moved to do something about it. He stood and walked towards the middle of the class and coughed to get their attention.

"Ahem," he cleared his throat. "I can tell you all have been studying hard. I know we haven't done any practice scenarios and because of the nature of the exam we can't practice them anyways. However, I can give you some tips per say." Captain Pole stretched and looked around the room.

"Yes, I know it may seem like all this studying is for nothing, but you'll need to know that information to make better informed decisions. Meaning, you'll need to know the names of the planets and space stations, so you won't think you're orbiting Ceapeaya when you're really orbiting Fandour. The test isn't about winning. There is no wrong way to complete the mission, however, and I'll say this again: your ability to work together and think critically is most important. Read the mission scenario carefully and monitor yourselves as well as your ship. On test day, you'll be split up into random groups of ten. Your score is calculated based on how each team completes the mission." the captain paused. The stares he was getting back didn't show any signs of relief, so he sighed. "So, in light of this, I have decided to end class early. Use this time to relax. You have a big day tomorrow."

The sounds of cheers and claps broke out all over the class room as the cadets filed out. It was noon and most headed to the dining hall, while others headed out to study. Murk and his friends passed Ester and Angel.

"I hope you enjoyed your free ride, dust rat," Murk said in passing.

"What did you say?" Ester growled, but Angel pulled her back.

"It's not worth it." Angel struggled to hold her back "One day, we'll be through with him and his nonsense."

"I hate that guy." The electricity surged through her veins shocking Angel.

"Ow!" Angel shouted and that snapped Ester out of her rage.

Others stopped and watched the scene unfold. Angel shook his hands.

"I'm so sorry, Angel." Ester drew her hands back.

"You know, you really have to stop letting that guy get under your skin." Angel inspected his hands. "That hurt like crazy. You gotta calm down, Ester."

"I know, I'm sorry." She lowered her head, feeling embarrassed as wandering eyes whispered as they passed.

"It'll be okay, just you wait this time next week. We'll be official rangers."

Ester nodded as Angel rubbed her back. She was nervous about the test tomorrow. This wasn't something she could do alone, and she didn't mind working with others. She just couldn't stand the idea that someone like Murk could get a chance to join ranger academy. Just thinking about him walking across the stage made her blood boil. She took a deep breath and re-focused. He did not matter right now. All that was important was that she was ready for the test tomorrow, the final obstacle in your journey to becoming a ranger.

Chapter Twelve

Test day arrived and the chatter reached a din in the dormitory. Cadets rushed around like rats, hopping in the showers and changing into their uniforms. Ester was up bright and early, mainly because her nerves wouldn't let her sleep. This was it, their last exam, and it burned Ester up inside knowing that she couldn't just rely on herself to get through it. Angel was up just as early prepping for the exam. Some cadets crammed on their beds, while others prayed. The excitement was both energizing and nerve racketing and because their house was only in third place, they would need to work hard if they were going to make it into the top ninety.

Angel powdered up and curled his hair as Ester pulled her feet through her uniform. From her bench she could see Murk and his friends laughing. She was sure they thought they had it in the bag, but this was still anyone's game. Kiakit caught her eye and scoffed, only turning Ester's mood sour. Ester clenched the shoulder of her uniform as she pulled it up, half ready to confront them, but then a body moved in front of her view. Ester looked up to find Samay and Fermit staring down at her.

"Yikes, we haven't lost yet," Fermit joked.

"And we're not going to." Angel turned as he padded the last bit of setting powder onto his face. "We're going to kick some ass, right guys?"

Samay averted her gaze with a nervous giggle, and Fermit laughed a little, but he was clearly tense.

"Come on guys," Angel said, "we totally got this."

Ester smiled at Angel's attempt to cheer up his friends, but he was right. They had worked too hard these past few weeks and hard work paid off.

"Yeah," Ester pulled up her ride suit. "We're going to own this test and come out on top." Ester raised her fist. The others nodded, and smiles shined brightly on their faces.

For their final exam, the cadets met in a large conference room on the other side of campus. The conference room was similar to their classroom, but instead, everyone was seated around a large oval table with a polished metal finish. The cadets were impressed by the elegance and style of the room. It looked like one of the rooms the rangers held their press conferences in.

Just like for their first exam, everyone wore their matching silver and blue ride suits, proudly showing the house they represented. Captain Pole was not there on time, which unnerved the cadets, but they waited patiently as usual. Angel eyed the art on the walls; it remained him of the pieces that hung in his home. Ester and Samay fell absolutely in love with the fancy dark silver chairs, which were the softest chairs they had ever sat in. Suddenly, the large black screen in the front of the conference room turned on and the cadets saw their captain.

"Good morning cadets. I am sorry I could not be there in person to see you off, but rules are rules. In a few minutes, each of your names will be posted on the screen in the groups you will be completing the exam in. They are pre-selected, meaning there will be no switching or substituting of any kind."

Ester threw Angel a nervous look.

"Read the directions carefully above the screen at the door of your testing room. Your positions have been chosen for you, once again no switching. You will have ten minutes to mentally prepare for the exam. Groups will go one at a time and the directions on the screen will tell you who is next. Follow the simulator and remember there is no wrong way to complete your mission. All that is important is that you work together. Good luck, cadets. May Rean be with you."

The screen turned black then a blue screen appeared with three columns of names on it. All the cadets crowded around the screen as they looked for their names, pushing and talking loudly over one another.

"Shit.," Ester cursed under her breath when she saw who she was paired with.

"Hey, Ester. I'm up first." Angel turned to her with his bright blue eyes full of excitement and a little nervousness. "Wish me luck, though I shouldn't need it because I wore my lucky Section 42 cologne today." Angel patted Ester on the shoulder and was struck by how tense she was. "What's wrong?"

"It's him." Her eyes were glued to the screen. Why couldn't it be anyone else, anyone.

Angel looked at the screen, not sure what she was referring to. "What?"

"Looks like we'll be on the same team." Murk grinned, with Bue and Kiakit by his side.

Ester stared him down, but Angel stepped in front of her.

"And you better not mess this up," Angel shouted making sure everyone heard.

That put Murk in his place, but he was fuming. Angel ignored him.

"Worry about yourself, brat," Murk scoffed and walked off.

Ester clenched her fist. She was really getting tired of him.

"Don't let him get to you." Angel placed his hands on her shoulders. Samay and Fermit stood behind him, rallying behind her.

The list with the names on it moved and the first group was called. Angel and Hue were the only people Ester really knew in the first group. The nine cadets started to file out, but Angel lingered. He didn't want to do this exam without Ester. Ester saw him and smiled.

"Angel," Hue called.

Angel jumped then turned back to Ester and his friends. "Wish me luck."

"Good luck, you got this," Ester mouthed as she watched Angel's back disappear out the door.

***

It was eerily quiet as the numbers died down. After an hour, there were only ten cadets left. Ester was very nervous and trying hard to focus over the loud boasting of Murk and his friends. She sat next to Samay and Fermit in silence as the two watched the screen for their team to be called. It was almost unbearable, as there was nothing else to do other than stare at the wall. Ester's leg shook up and down as she tried to focus on anything other than the clock. That's when she looked up and saw Samay fidgeting with her hands.

"Hey," Ester placed her hand over Samay's. "We got this."

Samay slowly nodded. She was a ball of nerves and so was Fermit.

"You hear me, Fermit?" Ester turned to him. "We're going to pass this exam. I know it." A small smile found its way to Fermit's face.

The screen changed and flashed the final team of the exam. Samay jumped up, as Ester rubbed her on the back and the two nodded. Fermit got up as well and nodded to his friends as the rest of the class made their way to the door.

"Let's go, lackeys." Murk and his friends were the first out the door.

Ester rolled her eyes but followed. Now was not the time to think about Murk. The group followed the green arrows down the hall to the scenario room. The hall was all black, a stark contrast to the silver and white halls of the rest of the school. Lit only by tiny yellow lights on the ceiling, it made it feel like they were really walking down a terminal to a space ship. The green arrows carried them to a black door, and above it was a bright red light. They waited and looked around and then the light turned green and the door slid open.

Inside was a small room with just enough space to fit all the cadets. The floor was steel and the walls were white. There was one door in front of them with a red light above it, and a digital clock that flashed ten minutes. Once everyone was in, the doors to the hallway promptly closed, leaving them with nothing but the hum of the machinery behind the scenario door. A screen above the door turned on and the intercom crackled.

"Good morning, cadets. For today's mission, you will be traveling to Nork Station orbiting Kees. You will rendezvous with Sergeant Jor for ship maintenance. Your positions have been selected for you. Complete your mission and return home."

The voice stopped and then the screen flashed a list of ship positions just like Captain Pole had said. The clock started. They had ten minutes to get ready before the test would begin.

"Way to go, Fermit. You got captain." Ester pat him on the back.

"Psh. That was a mistake," Murk complained, but Ester and the others ignored him.

Bue was second in command; Murk was assigned to weapons and defense. Samay was assigned to ship maintenance, and Ester and Kiakit were assigned to responding officers. Others were assigned various support positions. As the clock counted down, others prepared as Ester noticed that Samay was shaking.

"You can do this." Ester looked her in the eyes.

"I-I don't know about this." Samay was starting to sweat.

"You can," Ester reassured her.

"Time's up, babies," Murk said as he stood at the door as the clock counted down to zero. The light turned green and the door opened.

The cadets hurried in but were shocked at how realistic the testing area looked. It really looked like they were on the deck of a Rean forty-seven. The deck was outfitted with high-tech command stations with touch screen displays and flashing panels. The floors were carpeted with light gray carpet and the walls were a milky white. The ship's window showed an endless mass of stars cruising through space. Everyone walked to their stations as their eyes wondered everywhere.

"Damn," Ester muttered to Samay, "Fermit didn't say this place looked this nice."

Samay nodded as she headed to her station

Fermit walked over to the captain's chair and rubbed the smooth arm rest and sat down. This was his second time taking the test, and though the layout was the same, his position was not. He would have much rather preferred something less essential. Something to put him in the background, but since this was his second time he was sure it was intentional. He closed his eyes and took a deep breath. His classmates needed him at his best, and that's exactly what he was going to give them.

Ester and Kiakit took their seats at the front of the deck behind their monitors. Both girls sat with their mouth agape at the smooth sleek design. It gave them chills. If it hadn't been for the fact that they were taking a test this would have been so cool. Suddenly, all the displays on the deck lit up, bringing up course maps and status reports. The exam had begun.

"It looks like we are on course, Captain Doil," Kiakit said to Fermit.

Fermit startled to attention and nodded as he watched the stars.

"Fermit, I-I mean, Captain Doil," Samay called out. "It looks like one of the ship's engines needs repair. It's recommending that we take it slow."

"Um, okay." Fermit nodded.

"How fast can it take us?" Bue asked.

"It looks like about a 100 cosknots per hour," Samay replied, peering at her screen.

"Are you serious? That's way too slow," Murk barked. "We won't even last that long before the engine dies."

"It-it's true, Captain. The ship is using up too much power. It's taking away from the support engine." Samay turned and looked at the captain.

"Okay, let's see." Fermit pulled up the ships specs. "Maybe we can cut something."

Another cadet working the life support station turn around and pointed to their screen. "We can cut life support to the decks we're not using."

"We can't though," Samay looked closer, "because the ship's registration says there are people down there."

"Let me see," Murk left his station.

"Murk." Fermit looked up at him. "You can't leave your station."

"Can it, Doil. It's clear she's reading it wrong."

"I can read just fine!" Samay snapped back.

Bue laughed. "Are you sure? Because you practically have a jungle on your head." He laughed and pointed at her hair.

"That's enough. I need the reading," Fermit said as a red light started flashing on the captain's panel.

Murk pushed Samay aside and read the screen to Bue. "Hey Bue, looks like there are people there, even though we're the only ones taking the test. How annoying."

Ester rolled her eyes. "It's supposed to simulate a real ship, dumbass."

"What did you say?" Murk was getting riled up again.

"Go back to your station now, Neben!" Fermit called Murk by his last name this time. Murk growled, but ultimately did what he was told. "We need to save energy. What can we cut?"

Samay scrolled through the ships essential and non-essential functions. "We can cut weapons."

Murk turned and glared at Samay, then looked at Bue.

"I don't think that's a good idea," Bue said.

Samay looked at the controls. "They would only be down until we get to the station which would be in a few hours or so," she said. "It turns out the power from the engine always has the weapons charged up. If we disable weapons, we could save more energy, but we would still be able to use our weapons if we needed to."

Murk looked between Fermit and Samay. "But we would still be defenseless. It's common knowledge that it takes around twenty minutes for the weapons to come back online."

"That's true, but we still have our shields." Samay turned and looked at Fermit. "It's your call, Captain."

Fermit felt the eyes on him, but somehow the extra pressure cleared his mind. "Do it."

Fermit ignored the complaints from Murk and Bue. The ship needed more energy, and the scans showed that they were the only ship for hundreds of cosknots. With the weapons disabled, they were able to continue on their course without any issues and it looked like they had moved along quite nicely on the map. Fermit pulled up his captain's panel, and all the systems were maintaining with accuracy.

"Kiakit, how long till we reach Nork station?" Fermit asked.

"Four hours, sir." Kiakit clicked on her screen.

"Okay, thank you." Fermit was starting to relax and watched the stars fly by on the screen. He turned to Bue. "I sure hope we don't have to wait four hours in here. I don't think my nerves could take it," he joked. Bue just rolled his eyes.

"Captain Doil," Ester called out. "I think I'm getting a distress signal."

Everyone turned and looked at the front screen.

"And I think it's a video message. Should I play it?" Ester turned and looked at the captain.

Fermit looked at Bue then back at Ester, as he fidgeted in his seat. "Um, sure."

Ester tapped the button and the video message popped up on the screen before them.

"This is Second in Command Cordane Mechel of Joy Station. Our space station orbiting Kees has taken damage by a stray asteroid and has broken away from planetary orbit. Three of our four engines are disabled, and we have injured personnel. Can you assist?"

The video stopped, and the crew was shocked at the visuals they were seeing. The deck of the Joy was cast in red with blinking crimson lights going off everywhere. Commander Mechel's face was covered in blood from a large cut on his forehead, and his crew didn't look any better. The people aboard were native Keesians, tall and boney with deep orange skin, and the sight of their bodies bruised and broken were so graphic it turned their stomachs upside down. Everyone sat in silence. Fermit swallowed hard. He knew this wasn't going to be easy.

"Um…Captain? What do we do?" Kiakit looked at him, and for the first time, her tough exterior faltered.

"Um, um," he stuttered.

"We-we can't stop," Murk spoke up, but his voice was shaky.

No one said a word. They knew this was an exam, but it felt so real. Fermit raked his brain for what to do, but this was much different from the exam he took before. He didn't have the answer. He knew one wrong move could deliver them bad marks on the test.

"We can't leave them," Ester blurted. "I mean if we're seeing this, it must be important, right?"

Fermit nodded. She was right, but his gut still churned.

Bue turned to Fermit. "You can't be serious?"

Fermit shook his head. rRanger protocol said that they were to prioritize people in danger and assist whenever possible. "Ester, how far is their station?" Everyone looked at him. He was dead serious now.

"About forty minutes away," Ester responded quickly.

"Samay, how much power do we have? Do we have enough to make a quick stop?"

Samay hit a few buttons and pulled up the ships energy panel. "Only a little, but we'll have to power a lot of things down to make it to the Joy in time."

"Do it. Disable all non-essential functions." Fermit leaned forward in his chair. "Ester, message the Joy and tell Commander Mechel we're on our way."

"Yes sir." Ester spun around and typed the message.

Time aboard the ship sped forward to move the simulator along, startling some of the cadets. Fermit smiled. This must have been the right decision. When they arrived, they saw the damaged space station on the screen. There were darkened parts from fire around some areas of the ship, and half the lights were out. A message blinked on Kiakit's screen.

Kiakit pulled up the message. "Captain, it's the Joy."

"Pull it up," Fermit ordered.

"Thank you, thank you so much." Commander Mechel turned to who was left of his crew.

"We are," Fermit cleared his throat. "I am Captain Fermit Doil of the Rean forty-seven, twenty-twenty-four. We are here to assist you. What do you need?" The screen fuzzed in and out.

"Our bay doors are stuck. We need to open them to free our escape pods. They can only be opened from the outside, but we cannot access them as the system controlling the single exit terminal is down."

"Okay, we'll see what we can do. Hold tight." Fermit held up his hand.

"Thank you, Captain." Commander Mechel winced.

The screen went back to a picture of the space station. "Do we have some way to get that door open?" Fermit asked around.

A cadet monitoring their ship cargo area turned around in their seat. "Yes, Captain. We have smaller ships that I think are used for external repairs. They can be controlled from the deck."

"Okay, do you think they can get that door open?"

The cadet looked through what was aboard the mini repair ship. "It has a tiny claw and a laser cutter that might help."

"Okay, let's use that." Fermit turned to the screen. "Kiakit, pull up the section that is jammed. Let's get a closer look at the damaged portion of the ship."

"Yes, sir." Kiakit zoomed in.

The shuttle door was dented, but it looked like it could be budged open. "Ester, contact Commander Mechel."

"Yes sir." Ester opened up the communication line.

"Yes, Captain?"

Commander Mechel was the only one on the deck, and it was obvious that their situation was deteriorating.

"We're sending a repair ship to open the cargo bay door," Fermit said has he waved his hand to dispatch the ship.

"Thank you!"

The image faded in and out. Then suddenly a loud siren sounded on the deck of the Joy.

"What is it, Commander?" Fermit stood from his chair.

"Our-our life support is failing. We won't be able to maintain power long enough to get everyone on board the escape pods."

The video faded in and out.

"We need more power!"

The message cut out. Everyone looked to Fermit as he stood and paced the deck.

"What are we going to do?" Bue started to panic.

Fermit continue to pace. Their ship was low on power too, but if they could only find a way to transfer them enough power while they worked on the door. Fermit stopped dead in his tracks and turned to the cadet guiding the repair ship. "How long do you think it would take for the repair ship to open the door?"

The cadet guiding the ship looked up at the screen. "Maybe ten to fifteen minutes, maybe longer."

Fermit nodded. "Samay, is there a way to transfer them power, like a jump start?"

Samay looked at her screen. "Yes, I think so, but it might be risky. With our support engine using up most of our power, we could be left dead in space."

Fermit stopped and pinched the bridge of his nose.

Murk turned and looked at Samay. "Dead in space? That would put us in the same position as the Joy. Doing that would strand us all."

"Well, do you have any better ideas?" Ester turned and snapped.

"We can't help them if we can't help ourselves in the end," Murk shouted back. "Use your brain."

"Can it." The look on Fermit's face was intense now. "We're not going to let them die." Murk glared at him. "Yeah, our ship would be dead in space, but at least we can say we tried."

Kiakit turned and looked at Fermit. "That's all well and dandy, but we still need a backup plan for when the people get here. Some of them on the Joy are really injured. How are we going to help them with the ship dead?"

This time Kiakit didn't have an attitude. She was really concerned, and all of her points were valid. They couldn't risk their ship. Many would die, but they couldn't leave the Keesians on the Joy to die either. They were in a real dilemma.

Fermit paced the deck again. "Do we have any ships that can make it to Nork Station?"

Ester pulled up the ship information. "Looks like we have five."

"How many can they seat?" Fermit walked over to Ester's screen.

Ester looked at the size recommendation. "Fifteen each."

"That's seventy-five max. How many people are aboard this ship?" Fermit looked over Ester's shoulders.

"Looks like twenty-five." Ester looked up at him. "I mean, ten of us plus the fake simulation people."

Bue got up. "What? That's not fair!"

Samay turned around. "We have to count them, too."

Fermit nodded. "How about we get the people off the Joy on our ship and load them on the smaller ships. They could go for help, while we float through space." Everyone was starting to like the idea and nodded. Murk rolled his eyes, but he was outnumbered here. "Okay, Samay, jump them. Kiakit, message the Joy we would like to commence an energy transfer."

"I can try." Kiakit sent the message, and within seconds they got the okay. "Got it."

"Great. Samay begin the transfer." Fermit pointed to her.

"Yes Captain." Samay slid the power button up and focused an energy beam to be absorbed by the Joy. The space station responded immediately, and the station came back to life. The repair ship was just about finished and close to opening the bay door.

Then on their deck an alert flashed on the screen and the panels went haywire.

"What's wrong?" Fermit turned to Samay.

"Our ship! Turns out we had circuit damage, too. I must have missed that." Samay fretted. "We can't maintain the transfer for much longer."

"Idiot!" Murk yelled. "Now, we're all dead."

"I'm-I'm sorry." Samay was near tears.

"It's okay. There's nothing we can do about it now. How much time do we have until the ship shuts down?"

Samay tapped some buttons on the screen. "I think like fifteen minutes or so." Samay looked at the controls.

Fermit walked to the screen. "Get everyone non-essential to the escape pods. When the Keesians from the Joy get here, we'll load them up and leave. Samay, can you buy us anymore time?"

Samay clicked around. "I think so." She looked around. "I think if we re-direct the power from the mainframe to the beam I can buy us thirty more minutes, but it would put us in grave danger. The ship might not make it."

Fermit nodded. "Do it."

Bue looked at Fermit. "Fermit, the repair pod has opened the door. The Keesians are boarding their ships, but there are too many of them. All of us won't fit in our pods."

There was silence building on the deck. With their own ship damaged beyond repair, the captain would have to make the tough call of who to let on the escape pods and who would stay behind. Fermit turned and looked at all the faces on the deck, their faces were riddled with panic and fear. Fermit swallowed hard and tightened up his posture. "Bue and Ester, head to the escape pods."

Fermit pointed to a few other cadets before Murk shot out of his chair.

"Are you serious? You can't be?" Fermit ignored his complaints. "You're going to kill us all. What about sticking together? I'm sure the mission wasn't about sacrificing our team."

"Could you be any denser!" Ester shouted as she got up from her seat. "He's making the best call to save the injured Keesians. It's the only option."

"So? What gives? Some of them won't make it anyways. Why not just take the ones we know we can save instead of sacrificing all the perfectly healthy lives of the rangers on board?" Murk was now in Ester's face.

"I don't want to hear it!" Fermit shouted. "Bue, Ester, head to the escape pods, now!"

"Please let me stay with you," Ester pleaded, "I don't care about my life. Let me help you."

Fermit was getting frustrated.

"I'll go," Kiakit stood and nodded to Ester. "I'll make sure everyone gets on board the escape pods."

Ester looked at Kiakit. "Kiakit…"

She turned to Ester. "Better you than me," she half-heartedly joked.

Ester stood and took a deep breath and extended her hand. "Wish I could say it was a pleasure."

Kiakit shook her hand. "Same." The two exchanged one final look. "Bue, you ready?" Bue nodded, and like magic, a door opened for Bue and Kiakit along with four others to exit.

"Okay, it's just us." Fermit walked over to Samay. "Are the

Keesians on board?"

"Yes, sir." Samay checked the dock. "Wait! I'm getting some better readings. If we withdraw power from the beam and reroute it to the cooling systems, we may be able to save the ship."

"Really?" Fermit walked over to her screen.

"Yeah, I think so." Samay looked at the ship map.

Murk walked up behind her. "You think or you know?"

"I-I think." Samay scratched her head.

Murk rolled his eyes. "Move. We don't need a scatter brain like you at the controls."

"Murk get back to your station!" Fermit demanded.

"It's-it's okay, I give up. He can have it." Samay backed away.

"Samay," Ester turned to her friend.

"It's okay." She stepped away and walked off to the side.

Fermit walked over to her. "Are you sure?" Samay nodded as she tried to fight back the tears.

"Red alert!" Murk shouted. "The engines are overheating! Samay, you idiot! You were looking at the wrong screen. Those weren't the engine panels! That was the life support system! The engines are going nuclear in five minutes!" Murk turned to the captain.

"Ester! Are the people boarding the ships?" Fermit ran to her as the alarms on the ship went haywire.

"Yes, some of them, but everyone hasn't gotten on yet."

"Tell them to hurry!" Fermit pulled at his hair.

"Yes, sir!" Ester sent down a message, but it was too late. The engines over-heated and exploded from stress and the simulator ended.

Everyone looked at each other as the lights turned back on and the simulator shut down. Samay watched in horror as she looked at her classmates faces.

"I'm-I'm…" Samay broke down.

Murk got up, electricity pulsed through his veins. "You bumbling idiot!" Murk crossed the room and slammed Samay into the wall. "You ruined us all."

Fermit tried to step in, but Murk wouldn't let Samay go. Tears streamed down her face. "Murk, back off!" Fermit yelled

"No!" He pushed Fermit to the ground. "We failed because of her." He turned to her, sparks of electricity coming from his fist.

"Murk, back off." Ester walked towards Murk. Fire burned in her eyes.

Murk turned to her, his mouth snarled open. "You, this is your fault too, for believing in this twill."

"She did her best!" Ester closed the gap between them.

Murk laughed as he stood his ground. "Are you sure about that? It's weaklings like you that cause all the problems for real cadets like me."

"Cadets like you shouldn't even be in this academy," Ester hollered.

She raised her fist and punched him dead in the face.

A fight erupted on the deck with Murk and Ester throwing spark filled punches. This was a long time coming as Ester let her rage pour out of her. She would take care of Murk once and for all. Murk dodged and landed a few hints in himself; he wasn't going to be shown up by a poor girl from Adum-la. The two locked hands and struggled to get one another to ground. Murk tripped Ester with his foot, but she brought him down with her. On the floor, they exchanged punches and kicked each other like a bunch of animals.

"Enough!"

A voice on the intercom blasted through the speakers breaking up Ester and Murk. Fermit rushed to pull Ester away. He helped her up, all while glaring at Murk.

"This portion of your exam is over. Please exit and go to the waiting area."

Chapter Thirteen

Ester and Murk stormed out of the testing area and into the waiting area with the rest of their teammates. Everyone had seen what happened. Samay and Fermit ran after Ester to try and cool her down, but Murk stormed up to her first.

"This is all your fault!" Murk shouted.

"My fault?" Ester yelled.

Fermit stepped in between them as sparks crackled around Ester and Murk. Fermit pushed his friend aside with the help of Samay. Their group had been through enough. There was no telling how many points they lost from that little hiccup, but Fermit was going to see to it that they didn't lose anymore.

"Come on, let's go." Fermit dragged Ester away by the arm.

"That's right, run! Run away, you brainless twills." Murk turned to Kiakit and Bue. "Can you believe them?" Murk said, but Kiakit stepped back. "What?" Murk glared.

Kiakit balled her fists up. "You went too far this time, Murk."

"Bullshit, you saw what they did?"

"It doesn't matter!" she snapped. "Your little fight could have cost us the test."

"Whatever," Murk said as he folded his arms.

Kiakit scoffed and stormed off.

"What a bitch." Murk turned to Bue.

"No, Murk," Bue shook his head. "You really overdid it this time." Bue turned and walked off too, leaving Murk alone.

Ester exited the testing area into the hallway. She was seething mad and wanted nothing more than to pound Murk into the ground. Fermit and Samay caught up with her and tried to calm her down, but she pushed them away. She needed sometime to calm herself. Fermit and Samay watched her leave, both with frowns on their faces. Ester walked through the side doors out into the courtyard where the testing center was. She didn't want to see anyone right now. She walked down the path ignoring the glances she was getting. Everything about the test could have gone a lot smoother if it hadn't been for Murk. He messed everything up with his bad attitude and arrogance. Why was he even allowed in? Ester wanted to pull her hair out. Sparks flew when Ester punched a tree and hissed when she felt a sting go up her arm. Sounds of crunching grass distracted her. She looked behind her and saw Angel.

"Damnit, Ester." Angel's face was red, his hair frizzy.

"What?"

"What do you mean 'what'?" Angel's face twisted in disgust. "I saw what happened."

"Then you know it's not my fault."

"No, Ester." Angel balled his fists. "You could have walked away."

"Walked away? You saw what he was going to do to Samay. I couldn't stand by and let him hurt her."

Angel lowered his head, but she could tell he was still mad. "No, you could have walked away. Stood between him, something. You should have taken the high road."

"I can't believe what I'm hearing and from you of all people," Ester said in anger.

"It's not just about you, Ester. Everyone's dream rides on the cooperation of everyone. When you act you have to think about the consequences."

Ester's heart raced as the sparks started to flare up her arms. Angel was mad at her for something Murk did.

"Whatever Angel, just leave me alone." Ester turned her back to him.

Angel stood and stared at her for a while, then she heard the sounds of footsteps walking away. Ester cursed under her breath. Everything was falling apart, and now she wasn't even sure she would make it into the academy.

***

The day after the test Ester woke up to find that Angel had already gone to breakfast without her. She got up and walked to the locker room and no one spoke to her, she only received side glances. The whispers were getting under her skin, but she ignored them. Samay found her and tried to cheer her up, but all Ester wanted to do was be alone. She sat alone in the garden outside of the crossroads leading to her dorm. The clouds rolled in and threatened rain, but Ester didn't care. She was still in shock about what happened at the test. She couldn't believe how awful Murk acted. It was embarrassing, but now things were all wrong. Her class only had sixty-four points going into the exam and who knew how many points they lost yesterday. Ester shoved her head in her palms. She wanted to scream.

She looked up. From where she was sitting, she could see the fountain with all the leaders of old. She was sure there was a lot of in fighting in their group too, but somehow, they'd seemed to put their differences aside for the greater good. Why couldn't he have done that? This was all his fault. Ester heard footsteps approach her, but she didn't look up.

"I don't want any company, guys," Ester said. When she didn't hear anyone, she looked up and saw Kiakit standing before her. "What do you want?"

Kiakit glared at her, but averted her eyes and folded and unfolded her arms. "I just wanted to say… I just wanted to come and apologize."

Ester rolled her eyes.

"I don't care if you don't like me, but how Murk acted…it was just unacceptable."

"Pshh, like you care. Ya'll have been acting this way all semester. Why should I accept your apology?"

"I've known Murk for a long time. He's a strong and worthy fighter, and I believed, no I still believe, that he is the only one who can lead this class to greatness," Kiakit said as she loosened her fist.

"But as the weeks went by, somehow he became consumed with being better and for that weakness I am sorry. Take my apology or not. I just thought you'd like to know that not everyone follows someone blindly around."

Ester watched Kiakit leave. To Ester, there was nothing good about Murk. He was hot headed and a bully, and that was not the kind of person anyone should follow. With the weekend coming up, she wasn't sure how she was going to survive having to wait and hear her test results. She just hoped that the fight hadn't hurt them too much.

***

It was the start of the week and the class sat in silence. By now, everyone had heard about what happened during the last exam. They were right to be mad at Ester and Murk, but it was judgement day now and most spent their time praying for good news. Some days after the fight, Murk mumbled an apology to Samay, but that only made Ester angrier. Samay was still shaken up about the test. She felt that their failure was her fault, even though her friends tried to reassure her. Ester looked over at Angel. He was still mad at her, but at least he walked in a group with her to class. Ester lowered her eyes. The door opened, and their captain walked in. He wasn't late today.

"Good morning, cadets." He quickly crossed the room and placed his mug on his desk.

He looked different today a little rattled. He took a sip from his mug, then patted his mouth dry with a handkerchief.

"I'm sure you're all anxious about your test scores," he said as he scanned the room, his eyes lingered over Murk and Ester. "I have some good news but also a bit of bad news."

The class looked around at each other. Ester's heart was starting to race as she reached up and touched her necklace on her chest.

"The good news," he paused, briefly and inhaled slowly, "is that you passed. Believe it or not, there were classes that did surprisingly worse than you."

Cheers erupted from the class once they realized he was serious. Cadets jumped up and hugged each other and gave high fives. Ester exhaled. She couldn't believe it. They passed. Ester looked over at Angel, and his face melted with joy. Fermit reached out to Ester and rubbed her shoulder. Ester was so relieved.

"But," Captain Pole raised his hand to silence the class, "there is a bit of bad news."

The class grew silent again. What could the news be? Was their class being penalized? Did they have to retake the exam again? The cadets sat on the edge of their seats.

"Here at Ranger Academy, we pride ourselves on our ability to work together. It is the primary reason for the second portion of the entrance exam. With that being said, the academy has no room for hot-headed individuals who cannot work together, even if their class proves victorious. Ester DuTain and Murk Neben, your behavior at the end of the exam was so deplorable the committee and admission staff has decided to decline your acceptance, permanently."

Ester gaped at the captain in pure shock. She started shaking as all the noise faded around her. This couldn't be happening, not to her, after all the work she had done.

Chapter Fourteen

It rained all over Ans-on as Ester stared out the window of the train. The ocean rocked with rage, agitated by thousands of tiny raindrops. The train was quiet, filled with sleeping passengers. She was dead inside, like an old mechanical clock that stopped ticking. Her life as she knew it ended on the day she was kicked out of the academy.

This would be her last train ride from Juw-ja, the island where ranger academy called home. She wanted to believe that this was all just a horrible nightmare and that any moment she would wake-up, but the reality sunk in when she packed up her bags and boarded the train for the last time. Angel was kind enough to let her stay with him at his parent's place, but she declined. She didn't want to be a burden on Angel or his parents. With nowhere to go, it didn't feel right to go back to Adum-la. After all, she had no family to return to. So Angel worked his magic and found her a small place on the outskirts of the main city. She remembered him cringing at the location, but she didn't care. He told her it was in a poorer area, if that were even possible in such a rich metropolis, but it didn't matter to her where she slept. Not anymore.

An old busted hover cab drove her down the narrow streets of the place that she would call home. Shadows walked under streetlights in a hurry to get out of the rain. While others huddled under overhangs, their faces shrouded by breaths of puffy air floating from their mouths. The cab driver turned to Ester and looked at her. She could tell that he wanted to say something, but one look into her eyes revealed more than she could ever say. He had already been paid but insisted on helping her move her bags to her new apartment. With nothing but two bags of clothes, Ester followed the cab driver to her room. He left her stuff at her door. She muffled a thank you, and he nodded and disappeared down the hall. The place smelt like damp carpet and cigarettes. It was run down with sloppy patchwork done on the hole ridden walls. Graffiti marked her door.

WelCum 2 the end, it said, but her journey ended a long time ago.

She took out the key Angel had given her, opened the door, and dropped her bags on the floor as the door closed with a click behind her. This place was cold and dark. She flipped the light switch revealing nothing but a crawl space with a couch in a small den, a closet of a kitchen, a bathroom, and bedroom. It was a far cry from the luxuries of ranger academy, not that she needed them to survive, but the atmosphere here was dead. Angel did his best to liven up the place, and to his credit, it looked cozy, but she didn't have the energy to enjoy it. She walked towards the window as the rain continued to pour.

"Are you crying for me?" she whispered as she found it hard to breathe.

Outside her window, she flinched at the sounds of sirens followed by red and blue lights that lit up the room. Was this her home now? Was this her life now? What would she even do? These were the questions that gained traction in her mind. She walked to her bedroom. Angel did a really good job decorating. The bedspread was brand new, and there was even a chest and dresser for her clothes. The floors were wooden and uneven, so Angel placed a few rugs about, complete with a pair of slippers to protect her feet. On the makeshift vanity he put together sat the picture they took just before they went to the concert some weeks ago.

Seeing that made her want to cry even harder. Who was that Ester? She looked at the picture. All that work she put in, only to have it washed away with the rain. Ester didn't bother unpacking. It wasn't like she had a lot of stuff anyways. She pulled out some night clothes and undergarments and drew herself a bath. She made the water as hot as she could take it and let the sadness pour from her. An entire ocean would not be enough to hold her tears that night.

***

Morning came without her permission, inviting itself in with sunlight breaking through the clouds. Ester turned around in bed and tried to move the covers over her head, but the rogue sunlight wouldn't leave her be. She hadn't ventured out of her apartment in three days, eating through all the rations Angel had stocked for her. She didn't have the energy to face the world, so she curled up into a little ball and laid there until sleep would take her once more. Her eyes grew heavy and she was just about to fall asleep when she heard a loud knock on the door. She opened her eyes, hoping whoever it was would go away, and then closed her eyes again. However the knocking persisted.

"Ester! I know you're in there." The muffled sound of Angel's voice could be heard from her room. "Ester!"

Ester pulled the covers further over her head, but it was useless trying to hide from Angel. He was as persistent as a light driven moth. She rolled over to the other side of the bed and threw her legs over the edge. She sat there for a few seconds as Angel continued to pound on the door. She really wished he would go away. When she finally got up and opened the door, she was greeted by a pair of angry blue eyes. He said something sassy to her, but her ears hadn't quiet gotten up yet. She just wanted to go back to the pit of her bed and sleep and never wake up.

"Are you listening to me?" Angel turned around with a large box in his hands.

Ester stared at him for a few seconds then nodded.

"No, you're not." Angel rolled his eyes. "Ester, I'm worried about you. Here." Angel handed her a card. "I put a few tones on here so you can buy yourself some food and new clothes. A girl has to have a new set of clothes for each new chapter of her life."

But was this really a new chapter? Ester thought, *or was this the epilogue?*

Angel couldn't ignore the vacant stares of his friend. He wanted so badly to go back in time and change her fate, but it was out his reach, even with civil councilors as parents.

"Hey, look what I got you." Angel cracked open a decent sized white box.

Ester stared at it, as if it had come from space.

"It's a hologram phone. It's my old one, but you can have it." He placed it on the small coffee table in the den. "Now we can make hologram calls to each other."

He clapped his hands in excitement, but Ester still looked sad. He frowned, making his icy blue eyes cloudy with sadness. This wasn't fair, and he hated that she got kicked out. He sat the phone aside and hugged her tight.

"It's going to be okay, Ester." Now he was getting teary eyed.

He hugged her tighter. His watch buzzed; it was time to go. He let her go and rubbed her shoulders.

"Take care of yourself, Ester," Angel said as he headed to the door.

When he looked back, Ester sort of smiled as he pushed himself to leave. He opened the door, tears overflowing. He turned and ran back to her, slamming into her with such intense force and grabbing her shoulders. He shook her, hard, then pulled her back to him.

"You better take care of yourself, darn it, because if you don't I'm going to cry all day until the dead returns you back to me." He broke the hug and looked into Ester's eyes.

She melted as she bit her lip, fighting back her own tears.

"Okay, Angel, I will try." She pat him on the head and drew him closer.

"You better." Angel hugged her tighter for the last time.

Angel left and with him went all the sunlight and life. Angel was from a part of her life she could never go back to, and soon, she was sure he would disappear too. There was no way she could maintain a friendship with someone who was from such a different world. He was normal. He had a family and a career and Ester was just a jobless orphan with nothing and no one to go back to. She sat alone in her apartment and stared at the floor. Tiny bugs hugged the walls racing from one side of the room to the other. It seemed like everyone had a purpose, everyone except her.

***

As the days dragged on, Ester felt as if she had gotten more sleep than she ever needed. She was twice as tired, but she was getting hungry.

The sounds from outside got her a little curious and maybe a little fresh air could do her some good. She drew a bath because she hadn't showered in days. The water felt like pellets on her skin, reminding her that this was her life now. She fought her emotions as it turned to rage.

"Why!" she screamed. "Why!"

This wasn't supposed to happen. She wasn't supposed to be here, and yet the cold unforgiving reality was starting to sink in. If it hadn't been for Murk she wouldn't be here, at least that was the lie she replayed in her mind a hundred times. It was his fault and he had been punished too, but his expulsion did nothing to ease her mind.

There was little to eat in her apartment, expect for a few meal bars. She opened one package labelled sweet and salty. She took one bite and spit it out. It tasted like dirt. Who would buy these? She made a face as she read the package ingredients then tossed it out. It was sunny outside at least, so she threw on a nice sleeveless lavender ride suit and heavy jacket that Angel had bought for her.

Today, in the apartment hallway, it smelled like old wood and rust. She'd smelt worst. She looked at her graffiti tagged door and glared. She was starting to hate this place again. This place, she was sure, would be her tomb.

As she turned to head down the stairs, she heard a crashing sound just down the hall.

She stopped and looked in the direction where she heard the noise. Then she heard another crashing sound. She hoped no one was in trouble, but she wasn't a ranger now. She paused and thought about it. She wasn't a hero, but her mind wouldn't let her move on, especially if someone was actually in trouble. She sighed as the weight of her necklace hung heavy around her neck. These were her neighbors now; their trouble was her trouble. She sighed at her mother's words as she turned and walked down the hall, hoping there wasn't any danger. She turned around a corner and saw a slender, orange-skinned man wearing a white t-shirt hunched over a pile of spilt groceries.

"Oh no, let me help you." Without hesitation, Ester got to work helping the man pick up his groceries. "I know how frustrating it can be when your bag breaks."

She trailed off when the man started to stand, rising a full seven feet in the air. He wasn't Reanian but an entirely different species altogether. He towered over her, looking very thin and frail, wearing a dingy white crop top and loose-fitting pants tied tightly around the waist with a black belt. Ester mustered a smile and stretched out her hand to hand him his things. His large jet-black eyes stared down at her as he smiled and moved a few strands of greasy dark gray hair out of his face. He took the canned good from Ester, making her cringe slightly at his white less black eyes.

"Thank you, thank you so very much," he said with a thick foreign accent. "These old totes just are not what they use to be." He squatted down in front of her, bending his long legs that were almost as long as his arms.

"No-no problem." Ester forced a laugh as she tried to help him pick up the rest of his things.

"You must be our new neighbor. I saw a bright little boy who looked of sunshine come through here a few times. He was radiant." The leathery skinned man smiled, which only put more tension on his wrinkled skin.

Ester forced another smile, as she rubbed her arm, and looked away. When he noticed her uneasiness, he stood and clasped his hands to his chest.

"I don't mean to pry, I, um, I am just curious. We don't get many new neighbors, and I do so enjoy the company."

Ester nodded like she understood, but really, she just wanted to run and never come back.

"I'm sorry, forgive my manners. I have been on this planet for years, but my people are telepaths and we greet in here." He pointed to his head. "It is how we communicate, though sadly, it does not work on those outside our species."

Ester's expression changed. Her hunch was right. He wasn't from Rean. She had never met an alien before.

"My name is Sal Chu'pree. I immigrated here, well to Cha-la, but I moved to Ans-on for a friend." His turned to her and the sadness in his jet black eyes was so intense that Ester thought it would swallow her whole.

"It-it's nice to meet you, Sal." Ester felt the urge to change the subject, anything to escape the sadness in his eyes. "My name is Ester DuTain. I'm from here. I mean, of course I'm from here, I mean Rean. I'm from Adum-la originally." She laughed a little as she played with the curls on the back of her neck.

"It's very nice to meet you, Ester DuTain." Sal's smile softened.

Ester smiled back and placed his groceries in an untorn bag next to his door.

"Do you need help bringing them inside?" she offered.

"I don't want to keep you. You were so kind to help me. I must be inhibiting the start of your day." Sal reached down to pick up his bags. He struggled a bit but played it off best he could.

"I didn't have anything planned." Ester smiled. "I would be happy to help."

Sal stood and looked into Ester's eyes and smiled. "You are too kind, too kind." Sal looked like he was about to break down.

He unlocked the door and allowed Ester to help him. He thanked her a million times, even though she didn't feel like she had done anything that grand. She waved and said it was no big deal. After all, all she did was help him carry his groceries inside. As she left, she noticed all the pictures of Sal and what looked like his family or friends. She deduced that he must be from Kees, but despite the pictures, there didn't appear to be anyone living there but him. That made her a little sad. Loneliness. Was this her fate as well? Sal showered her with one last thanks as Ester left his apartment.

She didn't want to think about her future right now. Feeling a little tired, she drummed up the energy to continue her quest for food. She needed to get something to eat or at least find out where the local market was. She hurried down the stairs, looking forward to the fresh air, but the minute she stepped outside she was slapped in the face by the smell of warm sewage. She covered her nose with her forearm as she took a step back. The scene outside was just as dismal. The sky was overcast with dirty gray clouds, and the streets were filled with busy hover cars. The sidewalks were cluttered with people indifferent to those around them. It was the opposite of how she imagined a metropolis to be. Wanting to turn around and go back inside, she couldn't ignore the protest of her stomach. She looked up and down the street but didn't see a single eatery. She squinted a little longer and spotted what looked like a small convenience store down the street. *Perfect*, she said to herself, because she would do anything to get off this smelly street.

She started down the sidewalk as people zipped by with hard looks and jackets huddled close to their chest. No one made eye contact; it was like walking amongst the dead. Ester pulled her jacket closer together, hoping to end this little adventure as quickly as possible. On the streets, dented and dingy hover cars drove by with honking horns that startled her. Cab drivers picked up people and dropped them off abruptly causing her to nearly run into everyone. Cooling air units dropped water into puddles, and lingering people drew long drags from their cigarettes. It was so impersonal; she really did feel like she had walked into the afterlife. Ester shivered, feeling alone in the sea of cold faces. She made it to the convenience store hoping to find a change in scenery, but it was nothing but a hole in the wall. No bigger than a closet, people crowded in, picking up items and rushing to checkout. There was barely enough space to browse, but she settled on a few packaged sandwiches, as there was nothing fresh here like back at home. Just as she was grabbing a juice, a man bumped into her.

"Hey! Watch it," Ester snapped, but the man neither acknowledged her nor apologized.

He, like everyone else in this hell scape of a city, seemed preoccupied with their own business. Ester clenched her jaw. She wanted to run. Anywhere was fine, anywhere was better than living in this place. She paid for her things and headed back to her apartment.

For the rest of the day, Ester did the only thing that brought her comfort. She napped. When she woke up, she realized that the sun had set on yet another uneventful day. She had finished the last of her sandwiches and was now sitting on her couch watching teleshows. There were so many channels. She never had this sort of freedom before, and yet, it didn't bring her any happiness. She flipped through the channels, the flashing images pushing her further and further away. She couldn't make a life here. She felt like she was living in Ans-on's armpit, and that was saying a lot coming from someone who use to lived near a wind ravaged dessert. It was a cold and smelly place where she was sure people came to die. There seemed to be no hope of getting out, nothing to look forward to, or any reason to get out of bed. Here she was just another cold face, a forgotten soul, one destined to fade away.

Chapter Fifteen

Morning came, once again, with its offensive positivity in the form of sleep irritating sunlight. Ester flung the covers over her head, but that did little to stop the sun from illuminating the room. She huffed and clung to her covers tighter, but eventually gave in. She flung the sheets over her body and sat up and stared at the broken blinds. Something needed to be done about those blinds. She got up and picked at them. They were so old and frail, a single tug sent them creaking. She rolled her eyes. This may be her tomb, but that didn't mean it had to be a dump. She walked out of her room and tripped over a pile of clothes. She got up and growled when she realized the laundry box had broken. She rolled over and inspected the wood. It was old and worn, and she tossed it to the side. This place needed a total makeover. It was hard enough dealing with her feelings with her apartment falling apart around her.

All morning, Ester spent her time cleaning house. She swept and cleaned the windows. She took note of everything broken and made a list of supplies she would get later. She dusted and cleaned the kitchen, which needed a complete overhaul. Before she knew it, she found herself playing soft music from her tele and humming along as she scrubbed the bathroom floor. She was thankful for Angel giving her a gift basket of cleaning supplies. After hours of backbreaking work, her apartment looked like a whole new place. She smiled as she surveyed her work, wiping the sweat from her forehead. It wasn't as nice as Angel's place, and not even as nice as the orphanage, but it was clean and that made her happy. She grabbed one of her sandwiches she had forgotten she had left and sat on her loveseat. She looked up at the holes in the blinds on the window in the den. That's what she needed, the final thing to make her apartment livable.

She dreaded another trip outside of her apartment, but she could not stand the thought of another morning ruined by the sun. She took note of the measurements of the blinds by counting how many hands across they were. She only needed two, one for the den and one for the bedroom. Throwing on a dark purple ride suit, one that Angel had picked out, and her jacket, she started her quest. She didn't have the slightest idea where to buy blinds. She didn't even know if this area had markets or what kind of store to start her search. She looked around the streets; it was no use. All the buildings looked like shady bars and rundown apartment complexes, so she started at the only place she knew sold anything: the convenience store down the street. The weather was a little better today, even the streets smelt less like trash. She took a deep breath and walked into the crowded store to look around. Why was she surprised that a place that could be one of Angel's closets didn't sell blinds? She did not want to deal with this right now, but the sun had to be stopped. She squeezed in between customers and made her way to the cashier. Maybe they would be able to help. She popped up at the counter, thanking her ancestors that there was no line and managed an awkward smile.

"Um, excuse me," Ester twirled the hair on the back of her neck. "Is there a store around here that sells blinds?"

She laughed nervously, but the clerk seemed unamused. He must have been a distant relative of Captain Pole. The clerk allowed his magazine to flop over to get a better look at Ester. He snorted, and the sound of phlegm being pulled to the back of his throat made Ester want to gag. He grunted and lifted his chubby fingers towards to underground train station.

"South mall, you'll find what you're looking for there. Three stops west." He coughed as he motioned for the next customer to come forth.

"Thanks." Ester managed to get out.

She'd ridden the trains many times before but always with the help of a map or a guide. She had an idea where the station was, but it was still kind of intimidating. Even despite Angel's little breakdown of which lines went where. She was nervous about taking a train from around here, but she needed blinds. She exited the shop and looked around for any signs or post markings. Back home, there was always something that pointed to a bus station. She hoped there would be something similar here. She headed in the direction the clerk sent her, making her way through the wave of people. She would get nowhere trying to see through everyone, so she stopped and stood on her tippy toes. There had to be a sign somewhere, she just needed to search. A man down the street shouted for a cab another person just got out of and that caught Ester's attention. She saw a faded sign that looked like it had a train on it with an arrow. That had to be it.

She followed the arrows on the bent-up sign and walked down litter-filled streets until she reached the opening to the underground train system. The smell and heat coming from the ground made her feel like she was walking into a horse's ass. How can Ans-On, one of the most technologically advanced nation states, allow for such poor living conditions? Ester shook her head as others passed her with no problem. She watched them walk by unfazed by the smell, rushing up and down the stairs. She stood at the entrance like a rock, wondering if it were worth it at all, but what other choice did she have? This was her life now, and she really needed blinds. She cringed as she took her first steps. The heat got worse, and it was very humid and loud underground. The moving trains rumbled the entire station as the sounds of beeping and clicking turnstiles assaulted her ears. She looked around for a sign of anything familiar. The last time she was in a train station she was with Angel. He was from Ans-on, so everything he did was second nature to him. She twisted the curls on the back of her neck as she started to think. She needed to go west to South Mall, but there were no clear signs of routes or train lines. No kind person to help her out. She was on her own and moments away from giving up.

"Train cards! Have your train cards ready! Turnstile eight is down and we checkin'em manually!" A woman with a bell shouted over the crowd. "Train cards! Have'em ready!" She repeated.

Ester stared, then slowly moved her heads over her pockets and patted them down. She didn't have a train card, but she found the card

Angel had given her full of tones. She was lost, but before she could go anywhere she needed a train card and that was at least a place to start. She spotted the ticket booth on the other side of the station and breathed a sigh of relief. She stood in line as people inched closer and closer to buy their train cards. In front of her was a woman in a thick coat with her bouncing child pulled close to her. Ester looked down at the child and the child looked up at her and made a funny face. Ester made one back and the child giggled with excitement. The child bounced around once more but this time she tripped and stumbled over her own feet and fell onto Ester.

"Oops." Ester reached down to help her up.

The mother, once aware, turned to Ester with tired eyes and picked up her child right away.

"I am so sorry, miss." She looked at her daughter. "Sartine, what do you say?" The tired mother scolded.

"It's okay, ma'am." Ester's smile broke up the clouds on the mother's face, and the woman apologized again as she walked away to the next ticket window.

"Next!" An older man with greasy dark blond hair waved, tearing Ester away from her thoughts.

Ester ran right over to the ticket booth, which was nothing more than a closet space with a glass window and counter. Ester looked around the cramped room in discomfort and wondered if the people in Ans-on liked shopping and working in cramped places.

"Um, hi. I need to buy a train card." Ester hovered in front of the tiny voice box.

"Alright, you got a digi-id?" The man said over his computer.

"Yes, sir." Ester held up her card.

"Scan it." Ester did as she was told. "How much?"

"Excuse me?"

"How much you want on the card?" The man looked at her like he said this a million times.

Ester wasn't sure how much she needed per ride and she didn't feel like asking. "Twenty?"

The man looked at her as if she had gotten the question wrong.

"Okay, kid. Let's start with this." He gave her his full attention. "Where you headed?"

"Um, South Mall."

"Okay, and you gonna be using the train ere'day?"

"No, sir. Well, I'm not sure."

"Ere'day then. It cost two tones for local stops and five for non-local stops. Most folks load'em up for the month, depending on travel. Twenty for a doe like you won't get you far if you've never been around these parts. It's too easy for you to get lost down here." The man typed some information into his computer. "You got fifty tones?"

Ester thought for a second. When she last checked her balance, she thought she had about one hundred and twenty tones. "I think I have about one-twenty."

"Don't think, scan." The man pointed to the scanner. Ester scanned her tone card and she was off by thirty tones. "Always check." The man typed in some more info. "Now, I'm gonna load fifty tones on here. A train pass is worth its weight in ore. You gon use it a lot. Is that okay?" The man looked Ester in the eyes and she nodded.

"South Mall, do you know how to get there?" Ester squeezed in the question before her time was up.

The man pointed. "Scan and head to the non-local train seven. It's three stops. Don't get off on anything but your stop, save your tones. That's it?" The man looked at Ester and she nodded. "Next!" He waved on the next customer.

Ester left, feeling a little better. She walked over to the turnstile and scanned her new card. The light turned green and she headed as instructed to the non-local lines, line seven. It was crowded, but she made her way on the train. She stood in a sea of people, which was hot and uncomfortable. This was a far cry from the mega trains she took with Angel, but she guessed it served its purpose. She got off on the third stop and arrived at a much nicer train station. It smelled a little better and was cleaner too. She made her way to the exit and once outside she was greeted with the smell of cold fresh air. It was a nice change. She missed being able to breathe without the smell of sewer clogging her nose.

Above ground, the streets were crowded with people. She wasn't sure how she would find South Mall, but she was able to find a directory down the street. She rushed over to the display and found out she was in a shopping district and that South Mall was right across the street. She sighed with delight and bundled up as she waited on the opposite side of the street to cross.

Walking with the crowd, Ester marveled at the silver dome shaped building. She remembered the last time she was in a mall. It was with Angel, but that mall was on top of a skyscraper. It was huge and a little overwhelming and this one was no different. She wondered if Ans-on had malls like this all over the place. She wouldn't be surprised. She looked around wishing Angel was here to direct her. Taking a deep breath, she tried not to worry as she walked through the sliding doors. This mall was smaller but cluttered with shops stretching three stories high. She hadn't the slightest clue where to begin. There were so many sights, sounds, and smells, but she calmed her mind by remembering her trip to the markets when she was young. She remembered how scared she was and how it felt holding her father's hand. Her father's words stuck out in her mind, *what you seek will find you because it wants to be found.* Ester took a deep breath. What she wanted wanted to be found. She took a step forward past a few shops selling clothes. She looked through the displays and tried to piece together like products. If she was looking for blinds, then more than likely it would be sold in a shop that carried home décor. She looked up and saw a hover screen with a display of beautiful vases. Vases were home décor, so feeling optimistic, Ester headed to the second floor.

Ester found the store, but when she arrived, she found out that she didn't have enough money to buy blinds. She cursed under her breath as she looked at the prices. She couldn't even afford to buy the discounted blinds. She was so frustrated she left the store. She didn't know why she was so surprised. Places like these were bound to be out of her price range or maybe she was just naïve on exactly how much blinds cost. Either way, she felt like she had wasted her trip.

She left the mall and went back out into the cold, resigned on giving up and returning to her apartment. As she made her way back to the train station, she couldn't help but stop and look at the window displays. There were so many shops outside the mall, she barely noticed before. They all sold those ride suits Angel was crazy about. She kind of smiled as she remembered Angel fussing over which suit to wear the night of the concert. They weren't bad and definitely not as thin as they looked. The hardest part was going to the restroom and the fact that they were so tight. As she passed the shops, the smell of fresh manure grazed her noise. She stopped immediately as the distinct smell of home wafted in the air. She stood and inhaled. In what metropolis would a smell like this be coming from? She looked up and down the streets, searching for the source. Following her nose, she headed in the direction of where she thought the smell was coming from. She was in a metropolis, all the way in Ans-on, miles anyway from any farm. Was her mind playing tricks on her? Her pace quickened as the smell intensified, mixed with the aroma of fresh grilled food. She started jogging; this couldn't be real. She looked up ahead and down every alley she passed. The smells and sounds of large crowds intensified, but it all made her think of home. Could it be?

She jog-walked down one street and passed an alley. She double-backed when she thought she saw a pig. She stopped and looked down the short alley; there were lots of people on the other side walking by. She looked behind her trying to figure out if she was about to enter a portal or something. Laughter broke her train of thought, and she started moving. The closer she walked, the more intense the smells of grilled food, fresh produce, and animals got. Her ears were bombarded with sounds of chirping, snarling, heckling, and chatter. It reminded her so much of home, she thought she was really there. Coming out on the other side, she found herself in what she thought was another state. A huge bustling market was right in the middle of a metropolis in Ans-on. She looked around at all the vendors with their crates full of fruits and vegetables laid out. Herding animals were tied to post in the ground ready to be sold. There was a little bit of everything here. She walked through the crowd with ease, not at all stressed by the crowd of busy shoppers. This place felt like home, drawing up memories of riding horse drawn wagons with her parents. It was the Adum-la way of life, and it was right here in Ans-on. She passed a booth with rows of fresh ripe fruit. She picked up one and inspected it for blemishes or bugs. As she looked it over a heavy-set man with sweat covering his face eyed her. He leaned over his booth and snapped his fingers.

"Are you going to buy that? If not, move on." He folded his arms.

Ester glared at him and sat the fruit down. "I'm not now," she scuffed.

Rude vendors were a common thing at the markets. She continued around the booth to another area with fresh fruit. She looked them over and picked one up and smelled it. It was a mango and almost ripe too.

"Excuse me," an elderly lady grabbed Ester's attention. "I'm from out of town, and we don't have this variety of mango where I'm from. How do you tell if it's good to eat?"

Ester picked up another fruit. "Easy, ma'am. This one is near ripe. You can tell by the smell and feel." Ester smelled it. "See, it smells of dirt and its very firm, but this one," Ester squeezed it a little. It was softer and a little squishy, "this one is perfect. One hundred percent ripe. You know it's ripe because it practically turns to mush in your hands, and that's what you want in this variety of mango. I know farmers from my nation state who grow this, and these are best bought when they are firm. Sit them on your table if you don't intend on eating them in the next day or two. Or you can buy them super ripe like this and make the best thick mango jam you've ever had." Ester held out the two mangos for the lady to inspect.

"Thank you," The woman smelled and felt the mangos.

"No problem." Ester replied as the lady smiled and picked the super ripe fruit to buy.

Unknown to Ester, the rude vendor from before was watching. He was the boss of this entire four table booth. He walked closer to Ester and snapped his fingers at her again.

"Hey, you're good at this. I have a proposition for you."

Ester squinted her eyes but did not walk away. "Um, okay."

"We are short staff," the man continued. "If you need job, you can start tomorrow at eleven hundred hours."

A staff member tapped the man's shoulder, and he turned and addressed him. Ester didn't know what to say, but before she could think about it the man turned back around.

"Eleven hundred hours, come early, good pay," the man said, then returned to his work as if she wasn't there.

Ester gaped at his back, frozen in the spot. After his rude behavior, she couldn't believe he was offering her a job. She wasn't going to work for someone who was rude, even if she was almost broke. Ester left his booth, determined not to let that bit of drama ruin her day.

Despite the small amount of tones she had, she left the market with a lot of goods. She may not know about the prices in the malls, but in the markets, she knew how to shop. It had been so long since she'd had fresh produce. Now she could prepare a proper meal.

Back at her apartment, she cooked herself up some tasty stir-fry. It made her stomach very happy, but she couldn't help but think about what she was going to do with her dwindling allowance. Angel had been kind enough to pay her rent a few months in advance. It was cheap here, but it wasn't free, and she felt bad about relying on him for money. Angel was the type of person that would probably support her for life, but that kind of kindness was easy to take advantage of and Ester didn't want that. She was healthy and had no limitations to stop her from working. She just lacked the motivation to find a job. After all, finding a job wasn't how it was back home. Back home, she knew everyone and all she had to do was walk up and ask. It was an easy system based on trust, which was easy to earn because everyone knew each other. She would sleep on it and see how she felt in the morning.

Chapter Sixteen

In the shower the following morning, her mind was made up. She had had a terrible night's sleep because of the flashing lights on the emergency hover cars that seemed to run all night. There must have been something serious going down, but the bright multi-colored lights, did nothing to help her get a good night's sleep. She would not spend another night or morning being woken up because of her blinds. If just for the sake of getting a restful morning's sleep, she would take the job.

She got out of bed and flipped her bag upside down on her bed in search of a clean pair of undergarments. She'd barely unpacked and amongst her things was her kiko robe that Sister Genevieve made for her. A small bitter smile appeared on Ester's face. She didn't want to look at it, so she neatly folded it up and tucked it away in a drawer. From one of the folds, a picture frame fell out. Ester picked it up, it was her family portrait. Seeing their faces made her want to well up with tears.

What would they think of her now? Would they be disappointed? Ester looked at the faces of her mother, father, and brother.

No, she told herself. Failure only comes when you give up, she remembered her father saying and Ester broke out in tears, hugging her picture close to her chest. She placed the photo next to the one Angel had taken of them. She wiped her face and gathered her things for her shower.

The water ran down her back. Taking a market job felt like step back, but it was the best she could do. After all, this was her life now if she could even call it that. The smell of the market reminded her of home; it reminded her of Luck. She wouldn't know what to do if she ever ran into him again, and she wouldn't be surprised if he showed up with a hover car full of vegetables.

"You happy, Luck? I'm back to selling produce again." Ester laughed a little as she stared up at the shower head and frowned. "Back at the same place I was before."

Ester gave her hair a quick shake. Now was not the time to feel sorry for herself. Not sure what to wear, she put on a thick lavender ride suit with long sleeves and a white crew cut crop top. She put on some boots and grabbed her coat and headed out the door. She walked quickly, hoping to get to the train station fast. She ran down the stairs and turned the corner only to crash into a young boy.

"Watch it, hag!" The boy yelled as he got up and ran off.

"Screw you, twerp!" Ester yelled.

She groaned in disgust as she looked around. She landed in a wet spot and now her lavender suit had a big spot on it. She wiped and wiped it to get it clean, but it was no use. She didn't have time to change, and now she was pissed. This was one of the ride suits Angel had bought her, and now it had a stain on it. She tried one last attempt to cast the stain away, but it was fruitless. Maybe she could get it out later, but she had to run.

She made it to the market twenty minutes early and headed to the booth where the man had offered her a job. It wasn't hard to find the market this time around because it was on the directory outside the underground train station. She walked over to the man and tried to flag him down, but he seemed to ignore her at first until her recognized her face.

"Girl!" He walked over with open arms.

Ester cringed at the greeting but smiled anyways. He reached down and grabbed an apron and tossed to her. She barely had time to catch it as it landed in her hands just inches away from her face. His attitude had completely changed from before.

"I am J-Kolson, the boss. You come for job? Hmm?"

"Y-yes sir," Ester responded as she moved out of the way of the other workers.

"Good!" An employee tapped J-Kolson on the shoulder and

handed him some tones. J-Kolson nodded then turned back to Ester. "Name? You have name?"

"Ester, Ester DuTain." Ester put on the apron, trying to tie the worn straps together.

"DuTain! A good and hardy name," J-Kolson bellowed. "Well, welcome to J-Kolson's booth of fresh produce. I sell the best imports for my homeland Cha-la. You will load. You have loaded before, yes?"

Ester nodded.

"Good, new order in, load oldest to newest. Pay daily, but only for time worked. No breaks until slow time." J-Kolson threw his thumb back, pointing to where he wanted Ester to go.

Ester looked around. She had no idea where he was pointing at.

"Why do you stand around? Load is in back." He pointed again, then turned his attention to his arriving customers.

Ester looked passed him and finally saw where she was supposed to be working. She flipped up the door and walked over to a group of people off loading crates of vegetables. She fell in line and got up to the hover cart where a guy was passing crates. He stopped and looked at Ester for a second. She stood and looked at him back, extending her arms. He shrugged and passed her a crate. It was heavier than she thought. She looked inside; it was a crate full of mini-melons. She groaned but readjusted the weight and hauled the crate to the area where the mini-melons were stored. A person turned and nodded towards her as they took the crate and stocked and arranged the produce. Ester thanked him then headed back to the truck. She repeated this about forty more times, picking up more and more about the job from the staff as the day went on, and by closing time she was dead tired. It was true what they say, if you don't use it, you lose it and her stamina was being tested today. At the end of the day, the owner surveyed his booths. Everything was tidy and ready to go for tomorrow. Ester was paid 100 tones for her work.

"Good job, you come back on second, fourth, and sixth day and I pay the same for hard work." He reached down with his great big muscular hands to pick up a sack of melons. "Here, they're bad. Eat fast, first day welcoming gift," he hollered as he laughed.

Ester uttered a tired thank you and waved goodbye. Her first day wasn't terrible, but she was beyond tired. Now she dreaded her commute back to her apartment because she had to haul a bag full of melons. On the train ride home, she could barely keep awake. She would pass out right there if it were socially acceptable. She got off at her stop. The sun was setting, and it was nearly dark. She was starving but hadn't the energy to stop for anything. She was so exhausted that neither the sights nor smells bothered her, but there was something new growing inside of her. A small little seed of hope that things were finally starting to look up. She smiled to herself as her tired face blended in with all those around her.

***

Morning came, but this time Ester had won out on her war on sleep. She was far too tired for the rays to affect her today. She slept till a little after twelve hundred hours. When she finally got up, she felt well rested and refreshed for the day. She was eternally grateful she didn't have work today. When did she get so out of shape? She used to be in peak condition, then she remembered that it was all for ranger academy. She sighed as she stretched in her bed. She sat up and thought she heard a light knock at the door. She stopped and listened. The sound was faint, but there was a knock again. It couldn't be Angel. He would have practically knocked the door down by now. She got up and went to the door. There wasn't a peep hole.

"Who is it?"

"Forgive my intrusion, it is Sal Chu'Pree your neighborhood from down the–"

Ester opened the door and greeted her neighbor before he could finish introducing himself. Over the past few days, Sal had been making small talk with her in passing. She didn't mind now that she got to know him more. He was nice, but a little long winded at times.

"Hey Sal, what's up?" Ester causally smiled as she folded her arms.

Sal looked around confused. "I-I do not know. Was there some event in the news I should be made aware of?"

"No Sal, I mean, how are you?" Ester laughed.

"Oh, yes, I have heard that phrase before, but my mind could not summon its meaning in time. I am doing fine. What's up with you?" Sal stressed the phase as he forced a friendly smile.

All of Sal's smiles looked fake, but that was because his old skin was leathered and tight which always made him look like he was trying too hard.

"I'm fine," Ester returned his smile as she leaned against her door frame.

Sal nodded and smiled, waiting for Ester to elaborate, but suddenly he remembered why he stopped by.

"Oh, I had forgotten." Sal pulled a bruised melon out from his satchel. "You dropped this. I thought I'd return it to you in the morning. You looked gravely tired last night."

Ester looked at the melon. She had plenty of melons. She didn't need any more, especially since they were close to going bad anyways.

"Thanks, Sal, I got that from my new job. It's going to go bad soon, and I have plenty. Would you like to have it?"

Sal's face stretched into a painful looking smile as he inhaled a lung full of air in delight. "You are too kind, Ester, too kind."

"It's no biggie." Ester smiled as she watched Sal place the melon back into his satchel.

"I am happy you are adjusting well. This metropolis may seem cold and callus, but the people here have fine hearts."

Ester laughed to herself. "You don't say."

"I do say." Sal grinned widely, which reminded Ester of a horse's smile. "Just the other day I sat in Verdie's park and watched the birds. It was a beautiful day. The misses on the first floor had her children about. Oh, how I love the smiles of children." Sal clasped his hands together. "They say if the children are smiling then the neighborhood is bright and alive. It took me quite some time to see the beauty of this place, and one day you will see it too." Sal strained another smile.

"Okay Sal, I believe you." Ester yawned. She wouldn't mind relaxing in front of the tele screen for a bit before she started her day. She thought as she tried to let Sal go.

"I won't hold you." Sal reached down to pat his satchel. "And thank you for the melon."

"It's no biggie, really." Ester repeated.

Sal's smiled soften. It was her favorite part about talking to Sal. His genuine smiles and odd mannerisms made her wonder why he left his home planet for a dump like this. She waved at him one final time before closing her door. She walked over to her window and looked down at the street. She didn't see any beauty here but saw children running by with big smiles on their faces.

"Healthy neighborhood?" Ester muttered. She started to turn away, when a bright blue bird landed on her window ceil. It moved its head, chirped, then flew away. She watched the place where it once perched and mustered a smile as she settled on leftovers and spending the day relaxing in front of the telescreen.

***

After a few weeks on the job, she was really starting to get the swing of things. It wasn't as glamorous, but she liked it and she was good at it. She got up early and showered. This time she didn't bother wearing a nice ride suit, instead she wore some of her old clothes: a pair of thick pants and a heavy over shirt. She wanted to be warm but not too warm that she would over heat. She left her apartment and headed downstairs. As she got towards the middle of the stairs the sounds of arguments made her stop. Ester turned her ear and listened, it sounded like a mother and child.

"You're not my mom!" The same child that had bumped into her the other day yelled.

Ester stood in the shadows, some feet away.

"Gar," The woman tried to get control of the boy. Her face was tired and riddled with worry.

"I don't have to listen to you! Why don't you just leave me alone?" The boy ran away down the hall.

The woman looked as if she wanted to cry but didn't chase after him. Instead she placed her purse over her shoulder and left. Ester recognized the uniform, but she had remembered seeing the woman wear different uniforms other times. As the woman passed Ester, she lifted her head up giving Ester a weak smile, then moved on. Ester really didn't like that kid; he was a real brat. She wondered why he acted out so much, but she had little time to think about. She didn't want to miss to her train to work.

It was winter festival season in Ans-on and the markets were extremely packed. Her boss even asked her if she wanted to come in on her days off. She agreed but knew the next few days would take a lot out of her. After work, the trains were packed, making the lines long. She had never seen it this congested before. So, it took longer than expected to get home. She stopped by the convenience store to buy a sandwich, but they were out of the kind she liked and settled on drumming up something in the kitchen. The clouds were rolling in. Ester peaked out from the shop. She was only a few blocks from her apartment and could probably beat the rain if she ran. Just as she was about to start her sprint a ball of white fluff caught her eye. She looked and saw a pair of golden eyes staring back at her. It was a dog, a very old dog. She hadn't seen a dog in so long. Domestic pets were uncommon in Adum; most people only kept animals for work. She walked over to him and bent down as she extended her hand out close to the ground for them to sniff.

The dog sniffed her hand and wagged his tail. "What are you doing out here, old fella?" Ester petted him on the head. His fur was both soft but greasy. Then she felt a droplet fall on her cheek. "Ooo, looks like I've got to go." She looked up at the sky again, it was getting darker. "You got a place to go? It's going to rain soon."

The dog tilted its head and wagged its tail. She looked around. No one seemed to claim him. She reached down to pet him again and searched for a collar or tag.

"Here we go." She read the ID tag and to her surprise the dog was from her same apartment complex she lived in. "Chargie, huh?"

She stood up and looked around at the people passing by. Could the owner be in the convenience store? She wanted to wait, but the rain wasn't going to hold off while she played rescue mission.

"Okay, buddy, I can't sleep knowing you might get caught in the rain. Your owner lives in the same building as me, so I'll just take you home. Is that okay with you?"

The old dog tilted its head and stood slowly to his feet. He was a medium sized dog, about sixty pounds or so and looked it despite his fluff.

"You follow?" Ester started walking and the dog followed. "Good boy." She smiled and petted him once more.

The two beat the rain, just in time too, as it started to pour just moments after they entered the lobby. Ester shivered and looked down at the dog's collar again. His owner was in apartment A-3304 on the fourth floor. The two walked to the elevator and entered as Ester started down at the old white patch riddled dog.

"Boy, I hope your owner is okay." She wondered briefly if something could have happened to cause this old dog to be out on the streets alone.

The elevator came to a stop and the pair exited. Ester read the numbers of each apartment as she walked.

"Here's your stop." Ester looked down at the dog.

He lifted his head and his mouth opened, which made him look as if he were smiling. He pawed at the door and whined then stood on his hind legs and opened the door. Shocked, Ester couldn't believe she just watched a dog open a door.

"Chargie?" The voice of an old man could be heard in the distance. The man appeared at the door and was surprised to see Ester. "Oh hello." The old man, with dark tan skin and short wild white hair looked down at Chargie. "Did you bring back another girlfriend?" The old man laughed. "I am truly sorry miss if he gave you any trouble." The old white dog panted as he stood behind his owner and wagged his tail slowly.

"Not at all." Ester smiled.

"He has a habit of bringing guests over. I'm not lonely, you old fool." The man chuckled.

"He's a cute dog, smart, too." Ester eyed the dog. She guessed that he could have gone home at any time, seeing how he knew how to open the door. Chargie barked.

"Oh, hush." The old man petted his dog on the head. "Where are my manners? My name is InyOuty Applecom."

"It's nice to meet you sir, my name is Ester DuTain." Ester reached out her hand. The old man shook it with delight.

"DuTain? Haven't heard that name in a long time." The old man turned, expecting Ester to follow. "You're welcome to stay for dinner." He smiled. Ester looked surprised but figured why not. She didn't have anything good to eat back at her apartment and everyone in the building seemed friendly so far. "Where have I heard DuTain from? Ah yes. It was quite sad; vandals; miscreants, but that was decades ago."

Ester closed the door. "What was decades ago?"

The old man turned around and looked at Ester like he was looking at a friend he hadn't seen in a long time. "Before your time," he scratched his head. "Well, you look about the right age, but it was sad. Just a piss poor situation, but that's how it was back in my ranger days."

Ranger days? Ester thought to herself. Was InyOuty a retired ranger? Ester followed him to the kitchen looking around at all the pictures on the walls. Just like Sal, it looked like he was well traveled, but yet he made his home here. She stopped and looked at one picture taken in a massive freshly planted field. The man shuffled behind her.

"That one was taken at a place called Bluburry farms in north Adum-la. Back in those days, you could walk the land and see nothing but crops for miles." He smiled.

"It's still like that." Ester stood and turned to him. "Nothing but fields everywhere you look."

InyOuty's face lit up. "How wonderful. These days, nothing stays the same and when you get to my age you long to go back every day." InyOuty walked back to the kitchen.

Ester followed as the smell of fresh vegetable stew permeated the air as it simmered in a pot on the stove. Hanging on the walls were peppers and woven baskets of potatoes and bundles of spices. On the table sat a cornucopia of apples and pears and cinnamon incense burned lightly on a hand carved incense boat on the counter. Ester took a deep breath; this place was flooded with the smells of home. So much so that she half expected Sister Genevieve to walk around the corner carrying a tray of freshly baked bread.

The old man poured out some stew. "Is this enough?"

Ester snapped out of her memories and nodded. "Yes, that's fine." Chargie was by her side, wagging his tail and, looking quite content in the company of his new guest. Ester smiled at him and petted him on the head.

"Are you from Adum-la?" Ester said.

"What?"

"Are you from—"

"No, no. I was born in a tiny village in the Fortner locale in Who-da. When I was young, it was just called the traveling states, but you know we've got to have a name for everything."

InyOuty turned and walked to the table with two great big bowls of stew. The smells knocked at the doors of her memories and invited its self in.

"Haglin Who was the name of the man said to have brought peace to the traveling states, but all he did was show up and piss his pants, so they named it after him as consolation." InyOuty laughed, when Chargie pawed at his leg. "Oops, forgive me, old friend." InyOuty got up and walled to the refrigerator and took out a bowl for Chargie. He topped off his bowl with an extra spoonful of stew and stirred it. "This is for the lovely guest you brought over."

Ester smiled in between gobbling up a spoonful of stew. The stew was good. It reminded her of everything she missed. "So what made you want to live all the way down here, Mr. Applecom?"

"Applecom? Please call me InyOuty, Applecom is too formal for this old man." He sat back down and took in his stew sip by sip. "Here? Hmmm," he paused. "This place was the cheapest." He let out a hardy laugh. "You know, I've been alive for a very long time, but I wouldn't call myself a senior."

Ester eyed him.

"I'm only one hundred and thirty." InyOuty tried to flex. "And when you get to my age you realize any place you call your home is home."

Ester stopped eating and smiled as he continued to talk. He was right. She was slowly starting to realize this. A home could be anywhere, and she was beginning to realize that hers lived in her heart. She carried it with her wherever she went, ready to be planted and started a new, wherever life took her.

Chapter Seventeen

Work was incredibly busy the next day. Ester barely had time to sit down. People were buying up their stock faster than they could stock it. Ester moved loads in a hurry along with the other staff who didn't seem phased by all the craziness. The morning flew by and the crowds thinned out a little, giving Ester just enough time to enjoy a bruised tomato and a drink of water. She sat on a crate and people watched, wondering what the big fuss was about. She didn't know much about Ans-on's festivals, but she would call Angel and ask.

As she watched the crowd, she took interest in the families. She had forgotten how much she enjoyed playing with children, even though they could be little terrors at times. She laughed to herself as her memories came flooding in. When she looked up to scan the crowd again, she saw a young woman with gorgeous short midnight blue hair. Ester froze as her eyes followed her around the market. The woman's skin was a pale white and she was dressed in a dark gray ride suit with a long black cloak around her. Ester watched her move from booth to booth cautiously, as if she were lost or looking for something. The woman stopped many times at neighboring venders, but bought nothing, only stared and looked with her fingers drawn to her lips. Ester finished her tomato and wiped her hands on her pants. Her break was coming to an end, but she was captivated by the woman's beauty and guarded expression that fluttered every time someone bumped into her.

J-Kolson called Ester to the front to re-organize the vegetables. She was grateful that she could still watch the woman from her side of the booth as she worked. Ester moved some ears of corn, when she noticed the woman was heading her way. Ester averted her eyes, only stealing glances at her to not appear creepy. The woman walked over and looked at the vegetables as if she had never seen them before. Others moved around her, pushing her out of the way with quick grabby hands. The woman retracted her hands every time someone reached in front of her. It would be amusing to Ester if it wasn't so sad. Ester finished restocking some corn and walked over to the woman.

"Do you need any help?" Ester offered as she rubbed her hands off with a rag.

The woman looked up and that's when Ester noticed her silvery blue eyes. She had never seen someone with that type of eye color before. Ester pulled herself from her gaze, trying not to make things anymore awkward than it already was. The woman said nothing as she scanned the vegetables, as if she were in deep thought.

"It's okay, I know it's a lot to pick from. Are you from around here?"

The woman flinched.

"I don't mean to pry, but you look a little lost," Ester said. "These vegetables are imported from Cha-la, and a lot of them have similar counterparts to vegetables grown in other nation states. For example, this orange potato here may look a little weird if you're from Huma-ko, because Huma-ko potatoes are black, but this one is pretty much the same. It just has a little tartness in it that can be cooked out and sweetened if you want. The beans are the same way."

The woman poured over the vegetables, reaching out to them, then retracting her hands. Another customer pushed into her and Ester started to say something, but the woman shoved them away. The customer grunted and looked at the woman, but her glare extinguished any reaction they were thinking of having. Ester smirked watching the customer walk over to the other side of the booth.

"Vegetables?" The woman mumbled. Ester could barely understand her from her thick accent.

"Um, yes, all of these on this side are vegetables, on the other side is fruit."

"Fruit?"

"Yup, we have a pretty good stock of fruits as well, they're from Cha-la, but—"

"Green leaves, I would like to trade for green leaves." The woman said more assertively.

"Um, okay," Ester looked around. She didn't have many green leaves, but she had purple leaves. "These purple ones are like green spinach. They're just purple, but they taste the same."

"Same?"

"Yes," Ester nodded.

The woman stood there for a second. Ester could hear a few of the staffers call for her in the back. Ester looked around for another order staff. She couldn't take orders, but she really wanted to help this woman.

"I will have the purple leaf greens." The woman pointed to the spinach.

"Great, let me get you an order staff member," Ester turned and called one of the money takers to her side.

They came and finished up the woman's order. Ester watched from the back. The woman barely said a word and paid and walked away disappearing into the crowd. Ester scanned the crowd, but she couldn't find her again and returned to work. She hoped this wasn't the last time because she wouldn't mind getting to know her better.

***

For the rest of the week, Ester noticed an increase in energy. She was starting to regain the stamina she had back in Adum and this change didn't go unnoticed. Her boss was impressed at how fast she picked up the work and promoted her to taking orders. Ester felt honored. She was thriving in a place she thought she would die in, and it felt good to feel normal again. Ester ended her work day a hundred tones richer and was able to buy herself two sets of nice dark brown blinds. With a pantry full of veggies, she headed home with the idea of roasting vegetables for dinner.

She walked down the street with her coat huddled around her. It was the middle of winter now, and it was much colder after sunset. As she walked home, she started to notice how this placed had changed. The people who rushed by didn't seem like distant figures anymore. She spotted a man taking a drag off his cigarette next to a building. She had seen him before. He lived in that building with his girlfriend and child. In alleyways, once a place Ester dare not look, she saw sewer workers huddling around a fire lit trashcan. When they saw her approach, they smiled and she smiled back. Those were the men who offered extra food to the less fortunate. In the streets, she saw children and couples young and old, warmth covered their faces as they huddled close in the cold. This was a different city now, or rather it felt like her eyes had finally been opened.

Ester arrived home and sat her groceries on the counter. She tossed her coat on the couch and turned on the telescreen before washing her hands. While she prepped her vegetables, she thought about calling Angel. She hadn't spoken to him in a while, but she was sure he was busy in class or studying, so she would call him later tonight. The telescreen changed from a commercial to a program about a research station close to Labadora.

"Well, I can tell'ya first hand that these stones are from Verlin's Belt."

A dark skinned man said as he eyed the rock with glee.

"Now how it got all the way out here is the real mystery."

Ester watched the crew marvel over the specimen as she ran her vegetables under the water.

"But I'll tell ya, I'd give anything to visit the planet below."

"You're joking right?"

A woman laughed at the man's comment, but the man didn't seem bothered by it.

"No really, I can only imagine what wonders lie below."

Another man in the crew, wearing a blue suit, patted the man holding the rock on his back. The man in the blue suit shook his head.

"Trust me man," the man in the blue suit said. "Ain't nothing down there but chaos and headache."

The crew on the show continued to joke as Ester carried on with cooking. Were things really that hectic on Labadora? Ester paused as the screen panned to a beautiful shot of the large green planet. She couldn't imagine how such a beautiful planet could be all bad.

Later that night, Ester phoned Angel, using the device he bought her on his last visit. She rarely got to speak to him because he was so busy at school, but that didn't stop her from trying. It was twenty hundred hours; he should be finished with classes by now. Ester turned on the holograph phone; the device was pretty easy to use. They had something similar to this back at school. She found Angel's name under the contacts tab and tapped it. She waited a little as the icon on the screen pulsed in and out. She hoped she wasn't calling him at a bad time. The screen changed, prompting her to leave a message. Ester sighed; she guessed leaving a massage would have to do.

"Hey, it's Ester, call me back when you get this. I'll be up till zero one hundred hours," Ester said.

She guessed that she would have to wait. She wasn't mad about it, but she missed talking to her friends. She sat back on the couch and relaxed, watching the tele. There was a good drama on. This was quickly becoming her favorite thing to do. Just as she was starting to get into the show, her hologram phone sprang back to life, showing a goofy picture of Angel. Ester smiled and hit the green button.

"About damn time," she said with no real bite.

"About time? I'm the one who calls you!" Angel huffed.

It really had been awhile since they talked face to face. Because of Angel's school schedule, they only could talk in quick burst over text messages or whenever Angel called.

"How is everything?" Ester said.

Angel sat up and readjusted himself on his bed. "It's going."

Loud chatter could be heard in the background, and Angel looked away from the screen and smiled then turned back to Ester.

"It's super busy around here." Angel said.

"I bet," Ester said as she pulled her blanket over her.

"No, I mean, it's crazy busy. Even my parents are working, and you know it's busy if my parents are actually working."

Ester nodded. "Wow." She faked a smile and laughed.

Angel stuck out his tongue. "How's work? You need some extra tones?"

"Not bad, actually. I think I've finally got the swing of things. And no, I'm good on tones, so next time you come and visit I can take you out to lunch."

"Yes girl, I would love that, then we can go shopping because I have to get that everyday wear perfume volume two of Something Symple. I just got my sample in the mail, and it's really nice. They have a line in women's too. Be Remembered, I think it was called, but I would totally recommend it."

Ester could listen to Angel ramble on about cosmetics for hours. Even though she didn't have a clue what he was talking about. He was truly like the best friend she never had. On his next visit, they would have to go out and shop. She couldn't wait to show him South Mall.

"So when can I expect you?" Ester smiled.

"Huh?" Angel squinted at the screen. The picture was fading in and out. "Hold on." Ester heard some rattling noises and the screen showed his bedsheets then Angel picked up his tablet again. "The servers are slow today. Um, let's see." Angel swiped his fingers above the screen. "How about in two weeks?"

"That's perfect! Festival season will be winding down by then," Ester said in relief.

"That's right, I'm missing All's Day," Angel pouted.

"All's Day?"

"The festival of continuation; it's a festival about trains."

"Trains?" Ester said with a weird look.

Angel nodded. "Don't underestimate it. The instillation of the state train system revolutionized Ans-on. That's what we are famous for: our technology. Now the whole continent is connected because of it."

"Yay trains," Ester said unenthusiastically.

Angel stuck out his tongue again. "Whatever, I think it's cool."

"Lights out!"

Ester heard in the background.

"Okay, gotta go," Angel said.

"Okay, tell everyone I said hi and see you in two weeks."

Angel nodded as he made kissy faces on his tablet. "Will do! See you in two weeks. It's a date!"

Ester laughed and waved goodbye. The device turned off, and Ester stretched and resettled on the couch. Tomorrow was her day off. She would go to South Mall and explore the area for good places to shop and eat for when Angel arrived in town.

***

Finally, on her day off, Ester got to enjoy the full extent of her new blinds. She slept the entire morning, waking up at eleven hundred hours. It was the best sleep she'd had in weeks. She washed up and set out for her trip to the mall. It was cold and windy today, but that didn't bother her, especially since she could treat herself to some Fried Tuzan. Bundled up in a thick ride suit and coat, Ester headed to the train station. On her way there, she saw a shopkeeper wave a group of young kids out of his store. He yelled and shouted as the kids took off in different directions.

"Help! Thieves!" The man yelled in vein.

One of the children Ester recognized. It was the boy who lived in her apartment. She glared at him and took off after him. She was really getting tired of that kid. She ran after him down the street. He was fast but lacked the stamina. She chased him through the alley as he jumped over trashcans and side-stepped people. He was almost in the clear when he tripped on a pothole and fell to the ground, spilling his stolen goods on the concrete. Ester caught up to him, blocking him from escaping.

"Hey kid, cool it!" Ester shouted, towering over the glaring kid. He didn't look a day past ten. "What's your deal?" Ester stared him down.

"Piss off," Gar shouted and flung puddle water at her.

"Gross." Ester wiped her face, but by then the kid had regained traction and was off down the road again. She growled as the electricity coursed through her veins. She really hated that kid.

Despite her rocky morning, she had a fun time exploring South Mall. She saw very little of this area in her rush to and from work. The shopping locale was much bigger than she thought, and there were lots of shops dotted in and around the mall. She got to enjoy her lunch at Fried Tuzans, which was very busy today. Apparently, the owner was making a speech somewhere down the street. She only caught a glimpse of him, but it was his bluish gray skin that caught her eye. She watched the crowd move towards him and was about to turn away when she heard a beautiful voice over a microphone. She stopped and listened and swore it sounded familiar. The sound was deep and soulful, just like Galaxia's. She turned around to get a better look, but the crowd was thick. By the time she reached the front the singing had stopped.

"Thank you for that sample, Miss. Don't miss your chance to see her preform live this evening at The Noir," The man on the stage said as the crowd clapped. "Now a word from our President and CEO, Dell Inspread."

Ester watched the strange man take the stage in disappointment as she searched for the singer. She was less interested in hearing his speech and turned around to see if she could find out more information about what was happening at The Noir. She remembered that café from the directory. She was told they had amazing teas but never visited there herself. She pushed through the cheering crowd again that was now at a standstill. When she finally found herself back on the street, she was relieved to see that The Noir was just across the street. She walked to the café and looked around outside. She hoped there would be a flyer on the window or something that could tell her more about the concert.

"Ester?" A familiar voice called her name from outside a shop next door.

Ester looked up and gasped. "Samay?" Ester said. She couldn't believe her eyes and ran over to hug her. "What are you doing out here?"

"I was about to ask you the same thing," she said with a smile. "Do you live around here? I thought you went back home."

Ester nodded. "Sort of, I live in the Kahlizard Locale now. So only a few stops from here."

"Oh neat." Samay looked beyond Ester at the crowd outside.

"Hey, you wanna get something sweet?"

"Heck yes," Ester said.

Samay took her to a small café just a few blocks away. Ester had never been there before. She would have to make note of this place if it was any good for when Angel was coming to visit. The café was a small bakery and smelled of freshly baked cakes and pies. It looked antique, but modern at the same time—like a proper tea shop with wood furnishing, and polished figurines.

"I am so excited I get to try their new flavor of fried dough," Samay said as they stood in line.

Ester admired her tan lappa, a poncho like dress with big gapping sleeves that made it look like it was swallowing her up hole. Lappas weren't common in Ans-on, but they were big fashion in Cha-la, which was where Samay was from. Ester watched as Samay ordered two chocolate treats, then the two grabbed a table near the back to catch up.

"So, what's been up with you, besides academy stuff?" Ester said as she picked up her treat and took a big bite. Samay half smiled and avoided eye contact, causing Ester to put down her treat and look at her. "What?"

"Huh? Oh," Samay jumped. "Ester, I, uh, I quit the academy. Shortly after you left," Samay said poking at her fried dough.

There was silence between the two for a while, but then Ester shook herself out of it.

"What? why?" Ester gaped at her.

Samay looked away. "It wasn't for me. It was what my parents wanted. Being a ranger is a prestigious thing back home, but after what happened…well, my heart wasn't in it." Samay looked up at Ester. "I'm so sorry, Ester. I feel so bad after what happened."

"It's okay," Ester said.

"I know, but—"

"Samay, you're really smart. The Rangers could have used a badass like you, but if it's not what you want to do then I get that." Ester couldn't be mad at Samay for quitting. Ester was the one who let Murk get to her.

Samay broke out into a huge smile. "Ester, I swear you are too kind, but I am not a badass, at least not at that."

"Well, you can't change my mind," Ester said with a laugh. "So, what are you up to now?"

"Well, um, I sing now."

Ester stopped finger licking her plate. "Wait, were you the one singing back at the Fried Tuzan's?"

Samay nodded as she shied away.

"Oh my gosh! So you're playing at The Noir this evening?"

Samay nodded.

"Wow, you have some serious talent, girl!"

"You're too kind, but really I owe everything to my uncle. Remember when back at ranger academy over the break I met up with my uncle? I was scared at first, but I told him how I felt about the academy, and he told me that we all have our own lives to live and we should follow the strings of our heart." Samay smiled. "After the final exam, I knew then that I wasn't on the right path. Oh, Ester I'm so sorry things ended the way they did."

"Samay, it's okay, I'm fine really. Besides, at least they kicked that loser out as well."

Samay started to smile again. "It was a sight to see Murk a crying mess on the floor when he got permanently banned."

"And it serves him right too."

Samay giggled. Ester hadn't realized how much she missed her friends.

"So, how'd you land this gig? I mean you got to sing a little at the Fried Tuzan event."

"I have to thank my uncle again; he owns a small café on the other side of town. He told me I could stay with him for free, but only if I agreed to sing at his café. I was nervous at first, but then people started to come to the café just to see me. I couldn't believe it, and from there, things just started to take off."

"That's awesome," Ester said.

Samay nodded. She was happy to see that Ester was thriving and she wished her the best. "Hey, would you like another one? My treat."

"Heck yeah!" Ester threw her fist in the air.

"Okay, wait here." Samay got up and bounced back into line.

It was really nice seeing her friend again. Ester missed all of her friends from academy. Samay looked back and smiled. Her face lit up as her thick black pony-tailed fro bounced with her. Seeing old friends and eating treats after long days of window shopping was never a dream for Ester, but it was something she could get used to.

***

Attending Samay's show later that night was amazing. She was a goddess behind the mic, and Ester was convinced that Samay would become the next be thing—right up there with Glass Doll, who was a new electro-beat artist Angel was into and Ester was starting to like as well. After the show, Ester said her goodbyes to Samay. She promised to catch every show Samay was in town for. The girls exchanged numbers and hugged, promising to keep in contact.

After the show, Ester went back to Fried Tuzans and got dinner to take home. She headed back to the train station and while she waited, she caught sight of her neighbor. It was the woman who looked after that little brat that had stolen from the shop earlier today. Ester stared at the woman from a few feet away. She looked exhausted and yawned repeatedly on the platform. A train arriving for one of the north locales pulled into the station. It wasn't the train Ester was taking home. The woman jumped back to life and rushed quickly to get onboard. Once on board, the woman slipped on another shirt with a different logo on it. She must be heading to another job, but it was already so late. She was working really hard, and it couldn't be easy looking after a child like Gar. The train pulled off and Ester stood and watched it leave. Someone needed to talk to that boy.

When Ester arrived home, it was almost dark and very cold and rainy. It wasn't as bad as Adum's winters, but the wind tunnels created by the buildings made it extra cold. She wished it would snow like it did back at home. She could deal with the snow, but freezing rain was its own kind of hell. Ester shivered in the lobby; today had been a long day and she didn't feel like walking up three flights to her apartment, so she walked to the elevator and pressed the button. Machinery clanked and cracked, making her cringe, reminding her why she never took the elevators in the first place. She stepped back and shifted the weight of her bag from one hand to the other. The lobby doors from the outside opened, blowing in a mighty wind. Ester stiffened as the cold air bit at her back. She turned around and was surprised to see the woman with the short midnight blue hair from the market. She walked in briskly and headed straight for the stairs. Ester didn't know she lived in her apartment building or maybe she was just visiting.

"H-hey," Ester flagged her down. The woman froze and looked at Ester. "It's me, from the market. You bought some purple greens from the booth I was working at."

The woman seemed surprised that Ester noticed her and backed up when Ester approached.

"Sorry if I startled you," Ester said to ease the tension.

The woman only stared, as if she were calculating her words. Her hand hovered over the door handle, but then she pulled it away.

"Ah, yes. They market near the shop town," The woman said. Her body was tense and eyes focused.

"Yup, that's the one. Did you enjoy the greens?"

"They were edible," The woman said bluntly.

"Um, that's good. I mean that's all we can hope for, right? I'm Ester, by the way. I live on the third floor. Do you live here, too?"

The woman scanned Ester's eyes. Ester smiled to break the awkwardness, but that only sharpened the woman's glare. The elevator dinged, breaking the tense silence.

"Um, that's my ride, gotta go, but if you do live here hit me up. I'd love to chat." Ester rushed away.

Once she was in the elevator, she took a deep breath. That was awkward. She guessed some people were not as outgoing as she was, and she hoped she didn't seem rude running off like that. But there was something about her that put her off. Ester put those thoughts in the back of her mind as she got off the elevator. All she wanted to do now was eat dinner and take a nice long bath.

***

That night, Ester fell asleep on her couch in the den. The volume on her tele screen was on low as the images from the screen created shadows in the room. Bundled up tight in her blankets, she began to wake from the sound of scratching at her door. She grumbled and groaned as she tried to ignore it, but it wouldn't go away. Frustrated and half asleep, she fumbled around for the remote and turned the tele off. The scratching stopped, and she fell blissfully back to sleep. Then the scratching sounds started up again. She groaned and reached for the remote, but when she couldn't find it, she opened her eyes to a dark room. The tele was off, but the scratching noises persisted. Was someone at her door? An uneasiness crept through her mind, bringing her fully awake as the scratching sounds got louder. Who could it be at this hour? She looked at her wristband. Could it be Chargie? She'd never been visited by him this late at night, but given InyOuty's age, worry started to build inside of her. She got up and grabbed her long coat and zipped it up. Just before she got to the door, she thought for a brief second, what if it wasn't Chargie? What if it was some creep? She didn't have any weapons in her apartment, but she did have kitchen knives. She searched the kitchen and settled on a pan. It would be less deadly to swing a pan then it would be to swing a knife. The scratching continued, and Ester stood at her door ready to greet or chase off whatever woke her up from her sleep. She reached for the doorknob, unlocked it, and flung the door open.

"What is it!" she shouted, hoping to scare off whoever it was.

The boys fell back on themselves as they looked up at a rage filled Ester. She recognized one right away.

"You," she growled, and the rest of the boys scattered as she reached out to snatch up Gar.

Gar screamed and kicked as Ester lifted him off his feet high into the air. He looked for his friends, but they were long gone.

"Let-let me go." Gar wiggled.

Ester turned and looked at her front door. There were pictures of penises and curse words littered on her door on top of the graffiti that was already there.

"You little brat." She turned and slammed him against the wall.

She didn't care that he was a kid. If he was brazen enough to tag her door, then he was old enough to get his ass beaten. She clenched her fists, ready to pound the kid into dust. She growled then looked into his eyes. He reminded her of some of the kids back at the orphanage. Displaced and full of hatred, she remembered how Sister Genevieve would handle them. Ester softened her grip, and Gar took this opportunity to kick her. He barely missed her face.

"What's your problem kid? Why you picking with me?" Ester growled.

"Piss off!" He shouted.

"Okay, we'll try this again." She dropped him to the floor and he landed with a thud. She reached down and grabbed him by the ear.

"Ow ow ow, let go!" He squirmed.

"Not a chance. Your old lady is worried sick about you, I'm sure." Ester closed her apartment door and locked it and started dragging the kid back to his apartment. If he wasn't ready to talk, then she would take him home and let his guardian take care of him.

"Let go." He winced and wiggled, but Ester's grip was like a vice.

"You know, you got a lot of nerve tagging my door, and yes, I'm telling your old lady what you did."

"I-I don't care."

Ester continued to drag him along. He put on the breaks, but Ester continued to pull.

"I hope she's not sleeping." Ester headed downstairs.

"No, wait…" He gasped as he started to tear up. "You can't…because she's not home." Ester stopped and looked down at the boy. "She's-she's at work, and if she has to come back early they might fire her." Gar averted his eyes.

He lost the battle with his tear ducts and wiped his snotty face with his arms as he started to sniffle. Ester sighed and took a deep breath and let go of his ear. The boy grabbed it but made no attempt the run.

"Why are you causing trouble like this, kid?"

"What-what do you care?" His face was red, making his tan skin look darker.

"I don't," Ester said coldly. "But it's my door you've marked up and who's going to pay for that?" The boy said nothing. "Or should I leave the bill with your mother."

"No!" Gar blurted out, then he looked at the ground. "And, she's not my mom. She's my aunt."

"But she feeds you right? And takes care of you?" Ester plucked him on the forehead.

"Ow!" Gar rubbed his forehead.

"And this is how you repay her?" Gar didn't say anything. Ester sighed and relaxed her shoulders. She was familiar with the look of troubled kids, and sometimes they just needed a stern talking to instead of getting their folks involved. "I'll tell you what. You and your buddies fix my door, and I won't tell your aunt."

"What? How am I supposed to do that?"

"Don't know, don't care. You had balls enough to tag my door, but don't have much sense on how to fix it? Maybe I should just bill your aunt and have a service man come and do the job."

"No," Gar begged. "I'll-I'll fix it."

"You got till the end of the week and don't try and bail on me. I know where you live. Are we clear?" Ester stood over Gar.

"Ye-yeah." Gar lowered his head.

"Now scram."

Ester eyed him as she watched him run back to his apartment. She watched him go in and didn't leave until five minutes later. How long had it been since Ester had seen a fire like that in someone's eyes? Too long, she thought to herself on the way back to her apartment, but she knew from experience that a flame like that left unchecked would burn up everything.

***

Morning came bright and early, and this time it wasn't the scratching at her door that woke her up but a loud knock. She groaned as she once again dragged herself out of bed to answer the door. With her slippers and jammies on, she walked to the door, not even caring how she looked.

"Who is it?" Ester said from behind her door.

"Excuse me, miss. My name is Sky Tos. I am the aunt of Gar Su. We live downstairs." Ester opened the door and there stood Sky with Gar in tote. His face was puffy and wet. No doubt he looked like he got a stern talking to. "I am so sorry to bother you, but Mr. Chu'Pree said he saw my nephew and his friends drawing on your door, and we wanted to come and apologize." Sky pulled Gar forward by his arm. She forced his head down as they both bowed. "Please allow me to cover the cost of the damage to your door."

Ester looked down at them both and sighed. "It's okay, Miss Tos, I'm sure Gar knows better not to do this again."

Sky looked up at Ester, her eyes puffy and red and pleaded. "Please ma'am, please. It's the least I can do."

Ester looked between her and Gar. The boy looked like he was on the brink of tears. She didn't want to make a big deal of this. "How about this, I've got soap. You send your nephew over to clean this up, and we'll call it even. What do you say?"

Sky looked at Ester like she was going to cry and graciously thanked Ester.

"I actually have powdered soap at my apartment. Gar," she said sternly to the boy. "You are to go back to the apartment at once and grab the soap, bucket, and bushes. And I don't want to hear your mouth about it." Sky hissed, then she turned to Ester and forced a smile. Her watched buzzed. She gasped as she fretted. "I-I have to go, I'm so sorry." She looked at the place Gar once was. "I'm so sorry, but I promise to make him clean this up. I'm sorry."

"It's okay." Ester leaned against her doorframe and saw Sky off.

It must be hard raising someone else's child all on your own, but she could tell that she really cared about him. Gar returned as he was told and got to work cleaning the graffiti off of Ester's door. Ester sat on the floor of her apartment watching him in silence, as the angry ball of brown hair scrubbed away. She yawned and plucked a ripe mango from her fruit basket and looked back at Gar.

"Hey kid, you want one?" she said.

Gar looked up and saw the mango in Ester's hand. His mouth started to water, but he said nothing.

"Okay, fine with me, more mangos for me." Ester placed the mango back into the basket as she broke apart her mango and took a great big juicy bite.

Gar frowned as he watched her eat. He turned his head and pouted, but then spoke up. "Um, could I have one?" Gar mumbled.

"What was that?"

"Could-could I have a mango please?" he said a little louder.

She looked at him, then took out a knife and started to cut another mango. "Alright, come in and wash up."

Gar stood slowly and walked inside of her apartment. It was small like his, but with only one bedroom. Ester continued preparing the mango as Gar washed his hands in the sink.

"Here." She placed a plate of mangos on a small table in her kitchen and pulled up a chair.

"Thank you, um…" Gar trailed off, looking at her expectantly.

"It's Ester," she said as Gar continued to sit there, making himself look small.

"What's the deal with you, kid?" She sat down at the table. He didn't say anything at first then Ester slid the plate away. "Why are you acting up?"

Gar avoided eye contact. He looked like he wanted to yell, but instead he just stared at his fingers. "It's-it's nothing."

Ester slid the plate of mangos back over to him. "Doesn't sound like nothing."

He snatched a mango as if it would run away and bit into it. "I-I don't know. I just, I just hate it here."

Ester nodded. "I can see that. The place is run down and the outside smells like shit."

Gar looked up, his eyes giving his emotions away. "I just want to go home." He looked like he wanted to cry, but he didn't. "I just want to go home," he whimpered.

"But you can't, huh?"

Gar nodded. "My parents died in an accident two years ago, then my aunt lost her job and even though she would have been better off without me, she still took me in. But she works all the time to send me to that stupid prep school. I hate it, and everything around here is crappy and broken down. It's not fair."

"Life's not fair," Ester said bluntly as Gar slumped. "And I get that. My parents died when I was young too."

Gar looked at her in surprise.

"But your aunt really cares about you, and she's working her butt off to make sure you have the best life. Love like that isn't easy to come by and shouldn't be taken for granted. It's going to be hard for a while, but you have to do better—at least for her."

"I can't." Gar looked down at his hands.

"And why not?"

Gar didn't make eye contact. "I just can't."

"You can't or you won't?"

"You don't get it!" Gar snapped. "The kids at the prep school make fun of me. My uniform is always dirty, and they say I stink because I come from this place. I hate it there."

"Screw those kids." Ester took another bite of her mango. "Trust me, those kids are going to be sitting there with their jaws on the floor when they see you succeed. Bullies suck and you'll probably never get rid of them, but if you really want to stick it to them, succeed. Be the best person you can be and knock them all out by showing them it doesn't matter if you live in a dump with your aunt or that your uniform is stained. You came to that school to get an education. What do you want to be when you grow up, Gar?"

Gar looked up. This was the first time she had called him by his name. "I-I want to be an architect like my father."

"Okay then, well you better become the best damn architect Anson and the entire world as ever seen. You know why?"

Gar shook his head.

"Because you're Gar, that's why. You're not going to let anything get in the way of your dreams and there's nothing those snobby brats at your school can do about it."

"You really think so?"

"Trust me, kid. You work hard, and you'll be the one designing skyscrapers. Now opening: Gar's mega shopping center, an architectural wonder." Ester waved her hand around.

"I'm not going to make a mall!" Gar laughed.

Ester laughed with him. "Yeah well, whatever you make it's not going to happen if you keep cutting up. Hit the books, kid. I'm already booking my next destination at one of your buildings."

Gar smiled and happily finished his snack. By the end of the day, Ester's door was all cleaned up. She hoped that little pep talk helped him, but it stung a little telling a kid that hard work alone could make your dreams come true—knowing that hers was out of reach. There was something she knew for sure, and that was that the path he was heading down now would only led to more pain and trouble. It wasn't too late for him; it wasn't too late to turn it around.

Chapter Eighteen

With Angel's visit only days away, Ester poured hours into thinking of things to do. She was still new to this area, and she didn't know what people in the metropolises did for fun, besides shopping and she was sure Angel would love that. But she wanted to find other things to do. She turned to the local news hoping to find something interesting happening about, but Ans-on news was saturated in national news and very little aired that had anything to do with the area Ester lived in, unlike back home. Ester groaned as she laid back on her couch. It was her day off, and all she had on her list of things to do were a few dozen eateries and more than her lifetime's worth of shops. She checked the time; it was a little after ten hundred hours. She still had the entire day ahead of her to try and figure out something to do.

She fixed herself a quick breakfast and got dressed, thinking that she'd get more ideas exploring again. She stuffed her suit with her tone card and keys as she locked the door of her apartment. Maybe she could joyride through the different train stops, but she quickly tossed the idea remembering that train rides weren't free and she needed to manage her money carefully in order to pay her rent. She took the stairs down to the first floor and caught a glimpse of a tall figure in the mail room.

"Sal?" She ran over and peaked inside.

"Oh, Ester," Sal said as he turned to her.

Ester cracked a smile as she watched the wrinkles stretch around Sal's large black eyes.

"Hey Sal, you wouldn't happen to know of anywhere fun to hang out?"

Sal squinted as he drew his hand to his chin. "Fun? Well, I do recall a few places." He chuckled. "Yes, I do recall a few places indeed."

"Great! Where?"

"Let's see, there is the park just down the street. Oh, how the children look so happy when they play, and there is the park a little ways beyond that. Oh, that park is just lovely." Sal's mouth curled into a smile.

"Um, are there any other places besides parks?" Ester asked, trying to remain optimistic.

"Besides parks?" Sal blinked a few times. "Well, I, I do recall a place on the train line. Oh dear, my apologies, I am thinking of another park. Please forgive me."

"It's okay, Sal."

"But, I do believe next to that park, which is three stops east from here in the Hiji locale, is a center. It is rather loud, but the children seem to enjoy it."

"Center? What kind of center is it?"

Sal rubbed the skin of his chin, tugging at it gently. "If I recall correctly, it is a game center or a mall. No, it is both a game center and a mall." A smile found its way on Sal's face once more.

"A game center?"

Ester's eyes started to sparkle. She had never been to a game center before; they didn't have those anywhere near her back home. Ester clasped her hands together.

"Three stops east, Hiji locale, right?" Ester said.

"Yes, yes, I believe so."

"Great! Thanks Sal," Ester said as she left the mailroom.

"You're welcome!" Sal shouted.

Ester had practically forgotten about game centers. They had a few near the big fishing towns far south in Adum. She used to see them on the tele. Tel-sa was famous for their mega game centers that were so big that they had hover car racing in them. She would have to make it a point after Angel was done with school to do a little road trip. Maybe she could visit all the nation states in the future. She would love to visit Samay in Cha-la and maybe a few friends from the orphanage as well.

The train station wasn't as intimidating as it was before. Though she occasionally got lost from time to time, at least she was getting better at reading the maps. She stood in a crowd and looked at the arrival and departure screens. It looked like the next train for Hiji locale would be arriving in twenty minutes. Ester had plenty of money on her train card. Thank goodness she reloaded earlier this week. She looked down the corridor and spotted the woman with the short midnight blue hair who lived in her apartment. The one she had the awkward encounter with from before. She hated that she ran away so quickly and hoped it didn't put the woman off, so she walked over to her.

"Hey," Ester said, startling the woman, earning her one heck of a glare. Ester put her hands up in defense. "Sorry, didn't mean to startle you."

"You again. Do you not have anything better to do other than to pester others?" The woman snapped.

"Hey, I just said hi. You don't have to be rude," Ester bit back. What was up with this woman? She was always in a bad mood.

"Well, perhaps you should keep your nose in your own business." The woman's steely gaze made Ester's blood boil.

"You know what? I don't need this." Ester stormed off.

She didn't know what pissed her off, but she wanted nothing to do with it. She found her gate and sat and waited for her train. Today was going to be a good day, and she didn't need any drama to ruin it. The train pulled into the station on time. The doors opened, and people flooded out, then Ester boarded. It was tight, but she managed to grab a seat. She got comfy for the ten-minute ride, when she looked up and made eye contact with the rude woman again. The woman spotted her and glared as she searched around for any available seats, but the last seat was taken by a man talking on his phone. Now all that was left was a seat next to Ester. The conductor announced they would be departing in sixty seconds, leaving her with very little options other than to sit next to Ester. The woman grumbled and squeezed in between Ester and a larger woman with an armful of bags. It was uncomfortable, but better than standing. The train took off, causing the woman to shove into Ester.

"Ugh," Ester groaned.

The woman quickly readjusted herself but there was little space as her body was being smooshed by the woman carrying the large bags. It was awkward and hot. The trained reached full speed, then the conductor announced the next stop which was the Karlem locale.

"Karlem?" The woman seemed surprised.

Ester rolled her eyes. "Yeah, the next stop is Karlem."

Ester looked over at the woman, but where she expected to see a glare she saw a different expression; shock.

"Wait, you want to go to Karlem right?" Ester asked.

The woman grumbled, balling up her fist. "Ja, I wanted to go to Weleaf locale."

"Weleaf is four stops west; we're heading east."

"Ja," The woman groaned in a language Ester could not understand.

Ester sighed. She felt a little bad for her. Ester knew all too well the frustration of getting on the wrong train. Ester opened her mouth to say something but remembered how rude she was. She called Ester nosey, so she was on her own in getting to whatever she wanted to go. The two rode in silence, but a pinch of guilt was nagging at Ester. She could almost feel the weight of Sister Genevieve's eyes on her. Why should she help someone who was rude to her, but the feeling in her heart was growing and sprouting into frustration.

"If you get off on Hiji," Ester said, "you can take the express back to our locale's station, but you have to take the super orange not the red-violet. The red-violet will take you four stops past it."

Ester turned to the woman, whose eyes were vacant and confused. Ester sighed. She really wanted to go to the game center today, but this woman looked completely lost.

"You have taken an express before?" Ester asked.

The woman shook her head then frowned.

"Um, okay, let's see. If you go to the ticket office, a worker should be able to explain the express lines to you. It does cost a little more, but it's faster than taking another regular train back. Where are you heading? Maybe I can help you because I know for a fact Weleaf has three in locale stops."

The woman looked tense as if she was lost in deep thought. "Perhaps I am mistaken."

Ester groaned. It didn't seem like she knew where she was going at all, and she was still a little pissed about how she acted before. "Okay, I don't know what's up with you, but if we're going to be on speaking terms, you can't snap like that."

The woman looked at Ester, then lowered her gaze. "I am sorry."

"It's okay, these train lines can be a real bitch. So, you're not heading to Weleaf?"

The woman shrugged as her frown deepened. The conductor announced the next stop.

"Alright, get off with me and we'll figure this out. Before we get off, can I at least get your name?"

The woman gave Ester a long hard look then her body relaxed a little. "My name? My name is Pisces."

Ester nodded. "Nice to meet you, Pisces. I'm Ester."

They got off on the Hiji stop and headed towards the arrival and departure board. Pisces could barely recall the name of the locale she was trying to go to. Ester sighed. This was going nowhere fast. She didn't want to go all the way back home, but she didn't want to abandon Pisces either.

"Hey, you wanna go to the game center with me?" Ester said, seeing how she was already lost. "I mean if you're not pressed to get to wherever you're going."

"Game center? What is a game center?"

Ester shrugged. "Don't know, never been, but I wanted to check it out today. After that, I can help you get home. I won't be long, I promise."

Pisces stood and thought for a second then turned to Ester and nodded. Ester was low key starting to get excited again.

"Sweet! Let's go." Ester waved Pisces along through the dense crowd.

Stepping outside of the underground train station, the Hiji locale was nothing like the South Mall area. A breath of fresh air hit Ester's nostrils as the breath-taking scenery took her by surprise. In the middle of a sea of shop fronts and restaurants sat a beautiful park. This must have been the one Sal was talking about. The mix of technology and nature reminded her of Tel-sa. Lush and green, the park was about ten times bigger than any park Ester had ever seen. Shops and restaurants lined the roads facing the park and on the edges of the park. On the sidewalks, street venders cooed visitors over with smells of freshly cooked food. Ester could feel her stomach growling, but she had already eaten and didn't want to spend any extra tones. She turned to Pisces, who seemed just as amazed, then looked around to try and find the game center. Ester looked for an on-street directory, but there didn't seem to be any. Then Pisces tapped Ester on the shoulder and pointed. Ester looked where she was pointing and gasped. Just on the other side of the park was a huge silver building illuminated in bright flashing rainbow colors. Even in broad daylight, it was vibrant. In the center a screen showed images of children running and playing and holding prizes. The screen flashed to a cute bear creature and a name flashed across the mega screen, Mr. Peter's Game Center. This looked like a place Angel would love. Ester turned to Pisces with a great big smile on her face and waved her reluctantly along.

Sal was not exaggerating when he said this place was loud. Ear shattering sound blared from the speakers the moment they walked in. Ester hopped out of the way of a stampede of children as she tried to make her way to the entrance booth. It did not cost anything to get in, but they needed to purchase special wristbands which would hold their in-game center money. A tiny complaint escaped Pisces' lips as she wondered why she needed to transfer currency just to play a game. Ester wondered the same thing but made a mental note to save extra tones because each game had its own price. Pisces stepped aside as couple slurping drinks walked by. She eyed them suspiciously. Ester noticed this and laughed. She had no idea why Pisces was so tense.

"So, where to first?" Ester said, this was more of a rhetorical question, everything looked amazing and a little strange too.

"I am not sure. I have not been in such a strange place." Pisces eyed the loud, flashing machines.

"Okay," Ester stood on her tippy toes. The room stretched for yards, and there appeared to be a second and third level.

Thank goodness she had all day to explore. She hoped Pisces didn't mind. Out of the corner of her eye, she spotted something bright pink and yellow. Ester saw an image of Allura dancing across the screen. He was one of Angel's favorite singers.

"Let's give that one a try." Ester pointed to the flashy booth. Pisces followed along, tensing up every time a child screamed or a machine went off.

The machine looked about as big as a closet. It was bright yellow with images of some of Rean's biggest super stars. Ester watched the screen; it looked pretty interesting.

"Want to try?" Ester said.

Pisces shrugged, and Ester took that as a yes and followed the diagram to pay for the game. The two stepped in, and to their surprise, it was painted to look like the inside of a closet.

"Welcome fashion lovers to Superstar Dress Up!"

The machine turned on, startling them both. The music started at near deafening levels as a hologram man dressed in a soft pink ride suit materialized next to them. Pisces jumped back, but Ester grabbed her so she wouldn't fall back.

"I'm Harris, and I'll be your make over artist for today. Please select your body type, gender, and skin color on the screen."

Ester and Pisces looked at her each, then Ester raised her hands to select the required information.

"Excellent!"

A near nude hologram projected on their bodies causing both girls to rush and hide their exposed bits.

"Wait, wait, wait, not cool." Ester squealed, but when she felt her real clothes underneath the hologram she started to calm down.

"What is this dark craft?" Pisces hissed.

"This game is taking this a little too seriously." Ester laughed nervously.

"Now that your preferences have been selected, let's get shopping!"

An Allura song started to play along with the music video. Both girls stared uncomfortably at Allura's revealing outfit. Ester sort of laughed as she started to make her selection through the clothes. Whatever she clicked on was projected onto her body. It was weird but kind of fun. Ester heard Pisces gasp and looked at what Pisces was staring at.

"Yup, that's a butt," Ester said as she watched Allura dance with his butt cheeks fully exposed.

"Has-has his outfit malfunctioned?" Pisces cringed.

"Nope, I think he just likes to wear clothes with his butt out. I have no idea why, but he's super popular in Ans-on."

Ester caught a glimpse of Pisces' face and laughed. Ester felt the same way when Angel was showing her clips of his concerts. The man was eccentric. They finished the game, and at the end, it produced a tiny bear shaped hologram projector that when turned on produced an image of Ester and Pisces in their outfits. It was a neat little souvenir. Ester and Pisces checked out the other games which varied from ones you can physically touch to games that were based in virtual reality. This place was pretty amazing, and Ester was sure she looked like one big child as she wondered around. Pisces cracked a small smile which didn't go unnoticed by Ester. She was glad Pisces was having a good time too.

"Hey, they have an anti-gravity machine on the third floor. You can see what it feels like to float in space." Ester flipped through the map on her wristband.

"Interesting," Pisces said as she looked over her shoulder.

"Your accent, I've never heard it before," Ester said. "Are you from Huma-ko?"

Pisces stared at her for a second. "Um, yes."

"Sorry, I'm being nosey again, but it kind of sounds similar to a boy I use to know. Sorry if I'm acting crazy. I'm from Adum-la originally, and we don't have anything like this back at home."

"I do not have this in my homeland as well," Pisces said as her shoulders relaxed.

Ester smiled. She was glad to see Pisces starting to relax.

"Hey, let's try this fighting game over there."

Pisces nodded, and the two walked over to the machine.

"Now this is more my style." Ester and Pisces were thrust into a battle where they were fighting an army of evil robots.

Pisces nodded as she flipped a virtual android over her shoulder and punched its lights out with the game controller.

"Wow, you're really good at this." Ester watched Pisces rack up points as she kicked and punched robots as if it were nothing.

Pisces tensed, but relaxed when she saw how mesmerized Ester looked. "Th-thank you."

The game flashed red, and the robots were homing in on their final attack as the big boss appeared. Ester and Pisces hopped into their fighting stance as the boss opened its mouth showing off its serrated rotating teeth. Ester tried hard to contain her laughter. She looked over at Pisces and the two exchanged a nod. It was like they were a real fighting team and Ester hoped this was the beginning of a new friendship.

Chapter Nineteen

Angel's call was brief. He said he couldn't say much but that it would soon be all over the news. He was calling to say that he couldn't visit and that didn't bother Ester as much as the worry in his voice. She shook it off and carried on with her day because she had to get ready for work. She was sure whatever it was, the rangers could handle it. As she left her apartment, she spotted Gar down the street. He was talking to a group of kids. He was smiling and laughing. She hoped her little pep talk helped. She knew all too well how temping it could be to give up. She smiled to herself and promised to check in on him more.

Traffic was good today. The trains weren't as crowded, but she could feel a tension in the air. People avoided eye contact and talked in hush tones, but she wasn't sure if it was just the news from Angel clouding her mind. Regardless, she got off at her stop and walked towards the exit of the train station. As she walked she noticed a large crowd of people standing in front of one of the holo screens. Their faces were of shock as some whispered and gasped, drawing their hands to their mouths. Curious, Ester walked over. She squeezed through and caught sight of the broadcast. It was the national news.

"Breaking news. People of Ans-on, there has been an assassination of one of the Grand Councilman of Kees. Intergalactic experts are saying this could lead to war. Evidence found at the scene points to foreigners. The Grand Council of Kees are halting all traffic on and off the planet. More on this developing story later."

The story ran again and ran on all the holo screens in the station. People dispersed, chatting amongst themselves as Ester continued to watch. Could this be the news Angel was talking about? The idea of a war between planets was unheard of. She walked outside of the train station and the story was running on all the screens around the mall too. She looked at them in passing. For once, this was one thing she was starting to dislike about Ans-on as she blocked out the noise and flashing images as she walked to work.

***

The rains started mid-shift, and this, coupled with the recent news, caused a lot of stands to close early. Ester worked hard during the morning hours and didn't mind staying, but business was slow—especially during the rainy season which officially marked the end of winter. Her boss let he go home early, saying he would not be able to pay her a full day's work if business was slow. She didn't mind though and walked away with fifty tones. Before she left the markets, she bought herself some fresh fish as a treat. The rains did not let up, and judging by the causal attitudes of the people on the streets, it would seem that Ans-on rains were a part of their natural history. They would likely be around for the next few weeks much to Ester's displeasure. She thought about stopping at the convenience store and picking up an umbrella but decided to save up to buy a rain shield instead. She'd seen a few people walking from the mall with tiny hovering devices that created a shield to block the rain much like an umbrella. She didn't need one, a regular umbrella would do, but they looked so cool, so it would be her treat. At the cost of one hundred and fifty tones, a full day and a half days' work she would have to be responsible and save. Since the rains weren't going anywhere anytime soon, she figured she had plenty of time.

Back in the lobby of her apartment, she shook the excess rain from her coat sleeves and stomped on the carpet rug to dry her boots. She took the stairs today and turned the corner to find small boxes of dry goods in a trail on the floor. She looked down the hall and picked one up, wondering who they belonged to.

"Oh dear, oh dear." Sal came running over. "I am forever sorry, I am."

He fretted as he took the box from Ester and continued to pick up his goods. He stuffed his arms till they were full and dropped more than he could carry on his way back to his apartment.

"Sal, let me give you a hand." Ester pulled out an extra bag she had with her and filled it with items.

"I am so sorry, Ester. I am so sorry," he repeated over and over again.

"It's okay, really. I don't mind," she kept explaining to him.

His normal smiling face was riddled with worry, and she wondered if it had something to do with the assassination. He walked the halls like a drunkard, stumbling from the hallway to his room.

"I am so terribly sorry, I am," Sal kept repeating.

"Sal." She grabbed his hand and held it. "It's okay."

He stopped moving long enough to force a fake smile, but his eyes gave him away. She thought she heard the sound of his stomach growl, and she looked down at his narrow waist.

"Have you had lunch?"

Sal's frown increased. "I don't want to cause you any trouble. You're home early; you must have something important to do." He started to fret again.

Ester shook her head. "Nope, not at all. All I have plans for is to fry these fish and eat them with my good friend, Sal." She handed him her bag with his dry goods in them. "I'm going back to my apartment to get some things and then I'm coming right back, okay?"

She said quickly and took off before Sal could protest. He was a good neighbor, and she hoped making a little meal would cheer him up. She returned and knocked on his door. Sal appeared looking guilty, but Ester ignored his look and walked right past him. His place was small, but cozy. Sparkling rocks hung on threads spun with shiny tinsel from the ceiling. Hand woven rugs lined the hard wood floors and giant seashell bowls filled of fruits and nuts sat on the tables. It smelled like the sea, and Ester loved it.

"Sal, your place is very nice," she said, as this was the first time she had ever gotten a good look around.

Sal followed her to the kitchen as he nervously rubbed his hands together. "Thank you, you are too kind." He tried to make himself look small, but he was too tall for that. "I hope the vandals who ruined your door were taken care of."

Ester nodded. "Yes, thank you for reporting them. It turns out it was one of the little boys from our apartment."

"Miss Tos' nephew." Sal sunk his headed lower when Ester looked at him.

She smiled. "He's a good kid. I'll make sure he won't cut up again."

Sal nodded, scratching his head. He sat antsy in one of his small kitchen chairs. "It's quite rainy today," Sal forced.

"It is." Ester prepped the fish to be fried. She brought over some potatoes as well.

She could tell Sal was still anxious about something, but she didn't want to bring it up. As she washed the vegetables in the sink, she noticed a picture hanging on the wall. It was a faded postcard of clear blue waters dotted with tall rocky peaks.

"Sal, is this where you're from?" She pointed.

Sal got up and squinted, then smiled, a real smile this time. "I am not. That is a location called The Teller. I visited there when I was a child." Sal started to frown again.

Ester noticed then perked up. "Is that so? Looks like a fun place."

"It was. Younglings go there for a thing called camp."

"Camp?"

Sal nodded. "Camps were and are still very popular on my home world. Younglings go to camp to learn how to levitate and fly and how to manage and control their telepathy."

Ester turned from the sink in interest. She had almost forgotten that telepathy and levitation were powers unique to Keesians. "Telepathy, that's like reading minds right?"

Sal laughed a little. "That is what popular media wants you to think, but it is a form of communication between our species. So, not as dramatic but still essential for all Keesians. Camps help you learn how to control it, but if not taught early you'll be pledged with sound noise."

"What's that?"

"Interference. If not properly dealt with, it can cause headaches," Sal said in a matter-of-fact tone.

"Ouch, that sounds bad." Ester seasoned the flour. "I heard about your home world today. I'm so sorry about what happened. If you need someone to talk to, I'm here." She turned to Sal.

She was sure that was the reason why he was so upset. She wanted to acknowledge it, and let him know that he had a friend if he needed someone to talk to. Sal's frown returned as he started to scratch at his arms again.

"I'm sorry, I didn't mean to upset you again," Ester said.

Sal looked up at her. His black round eyes looked like they were going to spill over with water. He mustered up a smile then wiped his face.

"You are too kind Ester, too kind."

Ester smiled. "How would you like your potatoes?"

"Any way you prepare them is satisfactory to me," he said with a real smile.

"Alright then." Ester smiled as she finished their lunch.

Sitting at Sal's table, Ester got a better chance to look around. There were so many types of rocks and shells scattered everywhere, but what really captured her attention was how deep and beautiful the colors were. He had shells so blue that they matched the sky, and rocks that looked as smooth as marble. The variety reminded her of the stones her tribe used to create. She turned to Sal. He was staring at her. She felt a little uneasy, but then she realized he wasn't looking at her but past her at the holo screen on the wall behind her. She turned around and saw the newscaster covering the events leading up to the assassination.

"Sal." She turned back to him and placed her hand on his. He looked away from the screen when he felt her hand on his.

"I am so sorry," Sal said. He looked worse.

"Don't be." Ester reassured him.

"I just cannot help but think of the gross ramifications a crime of this magnitude will sure to have on intergalactic relations."

Ester stopped eating and looked at Sal. "I'm sure they'll find the person and put them in jail, then it'll be over and done with you'll see."

"If only it were that simple," Sal said with a deep frown. "Perhaps if the murderer were from Fandour or dare I say Kees itself."

"Why Fandour?"

"Fandour is the planet of heathens, but despite its reputation, a lot of mercenaries come from Fandour. Even if the heathen was caught, it would only further complicate the situation."

Ester had to think about what Sal was saying. She wasn't quite grasping what he was getting at.

"Okay, so they'll find whoever hired them and throw them in jail too."

"If it is discovered that it was, in fact, a mercenary hired from Fandour and if that person who hired them is Labadoran it would cause intergalactic war."

Ester stared at Sal. Her knowledge on intergalactic history was shaky at best. She did know, however, that the people of Labadora were locked in a vicious civil war—but what that had to do with Kees she did not know.

"They couldn't go to war just like that? What if the bad guy was working alone?"

"It wouldn't matter," Sal said with a sunken face. "Relations around the galaxy involving Labadora are very poor, and it has been that way for many decades."

"Decades? I mean I know the planet is in turmoil, but could it be that bad?"

Sal nodded slowly as he picked at his food. "They do not share intergalactic news on your planet's surface eagerly. What is common knowledge on Kees is kept secret on Rean. I learned that right away, but if it is discovered that a mercenary and a native Labadoran is involved, it would spell disaster for our worlds."

Ester shared a sympathetic look. It wasn't that she didn't believe Sal or even that she didn't want to believe him, she was just shocked. Her galaxy could be on the brink of war, and what part would Rean play in it? Would Rean even offer to help? She finished up dinner and left Sal's place a few hours later. He thanked and thanked her and seemed in better spirits after her visit.

***

That evening the rains let up just for a few hours. She ran out to pick up a snack at the convenience store, but the streets still felt cold. Hushed chatter echoed in the shadows. Citizens closed their windows and doors. It was as if a storm was coming. She made it to the convenience store, maneuvering herself around the crowd of people. She picked up a sandwich from the shelf and overheard two men talking.

"This isn't looking too good," one man said as the other nodded.

"Word on the streets says it might be thugs from Fandour," the other whispered.

"I heard it was one of those monsters from Labadora. You heard what their leader is doing right?"

The other nodded. "A friend of mine working the trading post near Al-Tex Station said their new leader is a real monster."

Ester didn't linger any longer. She paid for her sandwich and headed back to her apartment. She remembered studying galactic relations back at ranger academy, but nothing that hinted things were this bad. She decided if she wanted more information, she needed it straight from the source. So, she decided to call Angel.

"Hey Ester, everything alright?" Angel said via video call.

It was really late when he returned her call. She would have thought he would be in bed by now. He looked a little disheveled, but otherwise the same bubbly ball of blond hair.

"I was about to ask you the same thing," Ester said.

Angel laughed a little as he took peeks between his table and his surroundings.

"Shouldn't it be lights out?"

Angel stared at Ester for a few moments as if he were trying to find the right words to say.

"Yeah, um, things are little weird right now, so we're having a few extra classes."

"Extra classes? Like what?"

Angel leaned into the screen. "I really can't say," he whispered.

He was definitely more tense than usual.

"Is it because of the assassination?"

Angel nodded.

"Is something bad going to happen? I mean they haven't found the killer yet?"

Angel looked around. "This isn't something I should be passing around, but I mean, I trust you. My parents say that the Grand Council of Kees suspect it's a Labadoran."

Ester swallowed hard. Sal had been right.

"But you gotta swear not to say anything. They are trying to keep it hush hush."

"But why? People need to know what's really going on."

"We're talking about like maybe a war, one where Rean would have to join."

Ester sat in silence for a few seconds. A war? Rean has never been involved in a war between other planets.

"And you think Rean will fight?"

Angel nodded. "Truth be told, relations with Labadora have been bad, like, really really bad for years. Mother and Father are worried this might end the Compus Treaty."

Ester's eyes widened. The Compus Treaty was the cornerstone of peace in their galaxy. Signed here on Rean decades ago, planets promised to keep an open channel of communication and transparency in intergalactic relations and to never attack or invade established planets or colonies.

"But still, it could have been someone with a grudge. They don't know for sure," Ester offered.

"Yeah, but people like to blame people they don't like when things go wrong and with no planet or group coming forth to claim responsibility, plus the weird circumstances."

"Circumstances?"

Angel averted his eyes. "Dang it."

"Angel, just tell me," Ester said, rolling her eyes.

"Ester, this is like some top secret shit, like top *top* secret. I'm not even supposed to tell anyone. I could get in big trouble; my parents could get in big trouble."

Ester stared at Angel in amusement as her little blue-eyed friend started to fret. "Okay, okay, I'm not going to push you. Thanks for the update. A lot of people are talking about it down here too, and they seem really worried."

Angel sighed. "It's just a big fat mess."

"Agreed."

In the background, Ester could hear a few announcements and strained to listen.

"Oh, gotta go." Angel waved.

"See ya." Ester said and waved back. The image disappeared.

She sat back on her couch and turned the volume up on the tele screen. All the news outlets were covering the story, but none mentioned anything about Labadora. She flipped and flipped until she found a news station broadcasting from Adum-la. They were covering the start of the fishing season in south Adum. She smiled and settled on watching that. It was just like Adum to be completely disconnected from time. She was sure her people didn't need one more thing to worry about with growing season coming up. But still, it was hard to believe that the planet she had looked at in the sky all her life could be the catalyst to intergalactic war. Ester shivered and decided to focus on the news broadcast from Adum. It was nice to dive back into the slow and easy pace of Adum life, even if only for an evening.

***

A week went by, and the tension on the streets started to subside. The story still blared all over the place, but at this point, it was pure speculation. She hadn't heard anything from Angel, but that wasn't uncommon. They could go weeks without talking to each other. What was strange though was that she hadn't seen Pisces around. She wasn't exactly sure which apartment she lived in, but then again she never really asked either. Next time she saw her she would try and get her contact information so they could hang out again. Ester returned to work as the crowds started to pick up in the markets again. It was blooming season, and Cha-la imports were flooding into the market.

She was excited to try some of the strange produce famous in the land of the monks.

Her day ended the same as always. She walked away with her hundred tones and decided to do a little shopping. Fish and pink corn were on the menu, and she couldn't wait to get home and bake the fish and fry the special berry flavored sweet corn. Just before she left the markets for the day, she stopped at a store in the shopping area and looked at a very nice purple and lavender ride suit. Purple was her favorite color, and she was starting to develop a taste for fashion. She walked closer and admired the fabric and stitching from the window. Her rent was due, meaning she would have to wait to purchase any new clothes, but that gave her something to look forward to after she bought her mini umbrella.

The clouds moved in, setting the stage for a little rain, but the newscaster said it should clear up by tonight. Either way, she didn't want to get caught in it. She hurried home and cooked dinner—which was very delicious—and spent the rest of the night straightening up and listening to music on the tele. The sun set, but the rain persisted which was no surprise to her. She lifted her blinds to dust and looked down at the streets. There was Chargie again out on the sidewalk. It was drizzling, but even though spring was right around the corner, it was still chilly. Chargie was an old fluffy dog, and he didn't need to be out in this rain. She closed her blinds and got her rain jacket. He usually followed her wherever she went, so it would take no time at all to go outside and get him. She took the stairs down the three flights and the doors slid open.

When she looked around, Chargie was nowhere to be found. She searched towards the convenient store—his favorite spot—but didn't see him. She looked the other way and saw a big blur of fluff. They two made eye contact and she held out her hand and called him, but he turned and walked the other way. Ester groaned. The rains were letting up, but it was getting dark. She would have to collect him quickly. She chased after him, but he disappeared in the crowd. At the corner of an intersection, she looked for him. Why of all nights did he choose to play hide and seek? She saw what she thought was a tail a few blocks away and ran towards it. She rarely came this way. There wasn't much back here except the entrance to a parking garage and a bar or two.

"Chargie?" She called, then saw his big white head in the ally of one of the bars. Ester rolled her eyes.

"Is your owner in there or are you just skirt chasing?" She walked over to him and pet him with both hands. He barked and shook the rain from his fur. "Okay, I'll check, but I don't think they allow dogs in here."

She took her first step, and Chargie walked right in beside her. He took a few steps then looked back at her, just like before. Ester shook her head and smiled and followed him into the bar. The place was grimy, much like the rest of the city, but it was lively with people talking and playing slot machines. No one seemed to mind a dog and a girl walking in. Not that Ester wasn't allowed in bars. She was of age, but she was sure a big white dog would turn some heads. Most people just looked up and smiled as if it was common place.

The bartender called Chargie's name and waved a piece of meat over the bar. Chargie's tail slow wagged as the old dog took his treat. The bartender looked up at Ester and smiled, as if he was aware of Chargie's skirt chasing habits. Ester smiled back and continued to follow Chargie to the back. Past the chattering people and flashy machines, Chargie entered a hallway through a beaded curtain. Ester stopped. It was a little odd to her, but she guessed if Chargie was heading back there it was okay. Pass the beaded curtain was a series of rooms, some looked like bathrooms, maybe a janitor closet, and an office. It wasn't well lit, but there was definitely something towards the back as she noticed the faint red light. As she got closer, she heard voices.

She heard InyOuty greet his dog.

"Chargie."

"What is that mongrel?"

Ester heard a familiar voice and stopped.

InyOuty laughed. "Some would say the same of your beast."

There was silence.

"So will you help me? I do not have much time."

Ester heard InyOuty sigh and inched a little closer.

"I am but an old man now. There is little I can do."

There was a slam of hands on the table making Ester jump.

"I will not accept that! My mission is of the up most importance, and time is running out."

Ester stood with her back facing the wall. Who was InyOuty talking too?

"Shh shh, I know, but quiet down. Someone might hear you."

"I am sorry. I have traveled a long way from my home planet to find you Captain Applecom."

"Are you positive of the attack?"

"They are on route to Rean as we speak."

That's when Ester recognized the voice and barged into the room. Two faces stood in shock: one she recognized, and the other was a lean muscular creature with short dark midnight blue fur and onyx horns curled on her head. Ester stumbled back. She was wearing Pisces' clothes, but this couldn't be her. The creature before her was Labadoran.

Chapter Twenty

"Wait a minute, I know you," Ester said as she stepped closer. "Pisces?"

The air was tense as Ester looked between InyOuty and Pisces. What was Pisces doing here, and why did she look like that? Ester's mind raced. How did she know InyOuty? And an attack? What could she possibly mean by that? Meanwhile, Pisces cursed in a language Ester was unfamiliar with.

"I don't have time for this," Pisces growled.

InyOuty looked surprised, but Pisces only got angrier as she stared down Ester.

"This does not concern you," Pisces barked coldly.

"Excuse me?" Ester said.

Ester could feel her blood begin to boil. This woman, this Labadoran, was talking about a possible attack on her planet and had the gall to say that it wasn't any of Ester's business. She was tired of her secrets.

"Like hell it does!" Sparks spit from Ester's fingers.

Chargie barked as the two women looked like they were about to tear each other apart. InyOuty sighed. Things were becoming more complicated now. Chargie growled, breaking the silence.

"That's enough!" InyOuty raised his voice as he reached down to pet his dog. "Hush, hush, boy. I've got it."

"InyOuty, what's going on?" Ester said, looking into his eyes.

InyOuty pressed two fingers to the side of his head and winced.

"Calm down, you two." InyOuty took a deep breath. "Ester, I was not expecting you. How are you?"

Pisces growled. "Why are we wasting time? Has my message not convinced you?"

"Be quiet." InyOuty's words cut through Pisces' anger. "Ester this is Pisces, a member of the Unity Reform from her home planet of Labadora."

Pisces hissed, but Ester ignored her.

"Labadora? What's she doing here?" Ester said

Pisces silently stormed to the other side of the small room. "If you are not able to help me, I will find help elsewhere."

Chargie whined. "Easy." He petted his dog. "I did not say that I would not help you I said that I am an old man. But I may know of a retired ranger that maybe up for the job, but you are responsible for convincing him."

Ester couldn't believe what she was hearing. The word 'attack' rang in her ears and the weight of Sal's words turned her stomach into knots.

"InyOuty, someone please tell me what the heck is going on!" She started to panic.

InyOuty took a long and hard sigh. "You would be better off not knowing. Now, it's time for you to go."

"Bullshit. I will not go. This is my planet, my home. If someone is going to attack, it I want to know! I have friends in ranger academy. I even know someone who could talk to a civil councilor. Maybe if we tell them now, the rangers would be ready for the attack…"

Pisces' silver blue eyes glossed over. "It is no use," she interrupted.

"Have you tried?" Ester said.

Pisces grunted. "Your planet is on no terms to speak with me. They will not take my warnings to heart and attack fool heartedly. Without the right insight and knowledge, their attempts will fail."

"Then you can just give it to them."

"Weeks,"—Pisces slammed her hands on the table—"Months, *years* went into the planning of this take down! It is not something you can learn in a matter of days."

"Come now." InyOuty stood; he had heard enough. "I will give you what you seek, but you must go quick." InyOuty stood from his chair and walked over to a tweed bound book and opened it. "He lives in Cha-la, in the Furthert Locale. His name is Wildgrass Inspread. Tell him InyOuty sent you." InyOuty's eyes glared when he handed Pisces the address. "Do not lie to me, child. A great deal of lives are on the line, and I am extending my trust only because the stakes are too high not to."

Pisces took the note and bowed. "Then from the core of the Unity Reform under our great leader, Jordain, I will not let you down."

She turned and started to leave, but Ester blocked her exit. She was very familiar with the renegade ranger, Captain Wildgrass Inspread. He was her hero and currently the strongest man alive on the planet. If Pisces was up to no good, this could be a real danger for Rean. They couldn't risk losing their strongest warrior.

"I'm going with you." Ester glared.

"Ester, no," InyOuty protested, "it is too dangerous."

A blaze set behind Ester's deep brown eyes. She ignored him and focused on Pisces. "InyOuty may trust you, but you have not won my trust yet."

Pisces glared at both of them. She had already made the mistake of allowing someone to overhear her conversation. If she let Ester stay here, it could ruin her plan if she ran her mouth.

"Do as you please, but I am not responsible for your death." Pisces pushed past Ester and exited down the hall.

The old man frowned. This was not how he wanted this to go. He sat back down in his chair and rubbed the bridge of his nose. "Ester, I cannot allow you to go."

"It's okay, I can make sure she sticks to the plan," Ester said, even though she had no idea what the plan was.

"This isn't a game, Ester."

"I know, but something in my heart wants me to watch over her closely. I don't know how to explain it, but the electricity coursing through my veins tells me that this is the right thing to do."

InyOuty resisted the urge to sigh. He was all too familiar with the look in Ester's eyes. Young, driven, and foolish, he knew at this point there was little he could do to stop her. His old dog panted with his tongue out and looked up at him.

"Alright," InyOuty said. He rushed to scribble an address on a piece of paper for Ester and handed it to her. "This is the address to the garage I sent Pisces. I'll phone my old friend and tell him that there will be two making the trip, but you must hurry. She leaves at sun rise."

"Thank you! I won't let you down." Ester bounced on her heels and ran out.

InyOuty collapsed in his chair. "You better know what you're doing," He said to his dog, who barked by his side.

***

Ester rushed to catch up with Pisces. She didn't know what to think or do, so she just ran as fast as she could. There was going to be an attack on Rean. Should she call Angel? Could she trust a Labadoran? Her mind was flooded with questions. She ran down the street but couldn't find Pisces anywhere. InyOuty had given her the address of where Pisces was heading, but who's to say Pisces would follow through when she already knew where Wildgrass lived. Her heart jumped a beat. This road was taking her to Captain Wildgrass Inspread, her hero and idol. She wanted to enjoy this moment, but her mind was being taken over by images of Pisces trying to kill him. She couldn't let that happen.

The sliding doors of her apartment opened, and Ester headed straight for the stairs. She knew Pisces lived somewhere on the second floor, but she wasn't sure which room. She ran up the stairs and flung open the door and looked down the dank poorly lit halls. Ester clenched her fist. There were so many rooms. She couldn't search them all. Ester heard a door close and ran towards the sound. She looked at each door for any sign of identification, but it was useless in this rundown slum. She rounded a corner, and saw a man with a cigarette hanging from his lips. He looked up at her then went back to locking his door. *Shit.* Ester looked in the opposite direction. Pisces might as well be gone by now. She couldn't imagine her packing many things, so Ester decided to take a chance and try to catch Pisces at the garage.

Ester raided her closet and pulled out a dark royal purple ride suit and stuffed it in a bag. She ran to the kitchen and threw in a few meal bars and fruits. Her heart was racing; a voice in the back of her head begged her to call Angel. He would know what to do. He had all the connections, but she pushed that aside in a rush to pack. She ran to the bathroom and grabbed her tooth brush and soap then looked at them like they were offensive objects that had just slandered her name. She wasn't going on some vacation; she was following a possible assassin to her idol's house. She was way in over her head, and she knew it. Back in the den, she passed the large white hologram phone Angel had given her. It wasn't too late. She could still call Angel and warn him, but what then? Would the rangers descend on her apartment and capture Pisces? What if Pisces was right? What if this was the only way? Ester hollered in frustration, grabbed her bag, and was out the door, locking it behind her. Ester rushed to the stairs when she heard someone call her name. She spun around, thinking it was Pisces.

"Sal!" Ester forced a smile. He looked like he had just come from the convenience store.

"It is good to see you," he said as he noticed her bag. "Oh, my apologies. Am I keeping you?" Sal forced one of his big famous smiles.

"It's no biggie." Ester bit her lip. "I'm just going on a little trip."

"How lovely." Sal beamed. "If you have a visitor, should I tell them where you are?"

Ester thought for a second, "Sal, you remember the little blond boy?"

Sal thought for a second, then his face lit up again. "Yes, the little boy made of sunshine."

"Yes, his name is Angel Johnson. If he and only he comes looking for me, tell him I went to Cha-la for vacation, and that I'll be back soon."

"Cha-la for vacation, him only him. Angel Johnson, got it." Sal clasped his hands together.

"Thank you, Sal," Ester said as if this would be the last time she would see him.

"Enjoy your vacation." Sal stood at the top of the stairs as he watched Ester disappear around the corner.

She was actually relieved that she ran into Sal. She knew she could trust him to relay the message, plus she had her wristband, so she could call Angel at any time. That was her backup plan just in case anything went wrong.

The address InyOuty gave her to the garage was 2121 Fertlane Drive, but Ester had no idea where that was. She stood outside of her apartment complex and looked up and down the street. She looked at her wristband. It was twenty-two hundred hours. She had time, but not enough time to get lost. She ran to the convenience store, a place she knew she could ask for help. Her boots splashed in the puddles left by the rain as she pulled her windbreaker around her. The store was empty, much to her relief, as she ran past the shelves towards the counter. This time, the clerk was a young guy around her age that reeked of cigarettes.

"Do you sell digi-maps of this locale here?" she asked, out of breath.

The man sort of grinned as his gaze followed up and down Ester's body. "Where you headed? Maybe I can give you directions?"

Ester looked repulsed. "I'll take the map. Thank you."

The man grinned and folded his arms and leaned back. "And where's a pretty girl like you going this late at night?"

Ester did not have time for this. She reached over the counter and grabbed him by the shirt, nearly pulling him over the edge. "I'm in a hurry. You gonna sell me the map or what?"

She held him there as the man squirmed under her grip. He nodded, and she released him and he stumbled back

"Five tones."

Ester handed the man the money and took the map, rushing from the store out into the streets. She stood against a wall as she tore open the package, hoping the map would be easy to read. When she looked at it, she breathed a sigh of relief that it was similar to the map she had received from ranger academy. She scanned the chip over her wristband, and the map started to download. She pulled at the little curls on the back of her neck as she waited for the map to load, forcing a smile at the people passing her by. Then a hologram projection appeared showing her a layout of her locale.

"Okay, okay, where are you?" She looked around the map.

Her locale was a lot bigger than she thought, and she had no idea where to start. The last map she used the destination was already mapped for her. She looked at the box for directions, but there were none. She groaned. It would seem that the projection was just a basic map and not a step-by-step locator. Staring at the map, she scanned the streets for anything that looked familiar. She searched for her street or the underground train station, anything that would give her a starting point. Zooming in and out, she found something unexpected: the park. She knew that wasn't from here. That would give her a starting point. If she wanted to find a garage, more than likely there would be other garages around it. She searched the map for large similar shaped buildings. Then read through the streets when she found an area that looked like it could be garages: Hundoak, Camlan, Harvlane, Fertlane. Ester's eyes popped open. There it was, but it was located on the edge of her locale, meaning it would take her some time to get there. Ester looked down the street as the wind picked up. The temperature was dropping as if it were telling her to turn back, but it was a little too late for that. Ester swallowed hard and zipped up her windbreaker. Her planet needed her, and she wasn't going to turn back so easily.

Chapter Twenty-One

The warehouse district was large and confusing. The street sign for Fertlane had fallen down, which added nothing by time to her search. After about an hour of circling around, she finally found the place—a rundown building that looked like it was a violation away from being condemned. She stood at the door as the drizzle floated through the air. A dim yellow-orange light glowed against the scratched-up door of 2121 Fertlane drive. She took a deep breath and reached out to knock and it opened just as her fist was inches away. A tall skinny man with blue highlighted hair in a dirty t-shirt and jeans looked down at her.

"Ester?"

Ester nodded.

"Didn't think you were coming." The middle-aged man said with a smile, as he chucked a handful of seeds he pulled from his pocket.

She walked in from out of the rain and jumped when the door slammed loudly behind her. She winced, but the guy didn't seem phased at all. She followed him through the warehouse filled with dozens of different types of hover cars and jetters. He led her to an office on the other side of the show room.

"I'm Vertin by the way," the man introduced himself. "I gotta say, I haven't gotten a call from old InyOuty in a long time." The man moved around the office. "You don't need a digi-id do you?"

Ester shook her head.

"Thought so, but yeah, he was a friend of my old man." Vertin pulled out some more seeds and ate them. "Well, I'm not one to get in others business, but I wish you luck. Your jetter will be ready in a few hours. Traffic is low around dawn on the south tunnel out of the city. That's your best shot of getting out the quickest. Make yourself at home."

Vertin disappeared from the office leaving Ester there standing around. Ester looked around the small office. On the walls were old pictures of hover cars and jetters throughout the ages. Calendars and work sheets littered Vertin's desk, dotted with seeds. She turned around and saw a round table full of papers, weapons, maps, and other supplies, only adding more to the gravity of the situation. If she was being honest with herself, she didn't belong here. Maybe she jumped the gun a little. Maybe she should have let Angel and the other rangers handle this. After all, it was their job. She looked back at the clock. It was twenty-two thirty-five hundred hours, so she still had about eight hours or so until the sun rose. But first she needed to find Pisces. Ester sat her bag on one of the chairs that lined the walls and peaked out the office window into the show room. She saw Vertin, but no sign of Pisces anywhere. She doubted she got here before Pisces, but then again Pisces wasn't exactly the best at following directions. Ester paced the room. She could sneak out into the show room and look, but what if Pisces came back and sabotaged things somehow? After all, on the table were all the maps and most importantly weapons. She was at a loss of what to do until she heard voices behind the office door.

"Glad you could make it." She heard the soft causal voice of Vertin.

The door opened, and the same young woman Ester had seen at the market walked through the door. It was Pisces, but in her Reanian form. Vertin told her he would have her digi-id ready soon. He gave her the same run down as he had given Ester just moments before. Pisces nodded, but tensed when she saw Ester. It was just them now as Vertin left and went back to work.

"I see you made it," Ester said, but Pisces ignored her as she walked to the opposite side of the room and sat her things down. "And look you're wearing your little costume. Do you honestly think you can get away with this?"

"I have nothing to say to you," Pisces hissed.

"Fine, but I'm going to be keeping a sharp eye on you," Ester said as she sat on the other side.

The two sat in silence. It was dead quiet in the office. Only a few faint sounds of shop work could be heard in the background. Ester struggled the stay awake. The hum of the florescent lights was like a lullaby, and her body was threating sleep paralysis if she did not succumb to its needs. She couldn't let Pisces out of her sight, but if she stayed up all night she would be useless in watching her. Ester glanced over at her with tired watery eyes. It didn't look like Pisces even cared that Ester was there. Ester griped the bottom of her chair; she wanted to be mad, but she was too tired. She needed her rest, so she allowed herself to nap.

***

A rough push on her shoulder woke her. Ester startled awake only to find the piercing silver-blue eyes of Pisces looking down at her. Ester tensed immediately, but Pisces only glared. Pisces turned and left the office without uttering a word. What was her deal? Ester growled as she got herself together. Her eyes were still heavy with sleep, but her heart was pounding back to life. Pisces was really starting to get on her nerves. Ester looked at the clock, it was a zero five thirty-five hundred hours. She looked at the table; all the things on it the night before were gone, presumably packed. Ester muffled a yawn with her forearm and got up and stretched. She grabbed her bag and hurried into the shop area. Vertin was waiting for her. His face was tired, but his eyes said he could continue on like this for hours. In front of him stood a three-speed hover jetter, one of the fastest hover bikes on the planet. Ester gasped; she had only seen them on the tele.

"This should get you to where you're going in two and a half days if you're careful with your breaks," Vertin said, wiping his greasy hands off with a rag. "Don't take the main road. It's blooming season and there'll be too much traffic,"

He instructed as he put their bags in one of the side compartments.

"Here's a map. It should lead you to where you want to go. I'll get your helmets. They're not advanced or anything, but they'll protect your head."

Vertin walked away leaving Ester and Pisces alone.

"I still don't trust you," Ester said.

"I do not care," Pisces replied coldly.

Vertin returned with their helmets.

"Here and this is for you." He handed Pisces her digi-id. Pisces held it in her hands. It looked just like the real thing. "Keep your helmets on, act like you're just any other couple."

"Couple?" They both said in unison.

Vertin cracked a smile. "Easy, there's no deadline to returning the bike, just take care of it."

Both girls looked at each other in disgust but walked towards the bike. Pisces took the front, but Ester blocked her.

"Hey, how come you get to drive?"

"Have you driven a motor bike before?" Pisces cut Ester a sharp look.

"Have you?" Ester bit back.

Pisces rolled her eyes. "You may be native to this world, but you are still just a naïve child. I have far more experience than you, and you coming along will only hold me back."

Pisces pushed Ester out of the way and mounted the bike. Ester scoffed but swallowed her pride. A fight here would solve nothing. Her job was make sure Pisces didn't do anything to Captain Wildgrass.

"Oh, you're not getting rid of me that easy. I don't give a rat's ass about your experience. Like it or not, we're in this together." Ester put on her helmet and hopped on the back of the bike.

Pisces said something under her breath in a language Ester didn't understand and adjusted the settings. Pisces revved up the bike, and before Ester had a chance to get settled, she took off. Ester yelped as the two sped away. Vertin chuckled and shook his head and hit the button the close the garage door.

Ester held on tight as Pisces sped down the road. She navigated the streets with ease thanks to the map Vertin gave her that projected the path on the road made visible by their helmets. Buildings and people whizzed by as they ascended into the air. Pisces was really good at this, which made Ester wonder about her experience. What kinds of things did Pisces know? In her Reanian form, she didn't look much older than Ester, but she really didn't know a lot about her. In the wee hours of the sixth day of the week, traffic was nonexistent just like Vertin said. After all, it was a non-business day for many of the people in Ans-on. Ester's jacket flapped around her as they cruised above the city. She felt like a bird in the sky. This was an experience Ester had only dreamed about. It was bittersweet given the circumstances, but she couldn't help but allow herself to enjoy it if just for a little bit.

They arrived at the express tunnel leading to the south western part of Ans-on. Ester tensed when they arrived at the checkpoint. In the checkpoint office, a worker yawned as he read from his tablet. Pisces slowed to scan her digi-id loaded with her express pass as Ester watched the man. He didn't even look at them as the light turned green, and Pisces took off again into the tunnel. Ester gasped when they entered. It was breathtaking, shiny, and marbled white with green lights dotting the tunnel walls in blurred green streaks. Loud swooshing sounds buzzed over Ester's head as hover cars zoomed by. Ester unconsciously grabbed Pisces tighter, making Pisces roll her eyes. Ester couldn't help but be mesmerized by surrealism; she looked over at a pair riding an older model bike. It was a polished black with sleek silver lines outlining the body. It was an old Henderson model, one that was still very popular back home. It was cool to see one in such good condition. The pair took a hard right and exited down another tunnel. Ester felt Pisces pull left, they were coming up to their exit.

They came out and were now in the south western part of Ans-on. There were less taller buildings in this part of the state, reminding her a little of the towns around the markets of Tel-sa. Up ahead, Ester could see the final checkpoint, the one that would take them out of Ans-on. She was a little nervous about this one; she could even feel Pisces tense a little. This early in the morning there was little outgoing traffic. On the ground, Ester could see dozens of hover carts, no doubt importing goods from Who-da and Cha-la. Pisces descended to fall into line behind the cars exiting the metropolis.

"Take out your digi-id," Pisces said barely looking back.

Ester fumbled around for her id. She remembered going through this checkpoint the first time she entered Ans-on, but this time she wasn't at the train station. The checkpoint official waved them forward. He was a dark skin man with short blond hair and a round belly. He put up his hand to stop them and signaled for them to lift their helmets.

"Morning, ladies," The man said with a smile. "You gals sure are up early."

Pisces forced a smile, as Ester laughed nervously.

"Just heading out for a day trip," Ester said as she handed the man her id.

"Oh, I see," The man winked. He scanned both their ids, lifting them up to make sure the picture matched what they looked like. "Well, if you're heading to Promvo, there is a nice little restaurant that has the best roasted goat." He handed them back their ids.

"Thanks." Ester forced a smile as the checkpoint official waved them on.

Pisces took her id as well and put her helmet back on. Ester quickly did the same knowing that Pisces would not waste any time. They flew by the final checkpoint, and Ester breathed a sigh of relief looking back. They had finally arrived in Who-da, known as the birth place of all life on Rean. They cruised down the winding dirt roads for miles. It was a beautiful country. There was nothing but wide-open land for miles, dotted with small villages and fields of grazing cattle.

The two traveled all day, stopping only to eat. The sun was setting as Pisces started to slow down. They approached a wooded area, and Ester wondered if they would be camping here for the night. The hover jetter slowed to a crawl, and Pisces nodded for Ester to get off. She did, and Pisces started to pull away.

"Hey!" Ester yelled.

Pisces moved the hover jetter off the road and turned it off. Pisces took off her helmet and shook her dark midnight blue hair.

"If I wanted to leave you, I would have dumped you off on the first stop." Her piercing silver-blue eyes infuriated Ester.

Pisces parked the bike behind a tree and started to take out her things. Ester stormed over and slammed the compartment close.

"You know what, I'm getting real tired of your shit."

"Then leave then! Nobody asked you to come along."

"Right, so I'm supposed to ignore this big attack and trust you, someone who wears a disguise to trick everyone?"

"Ja!" Pisces screamed. "This is so much bigger than you. I am trying to save your stupid little planet and countless others!"

"Oh right, and I'm supposed to believe that? I barely understand this plan of yours, and what do you think others will think if you don't even trust them enough to explain?"

Pisces cursed and walked away, grabbing her bag to set up her tent. Ester rolled her eyes and grabbed her bag as well, slamming the door on the bike's compartment. All this yelling was getting her nowhere. What would Angel do? Ester took a deep breath and exhaled.

"Look," Ester said as she dropped her bag next to Pisces. "I'm not trying to give you a lot of flak. I'm just...I'm just scared."

Pisces stopped what she was doing.

"Okay, so maybe I jumped the gun by trying to muscle my way in on your mission, but I really do want to help. I just need to know what's going on."

Pisces took a deep sigh, revealing any part of her plan could jeopardize the mission, but ditching Ester could cause more problems.

"Promise me, promise me you won't leak a word."

"I promise."

Pisces studied her eyes. She was taking a big risk; her shoulders relaxed as she sighed. She stood and wiped the dirt from her pants.

"There is nothing I can offer you as proof, but as we speak, three Labadoran battleships under the command of General Tozork are heading this way."

"Tozork? Who the hell is that?"

"A vile evil man, driven by his lust for blood and power. Our planet has been locked in a vicious civil war for decades and there have been many warlords during this time trying to stake their clam over my homeland. But four seasons ago, General Tozork suddenly rose to power, wiping out whole armies and tribes, including mine."

Ester's eye's widened. She was no stranger to the pain of losing family. She sat as Pisces continued to set up their tent.

"But Commander Jordain stood against him. He united tribes all over the planet to try and stop him, but Tozork was too powerful. He enslaved thousands to build warships and has now set his sights on conquering other plants. Commander Jordain and the Unity Reform want to stop him, however, we don't know how Tozork became so powerful so quickly. He somehow developed a new weapon in secret. All we have are basic blueprints of the layout. We know very little about how it works, but we have seen enough of its power to know that General Tozork must be stopped."

"So, is that why they picked you to come here and stop him?"

"I volunteered, and yes, I am here to stop him. But since our worlds are on such bad terms, it was a very perilous journey trying to come here. And I have experienced further delays in locating Captain Applecom."

"Dang, sounds rough," Ester said as she reached in her bag and offered Pisces an apple.

Pisces eyed the fruit, but her stomach made the decision for her.

"Thank you."

Ester nodded and pulled out another apple. "Well, this Tozork guy sounds like a real pig."

"Pig?"

"It's like a fat round animal that rolls around in the mud."

"Ah, we have an animal similar to that on my world, but it is called a boar. They are as big as your hover cars and have long curved pointed tusk. They too enjoy the act of rolling in the mud."

"Wow, there are animals as big as hover cars on your planet?"

"Yes, all the animals on my world are large."

"That's so cool!" Ester's face lit up.

Pisces was not expecting Ester to be so interested. For so long Pisces was used to hearing the snide comments of others about Labadora and its culture; she thought no one would be interested in them. Pisces lightened up a bit and continued on with her story. As the night moved on, the two settled in their tent. Pisces had to admit she liked it on Rean, but she missed her home world very much. She hoped that her plan would be a success, so she could help restore it to its formal glory and maybe one day, she could show Ester just how great it was.

Chapter Twenty-Two

Sergeant Chi Vellumee sat at his desk re-playing one of the distress calls sent to him from one of the orbiting stations not far from Labadora. It was hard to make out what was being said. Each of the distress calls he had listened to were muffled and cut off abruptly as if some force had plucked them from the universe. He had been sent three so far from stations anchored near Labadora. He sent replies to the captains aboard the orbiting stations above Rean to continue monitoring the situation, but the mysterious circumstances raised alarms in his head. Sergeant Vellumee sighed and pushed away the tab containing the messages. He had a lot of paperwork to take care of and little time to dwell on the matter. He started to open a file when Sergeant Li-san Moore appeared at his door.

"There has been a meeting called," Sergeant Moore said with an uneasy coldness in her voice.

"Right." Sergeant Vellumee stood and logged out of his station.

The two hurried to the board room to meet with Assistant Director Collin Vibes of Ranger Academy and all three Grand Commanders of the Rean Coalition of Rangers. Sergeant Vellumee's gut instinct was right in that there was definitely something suspicious surrounding the distress signals they were receiving, after reading through the meeting notes on his wristband. He brought his colleague Sergeant Moore up to speed, on what he knew, as they walked to the board room ready to be briefed.

"Welcome Sergeant Moore, Sergeant Vellumee." The Assistant Director stood and nodded towards them. "I won't waste your time and get straight to the point." He pulled up a hologram, which showed a map of all the active stations from Rean to Labadora.

"Captains on research stations and ships are reporting a loss of communication from the following five stations."

"Five?" Sergeant Vellumee interrupted. "I thought there were only three reports of communication lost?"

Assistant Director Vibes nodded. "And you would be correct, if you were only counting ranger affiliated stations. Two outpost stations, Station K, a small private research station, and Station 43-07, a pit stop station, are now labelled inactive by their parent overseers." Vibes used his hands to zoom in on the map and drew a red line. "Why these stations, and not other more valuable stations, have been targeted is unknown. However, the path is clear. Each of these stations fall in the path of a line, one that leads directly to Rean."

The room drew quiet. Then Grand Commander Heaven Sanders cleared her throat. "Can we get a visual on any object heading our way?" She spoke in a regal but calm manner.

"We are having trouble relaying images; there seems to be some kind of interference and no ship can get close enough without disappearing." Assistant Director Vibes turned and faced her.

Grand Commander Sanders raised her hand to her thick lensed glasses and pulled them up the bridge of her nose. Without saying anything, she relayed a look of uneasiness. "Raise the base and school to high alert standby."

Grand Commander Calvin Xills looked at his senior commander tensely. "Is that really necessary Grand Commander? We do not have all the details. Raising levels to high alert standby might be too much."

Everyone in the room looked at Grand Commander Sanders, but nothing changed in her stoic demeanor. Grand Commander Xills sighed and nodded to Sergeant Moore and Sergeant Vellumee.

"I second then," Grand Commander Xills said.

"I third," Grand Commander J'Chives added. "It would not hurt to raise defense levels just in case."

With all in agreement, the sergeants were dismissed. Sergeant Moore and Sergeant Vellumee headed back to their offices with a feeling of uneasiness on their shoulders. Tension was building in the air, and they hoped nothing serious would come of it. If so, Rean was ready to fight, but if they could avoid it that would be a much better outcome for the peaceful and unknowing people of Rean.

Chapter Twenty-Three

Ester and Pisces left in the wee hours of the morning just after the dew settled on the leaves. They were only a day and a half from Cha-la. Ester road on the back of the jetter, but this time she didn't mind. She was more comfortable now knowing what was at stake. As Pisces speed down the dirt road, Ester thought about her friends. If this didn't work, what would that mean for them? The thought of the rangers losing seemed unreal. And what if Captain Wildgrass didn't want to help, or worse what if he wasn't able to like InyOuty? All these questions started to weigh heavily on her mind. She shook those thoughts from her head as she looked ahead. She hoped her boss wouldn't be too mad that she was missing work. Then again with a looming attack, who knew if there was going to be a job to come back to?

As the sun trekked across the sky, neither had wanted to stop and eat, but now it was well into the afternoon, and they were starting to pay the price of their skipped meal. They were coming up on the outskirts of a small village town. Ester spotted a caravan and asked Pisces if they could stop. It would be faster to eat somewhere outside of town to avoid the crowds. Pisces agreed and slowed to a stop and turned off the bike. Ester took off her helmet and breathed in the fresh air.

"Something smells good." Ester looked around. She wouldn't be surprised if this entire place was run by one family or two. Ester looked back at Pisces. She looked wary. "It's okay, I've been to places like this before. They have them back in my home state."

Pisces cut her a look, but her stomach didn't seem to care either way. Ester smiled and headed straight for the tent with Pisces not far behind. Hanging in the back, Pisces eyed every face, making sure to keep them at a comfortable distance.

Despite it being around lunch time, there were very little people here. A few faces eyed the pair, but none seemed to care. Ester walked up to the seller and looked over their menu. It was in a language she did not know, but the seller greeted them right away.

"Chup!" A woman with long dark brown wavy hair waved to them.

"Hi, um what's on your menu?" Ester asked, hoping the woman could understand her.

"Ah, oh! Ans-on? You from Ans-on?" The woman pointed in a thick accent.

"Yes," Ester said.

"Yes, hold on." The woman disappeared, and a tall, older man with gray hair replaced her.

"Welcome travelers to Hy's Food and Mead. On our menu we offer stir fried goat and vegetables, baked and fried sweets, along with our sweet mead."

Ester rubbed her hands together. She loved stir fried goat. She turned to Pisces. "Do you like goat?"

"G-goat?" Pisces shook her head as if she did not understand.

"It's good. Trust me." Ester turned to the man. "Can we get two orders of goat and veggies, water please, and what kind of sweets to you have?"

"Only the best sugar powdered bread." The man reached behind the counter and offered them a sample.

Ester gladly plucked two from the plate and offered one to Pisces. "Here."

Pisces pulled her hand back, but Ester would not take no for an answer. When Ester took a bite of hers and looked like she was in absolute bliss, Pisces inched forward. Pisces took her donut ball, still warm from the fryer and eyed it in discontent. She lifted it to her nose to smell and was captured by its sweet honey scent. She took a bite and made a face. The texture was foreign to her, but the taste was magical.

"You like, yes?" The man behind the counter said with a great big smile.

Pisces nodded and popped the entire thing in her mouth. Ester laughed and paid for their meal. They found a place to sit on the edge of the establishment. Kids ran around in the fields as the adults tended to their goats. In a matter of minutes, their food was brought to them by the woman they saw before.

"Thank you," Ester said as she started to scarf down the food. "Oh my gosh, this is amazing!"

Pisces cringed at Ester's manners then looked down at her own meal. It didn't smell as good as Ester led her to believe, but food for her had been very sparse over the past few weeks. She picked at a chunk of meat with her fork and brought it to her mouth.

"It's not going to bite you," Ester mumbled around her food.

"I am aware the creature in this food will not attack me." Pisces looked at the offensive piece of meat. "It is just not my taste."

"Well, it's either this or a meal bar."

Pisces frowned even more. She brought the piece of meat to her lips and opened her mouth. Ester watched as she chewed and waited patiently to see what she thought of it.

"Well?" Ester asked.

Pisces took another bite. "It is not bad."

"Good, I'm glad you like it because they don't make it like this in Ans-on, that's for sure."

Pisces watched Ester eat as she picked around her own meal. Ester looked up and paused.

"Do they have something like this on your home world?" Ester asked.

"Like this?"

"You know, like food venders?"

"I am not sure; I have only seen my village, and beyond that everything else lays in ruin."

Ester felt bad for prying, but Pisces didn't seem to mind and continued.

"On my world, tribes do not mingle with other tribes," Pisces offered. "I guess you can say that was the driving factor that tore us apart, but life was not always gloomy. When I was young, back when the conflict was many miles away, me and my people lived happily with our akumas."

"Akumas?"

"They are what you would consider dogs, but about the size of your world's horse. We ride them to hunt, but they are more than that. They are family."

"Whoa." Ester couldn't imagine such a beast.

"Yes. If I could share with you fired roasted ground bird, I know that you would love it."

"I do like a good cooked bird."

Ester laughed, and Pisces smiled. Somehow things didn't seem too different between Rean and Labadora. Pisces' people just wanted to live their life free from oppression and war. It was not that long ago, some hundreds of years, that Rean was locked in a similar battle. If peace could come to the people of Rean, Ester was sure it would find its way to Labadora.

***

The journey was long, but they finally arrived in Cha-la, the land of the ancient monks. Both Pisces and Ester were amazed by its rolling hills of rich purple grass that only grew here. Shrines and temples dotted the land, along with stone statues and herds of wild horses. They only had a half a day's ride from here and decided to power through and break when they got there.

It was late midday when they arrived on the dirt path leading to where Wildgrass lived. Ester was nervous. They didn't have much in the way of a plan. The two strolled by as Pisces looked at each dome-shaped house for the address numbers. They were about four or five houses away. From what was known about Captain Wildgrass, he was the son of a high-ranking ranger and a scientist. He came from wealth, just like Angel, but there was one big difference: he was the first and only native Reanian to have a ten on the natural ability scale. Most Reanians averaged a conductivity level of about three to five, but

Wildgrass was on a level all on his own. He rose through the ranks as a ranger fast, snatching crooks from Fandour, even visiting the elders of Kees. He was the best in his class and admired by all, but things changed when he suddenly quit and stepped out of the stoplight.

Pisces slowed to a stop at the house that matched the address InyOuty gave them. The house wasn't large like Ester imagined but modest and cozy. Smoke floated from the brick chimney as Pisces pulled up the long rocky drive way. She parked the jetter next to a chicken coup and stepped off. Ester hoped off and stretched.

"We're here." Pisces placed the helmet on the jetter then walked towards the door.

"Wait, aren't you going to rehearse what you're going to say?"

"Why?"

"I don't know, you're asking a complete stranger to help you. What's your game plan?"

Pisces thought for a second. "I plan to walk to his door and demand that he help me."

She started to turn away again, but Ester stopped her.

"Yeah, that's not going to work."

"It really isn't," called a voice from behind the house.

Ester and Pisces looked up and saw a tall, tanned middle-aged man with long vibrant green hair leaning against the house.

"Can I help you two?" He crossed his arms as a smirk found its way to his face.

Ester looked at Pisces who stepped forward.

"Are you Captain Wildgrass Inspread?" Pisces asked.

"Nope," The man picked in his ears. "I think his house is a few knocks that way."

Pisces nodded and was ready to leave, when Ester looked at the man closely.

"They say Captain Inspread has vibrant natural green hair," Ester said, stopping Pisces in her tracks.

"You don't say." The man kicked himself off the wall. "Well, you're old enough to not believe in rumors."

"He was about your height with tan skin, too," Ester added.

The man forced a smile and cut her a look. "I don't know, I think you might want to check down that way."

From around the house emerged a teenager with dark skin like Ester's, and a shaved head. She looked at the two women then at the man.

"Pops, who are they?" she said with a deadpan look.

"No one. Now go back in the house."

The teenager eyed the girls for a few seconds longer, then turned away. "I'm telling Dad."

"Amber, come on." The man waved his arms as the teen disappeared around the house. He turned towards Ester and Pisces and waved them along. "I'm so sorry I wasn't able to help you. Now if you don't mind hopping back on your bike and travel about I don't know forty knocks that way, I'm sure you'll find—"

"Wildgrass!" A man from the back of the house shouted. Wildgrass turned around and saw his husband walking over carrying their one-year-old son in his arms. "What is going on out here?" He looked at the two women. "Who are they?" He re-adjusted their son in his arms.

"I can explain, Taxes," Wildgrass protested as he looked back at the now glaring women.

"Well, explain inside. It's cold out here." His husband turned and hurried back in.

Wildgrass sighed and reluctantly waved for the woman to follow him inside of his home.

It was dinnertime, and the air around the table couldn't be anymore awkward as the family exchanged looks at their two uninvited guests. No one said anything for a while, while Taxes, Wildgrass' husband, prepared two more plates of food.

"Here you go." Taxes laid down their plates.

"Now, baby." Wildgrass tried to intervene.

"I don't want to hear it. We're just going to eat our meal and speak whatever needs to be spoken after." Taxes ignored him as he went around to his seat and started to feed their son.

Wildgrass sighed but didn't push any further.

Ester picked at her food in silence. It was far too awkward to chow down with that many eyes on her. Ester caught Pisces out of the counter of her eye picking at her food as well. This was not how Ester thought she would meet her hero. She glanced around the table at who she assumed to be Wildgrass's children. Besides Amber, the girl she saw before, there was another teenage girl with dark brown hair and tan skin. His husband looked like an adult version of Angel, with golden blond hair and tan skin, and the little baby was an adorable ball of red hair. Ester picked up her glass and finished off her water before sitting it down again.

"Oh, I'm sorry, where are my manners?" Taxes looked towards his guests. "I don't think we've been properly introduced."

Ester froze, "Um—"

"Forgive me," Pisces shot up and bowed. "My name is Pisces, and this is my partner, Ester."

Pisces sat back down as Ester melted a little over the word 'partner'.

"Regardless of the circumstances, it is a pleasure to meet you both," Taxes said. "I'm sure you know Wildgrass. I'm Taxes and these are our two daughters, Amber and Jasmine, and the little one is Monty."

Wildgrass coughed. "We're in the sharing mood tonight."

Taxes glared at him. "Of course, they are *your* guests after all."

Wildgrass and Taxes locked themselves into a staring battle, killing the mood completely. Ester slumped in her chair praying for this to be over.

After dinner Wildgrass, Ester, and Pisces sat in the living room staring at each other while Taxes prepared hot cocoa and biscuits. The house was clean, but lived in, with family pictures lining the walls and handmade knick-knacks on the tables and shelves. Toys littered the floor as the sweet aroma of cocoa wafted through the air. This would have been a house Ester would have liked to grow up in. Ester looked between Wildgrass and Pisces. He didn't seem bothered at all, reclining across from them with his leg resting on his knee. Pisces, on the other hand, sat with her hands curled up in a ball on her lap. Her jaw was clenched and her eyes focused. Ester looked away; she was starting to wish she was back at the dinner table. At least there she had the distraction of their cute son to look at. Taxes passed many times from the kitchen and den carrying saucers and tea cups. Ester watched as Wildgrass followed him with his eyes. Taxes returned again carrying napkins, and Wildgrass cleared his throat.

"Don't rush me!" Taxes snapped and returned to the kitchen.

Wildgrass cracked a smile but didn't say a word. He rested comfortably on his couch and let his husband do his thing. He heard a creak from the stairs but did not turn and look.

"Bed. Now, girls," he said calmly.

He heard the disappointed sighs of his two teenage daughters and listened to their footsteps as they went back to their rooms, then he turned and looked at Pisces.

"You can take that disguise off now," Wildgrass said as his green eyes sharpened.

Pisces gasped. "How did you know?"

Wildgrass smirked. "It's an older model. I can see the glitch."

Pisces frowned. Ester had been so used to seeing Pisces in her Reanian form she nearly forgot that it was a disguise. Pisces slowly looked down at her wristband and pushed a button. Her Reanian form faded revealing her thick short mid-night blue fur and large curved black horns. Ester inhaled, but Wildgrass didn't flinch.

"Much better. Now I'm not going to ask you why you're here because I already have an idea."

"Captain—" Pisces blurted, but Wildgrass raised his hand to stop her. He looked up at her with a sharp cold expression and she calmed back down.

"Whatever it is you're here for, the answer is no."

Pisces clenched and unclenched her jaw, a low growl rumbled from her throat. Ester placed her hand on Pisces' shoulder to calm her.

"But how can you say that when you have not heard what I am going to say?"

Wildgrass leaned back and switched legs placing his other leg over his knee. "Let me guess, the rangers sent you here to ask me to save the world, blah, blah, blah. Like I told them sixteen years ago, you don't need to come crying to me every time you've got a big problem."

Taxes strolled in with hot coco and biscuits.

"Help yourself, ladies." He placed the tray down with a smile, hoping to deflate the tension in the room.

"No rangers have sent me," Pisces hissed. "I was sent here by Captain Jordain of the Unity Reform on Labadora."

Wildgrass glared at them as his husband threw him a sharp look.

"Go on," Wildgrass motioned with his hand.

"I was sent here by my leader to find Rean's strongest warrior to help put a stop to General Tozork's invasion plan."

Taxes looked at Pisces as he brought his hands close to his chest. "Invasion plan?"

"Tozork you say?" Wildgrass said with a familiarity in his eyes.

"Are you familiar with that name?" Pisces said

"Yes, we are." Wildgrass stood and started walking to the door. "This is an official ranger matter. Whether they sent you or not, I cannot help you."

"Fools!" Pisces hissed, jumping to her feet. "Tozork's new weapon will put an end to the rangers, just as it did to all rival forces on my planet. Countless tribes have been destroyed. Our planet lay in waste all for his unquenchable thirst for power, and he will not stop until the whole galaxy is under his control."

This stopped Wildgrass in his tracks. He turned and looked at Pisces with hard eyes. He heard a creak in the floor boards and saw his two daughters standing in the doorway leading into the den.

"Girls," Wildgrass urged calmly.

Taxes turned to their children. "Hey, why don't we head upstairs?" Taxes eyed Wildgrass, his brown eyes pleading. Wildgrass sighed as his family left the room then continued.

"Even if I wanted to believe you, which I don't, I can't do anything without the ranger's help. I'm just one person. Granted I'm super powerful and super-hot, but one person nevertheless. I still have direct lines to the Grand Commanders."

Wildgrass moved towards a table and started to look for the

contact information. Pisces stood there with utter disappointment in her eyes. Her heart raced as her mind spun in circles. This plan had to work; there were no other options. Ester reached for Pisces' shoulder, but she turned away.

"Okay, so I think this is it; we can give it a try." Wildgrass walked over with the paper.

"Wildgrass!" Taxes shouted from the stairs. "You have to turn on the tele screen! *Now!*"

Wildgrass looked up as Taxes and their daughters came running past them. Taxes turned on the tele screen in the den and turned the volume up.

"Breaking news, live from Ans-on metropolis. Fire in the skies as ships invade the city."

Explosions could be heard as the anchor room shook. Everyone gasped as they walked closer.

"No," Pisces quivered.

"It appears we are under attack from an unknown enemy!"

The transmission frizzled in and out.

"The rangers have been deployed..."

The camera panned to the skyline, explosions dotted the sky as smoke rose from the streets.

"Oh my gosh," Ester drew her hands to her mouth.

"The Ans-on shields are going up. We're not sure how long we'll be able to broadcast!"

Another explosion could be heard in the background and the image quality faded to snow. The audio of the broadcast could still be heard as the sound of explosions boomeranged around the room mixed with the sound of shattered glass and screams.

"We'll—be—back—EVACUATE!"

The transmission cut off, and in a panic, Taxes flipped to another news station.

"It looks like Station Tower 13 has been hit. If you look in the sky you can see the shapes of ships! It looks like three of them. Holy smokes!"

Ester and everyone held their breath at the sight of three looming shadows breaking through the clouds. They watched the newscaster flinch as vibrations from the shields radiated through the building. Ester's stomach churned. This couldn't be happening.

"Wow, that was right above us!" The newscaster looked up, then back at the camera. "The shields are up, but for how long I'm not sure…"

Taxes muted the tele as Wildgrass swallowed hard. Wildgrass could see the rangers fighting above the shield. There were too many explosions bringing back too many memories for him to stick around. He turned to his husband, his eyes hard and brow tensed.

"What's your plan?" he demanded with his back facing Pisces, but it was clear he was talking to her.

"I have the maps of the main ship." Pisces pulled them up on her wristband. "There are three total, but it is the main ship in the middle that is the most important. I need to get on that ship, disable the shields, so I can destroy the weapon."

"What kind of weapon is it?" Wildgrass asked.

"We are not sure how Tozork got the technology or how it works, but we do know how to destroy it. It is a risky plan, but our only option. See, the source of its power comes from within the planet. Mines riddle our planet in search of a crystal, our sources say, and somehow Tozork has turned those crystals into a powerful weapon. None of our forces or attempts against him has worked, so our only option was to come to Rean and stop him here." Pisces looked around at the skeptical faces. "There are others. There are Reformers on the other two ships lying and waiting for the main ship's shields to go down so that they can take over and weaken the main ship, but they cannot move without the shields being disabled on the main ship."

"Okay," Wildgrass nodded as he paced and rubbed his chin. "So this big bad weapon, how are you going to bring it down if all other attempts have failed?"

"By focusing on this," Pisces zoomed in on the blueprints and showed the barrel of the weapon. "It is true we cannot directly destroy the weapon, but if we target the barrel, combined with the shields being down we will have a better chance. On our home world his forces proved to be impenetrable in our weakened state, so this plan combined with the help of the rangers we should be able to bring him down."

Wildgrass looked at the hologram. "Okay, so how come there isn't any back up on the main ship?"

"That is Tozork's stronghold. His loyalists are only on that ship. It would have been impossible to get anyone from the Unity Reform on board."

"And you think you can do the job when others have failed?" Wildgrass looked at her.

"With your help. Your people have the power of electricity. With this power, I can short circuit the board and get to the shields faster. I have memorized these maps; I know all the routes like I know the paths of my homeland."

"Sounds like a whole lot has been left to chance, and they sent you a kid to take down a war mongrel?" Wildgrass said.

"I have trained for over a year for this mission and many years prior in combat in servitude to our leader. I am no child, and I would not be standing here before you if I did not need your help. A distraction is needed for this plan. Tozork knows Rean has strong warriors, and it will be his arrogance that will open up a blind spot for me. Trust me, this is the only option."

"Sheesh. Alright, so you need a Reanian on the inside. Got a plan for that? And explain to me again how you're going to sneak on because I'm sure your body is going to burn up as soon as you get close to those shields."

"I am aware of this Captain—"

"Please, it's just Wildgrass."

Pisces nodded. "In the confusion of the distraction, I will board using my sensory disruptor bombs." Pisces held up two gray balls in her hands. "These will allow me to sneak on the ship undetected. They work by burning a small hole in the shields, but it only works for a few minutes and only something small like a person can pass. From there, I will make my way to the shields, disable them using the deciphered code, then I will plant a bomb on the barrel, which will disable the weapon."

"Heck, those would have been a real game changer if you would have come with more." Wildgrass marveled at the disruptor balls.

"Yes, if you like to die a slow and painful death. In large concentrations this stuff is radioactive. Our technology is new and largely untested. This is why we have struggled against Tozork for so long."

"Okay, we have a plan laid out." Wildgrass paced the den. "But you still haven't answered my first question. Who is going to be your number two to help you get on the main ship?"

Pisces stared at Wildgrass, then looked away. "I was hoping that you would have someone to recommend."

Wildgrass could feel a headache coming on. He grabbed the bridge of his nose. "So, let me get this straight, your great leader trained you, gave you maps and shield thingys, and sent you along your way without a second person to complete the plan? I know you need a Reanian, but it seems a tad bit risky."

"It was hard enough smuggling one person onto the planet. I sat in a crate for two months on route here."

Wildgrass threw his hands up in the air as Pisces started to growl.

"I'll go," Ester said.

Garnering confusion from Wildgrass, he looked up at Ester. She didn't look a day over seventeen, just a year older than his oldest daughter.

"Uh, no, that's going to be a negative for me."

"What?" Ester watched him roam around the room and look through stuff. "Why?"

Wildgrass looked up from the drawer where he was bent down at. "Hey, I respect your bravery, but you're just a kid. I mean a real *kid.*"

"Hey! I just turned nineteen." Ester placed her hand on her hips.

"Teen." Wildgrass stressed the word.

"Teen my ass. I got into ranger academy. I know how to hold my own." Ester flashed her fiery eyes.

Wildgrass stood. "You, um, what's your name again?"

"It's Ester."

Wildgrass paused then returned to searching around the room. "Okay, Ester, if I remember correctly second semester should still be in session and this is post festival season, so you should be in school."

Ester huffed and rolled her eyes.

"Right, so you're either lying, or you got kicked out."

"I'm not lying."

"Right." Wildgrass picked up an old address book, then called Taxes into the room. Taxes nodded without a word and took the address book. "I'm not going to let a child get herself killed."

"I'll go then." Taxes said.

"No," Wildgrass said a little too loudly. "And no to you, too." He pointed back to Ester. "Taxes, can you call around?"

Ester's blood started to boil as Wildgrass and Taxes talked amongst themselves. She was not a child, and if she was in ranger academy right now she would be preparing for the attack. She didn't have much training in the art of combat, but she was sure she could be an asset to the team.

"I can do this!" Ester yelled to the room.

Wildgrass crossed the room and stepped into Ester's space, his face just inches from hers. "This is not a game or a simulation. This is real life, real weapons, real chances of death, so unless you've seen a battlefield and looked death square in the face I'm going to have to ask you to sit down."

Nothing but passion flowed through Ester's eyes. Her heart raced as the electricity in her body began to rise; the surge was so powerful it could be seen coming off her body.

"I have seen plenty of death in my time, and this time I'm sure as hell not going to sit back and let it happen again. So think what you want about me, but I'm a lot strong than I look."

Wildgrass stepped back and looked at her. Her eyes said it all, burning with unwavering conviction. He sighed as he rubbed the back of his neck. "Alright, you can come, but it's your funeral."

"Wildgrass," Taxes protested.

"We're out of time, and no, I'm not going to allow you to put yourself in danger," Wildgrass said as he pushed his husband long.

"No," Taxes wiggled out of his grip.

"I can't. No, I won't," Wildgrass grabbed his husband by the shoulders. "One of us needs to stay behind." Wildgrass looked past Taxes at their children. Taxes followed his eyes, then sighed. Wildgrass smiled then turned to Ester.

"I like your heart, kid. So how far did you get in academy? Did you take combat 101?"

Ester shied away from the question.

"So, I'm guessing you don't know how to us a CuCore either?"

Ester looked down at the floor as Wildgrass pinched the bridge of his nose.

"Your passion is admirable, but you're probably going to die."

Taxes punched his husband.

"Ouch." He rubbed his arm. "We don't have a lot of time, but I know someone who can help. Amber, you're in charge, sweetie. Think you can handle it?"

Amber nodded.

"Thanks." Wildgrass kissed his daughter on the forehead. "Taxes, pack us a bag, please. I'm going to call Odie."

"Odie?" Pisces eyed him.

"Don't worry, he's the best damn mechanic the rangers ever had."

Pisces and Ester looked at each other. Things were heating up, but at least they had Wildgrass on their side. Ester walked to the window; it was calm and peaceful in Cha-la, but if this plan failed what would become of her world?

Chapter Twenty-Four

The cadets sat in a large classroom watching the chaos unfold on the screen. Hundreds of people ran the streets in terror as giant armored ships flew above them. Flashing lights and emergency officers shouted for people to return to their homes, but some had no homes to return to. The city was a fire, but it would recover, but only if help from the rangers came and came soon. The shields were up all around Ans-on, protecting them for the time being, but the officials had no idea how long they would last. All states were on high alert, as all forms of transportation shut down. The cadets watched helplessly, passing worried glances between their fellow peers.

"This is not happening." Fermit grabbed his head. "My family lives in the Fortuna locale." His face reddened as he fought back the tears.

"You don't think the Here-saw locale has been affected?" Bue said aloud. "They haven't shown anything about Here-Saw."

The chatter built as worried cadets started to panic. Soon the entire class was on edge eagerly wanting to check on their families.

Oh my gosh, Ester, I hope you're okay, Angel thought to himself, knowing his friend was all alone out there.

"Alright, cadets," Captain Pole limped in quickly with a tablet in his hands. "I won't waste time sugar coating anything. We're on high alert, and we could use every hand we've got. Evacuations of the people of Ans-on is now the top priority of all cadets here at Ranger Academy."

"Evacuations?" Kiakit blurted. "We should be fighting. Enemies are attacking the city!"

Captain Pole's expression did not change. "You are not trained to handle this level of combat. Your expertise will be best utilized on the ground, getting people out through the underground rail system." Captain Pole looked at his cadets; he knew they wanted to do more, but saving lives were just as important as fighting.

"It is the prime objective of the Rean Coalition of Rangers to protect the people of Rean. You are not expendable; you will follow your orders as assigned." Captain Pole pulled up a holograph of the list of assignments for the cadets. "Some of you will be assigned to ground work, others will be stationed in safe locations located outside the nation state. We are not sure how long the shields will hold, and evacuating people on this scale will produce a lot of chaos. It is your duty to keep the people calm and flowing. I understand this is your first mission and some of you will not be prepared. Remember why you became a ranger. Draw on that strength to help you get through this night because tomorrow will come whether Ans-on is here or not and Rean will need you."

Names popped up on the screen placing cadets in different groups and assignments. In an instant, the assignments were sent to their wrist bands.

"This is not happening." Fermit collapsed to the floor. "I don't know if I can handle this."

"Get up, come on." Angel helped Fermit to his feet. "It's going to be okay. The rangers always win, and this time will be no different," Angel said as he rubbed his friend's back.

Fermit sniffled and wiped his face with his arm then nodded. Angel and the others filed out, but there was a knot growing in Angel's stomach. He wanted to be brave, but he was shaking in his boots. The capital area looked like it was hit pretty hard, and that's where his parents lived. He was worried about Ester and Samay and all his friends. Part of him hoped this was a dream, but in his mind he knew this was real.

More than half of Angel's class was assigned to helping with the evacuations on the ground level. The academy built secret underwater tunnels that led to different coastal cities in Ans-on. Everyone assigned to the ground was packed tight into shuttles and sent underground. It was quiet, painfully so, and crammed full of cadets who would be seeing a battle zone for the first time. Angel sat squished next to Zime and Fermit in silence as the shuttle hummed along. Some cadets were shaking at every bump, worried they would be sunk at any minute. Finally, after what seemed like forever, the cadets emerged from the tunnel to a station that looked more like a military base. Rangers ran everywhere as the cadets stood on their tippy toes to get a look outside.

"Attention Rangers, please report to your crisis location at once. Crisis location and directions will be sent through your wristbands."

The message repeated many times before the doors opened. Then the rush of noise drowned out what was left of their calm reality. For Angel, it was the smell of something burning that pulled him back into reality. It was light, but somehow it found its way to wherever they were underground. Shouting, and loud footsteps, and announcements occupied every inch of Angel's mind.

"South locales! South Locales! Your shuttle is leaving in twenty minutes! South locales!" A man shouted across the platform.

Angel could barely hear as a hand reached out and grabbed him.

"This way, Angel," Fermit said.

Angel snapped out of his haze. Behind him Zime followed with the same overwhelmed look on her face.

"South locales!" The man shouted again as Angel and his friends hopped in line. "South locales only! Train leaving in fifteen minutes! Have wristbands out to be scanned!"

Angel looked at his wristband. He was as ready as he was ever going to be. He scanned his wristband and soon his friends were onboard. The shuffle took them up to the surface and when they arrived, the images on the holo screen could not compare to the fiery nightmare that had become his city. Buildings had collapsed in some areas; while other places were crowded with people walking with their families in tow through mazes of rumbled. He could see smoke in the distance in places he used to visit, and the thin translucent light blue shield breaking the horizon. He looked up and a true horror formed in his heart at the sight of the humongous ships above him. They dwarfed the size of Ans-on's tallest skyscrapers. He shivered in his bones, as his knees started to get weak. Fermit stood beside him and grabbed his hand and Angel turned to see his horrified expression as he looked up too. Everyone was looking up. As Angel looked around, he felt the terror grip his heart. Was this what he signed up for? Angel looked back to his childhood. He admired Grand Commander J'Chives, but he also remembered his scars—the bold reminders of the reality of being a ranger. Angel wasn't scared back then when he saw them. He remembered hugging him and running his fingers down the Commander's ridged face. He remembered Grand Commander J'Chives saying that his scars were earned protecting Rean and that he didn't regret a single one. A tear ran down Angel's cheek, and he quickly wiped it away. Angel took a deep breath and clenched his fists.

"Don't you worry, Grand Commander, I am here to return the favor."

Chapter Twenty-Five

Ester and Pisces sat in Odie's shop and watched Odie and Taxes run around and gather gadgets and items. It was late, but Taxes managed to get a hold of a friend of theirs they knew who could help. Time was limited, but Odie was more than willing to help. Odie was a mechanic and pilot before he retired from the Rean Coalition Rangers. He had been friends with Wildgrass long before he was even a ranger. Middle aged with golden blond hair and near balding, Odie rocked the stubble, beer belly look. He and Taxes talked and finalized plans as Ester and Pisces waited for their next move. Ester tried to watch the news updates, but it was getting to be too much. Things looked grim as reports flooded in that the shields would not hold for long, and this was the place Ester was heading to. The place she would be fighting. Her hearted pounded in her chest.

"Ya'll should get some sleep." Wildgrass walked over to them.

"I'm fine, really," Ester said.

Wildgrass chuckled and looked at Pisces. "And I guess you're going to say the same thing?"

"Our mission takes precedence over sleep."

"Is that so?" Wildgrass stretched, then tossed a rag he was holding in his hand into Pisces' face.

She startled back as she tried to block the offensive thing, but it flew right through her hands and landed on her shoulder. Ester looked between Pisces and Wildgrass as Pisces picked up the rag and glared at it.

"So, me and my rag are thinking that maybe sleep needs to come first?"

Both girls sighed, but he was right. They were no good to the mission if they were tired. They left Odie's shop and headed towards Odie's house. It was gorgeous at night. Stars littered the sky, fully visible in the absence of light pollution. Ester watched the perfect sky and wondered how it could look so breathtaking knowing miles away the nation state of Ans-on was being battered to its knees.

"So where are you from?" Wildgrass looked at Pisces as he reached in front of her to open the screen door.

"Labadora."

"I know that," Wildgrass said as he looked through the kitchen. Pisces' look was guarded as Ester followed close behind. "Okay, okay, I won't pry.

Pisces bit her lip. "FurQuill. FurQuill was the name of my tribe."

"Was?" Wildgrass offered them some water. Pisces turned it down, but Ester raised her hand.

"I'm sorry." Wildgrass handed a glass to Ester.

"Do not be." Pisces sharpened her look.

"Okay." Wildgrass raised his hands. "But I get it, seen it, lived through the aftermath. It's not fun watching the people you love slip through your fingers."

There was something in Wildgrass' eyes that made Ester second guess why she was here. Wildgrass and Pisces were both highly trained fighters and there was no doubt that they had seen a lot of battles. She knew she would be expected to fight as a ranger, but looking back on her own grim past would she be able to do something this time around?

"What about you?" Wildgrass' words cut through Ester's thoughts. "What's your story?"

"Orphaned," Ester said mechanically, as if she had been prompted like a robot.

Wildgrass stopped. "Orphaned?"

Ester shrugged. She was used to the look of pity in people's eyes, but when she looked up she was met with a warm smile.

"All my kids were orphans," Wildgrass said as he lead the way.

Ester chuckled. "You starting a collection?"

Wildgrass laughed as he opened a door and flicked on the light to a guest room. "No, but that's not a bad idea. There's too much suffering in the world not to reach out and help." He smiled. "Odie only has one guest room, so are ya'll okay with sharing?"

Ester and Pisces looked at each other and nodded.

"Cool, shower's through there. There's towels and stuff too. We wake at dawn." Wildgrass stood in the frame as Pisces headed to the bathroom.

"How do you do it?" Ester managed to get out before Wildgrass could leave.

"Hmm?" Wildgrass stopped.

"How did you do it all?"

"It was my job," he shrugged.

Ester stared for a few seconds. "But being a ranger is more than a job. It's a life's calling."

"Is that what they're telling you kids in academy? Look kid, the planet is always going to be in peril, no matter how many times you save it. This master plan, this life's purpose is all a load of crap. You can't stop the world from being destroyed, all you can do is hold onto the things that you love and fight like hell until you breathe your last breath."

Ester sat on the bed with a disappointed look on her face. Wildgrass was expecting this. She was still young.

"Whatever happens tomorrow, don't forget what you're fighting to protect. As long as you remember that your heart will never stray." He closed the door.

Ester smiled a little and took a deep breath. She didn't want tomorrow to come, but she hoped she had the strength to make it. Pisces opened the door to the bathroom and walked over to the bed. Ester looked at Pisces and was shocked to see that fur covered her entire body. Pisces scratched at her undergarments and looked up to find Ester staring at her.

"What?"

"There's so much fur…" Ester mused before she could stop herself.

Pisces examined her body. "I am confused."

"Oh no, I don't mean anything is wrong with it, it's just I've never see so much of it. On someone, I mean."

"Surely this is no different than your animals."

"I know, it's just cool."

Pisces stared at Ester for a minute then her expression warmed. *Cool*, she thought. That was not a word associated with Labadorans by foreigners. She opened her bag and pulled out her sleeping bag.

"Pisces, I'm not going to let you sleep on the hard-ass floor."

Pisces stopped as Ester flipped the sheets over. "I'm going to get changed. You hop in."

"I am fine with sleeping on the floor."

"Nope," Ester said in passing. "This could be our last night, and besides, I don't mind."

Pisces watched Ester close the bathroom door. When had she allowed her guard to drop this low? She came to Rean for one thing and one thing only, to stop Torzork, but she hadn't expected to find someone who treated her like a normal intelligent being. So much of the stigma that Labadorans were ruthless savages still remained. And yet, she was standing in her true form being offered a place to sleep by someone she barely knew. Pisces looked at the bed; she wondered if this could be foreshadowing for her people and the people of Rean. Peace was at the forefront of her mind, and if everything went according to plan tomorrow, she may actually live to see it come true.

Chapter Twenty-Six

The next day at sunrise, Ester was awoken from her sleep by the chatter coming from outside. She turned over in bed, half expecting to run into Pisces, but she barely noticed no one was there. Just as she was about to drift back to sleep she heard the loud roar of an engine and nearly fell off the bed. She stumbled to her feet and looked around. The room was empty, but the voices outside were getting louder. Outside Wildgrass and Odie were shouting and jumping up and down next to an old ranger's cargo ship. She stared in shock, mostly because she couldn't believe they got that relic to run. Ester hurried to get dressed and ran downstairs meeting everyone in the kitchen.

"Good morning." A beautiful tall blond woman said over a steaming hot stove.

Ester forced a smile as she tried to pull the stray strands of hair into a ponytail. She had seen that woman in a picture; she must be Odie's wife. Everyone, with the exception of Wildgrass and Odie, were in the kitchen, making Ester feel a little embarrassed for waking up later than everyone else. She took a seat next to Pisces, who of course looked alert and ready to go. Wildgrass opened the screen door and entered followed by Odie.

"Okay, gang," Wildgrass called everyone around the table. "I know this plan is super short notice, but hey, it could be worse."

"Worse?" Odie smirked.

"Well, I mean at least we get a nice warm breakfast before we all get blown to shit."

Wildgrass placed a mini projector on the table and pulled up the map of the ships supplied by Pisces.

"This is the map of all the ships. Luckily for me the other two ships are much smaller, meaning as Pisces said before, the meat is in the main one. Our plan is simple: distract and infiltrate. Odie will fly me to the closest small ship, I'll off load and do my thing, while Pisces and Ester sneak on. We good?"

Wildgrass looked around the table. Pisces nodded with assurance, but Ester not so much. She understandably was nervous, but she wasn't going to back out. Odie got up and walked over to the counter. He picked up a box and sat it on the kitchen table.

"Here, Ester, these are for you." Odie pulled out a pair of thick black and gray gloves. "I'm sorry that you've been thrown into this. I can't imagine what it feels like to have this be your first mission, but I hope theses gloves will give you a leg up."

He handed them to Ester. The material was thick, but the gloves were lightweight. In the center and on each of the five finger tips were round black circles. They were all connected to each other by a thin dark gray wire.

"They work just like a CuCore. They have a copper core which harnesses your natural conductivity and amplifies it into a pretty nasty shock."

Ester looked at them in amazement as Odie showed her how to turn them on and use them.

"And for you, Pisces, I modified this pocket gun into a stun gun. You won't have to worry about reloading it, but it packs a punch. One shot from this and your enemies won't be getting up anytime soon."

"Thank you." Pisces took the gun and placed in her utility belt.

"No problem," Odie said. "Oh! I forgot, in case things get a little overwhelming, I found these mini shields in the shop. Now they aren't super fancy, but they'll offer some protection from gunfire. They work in burst, so you can use them five minutes at a time, but they need a few minutes to recharge. Sorry I couldn't get you guys better models, but I hope these help. You wear them as rings on your thumb. To activate, squeeze the band, by clenching your fist." Odie handed them the rings.

"Thanks, Odie," Wildgrass said.

"Anytime, old friend." Odie patted Wildgrass on the shoulder.

"Hey, don't be giving me that old guy shit, we're coming back from this, all of us." He looked around the table. This was a hairball mess of a plan, but Wildgrass wasn't prepared to sign their death warrants just yet.

"Wildgrass!" Taxes snapped his fingers as he listened to the message from his connections at ranger academy over the phone. "The shields won't last much longer. Ya'll need to go now."

Wildgrass nodded. He stopped at the door and looked back at Taxes. His husband was near tears, and he could see the cracking flood gates behind his eyes. "No kisses."

"I know," Taxes stuttered.

"This isn't goodbye."

"Get out of here before I bet your ass," Taxes turned and pretended to be talking on the phone.

Wildgrass stole a glance of his husband one last time. They were going to make it back, just like he did a million times before. On the way out, Wildgrass passed Odie. He was saying goodbye to his family as well. Seeing the expressions on everyone's faces really hit home at how long it had been since he had to go away like this.

"Hey, Wildgrass," Odie shouted as he ran towards the plane. "You almost forgot your CuCore."

Ester and Pisces looked at the long scratched up bent copper rod Odie was waving. It looked like a piece of scrap metal.

"What's that?" Ester asked.

"My stick." Wildgrass hopped aboard.

Odie chuckled at Ester's confused face. "I know it doesn't look like much, but it's a copper core used in most CuCores. Usually they're found inside of the weapon, but Wildgrass over there always winds up metaling the casing. So he just uses the core as his weapon."

Ester stood in shock then rushed to catch up with everyone. Everyone loaded onto the plane. It was packed from top to bottom as if they were going on a week's long trip. Ester and Pisces struggled to find a place to sit as the engines started to turn on. Outside, the others watched the ship take off. Ester looked outside the window at the people she barely knew; she wished she could have met everyone under better circumstances. Odie and Wildgrass sat in the cockpit as the ship roared to life.

"Attention, everyone. Pray, chant, do what you have to do, we'll be in Ans-on in five hours. Buckle up because this ship's not your standard issue," Wildgrass announced over the intercom.

Ester and Pisces buckled themselves in next to each other as the ship began to take off.

"You ready?" Ester turned to Pisces.

"I am always ready," Pisces responded, but Ester only laughed.

The ship rattled as it took off. There was no turning back now. Ester's stomach was in knots as the ship flew through the sky. She ran through the plan over and over again, and each time it felt more and more unreal. Why was she so stressed out? Had she not gotten kicked out of ranger academy she would be on assignment in Ans-on right now. This is what she wanted, to save lives, to help people, but this had burst her bubble. The reality of going into battle terrified her now.

"Calm yourself." Pisces placed her hand on top of Esters. "We will be successful."

"But how do you know?" Ester started to panic.

"I believe." Pisces placed her hand to her chest. "Over the course of our fight, we have experienced many losses, our hope had been reduced to a flicker, but our leader never lost sight of the dream of a better life for Labadora. Even in our defeat on our home world, Jordain still forged a plan and that is the reason we are all here today. Because of his hope, because he believed we are closer than ever to seeing a future of peace."

Ester smiled a little. Pisces was right. Lots of people have worked hard to stop this nightmare from happening. People that weren't even her species were fighting to save her world. She needed to be brave, she wanted to be brave, even if she was terrified out of her mind.

"Here." Pisces took off her wristband. "On this wristband is the device I used to change my appearance. Loaded within its settings is the uniform worn by Tozork's elite. With this you will be unidentifiable."

"Thanks, but what about you?"

"I will be fine. I am Labadoran, so a disguise will do me little good, but it is important that they do not know a Reanian is on board. General Tozork believes he is invincible, even to the Unity Reform. He will think the intruders are Labadoran, thus less threatening."

"Gosh, he sure leaves a lot up to chance."

"With his weapon, he has no reason to fear chance," Pisces quipped.

***

The turbulence woke Ester from her short nap. They were right over Ans-on now, and the sky was crowded with ranger ships. She heard Odie over the intercom relaying the bare bones of the plan. Ester was ready to go, but her heart was racing. She still couldn't believe she was here and a small part of her wished she was back home safe in the fields of Adum-la. She took several deep breaths and rubbed the lump where her necklace was. *Mother, father, brother, if you can hear me, please give me the strength to overcome this.* She shut her eyes tight.

"Hey."

Ester jumped when she felt a hand on her shoulder. It was Wildgrass, in a light and dark gray ride suit, one that combat rangers wore, holding his large bent copper rod.

"You ready?"

Ester nodded, but it wasn't convincing anyone.

"It's okay if you want to sit this one out." Wildgrass had no seriousness in his voice. He was almost smiling, which made Ester flash a cocky grin.

"Yeah? And let you guys have all the fun."

Wildgrass laughed. "Okay kid, your funeral."

The intercom crackled on. "Okay everyone, we got a little backup and will be running in an arrow formation over the target ship. Our support is running flares, but we have to be on our game. Shields go down over Ans-on in thirty minutes, and I'm sure that's what our enemy is waiting for," Odie chimed off.

Ester nodded and looked for Pisces who was standing in the back of the plane with her eyes closed and hands clasped together. The cabin flashed red, which startled Ester. Wildgrass turned to her and smiled.

"I'm going out first." He stood by the bay door.

"With what?" Ester walked over to him. He didn't even have a hover pack on.

"Stand back. Wait for me to make contact before you jump."

"Jump?" Ester looked back at Pisces, who was ready and signaled Ester to put on her dive mask.

Ester looked back at Wildgrass, then the flashing lights turned green and the bay doors opened, flooding the plane with wind.

"Wildgrass: clear! Amplifiers launching in five, four, three, two, one."

Wildgrass jumped from the plane as the air blew like a wind storm around the cabin. Ester stuck her head out and watched through the cover of smoke bombs as his figure disappeared in the clouds. Shortly after, large metal balls fell from the back of the plane. Ester watched them drop into the clouds like acorns in the snow. Nothing happened for a long while as she scanned the horizon. Pisces joined her, and they both looked for Wildgrass then at each other.

Then suddenly from below, a shock waved rattled the ship.

Ester and Pisces held on for dear life as the clouds below them turned dark gray. Bolts of lightning mixed with the clouds in an electrifying storm. The last of the smoke bombs cleared and a shadowed figure in a tiny ball of green made contact with one of the secondary ships causing an explosion that nearly knocked the ship off course. Ester shielded her eyes with her arm. She gasped. This was the raw power of Rean's strongest warrior. She peeked over her arm and saw nothing but black smoke. Then the sounds of explosions came from the state below. The shields were going down early than expected. Pisces grabbed Ester's arm. It was time. Ester adjusted her dive mask and turned on her wristband as she stood next to Pisces inside the frame of the bay door.

The intercom crackled on. "Give me a second, ladies. I'm flying you to the target now. Turn your hover packs on." Ester and Pisces did as they were told.

"Getting into position now."

The ship tilted hard causing the women to wedge their feet into the frame to keep from slipping out. "Target in position. Five, four, three, two, one."

Pisces turned on the sensory disruptor balls and grabbed Ester's hand. They exchanged glances with a nod then jumped. Ester felt weightless for a few seconds, all of her worries disappeared as the instinct to survive took over. She gripped Pisces' hand as her suit powered on and gave them the ability to glide towards the main ship.

There was nothing in her wildest imagination she could compare to the size of this gigantic ship. It shadowed the city like a boot over an anthill. The two hovered down through the smoke and explosions. It was hard to see, but the ship had a thin grayish force field around it. Ester's breath hitched as she watched the balls Pisces had in her hands explode against it. Ester thought for sure they would crash and burn up upon contact, but as they fell closer to it, a small dark aura formed around them forming a mini shield. Pisces pulled Ester closer as they made contact with the shield. They stuck to it like soap bubbles. Their bodies lay on the shield, protected only by the thin dark layer from the balls. Within seconds, the aura melted a hole into the ship's shields, dissolving them away into nothing, creating a small opening. Ester and Pisces watched the hole expand as they stood crouched against the black aura waiting for the perfect opportunity to jump. The black aura flickered. This was all the space it could create as it fought against the ship's powerful shields. Pisces looked to Ester and pulled her close as the two slipped through the hole. Ester gasped and looked up. They were just in time too, because the tiny hole they had jumped through closed up right behind them.

Pisces powered on her hover pack and guided Ester to the ship. They landed hard against the metal. Ester released Pisces' hand to grab hold of the warm metal. She could feel the vibrations of the ship, as well as the ships buzzing over her. She opened her eyes and saw Pisces waving at her and pointing at her own feet. Ester looked down and had nearly forgot about the suit's magnetic soles. Ester reached down and turned hers on. She stood, then a rumble from the ship threatened to knock her over. Large doors opened up on the side of the ship just a few feet away from them, and huge guns emerged and aimed and fired at the ships above them. One explosion rocked Ester's entire body in the most terrifying way. She bent down and covered her head and saw the cannon gears turn, reload, and fire again. The sight of such a weapon had her frozen in place until a hand reached out to her and pulled her along.

Ester's body protested at first, but Pisces would not allow her to stop moving, So Ester focused her mind on that, moving. She was terrified, but the fear of these powerful ships arriving on the farms of Adum pushed her body to move her muscles and tendons along. The two made a quick cross to a spot where they could sneak in. Above them, rangers battled in full force. The shields were down over Anson, but the island of Juw-ja, home to ranger academy, still had its shields up, and it looked like the enemies were focusing on that first. Ester hunched over next to Pisces as she began unscrewing what looked like a small vent. It didn't seem like the enemies on board knew they were there, and Ester hoped it stayed that way. She looked in the sky and saw Odie's ship flying through the clouds. It was taking damage, but holding its own. Pisces pulled Ester along, tearing her from her thoughts into the hole.

The inside of the vent was pitch black and slippery like a metal slide. They slid along for what seemed like forever when they finally rolled to a stop. In the darkness, Ester stood to her feet but hit her head on the low laying ceiling. Pisces heard the thud and pulled Ester down. Pisces shushed her and pulled her towards a tiny light in the distance. They walked quickly as the vent began to get smaller again. It was better lit, but Ester was starting to prefer the darkness. The vents of the ship looked like black veiny snake skin but were hard like metal. They stopped, and Pisces turned around.

"Below," she whispered, "is the main hall leading to the ship's shield generator. We will not have long to make our next move after we attack the generator. By then they will know we are onboard, but it should cause enough confusion to give us the upper hand. Twenty-seven paces past the generator is where the machine room to the new weapon is. Get me there and we can bet them. Can you do that?"

Ester nodded and clenched her fists to turn on the gloves Odie had given her. She could feel them pulling her power to her hands. It was like nothing she had ever felt.

"Let's go." Pisces turned and began to open the vent door.

The vent cover swung open startling two guards. They came running over, only to be jumped by Pisces and Ester. Pisces landed on one and punched him out and Ester upper-cutted the other, zapping him into the air. He landed hard but did not get up. The two looked at each other and nodded and took off down the corridor. It was as dim as the vents, but the interior was a dark ashy brown with two sets of yellow lights coming from tiny bulbs in the ceiling. Ester followed Pisces as she cut turns and navigated forks. She really did know this place like the back of her hand. They ran until they came to their first door. It was locked by some kind of card reading mechanism. Pisces stepped out of the way so that Ester could fry the system. Ester stepped up to the panel and brought her hands over the controls. She concentrated on using enough electricity to fry it, but with little to no training, she let off a blast stronger than she intended. Pisces stepped back as the panel smoked and fizzled. Waving the smoke from her view Pisces turned to Ester with her eyes wide open.

"Sorry," Ester shrugged as she laughed a little.

"It is okay, now help me get this open."

They got to work and started to pry open the doors manually, but their actions did not go unnoticed. An alarm sounded that strobed the halls in red. Pisces and Ester looked at the ceiling. This was bad, but they couldn't turn back now. They pried open the door then took off down the corridor. From the shadows, guards appeared from unseen doors. Pisces withdrew her stun gun and shot down every guard she saw as they began to fire. Ester ducked and spotted the next door. Pisces saw it too, and they two ran faster. Ester sprinted forward as Pisces covered her. Ester placed her hand on the panel and didn't hold back. She blasted a hole right through it. Pisces slid into the door with her back to it as she shot down the guards heading their way. The door was still closed, and they needed time to open it. A wave of five guards appeared and shot at them. Pisces and Ester jumped out of the way as the door was taking hit after hit. They wouldn't last much longer hiding behind a support beam. Ester saw Pisces' taking aim and firing at the guards. She needed something like that. She needed to think.

"Pisces! Cover me!" Ester shouted as loud as she could.

"What?"

"I got a plan!" Ester turned the charge all the way up on her gloves.

For the most part, her people were immune to low levels of electricity. Their conductive bodies absorbed the brunt of it, meaning large amounts of electrical current could flow through their bodies and they would sustain little damage from it. If Ester created a flare, she could blind the guards and take them out one on one.

"Cover your eyes!" she shouted to Pisces.

Ester charged up her gloves and turned on her shield as she jumped out in front of the guards with her hands raised and let off a blinding electrical blast. Pisces covered her eyes and turned away. The guards were stunned and stumbled backwards. That's when Pisces charged forward and finished the job. Ester panted as she watched Pisces take down the last guard. She looked at her hands. She really loved these gloves.

"Let's go!" Pisces turned and started to pry the door open.

With help from Ester, it slowly slid open and the two slid through the crack just small enough for them to pass. Pisces lead the way down the hall to the last door and waved for Ester to open it. Ester placed her hands above the panel when suddenly Pisces heard a sound.

"Blast cannon!" she shouted as she pulled Ester out of the way.

The blast sent the women flying into the wall as smoke and debris filled the air. Ester coughed and winced. Her side was hurting quite badly. She looked over at Pisces. She was starting to get to her feet when gun fired rained through the hole. Both of them ducked and inched closer to the wall. The fire was heavy and with the threat of cannon fire, there was no way they were going to get through there. Behind them, they could hear gunshots in the distance. The corridor lit up with flashes and smoke started to pour in from behind. Pisces squinted in the dim smoke-filled hall. She didn't understand why gunshots would be coming from where they just left, but the echoes bounced louder in the hallway as Pisces and Ester crawled closer to the wall. Pisces turned her stun gun to high as Ester charged her gloves. The sound of footsteps came from down the hall. The guards appeared, but Pisces noticed the symbol on one of the guard's legs.

"Reformers." Pisces pointed to the symbol on their leg. It was hard to see at first, but Ester saw a giant serpent like beast on one of their legs. Somehow they managed to infiltrate the ship.

"I thought they couldn't get on?" Ester gasped.

"Jordain." Pisces raised her hand to her chest.

The men were armed with laser guns and shot back through the hole. Now it was a mess of laser fire on both sides. One of the Reformers rolled over to the other side of the door opposite of where Pisces and Ester were and threw a small hand grenade through the door. The Reformers stopped firing and ducked for cover. A loud explosion went off on the other side, filling the air with more black smoke and debris.

Pisces stood and looked at her fellow Reformers. They brought their right fist to their chest and Pisces did the same. They re-charged their weapons and nodded to her to follow. Pisces waved Ester along. Ester was relieved to see that they had some backup. On the other side of the door, the room was a mess of bodies and destruction. Many of the lights were damaged, and it was almost completely dark inside. Ester covered her nose as she stepped over the bodies of Tozork's men. It was weird. They were her enemy, but she would never get use to the sight of lifeless bodies on the ground. Pisces ran to the control panel and started to feverishly enter in codes. Ester stood around with the other Reformers. It was taking a lot of time for Pisces to bring down the system, and there was no telling when the next wave of guards would arrive. Ester turned and looked at the shield generator. It was a wall of panels, flashing lights and buttons. It looked all too confusing to her. Fire started up again in the hall as the Reformers rushed to defend the room. Time was running out. Ester ran over to Pisces.

"What's wrong?" Ester poured over the controls.

"I cannot…I cannot shut down the power. They must have changed the codes." Pisces mashed buttons but nothing seemed to work.

"Okay, it just needs to stop right?" Ester asked.

"Yes but finding the right codes to stop it is impossible." Pisces growled at another unauthorized message.

"What if we just break some of the parts, it's bound to stop some of it right?"

"It's not that easy, the generator has a lot of back up routes. It would more than likely recover."

"Okay, but what if we just completely wreck it?"

Pisces looked at her through the plastic shield of her helmet. "I cannot spare any of the bombs I brought to destroy the weapon."

Pisces looked down at Ester as she charged up her gloves.

"That is not enough. The exterior is virtually shock resistant. We need the right codes," Pisces said.

"We don't have time." Ester ran over to one of the deceased guards and pried the laser gun from their hands.

"What are you…?"

"Okay, the outside is shock resistant," Ester interrupted, "but what if I can create a small hole in the panel and focus my gloves' power in there. That would shock the inside."

Pisces looked down at the panel. The gunfire was getting louder. It was a crazy idea, but anything was worth trying at this point. The Reformers shot through the hole behind them, but one by one they were falling. Pisces took the gun and aimed it at a weak looking part of the panel. She fired and blasted out a fist sized hole. The panel flickered, but as Pisces suspected the shields generator returned to normal operation. Ester waved Pisces back. This was their only shot. If she could fry the panels on the doors, she could fry this. She charged her gloves up once more to the highest setting. Stepping closer, she hovered her hands over the hole. She drew all the electricity from her body into her hands and closed her eyes as she let it build. She had never focused this hard before, but she could feel her power getting stronger. She began to chant:

"Grand Mother in the sky, who watches over us and who we draw our strength from. Hear my pleas and open up a path for me to use your strength. Hear my pleas Grand Mother in the sky and grant me the ability to save my planet."

Ester opened her hands and something strange started to happen. Her necklace started to glow. From her chest, a great power began to form and take shape. The energy surged from her chest to her hands and exited out of her finger tips. The force blasted her and everyone else away and lit the entire wall a blaze with electricity and fire. Micro explosions rocked the entire room as the bodies of everyone in it landed and tumbled to the other side. Ester landed hard. Her hands were burning, and her body was screaming. She was half conscious when she felt the rumblings all around her. She could hear nothing, and her vision was blurry.

"What was that?" Pisces shouted as she stood over her. Ester could barely hear or see her. "That was incredible!"

Pisces' voice faded in and out. A hand reached out and started to drag Ester towards the wall. Reformers, just shadows in Ester's vison, rushed around the room as it became engulfed in flames. *What was that power?* Ester thought. It could not have been the gloves alone. Though she did not doubt the skills of Odie—she had seen his work firsthand—somehow that attack felt different. She lifted her arm to her chest where her necklace rested. It was still warm to the touch. Perhaps the Grand Mother in the sky had granted her power or maybe she just pushed the gloves to its limits. She turned her palm over and the little metal circles on the gloves were charred. She was defenseless now, but at least she completed her part.

Now it was up to Pisces.

One of the Reformers limped over to help Ester up. He hoisted her arm over his shoulder and walked her to the weapons room. The weapons room would not be as easy to destroy. It was built to withstand a direct hit and even the damage caused by the Reformers did little to affect the weapon incased behind the thick layers of metal. Pisces ran over to the hull and started to climb up the metal bar steps.

The few remaining Reformers below got to work prying open a small vent. Ester shook herself awake to see Pisces ascend. She was high off the ground climbing the massive weapon chamber. Lights and panels lit up as a slow pulsating hum vibrated through the floor.

Pisces stated to climb faster when she felt the vibrations. She was sure they were getting ready to use it. She reached the maintenance panel on the next level and hopped up only to be caught off guard by a guard with a laser gun. There was little time to withdraw her stun gun. She could only dodge, but she was not quick enough. She fell over and hissed as she held the wound on her arm. Blood started to bleed through the hole in her uniform. The guard stood over her, laser gun pointed at her head, then an explosion of blood coated the panels and the guard fell to the floor. Pisces used her arm to shield herself from the body then stood. She walked over to the rail and saw a Reformer on the floor holding a laser gun. The Reformer lowered their gun and raised their fist to their chest. Pisces smiled through the pain and did the same.

The pulsations continued and became strong at each passing second. They were running out of time. Pisces walked around the panel and found the upper maintenance stairs. They were locked, but she used the guard's laser gun to blast open the door and climb in. The weapon was reinforced inside and out and simply blowing it up would not be enough. That's why the Reformers choose to target the laser barrel. If the barrel were damaged the weapon would not function properly, thus giving the two remaining ships enough time to disable the main ship and rebel. Pisces counted her steps quickly as she crawled through the tiny maintenance vents. The laser weapon was revving up to fire and that's exactly what she wanted. She counted and followed the path, until she reached the interior of the barrel. Using a special laser cutter she had on her, she cut herself a small hole to plug a grappling hook into. She harnessed herself in and lowered herself into the barrel. Then the barrel shook, from the outside explosions. Pisces clenched onto her line; she could feel that it would not hold.

"Dammit." she shouted as she looked down.

She needed more time. She needed to place the bomb exactly two point seven four meters from the base, but it didn't seem like her line would hold for long. The barrel walls shook again, it sounded like charges, the weapon was nearly functional. Pisces held on tighter. There would be little time to set the bomb and get back up. She closed her eyes and took a deep breath.

"I will complete my mission," she said as she lowered herself down.

***

The Reformers back in the weapons room pried the vent door off and tossed it to the ground. They knew they couldn't hold the guards off forever. One Reformer checked the inside of the vent and nodded, then two others walked over to the sniper who had saved Pisces from before and exchanged a few words. The floor stopped pulsating and changed into one powerful hum. The sniper turned to Ester and raised his fist to his chest. Ester didn't know what to do, so she just nodded. She watched the sniper take off back the way they came along with a few others. That left just Ester and three other Reformers. Ester was starting to get up, using the wall to hoist herself upright. Pisces needed to hurry. It sounded like something bad was going to happen. She watched the panel for her come down when two reformers pulled her by the arm.

"Wait, what about Pisces? Shouldn't we wait for her?" Ester looked back at the maintenance panel. The Reformers tensed but ignored her pleas and dragged her along. "Wait!"

Ester shouted and tried to wiggle out of their hold, but it was no use with her body so weak. They pushed her through the vent and started crawling away from the weapon room.

"Hey, stop it!" Ester kicked, but the Reformer in front of her just pulled her by the arm faster.

A huge explosion from behind them stopped the group for just a second, then a rumble came from the vent. The Reformers looked at each other and then gasped.

"Move!" one shouted from the back as the group crawled faster.

The rumble got louder, and soon they started to feel the heat. The two Reformers in front and the one behind Ester pushed on, but the one in the back stopped and stayed behind. Ester looked over her shoulder.

"Wh-why is he stopping?" She saw him press a button and form a little blue shield. Ester's eyes widened. "Wait!" she screamed.

"There's no time!" One of the Reformers shouted from in front of her and pulled her along.

They came to an opening in the vents that went straight down, and a rough hand pushed Ester along sending them down the hole. Ester fell screaming but looked up only to see blue fiery flames coming from the place they just were. The group descended fast down the pitch-black vents. If they didn't find a way to stop, they would die from impact. One of the Reformers launched a grappling hook and it lodged itself into the side of the vent. That Reformer grabbed his buddy who in turn grabbed Ester's arm and the group stopped feet above the slide that lead to the exterior vent on the bottom of the ship. The rumbling continued as Ester could hear the fighting going on outside. The Reformer holding onto her used all their strength to hoist her up to grab the foot of the other Reformer. Ester saw what they were trying to do and reached out to grab it, but debris from above rained down and hit the Reformer holding her in the back causing them to lose their grip and Ester slipped away.

"No!" The Reformer shouted as they watched Ester hit the bottom of the chute and disappear down the vent. "We have to go down!"

"There's no time!" The Reformer grappled to the vent pointed up. Their rope wouldn't hold them for long. The other Reformer cursed and punched their hook into another section of the vent, and the two climbed back up.

Chapter Twenty-Seven

Fires raged all throughout General Tozork's ship. Flashing red lights turned the hallways into a warzone as guards raced to stop Reformers from advancing. On the deck, Tozork loyalists shouted over private channels in vain trying to get a grasp of the situation going on on the other ships. The secondary ship Core 3-2 had sustained heavy damage, and their other ship Core 3-3 was not doing any better. To further complicate the situation, it would appear that Reformers had taken over both ships and were now turning their weapons towards them. The shields were down, and their main weapon had just been disabled.

Vents burst on the main deck, spewing out hot gasses. Loyalist ran to their stations and armed up as the sound of gunshots echoed from behind the deck's door. In the captain's seat, General Tozork gripped the arm of his chair so tight that the cushions tore from the armrest. The six foot five Labadoran rose from his seat. He tore his robe from his chest revealing years of scared and burned flesh. He cracked his furless knuckles and rotated his neck, stepping into the light, making his large black horns more visible against the stitches on his face.

"General Tozork, the weapon is malfunctioning. What do you recommend we do?" A frantic guard said from their station.

General Tozork withdrew his weapon as the sounds of fighting increased from behind the deck door.

"Fire at the city below. If they think this battle is won, then they have grossly underestimated my power," General Tozork said with a sinister grin.

"Yes sir!"

General Tozork watched his ship set the city a blaze. From behind him, the deck door exploded open knocking his men off their feet.

General Tozork did not flinch as Reformers poured onto the deck and began firing at his men. His loyalists fired back, creating casualties on both sides. General Tozork withdrew his weapon, a fire sword, and slashed his way through the Reformers, relieving any opponent who stood in his way of their heads or limbs. Bodies dropped, but none could land a hit on Tozork because of the shield protecting him and soon more guards would arrive further bringing down the Reformer's numbers. General Tozork grabbed a Reformer by their head and used their body as a shield. Mangled and bullet ridden, Tozork lifted the body in the air and tossed it to the side with a grin. More guards arrived, firing from the hall as the ship shook from the on slot outside. General Tozork eyed a Reformer with a sniper gun and called his men to stand down.

"You can come out now, Jordain." General Tozork said with a grin.

Firing on both sides stopped, as the ship continued to rumble. The snipper that had saved Pisces from before stood and walked into the light. He removed his helmet, revealing a large scar on the right side of his head below his chipped black horn, nestled in his cornflower blue fur. He cast an anger look General Tozork's way. Tozork laughed, as arrogantly as ever, only making Jordain angrier.

"You failed to stop me on Labadora, and you think you can stop me here?" General Tozork said.

"Look around, you have been beaten," Jordain said.

"Beaten? I have been blessed by the motherland of Ceapeaya and raised from the ashes of fire. I will bring this planet to its knees."

"Give up. We have control of your ships."

General Tozork laughed, as tensions rose high as both sides rose their weapons.

"You know what separates me from you?" General Tozork circled around the bodies of his fallen men. "You rely on words and the actions of others to prove your worthiness. I do not need such things to command my following. If there is an opponent I take care of them myself. That is the Labadoran way."

Jordain glared at him but held his ground.

"Let's settle this now. Labadora does not need a warrior of words. It craves a warrior of action," General Tozork said.

General Tozork dropped his sword and turned off his shield and stood before Jordain. Guards on both sides kept their weapons on their enemies. Jordain glared at Tozork and handed his rifle to his fellow Reformer. The ship rattled as explosions continued to bombard the ship, but that did nothing to break the tension in the room. General Tozork grinned and opened up his arms wide taunting Jordain. Another vent exploded spewing out more thick white steam. Jordain used this opportunity to attack. Jordain ran low and slammed his body into Tozork's. Tozork fell back into a command panel, but there was only laughter coming from his gut as he slammed his fist into Jordain back. Jordain pulled back and punched Tozork in the face, then punched him again several times in the gut. Each blow knocked Tozork back, but not one of his blows knocked that grin off his face. Tozork was 240 pounds of pure muscle, which compared to Jordain's lean frame, gave him a clear advantage, but still Jordain was relentless in his attacks. Tozork stumbled into the screen, cracking it with his weight. Jordain had his speed as his advantage and Tozork knew that. Tozork blocked another punch and grabbed Jordain by the arm and swing him into the screen like a ragdoll. Tozork then stomped him in the gut until he felt ribs crack beneath his boots. Jordain coughed blood but swing around and punched Tozork in the knee. Tozork hollered and Jordain took this opening and punched him square in the nose. Tozork fell back and hissed as he wiped away the blood.

"No matter what you think will happen here, I will come out victorious." General Tozork's voice was briefly fainter as he searched for a weapon.

Jordain hollered and charged at Tozork, who pulled out a shard of metal and sliced Jordain across the gut. Jordain stumbled back and fell into a command station, holding his bleeding gut. The cut was shallow, but wide and blood soaked his fur and uniform.

"Coward!" Jordain shouted.

General Tozork got up and laughed.

"Words, words, words, it'll be all that is known of you!"

Tozork walled over to Jordain and grabbed him by the uniform and lifted him into the air. Tozork's dark green eyes revealed the true monster he was. He slammed Jordain against the panel, intent on breaking him into a million pieces. Jordain fought against his grip as Tozork laughed hysterically. Jordain could see the spots in his vision, but his heart would not give up. No amount of pain he endured could compare to the consequences his people would face if he died here today. Jordain kicked Tozork in the kidney. Tozork dropped him and hollered, moving his hands around wildly to catch him. Jordain dodged and kicked him in the gut again, causing Tozork to trip over one of the bodies of his own men. Jordain grabbed a pipe and struck Tozork across the head. White light flashed before Tozork's eyes as he went down, feeling blow after blow on his back and ribs. Tozork reached for a gun but Jordain slammed his foot into Tozork's knee, breaking it. Tozork hollered and rolled over, his breath hitched when he saw Jordain towering over him with his fire sword in hand.

"Wait!" Tozork yelled.

"You wanted a warrior of action. Well, let this be my inaugural statement," Jordain said as he brought the fiery hot blade across Tozork's neck, beheading him.

There was silence on the deck as Jordain reached down and picked up Tozork's head, holding it up for all to see. Loyalists dropped their weapons as more Reformers made it to the deck.

"Broadcast this to our home world. Let it be known that General Tozork is no more," Jordain said as his men took control over the ship.

***

Laser fire rained from the sky, causing debris to fall into the streets and onto people. Angel and Fermit struggled to funnel people into the tunnels. They thought they were in the clear when they saw one of the smaller ships begin to fire on the main ship, but suddenly the main ship started attacking Ans-on again. Rubble fell to the ground and shattered into pieces sending shards into buildings and hover cars.

Fermit jumped out of the way when one piece landed right where he was standing. He winced, as bits of glass cut into his hands. Angel hurried over to pull him out from the sidewalk. Another building went down not to fair from them causing a cloud of dust to sweep across the city. Citizens shielded their eyes as rangers and cadets continued to work.

"Fermit, let's take this batch down the tunnels," Angel said when he saw other rangers arriving.

The two had been working in pairs as most of their unit was either pulled elsewhere or injured. Dust burned Fermit's eyes as he struggled to his feet and stumbled after Angel down the tunnel. Citizens were still funneling through as Angel and Fermit waved for them to take the blue line deeper underground. All of the tunnels in Ans-on were triple reinforced. Angel praised the engineer's foresight as they directed the traffic deep underground.

Deep in the tunnels, citizens heathy enough to walk joined the long line of people exiting the city. Angel crouched down and to catch his breath. The air was thin down here and hard to breath, but it was no better on the surface. Angel wiped the blood and sweat from his face, when he thought he saw one of Ester's friends in the crowd. He wasn't that far from Ester's locale, but he couldn't get a hold of her and that scared him.

"I'll be right back, Fermit!"

"Angel!" Fermit shouted after him.

"Hey! Excuse me!" Angel shouted as he pushed through the crowd. "Excuse me! Sir."

Sal looked up and was surprised to see Ester's friend. He walked closer, closing the gap between them.

"Excuse me, do you know a girl named Ester DuTain?" Angel said.

"Yes! Yes, I do," Sal said. "You are Angel Johnson, Ester's friend."

"Yes, I am. Have you seen her? Is she with you?" Angel looked around.

"She is not, but to my knowledge she is okay. She left the nation state to visit Cha-la just a few days ago," he said, hoping that would help ease some of Angel's worries.

"Cha-la?" Angel said almost relieved. He didn't have time to dwell on it; he could fell his wristband beeping, Fermit was trying to reach him. "Thank you, thank you so much."

Sal waved as Angel ran back to Fermit. He didn't know why Ester had left for Cha-la but thank goodness. Fermit asked him what that was about, and Angel said he would explain later. Fermit pulled him along, back to the surface. They were being reassigned. Angel asked where and Fermit said they would know when they got there, but that did little to settle Angel's nerves. He barely wanted to be here. He wanted to go home and hide, but it was likely there wasn't even a home to go to.

Back on the surface, Fermit pulled up the directions and led them down the streets. It was mostly empty, but it was also littered with the bodies of civilians that were not so lucky. Angel tried to ignore it, but it was hard. The blasting stopped only to pick up again. Fermit and Angel took cover, but ran quickly to their new station, following the directions on Fermit's wristband. Straight ahead was a group of rangers shouting and directing others. A woman caught sight of the boys and waved them over.

"Hey! Are you the A-11 back-up?" The ranger standing next to a hover jetter said.

Fermit nodded as he tried not to look at the man groaning in the stretcher being taken away.

"Good, you're needed up top." The ranger turned on the bike. "You two take this up, the captain will give you more instructions when you get there."

Fermit hopped on first, as Angel took the back. Fermit gunned the hover jetter and ascended to the top of the skyscraper. Angel held on tight with his eyes closed as the ground was pummeled by lasers. Angel opened his eyes half way up and saw the extent of the damage. The main ship above them was firing at will and his poor nation state was being demolished. Angel held on tighter, wishing this nightmare would end. Fermit landed at the top and Angel was pulled away. Another ranger told Fermit to take another injured ranger down below.

Fermit and Angel exchanged glances, but Angel nodded to him that he would be okay. Angel watched Fermit leave as the ranger in charge directed him.

"Hey cadet, we could really use your help. Our canon is jammed. Help load so we can work," the captain shouted.

More shots hit the ground and Angel flinched. He could die here, just like those other rangers. He froze as the explosions blasted in his ears. All the stress of the day was catching up to him. The ranger working the cannon noticed this and ran over.

"What's your name, son?" the captain asked.

"An-Angel, Angel Johnson." Angel flinched when another hover screen plummeted to the ground.

"Well, Ranger Johnson, our team could really use your help. All you gotta do is help keep the cannon steady." The captain pointed to the cannon. "I know it's scary, but what Rean could really use is your help, are you ready?"

Angel turned and looked at the captain and slowly nodded. He swallowed his fear and ran over to the cannon and helped hold it in place. The sky was an ugly gray and droplets of metal rained from the sky as ranger pilots and enemy ships clashed. Angel took a deep breath and held the cannon steady.

"Thanks, Ranger," the captain said, as they re-loaded their cannon and fired at will.

Chapter Twenty-Eight

It was the sudden quietness that woke Ester. She was laying on a grate looking down at the metropolis a fire below. She slowly leaned up as the grate started to shake. There as a cracking noise and Ester looked around and noticed the platform she was laying on was starting to fall apart under her weight. She looked down. She was hundreds of feet in the air. She started to panic and looked up the slide. It was too steep for her to climb, but she tried away. She crawled slowly towards the chute, but it didn't seem like the grate would hold for much longer. Sweat formed on her brow as she inched closer and closer to the slide, with the grate creaking at every step, causing her to flinch as she moved. If she could just make it to the slide, she could perhaps wait there to be recused, but who would know she was there?

Her heart pounded against her chest as one end of the grate broke loose.

Ester froze.

She looked over her shoulder and saw where the grate had come loose from the vent. She gulped and slowly turned back around, carefully picking up her hand. Another side of the grate snapped, and the entire thing wobbled and bent. Ester cried out. She looked up at the slide, she was just inches away. She looked down and shut her eyes as she slowly moved her knee forward. Another latch on the grate failed and that combined with Ester's weight caused the vent door swing wide open, lunging Ester forward. She caught hold of the grate and was now hanging hundreds of feet in the air above Ans-on. She held on for dear life but didn't have the upper body strength to grip it for much longer.

She looked up at the vent above her. She wasn't sure what was going to give first: her fingers or the last latch on the grate. She dangled high in the air and struggled to do anything but hang. This couldn't be the end? Did they at least win? And what of Pisces? She couldn't have? Could she? Ester didn't even want to think about it. Her fingers burned as they pressed harder into the grate.

This was really it.

Warm tears cascaded down Ester's face. Her fingers began to slip as the latch whined.

"Well, I had a good run." She trembled as tears ran freely down her cheeks and the grate latches snapped sending her plummeting to the ground.

Ester watched the ship moved farther and farther away. This was the end. It would soon be over soon. She closed her eyes.

***

From the skyscraper where Angel was stationed, the captain broadcast a live feed from one of the pilots.

"We did it everyone!" the captain announced.

Cheers from the rest of the team erupted as the news spread of a surrender. Angel was relieved but extremely tired. He watched the feed of the ranger pilots boarding the ships.

"Hey, what's that?" one of the rangers said looking through a spy drone feed.

The Captain turned to her. "What are you seeing?"

"I'm not sure, sir, but it appears to be a person hanging from the underside of the main ship."

The Captain and the rest of the group walked over. "Is it one of ours?"

"Hard to tell sir, but I can zoom in closer." The ranger pressed the zoom button on their spy drone. "It looks like a ranger."

They could tell by the uniform. Angel examined the screen closer and gasped in fear.

"Ester!" Angel shouted as he looked to the main ship.

He could recognize that fly away hair anywhere. Without thinking Angel pushed his way pass the team and headed for the hover jetter.

"What? Wait!" the captain shouted as Angel hopped on and took off.

"Sorry! Gotta go!" Angel lifted in the air and made a sharp turn and gunned the jetter to full speed.

Ester hold on!

***

Ester was falling fast. Her eyes were closed as she accepted her fate. She was ready to go when a hand grabbed onto her arm, pulling her back into reality.

"You smoldering twill!" The blur of a voice mixed in with the sound of an engine whisked by her.

The force was enough to send them both spiraling out of control and Angel could not balance Ester's weight and wound up being pulled from his hover jetter. Now the two of them were falling together. When Ester finally got a look at who was trying to save her, she panicked. A red-faced ball of blond curly hair was falling alongside her. It was Angel and now they both were going to die. Yet, then a mess of rope and nets scooped them up into a tangled ball. Buzzing through the air, with Angel's big fat butt in her face, Ester looked up and saw Wildgrass hanging over the bay door.

"You idiots! Are ya'll trying to get yourselves killed?" His green hair blew through the wind as Angel whined about being afraid of heights.

Ester blinked several times as her brain tried to register what had just happened. The state was a blaze, but the sky was tented in purple, the color of surrender. They must have won, she thought as she leaned back and her vision faded.

Chapter Twenty-Nine

The enemies from Labadora surrendered, and the accused paid heavily for their crimes. It was revealed that a rouge under General Tozork's command spearheaded the assassination on Kees. So, the Grand Council on Rean saw to it that the conspirators were handed over to them to avoid intergalactic war. Captain Jordain of the United Reformers swore on and signed a new peace treaty as the new leader of Labadora. He knew there would be much work to do on his home world, but by signing this treaty he would begin to mend the tattered relationship between his world and the neighboring planets. As a sign of good faith, the Grand Council of Rean allowed Jordain and his Reformers to return to their home world under the condition they leave Tozork's main ship on Rean for further inspection. Jordain agreed and returned home with the hope that one day he could transform the way the galaxy perceived Labadora and its people.

Back at the ranger's base, Ester was still recovering from the battle. She wasn't too badly injured, seeing that most of the damage came from minor burns on her hands and cuts on her body. She wasn't sure what was going to happen to her or Angel or even Wildgrass. She wasn't a ranger and she was apprehended impersonating one. She sat in the hall, waiting to be called to stand before the Grand Commanders of the Rean Coalition of Rangers. She would be standing at the hearing alongside Wildgrass and Odie, but her mind was elsewhere. Pisces didn't make it, she later found out. Wildgrass managed to get a message from Jordain, thanking Ester and the rest of them personally for helping Pisces complete her mission, but to Ester it didn't feel like a win. She wanted to see Pisces one last time to at least kick her in the head for sacrificing herself like that. She died so that her people could be saved, and Ester would never forget that.

Wildgrass and Odie walked in, escorted by rangers. Ester looked up and stood as Wildgrass smiled at her. He looked a little nervous, but otherwise confident. After all, he did just help save to the planet. But even with that fact and the fact that he was the son of one of the highest ranking retired Grand Commanders, he knew that would not excuse his reckless behavior. Wildgrass, Ester, and Odie walked through the doors and stood before Grand Commander J'Chives, Grand Commander Sanders, and Grand Commander Xills, the highest-ranking commanders of the Rean Coalition of Rangers. They stood in silence as the commanders read the briefing. Ester had her head down; her nerves were a wreck. This was the second time in her short ranger career that she had landed in major trouble. She was already banned from ranger academy. She hoped she wouldn't be kicked out of Ans-on either.

Grand Commander Xills cleared his throat. He looked down at Wildgrass with displeasure. "Captain Inspread."

"Please, it's Wildgrass," Wildgrass interrupted and glanced up at the all too displeased face of the graying Grand Commander.

"Captain Inspread," Grand Commander Xills repeated again. "This mission report is absolute blasphemy; your executed plan could have cost thousands of lives."

"It was the only way, sir." Wildgrass looked up with a fake pleading look in his eyes, the Grand Commander's frown only deepened.

"Your plan could have resulted in the loss of thousands of lives—"

"Okay," Wildgrass cut him off. "I get it, thousands of lives. With all due respect, Calvin, we all know my life has been utilized on a number of occasions to save Rean and its precious people. Was this a plan on the fly? Yes. Did it endanger thousands of lives? Debatable. Was it our only option?" Wildgrass looked at the Grand Commanders, none of them said a word. "Yeah, I'm pretty sure it was."

Grand Commander J'Chives shuffled his paperwork. "We let you fight recklessly for many years Inspread, but this—"

"Let?" A glare formed behind Wildgrass' eyes. "As I recall, you found out I was super strong at birth and tested on me and groomed me to be the perfect solider. I'm not sure how much *letting* was done. *Letting* implies options, options imply I asked for this…"

Grand Commander J'Chives shifted in his seat and sighed, but Grand Commander Sanders raised her hand, silencing the group. She was the senior commander, and she sat in her chair looming over the group stoically.

"I have heard enough. My locale is currently a heaping pile of rubble and our neighbors aren't fairing any better. Captain Wildgrass Inspread, Captain Odie Noxx, and Ester DuTain, you conspired with an illegal immigrant to stop a plot against our planet. As reckless as that was, you did end up saving all of us from certain destruction. I will excuse your behavior, this one time, but from here on out, I do not care about the sensitivity of the circumstances, you will report to us first if you find yourself in this situation again. Is that clear?"

"Yes, ma'am," Wildgrass said a little too enthusiastically.

"With that being said, you are all assigned to one year of restorative duties." She adjusted her thick lensed glasses.

"Crap," Wildgrass groaned as Ester breathed a sigh of relief.

"You are lucky, Inspread." Grand Commander Xills interrupted with a disapproving look.

Wildgrass wanted to stick his tongue out like a child but settled on a grin.

Grand Commander J'Chives cleared his throat. "Well, we have much work to do, you are all dismissed."

"Before you go," Wildgrass interrupted as Odie and Ester looked at him, "you think you can do something for my friend here? I mean, after all, she did help save the planet."

Ester looked at Wildgrass and he smiled. Her breath hitched.

What was Wildgrass doing? Ester's heart started to race. They were nearly in the clear.

"The answer is no," Grand Commander Xills grunted, "and I

don't need to read minds to know what you are about to ask. We do not need another you in our ranks."

"Aww, is that your final answer, Cal?" Wildgrass whined as Grand Commander Xills glared.

"Okay." Wildgrass was about to turn and walk away, but stopped. "But, hypothetically?" The Grand Commander was about to blow a blood vessel. "I mean she not only saved us, but she also risked her life—just like any other ranger would do."

"Inspread," Grand Commander Xills growled.

So much for Wildgrass' big plan. He didn't like the idea of Ester becoming a ranger, but it was clear this was where she belonged. She stepped up when the time came and put herself in danger to save the lives of her people. That's what it really meant to be a ranger, not a flashy title or a powerful weapon. A ranger was someone who stood their ground in the face of danger and even if it took years, Wildgrass would fight to see that Ester walked among them. As he was about to turn around and leave, he heard a ruckus coming from outside the door. Voices raised, building up to shouts, to grunts, then yells. The Grand Commanders looked up as the door started to open.

"Hey, you can't—" A guard tried to reach for the intruder but was too slow.

A head of blond slipped through and threw themselves on the floor before the commanders. Ester gasped as Angel bowed then looked up.

"Please forgive my intrusion, Grand Commanders. I am Ranger Cadet Angel Johnson and I am petitioning you to re-consider Ester DuTain's expulsion."

"What? What order?" Grand Commander Xills barked.

Grand Commander Sander's eyes sharpened, but she did not raise her hand to stop Angel, surprising everyone, even Grand Commander J'Chives.

"By order of the Civil Council," Angel's chin stuck out as he spoke loudly. "I have procured all fifty-two signatures, along with forty-five Captain signatures and one-hundred and fifty ranger signatures recommending a special waive of punishment."

Wildgrass looked between Odie and Ester. He was impressed. This was a risk, a big risk.

Angel swallowed hard, but he could not bear to see his friend cast from the very academy she helped save. If there was one thing he learned from his parents, it was there was great power in connections. He knew the minute he got back that he wanted help get Ester back in the academy, and with his parents' help, he was able to gather over two hundred signatures.

The Grand Commanders looked at each other as Grand Commander J'Chives waved to a court guard to take the list from Angel.

Grand Commander Xills was near boiling. "I do not care—"

"Hold on." Grand Commandeer J'Chives waved his hand to calm his colleague. He had known Angel since he was a child. He was proud to see him now as a cadet, but even this was out of his hands. "Angel, I'm sorry. I commend your efforts, but we cannot go back on a permanent ban."

Angel was shaking, but a hand on his shoulder calmed him. It was Ester, and she was overwhelmed with gratitude. Angel had stood up for her and so did Wildgrass, but it was okay. Even if she couldn't have the life she dreamed of, she knew she would be happy carving out her own path.

"Aw, come on," Wildgrass whined. "that was a lot of signatures. I mean—"

"I overturn the ban," Grand Commander Sanders said, bringing the room to silence.

"Wait, what…" Wildgrass paused mid-sentence and stared at senior Grand Commander Sanders.

Everyone froze in shock, waiting for someone to make a comment. Grand Commander Sanders took off her glasses and used a soft cloth to clean them and put them back on.

"Our rangers are comprised of ordinary people who have the courage to stand up and fight against injustice wherever it grows. It is not easy to answer the call when danger is knocking at your door, but to take up arms even at the cost of your life in order to protect the lives of others is the core fundamental in which our military was founded on. This is not something that can be taught. It is instinct, and you, child, have it." Grand Commander Sanders stood and flattened out the wrinkles in her rode. "Grand Commander J'Chives, Grand Commander Xills, I will be writing in my request to President Le later. Given the circumstances, I believe we can overlook the ban just this once. Now are there any more topics that need to be addressed? I have a lot of paperwork to do and a nation state to help rebuild?"

No one said a word.

"Good. Now, if you will excuse us." Grand Commander Sanders got up and started to leave.

Ester was frozen in place as the others whispered congratulations and cheers in her ear. Grand Commander Sanders stopped before exiting and turned around.

"I hope you will make better choices this time around, DuTain. This is a rare exception, and it would be wise of you not to take it for granted."

Ester stood up straight, chin pointed out, hands clasped behind her. "Yes, ma'am."

Grand Commander J'Chives smiled and stood as well. "You can count on my recommendation. I think you'll make a fine ranger." He smiled at Ester then turned to Angel. The commander scrolled through Angel's impressive number of signatures. "And are you sure you don't want to become a civil councilor?"

"No, sir. My place is on the battlefield with my comrades." Angel stood proud.

Grand Commander J'Chive chuckled. "Okay, very well, you take care now."

Angel bowed. "You do the same, Grand Commander."

Grand Commander Xills stood and cast a glare at the group.

"Oh, and thanks, Cal," Wildgrass shouted. The Commander growled and ignored him.

The group watched the Grand Commander's exit, and the doors were opened for them to leave.

"Holy cow, that was close!" Wildgrass grabbed Angel by the

shoulders. "You got some balls on you for that one, kid!"

Angel blushed.

Odie chuckled and turned to Wildgrass. "Look who's talking. Calvin is going to have you killed one day."

"Aww, he loves me, and he knows it." Wildgrass laughed.

Ester hung back as the voices of her friends started to fade. Was this real? Was this actually real? Her heart wouldn't take it if she were to wake up in her bed right now and this all be a dream. Odie and Wildgrass' laughter stirred her back to reality. She rushed to catch up with everyone.

"Angel, I…" Ester could barely form the words.

"Don't mention it," Angel said, "I just did what any cute boy would do for his best friend." He smiled brightly.

Ester looked him in the eyes, tears threatening to break loose. She sniffled then burst out into laughter. "Does your cuteness have any limits?"

Wildgrass smirked in amusement and watched the two friends enjoy their moment. He knew they would face many tough trials ahead, but at least they had each other.

"Okay, okay," Wildgrass said as he broke up their little moment. "I have an angry husband to get home to, so I'm going to need ya'll to wrap this up."

Angel whined as Ester pulled him along. Ester was glad to see that this whole conflict was over. All she wanted to do was rest. There would be plenty time to fix things later.

Chapter Thirty

Ester sat in her room on her bed as guests flooded in and out of her apartment. It was a month after the attack, and she was lucky her apartment was still standing in one piece. Angel was throwing her a little party; it was a nice break from the clean-up taking place all of over the state. The city was in ruins and all cadet classes were postponed for reconstruction, but Ester had no doubt things would be up and running in no time. There were already hover screens floating in the sky, but this time advertising shelters and places to apply for aid.

Ester fingered the tiny projector she had gotten from the game center. The device turned on, projecting the picture Ester and Pisces took in their outfits from the dress-up game. It was the only picture of Pisces she had. Ester smiled at the Reanian form Pisces wore. It was funny seeing her without her mid-night blue fur, but at least it showed her beautiful silver blue eyes and her soft smile. Ester heard a loud laugh, and she guessed it was time to head back to the party. Ester walked out of her room wearing a new lilac and lavender ride suit. She saw Sal in the back talking to InyOuty and Angel fussing over the food table. Ester scanned the room for Wildgrass, but she couldn't find him. She walked into the den when a body slammed into her. Ester jumped and looked down to see Gar, his eyes brimming with tears.

"Gah! You can't be leaving! You can't!" he whined.

"Gar," Ester wrapped her arms around him, but he turned away.

"You moved here and just like that you're going to move away. You're gonna turn out to be just like those kids in my class and forget about us."

"Gar, I would never do that, and besides, I'm not leaving anytime soon. I meant what I said. I want to be the first in line to one of your new buildings. So you better do well in school and make your aunt and your parents proud," Ester said. "Can you do that for me?"

Gar's lip quivered. "I-I'm going to do better than that. I'm going to be the greatest architect the world as ever seen."

Ester smiled and rubbed his head. "You better."

She hugged him tight and continued her search for Wildgrass. She hoped he hadn't left. In the kitchen, her boss from the market bellowed as he lifted his drink to her. He had been kind enough to donate food to families in need. Ester was grateful for that. She smiled back at him and slipped out the front door into hall. She didn't see him but was surprised the find Chargie lounging on the floor.

"Hey, Chargie, you think you can do me a favor?" she asked, and the dog lifted up his head and wigged his tail. "Can you find Wildgrass for me?"

The dog barked and stood up slowly. He turned his head down the hall then looked back at Ester. She knew what to do. Chargie led her to the stairs and pawed at the door.

"Down here?"

Chargie wagged his tail. Ester opened the door and Chargie took off down the three flights of stairs to the lobby.

"Chargie, hold up," Ester said as Chargie walked through the sliding doors. "Chargie?"

She looked outside and found Chargie sniffing and bouncing around Wildgrass, who was sitting on a crate outside of her apartment.

"Trying to ditch my party?" Ester folded her arms.

Wildgrass looked up. "I would never." he turned to Chargie. "Wait a minute. Did you do this?"

Chargie tilted his head and panted then settled at Wildgrass' feet.

"I hope I'm not keeping you," Ester said. "You can leave if you need to."

"Nah," Wildgrass leaned back into the building. "Can't anyways. I'm stuck on clean up duty, remember?"

"Oh yeah," Ester said. She was assigned to clean up duty too, but she didn't mind.

Ester watched Wildgrass stare at the street. He was still very much the hero she remembered him as, but there was something on her mind that she wanted to ask.

"Hey, Wildgrass?"

"Yeah?" He looked up at her.

"Why did you decide to quit the Rean Coalition of Rangers?"

Wildgrass paused, then stretched out his arms. "I left because it wasn't the place for me."

"I don't understand. You were the best ranger we ever had."

Wildgrass smirked. "In this world, there's always going to be something that needs saving, be it a space station or planet, but even with all that going on, you can't forget about yourself. You can't be afraid to take charge of your life and make decisions that are best for you, even if others are hurt by it. I left because I found something greater."

Wildgrass looked up at her. She didn't understand what he meant, and he knew it, but she had plenty of time to figure that out.

"Just don't forget about the people that love you. Cherish them, but most of all don't lose that spark that gets you out of bed every morning—that's the only way you'll make it through life."

Ester blinked a few times, then smiled.

"Thank you. Now, are you going to be around to help me move when I go back to the academy?"

"Sure, but you'll need to pack everything up nice and tight if it's going to make it all the way to Cha-la."

"Cha-la? Why the heck is it going all the way out there?"

Wildgrass smirked. "I collect orphans, remember?

Ester's eye's widened.

"Besides, you're going to need a place to go, you know, a home for when you have downtime. So come visit us. I'm sure Taxes would love the company."

"Really?" Ester was starting to get teary-eyed.

"Hey, no waterworks."

But it was too late, Ester had already tackled him.

"Hey easy!"

Wildgrass embraced the hug despite his protests. She was a good kid and family now, and he would see to it that she was looked after.

***

Dirt and sand drew up along the tunnels of a torch lit cave. Tall figures dressed in black robes walked by as if they were levitating. The lights flickered as the old stone doors were pushed open, revealing a room ancient and frozen in time. Five figures bowed in front of a shrine made of clear crystal. Others lined the walls in the shadows with their hoods covering their faces, as their leader rose. He moved across the room like an apparition and stood above his followers.

"Have you retrieved it?" His voice was deep and mincing.

"Yes, my lord."

One of the followers pulled from their robe a crystal the size of their hand. It was dull and green and lifted it up to their master. The leader waved his fingers, lifting it with their magic. He examined the crystal with his large round black eyes then whispered a spell, bringing the crystal back to life. The leader turned and placed it on the shrine next to three others, nearly completing the set, with one missing. The leader waved away the others, and they joined their brethren along the walls. The leader stepped back and lifted his arms, extending his fingers as he chanted in an ancient language. The more he chanted, the more the shrine began to glow and glow until it radiated with energy. A whisk of wind blew out the lights as fog fell from the edges of the shrine and poured out onto the ground. In the middle, a shadowed figure appeared.

"Is it done?" a voice echoed from another world.

"Almost, my lord. We are still missing one stone." The leader in the dark robe said with his head bowed.

There was a low growl of displeasure from the figure in the shadows, but that did not phase the leader in the robe. A smirked appeared on his face as he lifted his head to face his one true master.

"Fret not, my lord. Our plan was not for nothing. For we now know the location of the final crystal." The robed leader formed a ball in his hands revealing a group of tribal people traveling together by hover cart.

"Are you sure this time?" The figure grumbled.

"Yes, my lord. Word is being sent to a highly efficient group of mercenaries as we speak."

"Excellent!" The voice bellowed. "Secure the final crystal, and you and your followers will be rewarded with power beyond your imagination."

"Thank you, Lord Vloss." The leader bowed his head as the shrine faded to black.

Thanks for reading!

Ester and the gang will be back soon. To keep up with all the updates on this series and the many others, please visit my website at https://theofficebc.wordpress.com.

If you enjoyed the story feel free to leave me a review on Amazon and/or Goodreads, I'd love to hear from you.

Thanks again and take care,
-Blair

Photo Credit - Brittany Rose Photography

Blair Cousins is an author and avid genre hopper of many stories. In her free time, she enjoys pursuing the great American pass time of sleeping. During her waking hours, she grinds hard to make her dreams come true.

42245843R00192

Made in the USA
Lexington, KY
14 June 2019